OTHER HARLEM MOON CLASSICS

Pride of Family: Four Generations of American Women of Color by Carole Ione

Soulscript: A Collection of African American Poetry edited by June Jordan

THE QUEST OF THE
SILVER FLEECE

*

A Novel

W.E.B. DU BOIS

HARLEM MOON

Broadway Books

New York

CLASSIC

Published by Harlem Moon, an imprint of Broadway Books, a division of Random House, Inc.

A hardcover edition of this book was originally published in 1911 by A.C. Mc-Clurg & Co.

PRINTED IN THE UNITED STATES OF AMERICA

HARLEM MOON, BROADWAY BOOKS, and the HARLEM MOON logo, depicting a moon and a woman, are trademarks of Random House, Inc. The figure in the Harlem Moon logo is inspired by a graphic design by Aaron Douglas (1899–1979).

Harlem Moon Classics series advisor: Gina Dent, Associate Professor of Women's Studies and History of Consciousness, University of California, Santa Cruz

Visit our website at www.harlemmoon.com

First Harlem Moon trade paperback edition published 2004

Book design by Amanda Dewey

Library of Congress Cataloging-in-Publication Data

Du Bois, W.E.B. (William Edward Burghardt), 1868–1963.
    The quest of the silver fleece : a novel / W.E.B Du Bois.—1st Harlem Moon trade pbk. ed.
      p. cm.
     1. Power (Social sciences)—Fiction. 2. African American women—Fiction. 3. Rejection (Psychology)—Fiction. 4. Social classes—Fiction. 5. Cotton trade—Fiction. 6. Swamps—Fiction 7. Race—Fiction. I. Title

PS3507.U147Q46 2004
813'.52—dc22   2004047414

ISBN 0-7679-1845-2

10 9 8 7 6 5 4 3 2 1

Contents

Introduction by Arnold Rampersad   ix

THE QUEST OF THE SILVER FLEECE

Note from the Author   3

One: DREAMS   5

Two: THE SCHOOL   12

Three: MISS MARY TAYLOR   16

Four: TOWN   23

Five: ZORA   33

Six: COTTON   42

Seven: THE PLACE OF DREAMS   53

Eight: MR. HARRY CRESSWELL   66

Nine: THE PLANTING   74

Ten: MR. TAYLOR CALLS   84

Eleven: THE FLOWERING OF THE FLEECE   99

Twelve: THE PROMISE   108

Thirteen: MRS. GREY GIVES A DINNER   122

Fourteen: LOVE   128

Fifteen: REVELATION   134

Sixteen: THE GREAT REFUSAL   146

Seventeen: THE RAPE OF THE FLEECE   154

Eighteen: THE COTTON CORNER   162

Nineteen: THE DYING OF ELSPETH   171

Twenty: THE WEAVING OF THE SILVER FLEECE   182

Twenty-one: THE MARRIAGE MORNING   191

Twenty-two: MISS CAROLINE WYNN   199

Twenty-three: THE TRAINING OF ZORA   210

Twenty-four: THE EDUCATION OF ALWYN   218

Twenty-five: THE CAMPAIGN   230

Twenty-six: CONGRESSMAN CRESSWELL   244

Twenty-seven: THE VISION OF ZORA   254

Twenty-eight: THE ANNUNCIATION   263

Twenty-nine: A MASTER OF FATE   *271*

Thirty: THE RETURN OF ZORA   *283*

Thirty-one: A PARTING OF WAYS   *293*

Thirty-two: ZORA'S WAY   *309*

Thirty-three: THE BUYING OF THE SWAMP   *316*

Thirty-four: THE RETURN OF ALWYN   *328*

Thirty-five: THE COTTON MILL   *339*

Thirty-six: THE LAND   *350*

Thirty-seven: THE MOB   *364*

Thirty-eight: ATONEMENT   *371*

Reader's Companion   *379*

Introduction

When W.E.B. Du Bois's first novel, *The Quest of the Silver Fleece*, appeared in 1911, he had bravely begun only a year before a new, exciting, but also potentially disastrous adventure. After thirteen years as a professor at Atlanta University, Du Bois dumped his academic robes in 1910 and joined an upstart civil rights organization in New York City, the National Association for the Advancement of Colored People. Specifically, he joined the NAACP as its first director of publicity and the founding editor of its crusading monthly magazine, *The Crisis*. For the next twenty-four years, he made this magazine a clarion call to blacks across America who were dedicated to their rise as a people.

As a novel, *The Quest of the Silver Fleece* was an audacious departure from the kind of books that had established Du Bois not only as the premier black academic in America but as one of the leading American academics in almost any field. His first book, *The Suppression of the Slave-Trade to the United States,* was a major work of history; his second, *The Philadelphia Negro,* a pioneering example of empirical sociology based on an exhaustive study of blacks in that city. At Atlanta, he edited an annual series of sociological studies on subjects pertaining to black American life, based on conferences he organized at his university. (The publications started in 1897 and continued beyond his departure from Atlanta.)

Educated at Fisk University, Harvard University (where he earned a doctorate in history), and the University of Berlin, Du Bois labored to be a scholar according to the strictest standards of the profession. Although no white college or university would dare to hire him as a professor, he succeeded in establishing an excellent reputation as an academic writer. However, he also failed, as he saw it, because all of his vaunted scholarly texts had done virtually nothing to alter the appalling conditions under which black Americans lived, especially after the U.S. Supreme Court decision of 1896, *Plessy v. Ferguson,* which justified and encouraged the practice of racial segregation.

Before this novel, in addition to the works already mentioned, Du Bois wrote a biography of the abolitionist martyr John Brown, edited journals of news and opinion aimed at a black audience, and published poems that expressed the powerful emotions evoked by the horrors of Jim Crow. His single most influential work before 1910—perhaps the finest work of his long life—was *The Souls of Black Folk* (1903). In this volume, Du Bois brought together his talents in history, sociology, fiction, religious and musical studies, biography, and autobiography. It boldly announced his differences with Booker T. Washington, the most powerful black American of his day and the founder of Tuskegee Institute in Alabama. *The Souls of Black Folk* showed Du Bois's intimate knowledge, despite his New England origins, of black life in the South. It reflected his sense of a perpetual crisis in black American life, caught between the cruel fact of segregation and the promise of freedom. It declared famously that "the problem of the twentieth century is the problem of the color line."

In many ways, *The Quest of the Silver Fleece* renders in novel form the essence of *The Souls of Black Folk* and the knowledge and insights gained by Du Bois about white Americans, black Americans, himself, and life since 1903. Despite the success of *The Souls of Black Folk* in establishing him and his vision as the main rivals to the authority of Booker T. Washington, Du Bois saw the limitations of the book even as it appeared. By 1911, when *Quest* was published, he had an even more acute sense of how much (as he would later publicly regret) his 1903 volume suffered from his lack of a deep understanding of, and sympathy for, the works of Marx and Freud—that is, dialectical materialism and psychology. Because of his reading of these two major thinkers and because the novel as a form invited psychological probing, *The Quest of the Silver Fleece* took Du Bois into areas he had barely touched as a commentator on the predicament of being black in America. In so doing, it broke new ground among black novels.

By our standards of fiction today, *The Quest of the Silver Fleece* is in some ways a quaint, old-fashioned work of art. Based on the "marriage" plot (that staple of bourgeois fiction in which the complexities of a story are resolved by the triumph of love in a wedding), it is aimed at least as much at middle-class women, who then as now made up the majority of the American readership of fiction, as at middle-class men. Because of that strategy, as well as for other reasons, the tale is often sentimental and idealistic. It employs, at times, archaic diction. Du Bois also uses black dialect as a marker of social and educational inferiority in ways that were common at the time but which now often seem to us condescending and stereotypical.

Nevertheless, this novel is a remarkable accomplishment, an always entertaining work that, unlike perhaps any other novel of its time, throws open a wide window on black life—urban and rural, rich and poor—in the first years of the century. As much concerned with its heroine, Zora, as with its hero, Bles, it is set in the South and the North, as well as in the middle territory of Washington, D.C. It involves electoral politics, with the Republicans (the party of Abraham Lincoln) vying for the black vote against the Democrats (the party of the white South).

Most striking among black novels before and of its time, it reveals a shrewd interest in economics. Like the white novelist Frank Norris' trilogy about the production and marketing of wheat, *The Quest of the Silver Fleece* is anchored in the production and sale of cotton—including the people (most often black) who plant and pick it, the farmers (typically white) who control its production at a primary level, the bankers (all white) who control these farmers, the speculators on Wall Street who make and lose fortunes as the price of cotton rises and falls, and the purchasers of cotton garments who typically understand little of the drama and, often, the tragedy involved in the production and sale of the fabric.

Du Bois's novel, which starts in the South, is also about education. It reprises the most famous antagonism of his life to this point, pitting him as a lover of culture and the liberal arts against Booker T. Washington, who stressed manual and vocational training as the main way for Southern black masses to rise out of poverty. Compelling in its concern for morality (although unconcerned with formal religion), the story scrutinizes the values of American culture from top to bottom. The child of an evil woman, compromised early by exposure to sexual license, Zora must remake herself into a woman of virtue in order to be worthy of the hero, Bles, who himself strays from the path of righteousness before regaining his moral balance. Both redeem themselves and their lives by recognizing the importance of self-control, moral integrity, formal education, a dedication to hard work, and a commitment to toil, above all, for the uplift of other black people.

Black American character runs the complete gamut here, from our virtuous hero and heroine to villains such as Zora's witch of a mother and the coolly sophisticated but unscrupulous woman, Carolyn Wynn, who almost leads Bles permanently astray. So, too, are the white characters of various types. Sarah Smith, a veteran New Englander who has made her life's work the education of poor black folk, is the absolute beacon of moral light that guides the blacks she serves, including Bles and Zora. She shares the stage with more lamentable characters—the profligate Southern plantation owner and his son, who exemplify the corrupted white aristocracy of the region; the poor whites, who are typically pawns exploited by those rich whites who foment the racial antagonism between them and blacks; and cynical Northern whites, who are but a mere shadow of the radical moral energy that led decades before to the Civil War.

Writing with comparative ease, Du Bois spins a complex tale. The novel ends in the triumph of idealism, education, and the will to work hard over both those blacks who would surrender, in one way or another, to the miasma of their lives under white domination and those whites who would make a mockery of their own vaunted standards of morality and culture by worshipping money and denying the principles of democracy. Far more so than in *The Souls of Black Folk*, Du Bois shows a sure understanding of how economic interests underlie most aspects of life. Similarly, in touching almost sensationally on such matters as miscegenation between black men and white women, and the possibility that some white women might actually desire, if mainly in an unconscious way, black men (certainly a black man as attractive as Bles), the novelist takes us into psychological and subliminal territory barely acknowledged before in fiction by writers black or white.

The Quest of the Silver Fleece was not a commercial success. Nevertheless, Du Bois so enjoyed writing this novel that he would produce another, *Dark Princess*, in 1928. Much later, near the end of his life, he published a trilogy of novels of black life on an epic scale, spanning several generations. A historian and sociologist by training, he loved the arts, especially music and literature. He clearly valued the novel as a form. The fiction he wrote is an important index to his superb intelligence and imagination, and *The Quest of the Silver Fleece* should be read by all those who respect his matchless gifts as perhaps the premier black intellectual in our long history.

ARNOLD RAMPERSAD
Stanford University

Professor Arnold Rampersad is cognizant dean of the School of Humanities and Sciences at Stanford University. An acclaimed biographer, he has written books on Langston Hughes and Jackie Robinson, and cowrote Arthur Ashe's memoir, Days of Grace.

THE QUEST OF THE SILVER FLEECE

TO ONE

whose name may not be written but to whose tireless
faith the shaping of these cruder thoughts to forms
more fitly perfect is doubtless due, this
finished work is herewith dedicated

*

Note

He who would tell a tale must look toward three ideals: to tell it well, to tell it beautifully, and to tell the truth.

The first is the Gift of God, the second is the Vision of Genius, but the third is the Reward of Honesty.

In *The Quest of the Silver Fleece* there is little, I ween, divine or ingenious; but, at least, I have been honest. In no fact or picture have I consciously set down aught the counterpart of which I have not seen or known; and whatever the finished picture may lack of completeness, this lack is due now to the story-teller, now to the artist, but never to the herald of the Truth.

NEW YORK CITY
August 15, 1911
THE AUTHOR

One

DREAMS

Night fell. The red waters of the swamp grew sinister and sullen. The tall pines lost their slimness and stood in wide blurred blotches all across the way, and a great shadowy bird arose, wheeled and melted, murmuring, into the black-green sky.

The boy wearily dropped his heavy bundle and stood still, listening as the voice of crickets split the shadows and made the silence audible. A tear wandered down his brown cheek. They were at supper now, he whispered—the father and old mother, away back yonder beyond the night. They were far away; they would never be as near as once they had been, for he had stepped into the world. And the cat and Old Billy—ah, but the world was a lonely thing, so wide and tall and empty! And so bare, so bitter bare! Somehow he had never dreamed of the world as lonely before; he had fared forth to beckoning hands and luring, and to the eager hum of human voices, as of some great, swelling music.

Yet now he was alone; the empty night was closing all about him here in a strange land, and he was afraid. The bundle with his earthly treasure had hung heavy and heavier on his shoulder; his little horde of money was tightly wadded in his sock, and the school lay hidden somewhere far away in the shadows. He wondered how far it was; he looked and harkened, starting at his own heartbeats, and fearing more and more the long dark fingers of the night.

Then of a sudden up from the darkness came music. It was human music, but of a wildness and a weirdness that startled the boy as it fluttered and danced across the dull red waters of the swamp. He hesitated, then impelled by some strange power, left the highway and slipped into the forest of the swamp, shrinking, yet following the song hungrily and half forgetting his fear. A harsher, shriller note struck in as of many and ruder voices; but above it flew the first sweet music, birdlike, abandoned, and the boy crept closer.

The cabin crouched ragged and black at the edge of black waters. An old chimney leaned drunkenly against it, raging with fire and smoke, while through the chinks winked red gleams of warmth and wild cheer. With a revel of shouting and noise, the music suddenly ceased. Hoarse staccato cries and peals of laughter shook the old hut, and as the boy stood there peering through the black trees, abruptly the door flew open and a flood of light illumined the wood.

Amid this mighty halo, as on clouds of flame, a girl was dancing. She was black, and lithe, and tall, and willowy. Her garments twined and flew around the delicate moulding of her dark, young, half-naked limbs. A heavy mass of hair clung motionless to her wide forehead. Her arms twirled and flickered, and body and soul seemed quivering and whirring in the poetry of her motion.

As she danced she sang. He heard her voice as before, fluttering like a bird's in the full sweetness of her utter music. It was no tune nor

melody, it was just formless, boundless music. The boy
and all the world besides. All his darkness was sudde
he crept forward, bewildered, fascinated, until with o
the elf-girl paused. The crimson light fell full upon the warm
vet bronze of her face—her midnight eyes were aglow, her full purple
lips apart, her half hid bosom panting, and all the music dead. Involuntarily the boy gave a gasping cry and awoke to swamp and night and
fire, while a white face, drawn, red-eyed, peered outward from some
hidden throng within the cabin.

"Who's that?" a harsh voice cried.

"Where?" "Who is it?" and pale crowding faces blurred the light.

The boy wheeled blindly and fled in terror stumbling through the
swamp, hearing strange sounds and feeling stealthy creeping hands
and arms and whispering voices. On he toiled in mad haste, struggling
toward the road and losing it until finally beneath the shadows of a
mighty oak he sank exhausted. There he lay a while trembling and at
last drifted into dreamless sleep.

It was morning when he awoke and threw a startled glance upward
to the twisted branches of the oak that bent above, sifting down sunshine on his brown face and close curled hair. Slowly he remembered
the loneliness, the fear and wild running through the dark. He laughed
in the bold courage of day and stretched himself.

Then suddenly he bethought him again of that vision of the night—
the waving arms and flying limbs of the girl, and her great black eyes
looking into the night and calling him. He could hear her now, and
hear that wondrous savage music. Had it been real? Had he dreamed?
Or had it been some witch-vision of the night, come to tempt and lure
him to his undoing? Where was that black and flaming cabin? Where
was the girl—the soul that had called him? *She* must have been real;
she had to live and dance and sing; he must again look into the mystery
of her great eyes. And he sat up in sudden determination, and, lo!
gazed straight into the very eyes of his dreaming.

She sat not four feet from him, leaning against the great tree, her eyes now languorously abstracted, now alert and quizzical with mischief. She seemed but half-clothed, and her warm, dark flesh peeped furtively through the rent gown; her thick, crisp hair was frowsy and rumpled, and the long curves of her bare young arms gleamed in the morning sunshine, glowing with vigor and life. A little mocking smile came and sat upon her lips.

"What you run for?" she asked, with dancing mischief in her eyes.

"Because—" he hesitated, and his cheeks grew hot.

"I knows," she said, with impish glee, laughing low music.

"Why?" he challenged, sturdily.

"You was a-feared."

He bridled. "Well, I reckon you'd be a-feared if you was caught out in the black dark all alone."

"Pooh!" she scoffed and hugged her knees. "Pooh! I've stayed out all alone heaps o' nights."

He looked at her with a curious awe.

"I don't believe you," he asserted; but she tossed her head and her eyes grew scornful.

"Who's a-feared of the dark? I love night." Her eyes grew soft.

He watched her silently, till, waking from her daydream, she abruptly asked:

"Where you from?"

"Georgia."

"Where's that?"

He looked at her in surprise, but she seemed matter-of-fact.

"It's away over yonder," he answered.

"Behind where the sun comes up?"

"Oh, no!"

"Then it ain't so far," she declared. "I knows where the sun rises, and I knows where it sets." She looked up at its gleaming splendor glinting through the leaves, and, noting its height, announced abruptly:

"I'se hungry."

"So'm I," answered the boy, fumbling at his bundle; and then, timidly: "Will you eat with me?"

"Yes," she said, and watched him with eager eyes.

Untying the strips of cloth, he opened his box, and disclosed chicken and biscuits, ham and corn-bread. She clapped her hands in glee.

"Is there any water near?" he asked.

Without a word, she bounded up and flitted off like a brown bird, gleaming dull-golden in the sun, glancing in and out among the trees, till she paused above a tiny black pool, and then came tripping and swaying back with hands held cupwise and dripping with cool water.

"Drink," she cried. Obediently he bent over the little hands that seemed so soft and thin. He took a deep draught; and then to drain the last drop, his hands touched hers and the shock of flesh first meeting flesh startled them both, while the water rained through. A moment their eyes looked deep into each other's—a timid, startled gleam in hers; a wonder in his. Then she said dreamily:

"We'se known us all our lives, and—before, ain't we?"

He hesitated.

"Ye—es—I reckon," he slowly returned. And then, brightening, he asked gayly: "And we'll be friends always, won't we?"

"Yes," she said at last, slowly and solemnly, and another brief moment they stood still.

Then the mischief danced in her eyes, and a song bubbled on her lips. She hopped to the tree.

"Come—eat!" she cried. And they nestled together amid the big black roots of the oak, laughing and talking while they ate.

"What's over there?" he asked pointing northward.

"Cresswell's big house."

"And yonder to the west?"

"The school."

He started joyfully.

"The school! What school?"

"Old Miss' School."

"Miss Smith's school?"

"Yes." The tone was disdainful.

"Why, that's where I'm going. I was a-feared it was a long way off; I must have passed it in the night."

"I hate it!" cried the girl, her lips tense.

"But I'll be so near," he explained. "And why do you hate it?"

"Yes—you'll be near," she admitted; "that'll be nice; but—" she glanced westward, and the fierce look faded. Soft joy crept to her face again, and she sat once more dreaming.

"Yon way's nicest," she said.

"Why, what's there?"

"The swamp," she said mysteriously.

"And what's beyond the swamp?"

She crouched beside him and whispered in eager, tense tones: "Dreams!"

He looked at her, puzzled.

"Dreams?" vaguely—"dreams? Why, dreams ain't—nothing."

"Oh, yes they is!" she insisted, her eyes flaming in misty radiance as she sat staring beyond the shadows of the swamp. "Yes they is! There ain't nothing but dreams—that is, nothing much.

"And over yonder behind the swamps is great fields full of dreams, piled high and burning; and right amongst them the sun, when he's tired o' night, whispers and drops red things, 'cept when devils make 'em black."

The boy stared at her; he knew not whether to jeer or wonder.

"How you know?" he asked at last, skeptically.

"Promise you won't tell?"

"Yes," he answered.

She cuddled into a little heap, nursing her knees, and answered slowly.

"I goes there sometimes. I creeps in 'mongst the dreams; they hangs there like big flowers, dripping dew and sugar and blood—red, red blood. And there's little fairies there that hop about and sing, and devils—great, ugly devils that grabs at you and roasts and eats you if they gits you; but they don't git me. Some devils is big and white, like ha'nts; some is long and shiny, like creepy, slippery snakes; and some is little and broad and black, and they yells—"

The boy was listening in incredulous curiosity, half minded to laugh, half minded to edge away from the black-red radiance of yonder dusky swamp. He glanced furtively backward, and his heart gave a great bound.

"Some is little and broad and black, and they yells—" chanted the girl. And as she chanted, deep, harsh tones came booming through the forest:

"*Zo-ra! Zo-ra!* O—o—oh, Zora!"

He saw far behind him, toward the shadows of the swamp, an old woman—short, broad, black and wrinkled, with fangs and pendulous lips and red, wicked eyes. His heart bounded in sudden fear; he wheeled toward the girl, and caught only the uncertain flash of her garments—the wood was silent, and he was alone.

He arose, startled, quickly gathered his bundle, and looked around him. The sun was strong and high, the morning fresh and vigorous. Stamping one foot angrily, he strode jauntily out of the wood toward the big road.

But ever and anon he glanced curiously back. Had he seen a haunt? Or was the elf-girl real? And then he thought of her words:

"We'se known us all our lives."

Two

THE SCHOOL

Day was breaking above the white buildings of the Negro school and throwing long, low lines of gold in at Miss Sarah Smith's front window. She lay in the stupor of her last morning nap, after a night of harrowing worry. Then, even as she partially awoke, she lay still with closed eyes, feeling the shadow of some great burden, yet daring not to rouse herself and recall its exact form; slowly again she drifted toward unconsciousness.

"*Bang! bang! bang!*" hard knuckles were beating upon the door below.

She heard drowsily, and dreamed that it was the nailing up of all her doors; but she did not care much, and but feebly warded the blows away, for she was very tired.

"*Bang! bang! bang!*" persisted the hard knuckles.

She started up, and her eye fell upon a letter lying on her bureau. Back she sank with a sigh, and lay staring at the ceiling—a gaunt, flat, sad-eyed creature, with wisps of gray hair half-covering her baldness, and a face furrowed with care and gathering years.

It was thirty years ago this day, she recalled, since she first came to this broad land of shade and shine in Alabama to teach black folks.

It had been a hard beginning with suspicion and squalor around; with poverty within and without the first white walls of the new school home. Yet somehow the struggle then with all its helplessness and disappointment had not seemed so bitter as today: then failure meant but little, now it seemed to mean everything; then it meant disappointment to a score of ragged urchins, now it meant two hundred boys and girls, the spirits of a thousand gone before and the hopes of thousands to come. In her imagination the significance of these half dozen gleaming buildings perched aloft seemed portentous—big with the destiny not simply of a county and a State, but of a race—a nation—a world. It was God's own cause, and yet—

"*Bang! bang! bang!*" again went the hard knuckles down there at the front.

Miss Smith slowly arose, shivering a bit and wondering who could possibly be rapping at that time in the morning. She sniffed the chilling air and was sure she caught some lingering perfume from Mrs. Vanderpool's gown. She had brought this rich and rare-apparelled lady up here yesterday, because it was more private, and here she had poured forth her needs. She had talked long and in deadly earnest. She had not spoken of the endowment for which she had hoped so desperately during a quarter of a century—no, only for the five thousand dollars to buy the long needed new land. It was so little—so little beside what this woman squandered—

The insistent knocking was repeated louder than before.

"Sakes alive," cried Miss Smith, throwing a shawl about her and leaning out the window. "Who is it, and what do you want?"

"Please, ma'am. I've come to school," answered a tall black boy with a bundle.

"Well, why don't you go to the office?" Then she saw his face and hesitated. She felt again the old motherly instinct to be the first to welcome the new pupil; a luxury which, in later years, the endless push of details had denied her.

"Wait!" she cried shortly, and began to dress.

A new boy, she mused. Yes, every day they straggled in; every day came the call for more, more—this great, growing thirst to know—to do—to be. And yet that woman had sat right here, aloof, imperturbable, listening only courteously. When Miss Smith finished, she had paused and, flicking her glove,—

"My dear Miss Smith," she said softly, with a tone that just escaped a drawl—"My dear Miss Smith, your work is interesting and your faith—marvellous; but, frankly, I cannot make myself believe in it. You are trying to treat these funny little monkeys just as you would your own children—or even mine. It's quite heroic, of course, but it's sheer madness, and I do not feel I ought to encourage it. I would not mind a thousand or so to train a good cook for the Cresswells, or a clean and faithful maid for myself—for Helene has faults—or indeed deft and tractable laboring-folk for any one; but I'm quite through trying to turn natural servants into masters of me and mine. I—hope I'm not too blunt; I hope I make myself clear. You know, statistics show—"

"Drat statistics!" Miss Smith had flashed impatiently. "These are folks."

Mrs. Vanderpool smiled indulgently. "To be sure," she murmured, "but what sort of folks?"

"God's sort."

"Oh, well—"

But Miss Smith had the bit in her teeth and could not have stopped. She was paying high for the privilege of talking, but it had to be said.

"God's sort, Mrs. Vanderpool—not the sort that think of the world as arranged for their exclusive benefit and comfort."

"Well, I do want to count—"

Miss Smith bent forward—not a beautiful pose, but earnest.

"I want you to count, and I want to count, too; but I don't want us to be the only ones that count. I want to live in a world where every soul counts—white, black, and yellow—all. *That's* what I'm teaching these children here—to count, and not to be like dumb, driven cattle. If you don't believe in this, of course you cannot help us."

"Your spirit is admirable, Miss Smith," she had said very softly; "I only wish I could feel as you do. Good-afternoon," and she had rustled gently down the narrow stairs, leaving an all but imperceptible suggestion of perfume. Miss Smith could smell it yet as she went down this morning.

The breakfast bell jangled. "Five thousand dollars," she kept repeating to herself, greeting the teachers absently—"five thousand dollars." And then on the porch she was suddenly aware of the awaiting boy. She eyed him critically: black, fifteen, country-bred, strong, clear-eyed.

"Well?" she asked in that brusque manner wherewith her natural timidity was wont to mask her kindness. "Well, sir?"

"I've come to school."

"Humph—we can't teach boys for nothing."

The boy straightened. "I can pay my way," he returned.

"You mean you can pay what we ask?"

"Why, yes. Ain't that all?"

"No. The rest is gathered from the crumbs of Dives' table."

Then he saw the twinkle in her eyes. She laid her hand gently upon his shoulder.

"If you don't hurry you'll be late to breakfast," she said with an air of confidence. "See those boys over there? Follow them, and at noon come to the office—wait! What's your name?"

"Blessed Alwyn," he answered, and the passing teachers smiled.

Three

MISS MARY TAYLOR

Miss Mary Taylor did not take a college course for the purpose of teaching Negroes. Not that she objected to Negroes as human beings—quite the contrary. In the debate between the senior societies her defence of the Fifteenth Amendment had been not only a notable bit of reasoning, but delivered with real enthusiasm. Nevertheless, when the end of the summer came and the only opening facing her was the teaching of children at Miss Smith's experiment in the Alabama swamps, it must be frankly confessed that Miss Taylor was disappointed.

Her dream had been a post-graduate course at Bryn Mawr; but that was out of the question until money was earned. She had pictured herself earning this by teaching one or two of her "specialties" in some private school near New York or Boston, or even in a Western college. The South she had not thought of seriously; and yet, knowing of its delightful hospitality and mild climate, she was not averse to Charleston or New Orleans. But from the offer that came to teach Negroes—country Negroes, and little ones at that—she shrank, and, indeed, probably would have refused it out of hand had it not been for her queer brother, John. John Taylor, who had supported her through college, was interested in cotton. Having certain schemes in mind, he had been struck by the fact that the Smith School was in the midst of the Alabama cotton-belt.

"Better go," he had counselled, sententiously. "Might learn something useful down there."

She had been not a little dismayed by the outlook, and had protested against his blunt insistence.

"But, John, there's no society—just elementary work—"

John had met this objection with, "Humph!" as he left for his office. Next day he had returned to the subject.

"Been looking up Tooms County. Find some Cresswells there—big plantations—rated at two hundred and fifty thousand dollars. Some others, too; big cotton county."

"You ought to know, John, if I teach Negroes I'll scarcely see much of people in my own class."

"Nonsense! Butt in. Show off. Give 'em your Greek—and study Cotton. At any rate, I say go."

And so, howsoever reluctantly, she had gone.

The trial was all she had anticipated, and possibly a bit more. She was a pretty young woman of twenty-three, fair and rather daintily moulded. In favorable surroundings, she would have been an aristocrat and an epicure. Here she was teaching dirty children, and the smell of confused odors and bodily perspiration was to her at times unbearable.

Then there was the fact of their color: it was a fact so insistent, so fatal she almost said at times, that she could not escape it. Theoretically she had always treated it with disdainful ease.

"What's the mere color of a human soul's skin," she had cried to a Wellesley audience and the audience had applauded with enthusiasm. But here in Alabama, brought closely and intimately in touch with these dark skinned children, their color struck her at first with a sort of terror—it seemed ominous and forbidding. She found herself shrinking away and gripping herself lest they should perceive. She could not help but think that in most other things they were as different from her as in color. She groped for new ways to teach colored brains and marshal colored thoughts and the result was puzzling both to teacher and student. With the other teachers she had little commerce. They were in no sense her sort of folk. Miss Smith represented the older New England of her parents—honest, inscrutable, determined, with a conscience which she worshipped, and utterly unselfish. She appealed to Miss Taylor's ruddier and daintier vision but dimly and distantly as some memory of the past. The other teachers were indistinct personalities, always very busy and very tired, and talking "school-room" with their meals. Miss Taylor was soon starving for human companionship, for the lighter touches of life and some of its warmth and laughter. She wanted a glance of the new books and periodicals and talk of great philanthropies and reforms. She felt out of the world, shut in and mentally anæmic; great as the "Negro Problem" might be as a world problem, it looked sordid and small at close range. So for the hundredth time she was thinking today, as she walked alone up the lane back of the barn, and then slowly down through the bottoms. She paused a moment and nodded to the two boys at work in a young cotton field.

"Cotton!"

She paused. She remembered with what interest she had always read of this little thread of the world. She had almost forgotten that it was here within touch and sight. For a moment something of the vision of Cotton was mirrored in her mind. The glimmering sea of delicate leaves whispered and murmured before her, stretching away to the

Northward. She remembered that beyond this little world it stretched on and on—how far she did not know—but on and on in a great trembling sea, and the foam of its mighty waters would one time flood the ends of the earth.

She glimpsed all this with parted lips, and then sighed impatiently. There might be a bit of poetry here and there, but most of this place was such desperate prose.

She glanced absently at the boys.

One was Bles Alwyn, a tall black lad. (Bles, she mused,—now who would think of naming a boy "Blessed," save these incomprehensible creatures!) Her regard shifted to the green stalks and leaves again, and she started to move away. Then her New England conscience stepped in. She ought not to pass these students without a word of encouragement or instruction.

"Cotton is a wonderful thing, is it not, boys?" she said rather primly. The boys touched their hats and murmured something indistinctly. Miss Taylor did not know much about cotton, but at least one more remark seemed called for.

"How long before the stalks will be ready to cut?" she asked carelessly. The farther boy coughed and Bles raised his eyes and looked at her; then after a pause he answered slowly. (Oh! these people were so slow—now a New England boy would have answered and asked a half-dozen questions in the time.)

"I—I don't know," he faltered.

"Don't know! Well, of all things!" inwardly commented Miss Taylor—"literally born in cotton, and—Oh, well," as much as to ask, "What's the use?" She turned again to go.

"What is planted over there?" she asked, although she really didn't care.

"Goobers," answered the smaller boy.

"Goobers?" uncomprehendingly.

"Peanuts," Bles specified.

"Oh!" murmured Miss Taylor. "I see there are none on the vines yet. I suppose, though, it's too early for them."

Then came the explosion. The smaller boy just snorted with irrepressible laughter and bolted across the fields. And Bles—was Miss Taylor deceived?—or was he chuckling? She reddened, drew herself up, and then, dropping her primness, rippled with laughter.

"What is the matter, Bles?" she asked.

He looked at her with twinkling eyes.

"Well, you see, Miss Taylor, it's like this: farming don't seem to be your specialty."

The word was often on Miss Taylor's lips, and she recognized it. Despite herself she smiled again.

"Of course, it isn't—I don't know anything about farming. But what did I say so funny?"

Bles was now laughing outright.

"Why, Miss Taylor! I declare! Goobers don't grow on the tops of vines, but underground on the roots—like yams."

"Is that so?"

"Yes, and we—we don't pick cotton stalks except for kindling."

"I must have been thinking of hemp. But tell me more about cotton."

His eyes lighted, for cotton was to him a very real and beautiful thing, and a life-long companion, yet not one whose friendship had been coarsened and killed by heavy toil. He leaned against his hoe and talked half dreamily—where had he learned so well that dream-talk?

"We turn up the earth and sow it soon after Christmas. Then pretty soon there comes a sort of greenness on the black land and it swells and grows and, and—shivers. Then stalks shoot up with three or four leaves. That's the way it is now, see? After that we chop out the weak stalks, and the strong ones grow tall and dark, till I think it must be like the ocean—all green and billowy; then come little flecks here and there and the sea is all filled with flowers—flowers like little bells, blue and purple and white."

"Ah! that must be beautiful," sighed Miss Taylor, wistfully, sinking to the ground and clasping her hands about her knees.

"Yes, ma'am. But it's prettiest when the bolls come and swell and burst, and the cotton covers the field like foam, all misty—"

She bent wondering over the pale plants. The poetry of the thing began to sing within her, awakening her unpoetic imagination, and she murmured:

"The Golden Fleece—it's the Silver Fleece!"

He harkened.

"What's that?" he asked.

"Have you never heard of the Golden Fleece, Bles?"

"No, ma'am," he said eagerly; then glancing up toward the Cresswell fields, he saw two white men watching them. He grasped his hoe and started briskly to work.

"Some time you'll tell me, please, won't you?"

She glanced at her watch in surprise and arose hastily.

"Yes, with pleasure," she said moving away—at first very fast, and then more and more slowly up the lane, with a puzzled look on her face.

She began to realize that in this pleasant little chat the fact of the boy's color had quite escaped her; and what especially puzzled her was that this had not happened before. She had been here four months, and yet every moment up to now she seemed to have been vividly, almost painfully conscious, that she was a white woman talking to black folk. Now, for one little half-hour she had been a woman talking to a boy— no, not even that: she had been talking—just talking; there were no persons in the conversation, just things—one thing: Cotton.

She started thinking of cotton—but at once she pulled herself back to the other aspect. Always before she had been veiled from these folk: who had put the veil there? Had she herself hung it before her soul, or had they hidden timidly behind its other side? Or was it simply a brute fact, regardless of both of them?

The longer she thought, the more bewildered she grew. There seemed no analogy that she knew. Here was a unique thing, and she climbed to her bedroom and stared at the stars.

Four

TOWN

John Taylor had written to his sister. He wanted information, very definite information, about Tooms County cotton; about its stores, its people—especially its people. He propounded a dozen questions, sharp, searching questions, and he wanted the answers tomorrow. Impossible! thought Miss Taylor. He had calculated on her getting this letter yesterday, forgetting that their mail was fetched once a day from the town, four miles away. Then, too, she did not know all these matters and knew no one who did. Did John think she had nothing else to do? And sighing at the thought of to-morrow's drudgery, she determined to consult Miss Smith in the morning.

Miss Smith suggested a drive to town—Bles could take her in the top-buggy after school—and she could consult some of the merchants and business men. She could then write her letter and mail it there; it would be but a day or so late getting to New York.

"Of course," said Miss Smith drily, slowly folding her napkin, "of course, the only people here are the Cresswells."

"Oh, yes," said Miss Taylor invitingly. There was an allurement about this all-pervasive name; it held her by a growing fascination and she was anxious for the older woman to amplify. Miss Smith, however, remained provokingly silent, so Miss Taylor essayed further.

"What sort of people are the Cresswells?" she asked.

"The old man's a fool; the young one a rascal; the girl a ninny," was Miss Smith's succinct and acid classification of the county's first family; adding, as she rose, "but they own us body and soul." She hurried out of the dining-room without further remark. Miss Smith was more patient with black folk than with white.

The sun was hanging just above the tallest trees of the swamp when Miss Taylor, weary with the day's work, climbed into the buggy beside Bles. They wheeled comfortably down the road, leaving the sombre swamp, with its black-green, to the right, and heading toward the golden-green of waving cotton fields. Miss Taylor lay back, listlessly, and drank the soft warm air of the languorous Spring. She thought of the golden sheen of the cotton, and the cold March winds of New England; of her brother who apparently noted nothing of leaves and winds and seasons; and of the mighty Cresswells whom Miss Smith so evidently disliked. Suddenly she became aware of her long silence and the silence of the boy.

"Bles," she began didactically, "where are you from?"

He glanced across at her and answered shortly:

"Georgia, ma'am," and was silent.

The girl tried again.

"Georgia is a large State,"—tentatively.

"Yes, ma'am."

"Are you going back there when you finish?"

"I don't know."

"I think you ought to—and work for your people."

"Yes, ma'am."

She stopped, puzzled, and looked about. The old horse jogged lazily on, and Bles switched him unavailingly. Somehow she had missed the way today. The Veil hung thick, sombre, impenetrable. Well, she had done her duty, and slowly she nestled back and watched the far-off green and golden radiance of the cotton.

"Bles," she said impulsively, "shall I tell you of the Golden Fleece?"

He glanced at her again.

"Yes'm, please," he said.

She settled herself almost luxuriously, and began the story of Jason and the Argonauts.

The boy remained silent. And when she had finished, he still sat silent, elbow on knee, absently flicking the jogging horse and staring ahead at the horizon. She looked at him doubtfully with some disappointment that his hearing had apparently shared so little of the joy of her telling; and, too, there was mingled a vague sense of having lowered herself to too familiar fellowship with this—this boy. She straightened herself instinctively and thought of some remark that would restore proper relations. She had not found it before he said, slowly:

"All yon is Jason's."

"What?" she asked, puzzled.

He pointed with one sweep of his long arm to the quivering mass of green-gold foliage that swept from swamp to horizon.

"All yon golden fleece is Jason's now," he repeated.

"I thought it was—Cresswell's," she said.

"That's what I mean."

She suddenly understood that the story had sunk deeply.

"I am glad to hear you say that," she said methodically, "for Jason was a brave adventurer—"

"I thought he was a thief."

"Oh, well—those were other times."

"The Cresswells are thieves now."

Miss Taylor answered sharply.

"Bles, I am ashamed to hear you talk so of your neighbors simply because they are white."

But Bles continued.

"This is the Black Sea," he said, pointing to the dull cabins that crouched here and there upon the earth, with the dark twinkling of their black folk darting out to see the strangers ride by.

Despite herself Miss Taylor caught the allegory and half whispered, "Lo! the King himself!" as a black man almost rose from the tangled earth at their side. He was tall and thin and sombre-hued, with a carven face and thick gray hair.

"Your servant, mistress," he said, with a sweeping bow as he strode toward the swamp. Miss Taylor stopped him, for he looked interesting, and might answer some of her brother's questions. He turned back and stood regarding her with sorrowful eyes and ugly mouth.

"Do you live about here?" she asked.

"I'se lived here a hundred years," he answered. She did not believe it; he might be seventy, eighty, or even ninety—indeed, there was about him that indefinable sense of age—some shadow of endless living; but a hundred seemed absurd.

"You know the people pretty well, then?"

"I knows dem all. I knows most of 'em better dan dey knows demselves. I knows a heap of tings in dis world and in de next."

"This is a great cotton country?"

"Dey don't raise no cotton now to what dey used to when old Gen'rel Cresswell fust come from Carolina; den it was a bale and a half to the acre on stalks dat looked like young brushwood. Dat was cotton."

"You know the Cresswells, then?"

"Know dem? I knowed dem afore dey was born."

"They are—wealthy people?"

"Dey rolls in money and dey'se quality, too. No shoddy upstarts dem, but born to purple, lady, born to purple. Old Gen'ral Cresswell had niggers and acres no end back dere in Carolina. He brung a part of dem here and here his son, de father of dis Colonel Cresswell, was born. De son—I knowed him well—he had a tousand niggers and ten tousand acres afore de war."

"Were they kind to their slaves?"

"Oh, yaas, yaas, ma'am, dey was careful of de're niggers and wouldn't let de drivers whip 'em much."

"And these Cresswells today?"

"Oh, dey're quality—high-blooded folks—dey'se lost some land and niggers, but, lordy, nuttin' can buy de Cresswells, dey naturally owns de world."

"Are they honest and kind?"

"Oh, yaas, ma'am—dey'se good white folks."

"Good white folk?"

"Oh, yaas, ma'am—course you knows white folks will be white folks—white folks will be white folks. Your servant, ma'am." And the swamp swallowed him.

The boy's eyes followed him as he whipped up the horse.

"He's going to Elspeth's," he said.

"Who is he?"

"We just call him Old Pappy—he's a preacher, and some folks say a conjure man, too."

"And who is Elspeth?"

"She lives in the swamp—she's a kind of witch, I reckon, like—like—"

"Like Medea?"

"Yes—only—I don't know—" and he grew thoughtful.

The road turned now and far away to the eastward rose the first straggling cabins of the town. Creeping toward them down the road rolled a dark squat figure. It grew and spread slowly on the horizon until it became a fat old black woman, hooded and aproned, with great round hips and massive bosom. Her face was heavy and homely until she looked up and lifted the drooping cheeks, and then kindly old eyes beamed on the young teacher, as she curtsied and cried:

"Good-evening, honey! Good-evening! You sure is pretty dis evening."

"Why, Aunt Rachel, how are you?" There was genuine pleasure in the girl's tone.

"Just tolerable, honey, bless de Lord! Rumatiz is kind o' bad and Aunt Rachel ain't so young as she use ter be."

"And what brings you to town afoot this time of day?"

The face fell again to dull care and the old eyes crept away. She fumbled with her cane.

"It's de boys again, honey," she returned solemnly; "dey'se good boys, dey is good to de're old mammy, but dey'se high strung and dey gits fighting and drinking and—and—last Saturday night dey got took up again. I'se been to Jedge Grey—I use to tote him on my knee, honey—I'se been to him to plead him not to let 'em go on de gang, 'cause you see, honey," and she stroked the girl's sleeve as if pleading with her, too, "you see it done ruins boys to put 'em on de gang.

Miss Taylor tried hard to think of something comforting to say, but words seemed inadequate to cheer the old soul; but after a few moments they rode on, leaving the kind face again beaming and dimpling.

And now the country town of Toomsville lifted itself above the cotton and corn, fringed with dirty straggling cabins of black folk. The road swung past the iron watering trough, turned sharply and, after passing two or three pert cottages and a stately house, old and faded, opened into the wide square. Here pulsed the very life and being of the land. Yonder great bales of cotton, yellow-white in its soiled sacking, piled in lofty, dusty mountains, lay listening for the train that, twice a day, ran out to the greater world. Round about, tied to the well-gnawed hitching rails, were rows of mules—mules with back cloths;

mules with saddles; mules hitched to long wagons, buggies, and rickety gigs; mules munching golden ears of corn, and mules drooping their heads in sorrowful memory of better days.

Beyond the cotton warehouse smoked the chimneys of the seed-mill and the cotton-gin; a red livery-stable faced them and all about three sides of the square ran stores; big stores and small wide-windowed, narrow stores. Some had old steps above the worn clay side-walks, and some were flush with the ground. All had a general sense of dilapidation—save one, the largest and most imposing, a three-story brick. This was Caldwell's "Emporium"; and here Bles stopped and Miss Taylor entered.

Mr. Caldwell himself hurried forward; and the whole store, clerks and customers, stood at attention, for Miss Taylor was yet new to the county.

She bought a few trifles and then approached her main business.

"My brother wants some information about the county, Mr. Caldwell, and I am only a teacher, and do not know much about conditions here."

"Ah! where do you teach?" asked Mr. Caldwell. He was certain he knew the teachers of all the white schools in the county. Miss Taylor told him. He stiffened slightly but perceptibly, like a man clicking the buckles of his ready armor, and two townswomen who listened gradually turned their backs, but remained near.

"Yes—yes," he said, with uncomfortable haste. "Any—er—information—of course—" Miss Taylor got out her notes.

"The leading land-owners," she began, sorting the notes searchingly, "I should like to know something about them."

"Well, Colonel Cresswell is, of course, our greatest landlord—a high-bred gentleman of the old school. He and his son—a worthy successor to the name—hold some fifty thousand acres. They may be considered representative types. Then, Mr. Maxwell has ten thousand acres and Mr. Tolliver a thousand."

Miss Taylor wrote rapidly. "And cotton?" she asked.

"We raise considerable cotton, but not nearly what we ought to; nigger labor is too worthless."

"Oh! The Negroes are not, then, very efficient?"

"Efficient!" snorted Mr. Caldwell; at last she had broached a phase of the problem upon which he could dilate with fervor. "They're the lowest-down, ornriest—begging your pardon—good-for-nothing loafers you ever heard of. Why, we just have to carry them and care for them like children. Look yonder," he pointed across the square to the court-house. It was an old square brick-and-stucco building, sombre and stilted and very dirty. Out of it filed a stream of men—some black and shackled; some white and swaggering and liberal with tobacco-juice; some white and shaven and stiff. "Court's just out," pursued Mr. Caldwell, "and them niggers have just been sent to the gang— young ones, too; educated but good for nothing. They're all that way."

Miss Taylor looked up a little puzzled, and became aware of a battery of eyes and ears. Everybody seemed craning and listening, and she felt a sudden embarrassment and a sense of half-veiled hostility in the air. With one or two further perfunctory questions, and a hasty expression of thanks, she escaped into the air.

The whole square seemed loafing and lolling—the white world perched on stoops and chairs, in doorways and windows; the black world filtering down from doorways to side-walk and curb. The hot, dusty quadrangle stretched in dreary deadness toward the temple of the town, as if doing obeisance to the court-house. Down the court-house steps the sheriff, with Winchester on shoulder, was bringing the last prisoner—a curly-headed boy with golden face and big brown frightened eyes.

"It's one of Dunn's boys," said Bles. "He's drunk again, and they say he's been stealing. I expect he was hungry." And they wheeled out of the square.

Miss Taylor was tired, and the hastily scribbled letter which she dropped into the post in passing was not as clearly expressed as she could wish.

A great-voiced giant, brown and bearded, drove past them, roaring a hymn. He greeted Bles with a comprehensive wave of the hand.

"I guess Tylor has been paid off," said Bles, but Miss Taylor was too disgusted to answer. Further on they overtook a tall young yellow boy walking awkwardly beside a handsome, bold-faced girl. Two white men came riding by. One leered at the girl, and she laughed back, while the yellow boy strode sullenly ahead. As the two white riders approached the buggy one said to the other:

"Who's that nigger with?"

"One of them nigger teachers."

"Well, they'll stop this damn riding around or they'll hear something," and they rode slowly by.

Miss Taylor felt rather than heard their words, and she was uncomfortable. The sun fell fast; the long shadows of the swamp swept soft coolness on the red road. Then afar in front a curled cloud of white dust arose and out of it came the sound of galloping horses.

"Who's this?" asked Miss Taylor.

"The Cresswells, I think; they usually ride to town about this time." But already Miss Taylor had descried the brown and tawny sides of the speeding horses.

"Good gracious!" she thought. "The Cresswells!" And with it came a sudden desire not to meet them—just then. She glanced toward the swamp. The sun was sifting blood-red lances through the trees. A little wagon-road entered the wood and disappeared. Miss Taylor saw it.

"Let's see the sunset in the swamp," she said suddenly. On came the galloping horses. Bles looked up in surprise, then silently turned into the swamp. The horses flew by, their hoof-beats dying in the distance. A dark green silence lay about them lit by mighty crimson glories beyond. Miss Taylor leaned back and watched it dreamily till a sense of oppression grew on her. The sun was sinking fast.

"Where does this road come out?" she asked at last.

"It doesn't come out."

"Where does it go?"

"It goes to Elspeth's."

"Why, we must turn back immediately. I thought—" But Bles was already turning. They were approaching the main road again when there came a fluttering as of a great bird beating its wings amid the forest. Then a girl, lithe, dark brown, and tall, leaped lightly into the path with greetings on her lips for Bles. At the sight of the lady she drew suddenly back and stood motionless regarding Miss Taylor, searching her with wide black liquid eyes. Miss Taylor was a little startled.

"Good—good-evening," she said, straightening herself.

The girl was still silent and the horse stopped. One tense moment pulsed through all the swamp. Then the girl, still motionless— still looking Miss Taylor through and through—said with slow deliberateness:

"I hates you."

The teacher in Miss Taylor strove to rebuke this unconventional greeting but the woman in her spoke first and asked almost before she knew it—

"Why?"

Five

___

ZORA

Zora, child of the swamp, was a heathen hoyden of twelve wayward, untrained years. Slight, straight, strong, full-blooded, she
had dreamed her life away in wilful wandering through her dark and
sombre kingdom until she was one with it in all its moods; mischievous, secretive, brooding; full of great and awful visions, steeped body
and soul in wood-lore. Her home was out of doors, the cabin of Elspeth her port of call for talking and eating. She had not known, she
had scarcely seen, a child of her own age until Bles Alwyn had fled
from her dancing in the night, and she had searched and found him
sleeping in the misty morning light. It was to her a strange new thing
to see a fellow of like years with herself, and she gripped him to her
soul in wild interest and new curiosity. Yet this childish friendship was
so new and incomprehensible a thing to her that she did not know how
to express it. At first she pounced upon him in mirthful, almost impish

glee, teasing and mocking and half scaring him, despite his fifteen years of young manhood.

"Yes, they is devils down yonder behind the swamp," she would whisper, warningly, when, after the first meeting, he had crept back again and again, half fascinated, half amused to greet her; "I'se seen 'em, I'se heard 'em, 'cause my mammy is a witch."

The boy would sit and watch her wonderingly as she lay curled along the low branch of the mighty oak, clinging with little curved limbs and flying fingers. Possessed by the spirit of her vision, she would chant, low-voiced, tremulous, mischievous:

"One night a devil come to me on blue fire out of a big red flower that grows in the south swamp; he was tall and big and strong as anything, and when he spoke the trees shook and the stars fell. Even mammy was afeared; and it takes a lot to make mammy afeared, 'cause she's a witch and can conjure. He said, 'I'll come when you die—I'll come when you die, and take the conjure off you,' and then he went away on a big fire."

"Shucks!" the boy would say, trying to express scornful disbelief when, in truth, he was awed and doubtful. Always he would glance involuntarily back along the path behind him. Then her low birdlike laughter would rise and ring through the trees.

So passed a year, and there came the time when her wayward teasing and the almost painful thrill of her tale-telling nettled him and drove him away. For long months he did not meet her, until one day he saw her deep eyes fixed longingly upon him from a thicket in the swamp. He went and greeted her. But she said no word, sitting nested among the greenwood with passionate, proud silence, until he had sued long for peace; then in sudden new friendship she had taken his hand and led him through the swamp, showing him all the beauty of her swamp-world—great shadowy oaks and limpid pools, lone, naked trees and sweet flowers; the whispering and flitting of wild things, and the winging of furtive birds. She had dropped the impish mischief of her way, and up from beneath it rose a wistful, visionary tenderness; a mighty half-confessed, half-concealed, striving for unknown things. He seemed to have found a new friend.

And today, after he had taken Miss Taylor home and supped, he came out in the twilight under the new moon and whistled the tremulous note that always brought her.

"Why did you speak so to Miss Taylor?" he asked, reproachfully. She considered the matter a moment.

"You don't understand," she said. "You can't never understand. I can see right through people. You can't. You never had a witch for a mammy—did you?"

"No."

"Well, then, you see I have to take care of you and see things for you."

"Zora," he said thoughtfully, "you must learn to read."

"What for?"

"So that you can read books and know lots of things."

"Don't white folks make books?"

"Yes—most of the books."

"Pooh! I knows more than they do now—a heap more."

"In some ways you do; but they know things that give them power and wealth and make them rule."

"No, no. They don't really rule; they just thinks they rule. They just got things—heavy, dead things. We black folks is got the *spirit*. We'se lighter and cunninger; we fly right through them; we go and come again just as we wants to. Black folks is wonderful."

He did not understand what she meant; but he knew what he wanted and he tried again.

"Even if white folks don't know everything they know different things from us, and we ought to know what they know."

This appealed to her somewhat.

"I don't believe they know much," she concluded; "but I'll learn to read and just see."

"It will be hard work," he warned. But he had come prepared for acquiescence. He took a primer from his pocket and, lighting a match, showed her the alphabet.

"Learn those," he said.

"What for?" she asked, looking at the letters disdainfully.

"Because that's the way," he said, as the light flared and went out.

"I don't believe it," she disputed, disappearing in the wood and returning with a pine-knot. They lighted it and its smoky flame threw wavering shadows about. She turned the leaves till she came to a picture which she studied intently.

"Is this about this?" she asked, pointing alternately to reading and picture.

"Yes. And if you learn—"

"Read it," she commanded. He read the page.

"Again," she said, making him point out each word. Then she read it after him, accurately, with more perfect expression. He stared at her. She took the book, and with a nod was gone.

It was Saturday and dark. She never asked Bles to her home—to that mysterious black cabin in mid-swamp. He thought her ashamed of it, and delicately refrained from going. So tonight she slipped away, stopped and listened till she heard his footsteps on the pike, and then flew homeward. Presently the old black cabin loomed before her with its wide flapping door. The old woman was bending over the fire, stirring some savory mess, and a yellow girl with a white baby on one arm was placing dishes on a rickety wooden table when Zora suddenly and noiselessly entered the door.

"Come, is you? I 'lowed victuals would fetch you," grumbled the hag.

But Zora deigned no answer. She walked placidly to the table, where she took up a handful of cold corn-bread and meat, and then went over and curled up by the fire.

Elspeth and the girl talked and laughed coarsely, and the night wore on.

By and by loud laughter and tramping came from the road—a sound of numerous footsteps. Zora listened, leapt to her feet and started to the door. The old crone threw an epithet after her; but she flashed through the lighted doorway and was gone, followed by the oath and shouts from the approaching men. In the hut night fled with wild song and revel, and day dawned again. Out from some fastness of the wood crept Zora. She stopped and bathed in a pool, and combed her close-clung hair, then entered silently to breakfast.

Thus began in the dark swamp that primal battle with the Word. She hated it and despised it, but her pride was in arms and her one great life friendship in the balance. She fought her way with a dogged persistence that brought word after word of praise and interest from Bles. Then, once well begun, her busy, eager mind flew with a rapidity that startled; the stories especially she devoured—tales of strange things and countries and men gripped her imagination and clung to her memory.

"Didn't I tell you there was lots to learn?" he asked once.

"I knew it all," she retorted; "every bit. I'se thought it all before; only the little things is different—and I like the little, strange things."

Spring ripened to summer. She was reading well and writing some.

"Zora," he announced one morning under their forest oak, "you must go to school."

She eyed him, surprised.

"Why?"

"You've found some things worth knowing in this world, haven't you, Zora?

"Yes," she admitted.

"But there are more—many, many more—worlds on worlds of things—you have not dreamed of."

She stared at him, open-eyed, and a wonder crept upon her face battling with the old assurance. Then she looked down at her bare brown feet and torn gown.

"I've got a little money, Zora," he said quickly.

But she lifted her head.

"I'll earn mine," she said.

"How?" he asked doubtfully.

"I'll pick cotton."

"Can you?"

"Course I can."

"It's hard work."

She hesitated.

"I don't like to work," she mused. "You see, mammy's pappy was a king's son, and kings don't work. I don't work; mostly I dreams. But I can work, and I will—for the wonder things—and for you."

So the summer yellowed and silvered into fall. All the vacation days Bles worked on the farm, and Zora read and dreamed and studied in the wood, until the land lay white with harvest. Then, without warning, she appeared in the cotton-field beside Bles, and picked.

It was hot, sore work. The sun blazed; her bent and untrained back pained, and the soft little hands bled. But no complaint passed her lips; her hands never wavered, and her eyes met his steadily and gravely. She bade him good-night, cheerily, and then stole away to the wood, crouching beneath the great oak, and biting back the groans that trembled on her lips. Often, she fell supperless to sleep, with two great tears creeping down her tired cheeks.

When school-time came there was not yet money enough, for cotton-picking was not far advanced. Yet Zora would take no money from Bles, and worked earnestly away.

Meantime there occurred to the boy the momentous question of clothes. Had Zora thought of them? He feared not. She knew little of clothes and cared less. So one day in town he dropped into Caldwell's

"Emporium" and glanced hesitantly at certain ready-made dresses. One caught his eye. It came from the great Easterly mills in New England and was red—a vivid red. The glowing warmth of this cloth of cotton caught the eye of Bles, and he bought the gown for a dollar and a half.

He carried it to Zora in the wood, and unrolled it before her eyes that danced with glad tears. Of course, it was long and wide; but he fetched needle and thread and scissors, too. It was a full month after school had begun when they, together back in the swamp, shadowed by the foliage, began to fashion the wonderful garment. At the same time she laid ten dollars of her first hard-earned money in his hands.

"You can finish the first year with this money," Bles assured her, delighted, "and then next year you must come in to board; because, you see, when you're educated you won't want to live in the swamp."

"I wants to live here always."

"But not at Elspeth's."

"No-o—not there, not there." And a troubled questioning trembled in her eyes, but brought no answering thought in his, for he was busy with his plans.

"Then, you see, Zora, if you stay here you'll need a new house, and you'll want to learn how to make it beautiful."

"Yes, a beautiful, great castle here in the swamp," she dreamed; "but," and her face fell, "I can't get money enough to board in; and I don't want to board in—I wants to be free."

He looked at her, curled down so earnestly at her puzzling task, and a pity for the more than motherless child swept over him. He bent over her, nervously, eagerly, and she laid down her sewing and sat silent and passive with dark, burning eyes.

"Zora," he said, "I want you to do all this—for me."

"I will, if you wants me to," she said quietly, but with something in her voice that made him look half startled into her beautiful eyes and feel a queer flushing in his face. He stretched his hand out and taking hers held it lightly till she quivered and drew away, bending again over her sewing.

Then a nameless exaltation rose within his heart.

"Zora," he whispered, "I've got a plan."

"What is it?" she asked, still with bowed head.

"Listen, till I tell you of the Golden Fleece."

Then she too heard the story of Jason. Breathless she listened, dropping her sewing and leaning forward, eager-eyed. Then her face clouded.

"Do you s'pose mammy's the witch?" she asked dubiously.

"No; she wouldn't give her own flesh and blood to help the thieving Jason."

She looked at him searchingly.

"Yes, she would, too," affirmed the girl, and then she paused, still intently watching him. She was troubled, and again a question eagerly hovered on her lips. But he continued:

"Then we must escape her," he said gayly. "See! yonder lies the Silver Fleece spread across the brown back of the world; let's get a bit of it, and hide it here in the swamp, and comb it, and tend it, and make it the beautifullest bit of all. Then we can sell it, and send you to school."

She sat silently bent forward, turning the picture in her mind. Suddenly forgetting her trouble, she bubbled with laughter, and leaping up clapped her hands.

"And I knows just the place!" she cried eagerly, looking at him with a flash of the old teasing mischief—"down in the heart of the swamp—where dreams and devils lives."

Up at the school-house Miss Taylor was musing. She had been invited to spend the summer with Mrs. Grey at Lake George, and such a summer!—silken clothes and dainty food, motoring and golf, well-groomed men and elegant women. She would not have put it in just that way, but the vision came very close to spelling heaven to her mind. Not that she would come to it vacant-minded, but rather as a trained woman, starved for companionship and wanting something of the beauty and ease of life. She sat dreaming of it here with rows of dark faces before her, and the singsong wail of a little black reader with his head aslant and his patched kneepants.

The day was warm and languorous, and the last pale mist of the Silver Fleece peeped in at the windows. She tried to follow the third-reader lesson with her finger, but persistently off she went, dreaming, to some exquisite little parlor with its green and gold, the clink of dainty china and hum of low voices, and the blue lake in the window; she would glance up, the door would open softly and—

Just here she did glance up, and all the school glanced with her. The drone of the reader hushed. The door opened softly, and upon the threshold stood Zora. Her small feet and slender ankles were black and bare; her dark, round, and broad-browed head and strangely beautiful face were poised almost defiantly, crowned with a misty mass of waveless hair, and lit by the velvet radiance of two wonderful eyes. And hanging from shoulder to ankle, in formless, clinging folds, blazed the scarlet gown.

Six

COTTON

The cry of the naked was sweeping the world. From the peasant toiling in Russia, the lady lolling in London, the chieftain burning in Africa, and the Esquimaux freezing in Alaska; from long lines of hungry men, from patient sad-eyed women, from old folk and creeping children went up the cry, "Clothes, clothes!" Far away the wide black land that belts the South, where Miss Smith worked and Miss Taylor drudged and Bles and Zora dreamed, the dense black land sensed the cry and heard the bound of answering life within the vast dark breast. All that dark earth heaved in mighty travail with the bursting bolls of the cotton while black attendant earth spirits swarmed above, sweating and crooning to its birth pains.

After the miracle of the bursting bolls, when the land was brightest with the piled mist of the Fleece, and when the cry of the naked was loudest in the mouths of men, a sudden cloud of workers swarmed between the Cotton and the Naked, spinning and weaving and sewing and carrying the Fleece and mining and minting and bringing the Silver till the Song of Service filled the world and the poetry of Toil was in the souls of the laborers. Yet ever and always there were tense silent white-faced men moving in that swarm who felt no poetry and heard no song, and one of these was John Taylor.

He was tall, thin, cold, and tireless and he moved among the Watchers of this World of Trade. In the rich Wall Street offices of Grey and Easterly, Brokers, Mr. Taylor, as chief and confidential clerk surveyed the world's nakedness and the supply of cotton to clothe it. The object of his watching was frankly stated to himself and to his world. He purposed going into business neither for his own health nor for the healing or clothing of the peoples but to apply his knowledge of the world's nakedness and of black men's toil in such a way as to bring himself wealth. In this he was but following the teaching of his highest ideal, lately deceased, Mr. Job Grey. Mr. Grey had so successfully manipulated the cotton market that while black men who made the cotton starved in Alabama and white men who bought it froze in Siberia, he himself sat—

"High on a throne of royal state
That far outshone the wealth
Of Ormuz or of Ind."

Notwithstanding this he died eventually, leaving the burden of his wealth to his bewildered wife, and his business to the astute Mr. Easterly; not simply to Mr. Easterly, but in a sense to his spiritual heir, John Taylor.

To be sure Mr. Taylor had but a modest salary and no financial interest in the business, but he had knowledge and business daring— effrontery even—and the determination was fixed in his mind to be a millionaire at no distant date. Some cautious fliers on the market gave him enough surplus to send his sister Mary through the high school of his country home in New Hampshire, and afterward through Wellesley College; although just why a woman should want to go through college was inexplicable to John Taylor, and he was still uncertain as to the wisdom of his charity.

When she had an offer to teach in the South, John Taylor hurried her off for two reasons: he was profoundly interested in the cotton-belt, and there she might be of service to him; and secondly, he had spent all the money on her that he intended to at present, and he wanted her to go to work. As an investment he did not consider Mary a success. Her letters intimated very strongly her intention not to return to Miss Smith's School; but they also brought information—disjointed and incomplete, to be sure—which mightily interested Mr. Taylor and sent him to atlases, encyclopædias, and census-reports. When he went to that little lunch with old Mrs. Grey he was not sure that he wanted his sister to leave the cotton-belt just yet. After lunch he was sure that he did not want her to leave.

The rich Mrs. Grey was at the crisis of her fortunes. She was an elderly lady, in those uncertain years beyond fifty, and had been left suddenly with more millions than she could easily count. Personally she was inclined to spend her money in bettering the world right off, in such ways as might from time to time seem attractive. This course, to her husband's former partner and present executor, Mr. Edward Easterly, was not only foolish but wicked, and, incidentally, distinctly unprofitable to him. He had expressed himself strongly to Mrs. Grey last night at dinner and had reinforced his argument by a pointed letter written this morning.

To John Taylor Mrs. Grey's disposal of the income was unbelievable blasphemy against the memory of a mighty man. He did not put this in words to Mrs. Grey—he was only head clerk in her late husband's office—but he became watchful and thoughtful. He ate his soup in silence when she descanted on various benevolent schemes.

"Now, what do you know," she asked finally, "about Negroes—about educating them?" Mr. Taylor over his fish was about to deny all knowledge of any sort on the subject, but all at once he recollected his sister, and a sudden gleam of light radiated his mental gloom.

"Have a sister who is—er—devoting herself to teaching them," he said.

"Is that so!" cried Mrs. Grey, joyfully. "Where is she?"

"In Tooms County, Alabama—in—" Mr. Taylor consulted a remote mental pocket—"in Miss Sara Smith's school."

"Why, how fortunate! I'm so glad I mentioned the matter. You see, Miss Smith is a sister of a friend of ours, Congressman Smith of New Jersey, and she has just written to me for help; a very touching letter, too, about the poor blacks. My father set great store by blacks and was a leading abolitionist before he died."

Mr. Taylor was thinking fast. Yes, the name of Congressman Peter Smith was quite familiar. Mr. Easterly, as chairman of the Republican State Committee of New Jersey, had been compelled to discipline Mr. Smith pretty severely for certain socialistic votes in the House, and consequently his future career was uncertain. It was important that such a man should not have too much to do with Mrs. Grey's philanthropies—at least, in his present position.

"Should like to have you meet and talk with my sister, Mrs. Grey; she's a Wellesley graduate," said Taylor, finally.

Mrs. Grey was delighted. It was a combination which she felt she needed. Here was a college-girl who could direct her philanthropies and her etiquette during the summer. Forthwith Mary Taylor received an intimation from her brother that vast interests depended on her summer vacation.

Thus it had happened that Miss Taylor came to Lake George for her vacation after the first year at the Smith School, and she and Miss Smith had silently agreed as she left that it would be better for her not to return. But the gods of lower Broadway thought otherwise. Not that

Mary Taylor did not believe in Miss Smith's work, she was too honest not to believe in education; but she was sure that this was not *her* work, and she had not as yet perfected in her own mind any theory of the world into which black folk fitted. She was rather taken back, therefore, to be regarded as an expert on the problem. First her brother attacked her, not simply on cotton, but, to her great surprise, on Negro education; and after listening to her halting uncertain remarks, he suggested to her certain matters which it would be better for her to believe when Mrs. Grey talked to her.

"Interested in darkies, you see," he concluded, "and looks to you to tell things. Better go easy and suggest a waiting-game before she goes in heavy."

"But Miss Smith needs money—" the New England conscience prompted. John Taylor cut in sharply:

"We all need money, and I know people who need Mrs. Grey's more than Miss Smith does at present."

Miss Taylor found the Lake George colony charming. It was not ultra-fashionable, but it had wealth and leisure and some breeding. Especially was this true of a circumscribed, rather exclusive, set which centred around the Vanderpools of New York and Boston. They, or rather Mr. Vanderpool's connections, were of Old Dutch New York stock; his father it was who had built the Lake George cottage.

Mrs. Vanderpool was a Wells of Boston, and endured Lake George now and then during the summer for her husband's sake, although she regarded it all as rather a joke. This summer promised to be unusually lonesome for her, and she was meditating a retreat to the Massachusetts north shore when she chanced to meet Mary Taylor, at a miscellaneous dinner, and found her interesting. She discovered that this young woman knew things, that she could talk books, and that she was rather pretty. To be sure she knew no people, but Mrs. Vanderpool knew enough to even things.

"By the bye, I met some charming Alabama people last winter, in Montgomery—the Cresswells; do you know them?" she asked one day, as they were lounging in wicker chairs on the Vanderpool porch. Then she answered the query herself: "No, of course you could not. It is too bad that your work deprives you of the society of people of your class. Now my ideal is a set of Negro schools where the white teachers *could* know the Cresswells.

"Why, yes—" faltered Miss Taylor; "but—wouldn't that be difficult?"

"Why should it be?"

"I mean, would the Cresswells approve of educating Negroes?"

"Oh, 'educating'! The word conceals so much. Now, I take it the Cresswells would object to instructing them in French and in dinner etiquette and tea-gowns, and so, in fact, would I; but teach them how to handle a hoe and to sew and cook. I have reason to know that people like the Cresswells would be delighted."

"And with the teachers of it?"

"Why not?—provided, of course, they were—well, gentlefolk and associated accordingly."

"But one must associate with one's pupils."

"Oh, certainly, certainly; just as one must associate with one's maids and chauffeurs and dressmakers—cordially and kindly, but with a difference."

"But—but, dear Mrs. Vanderpool, you wouldn't want your children trained that way, would you?

"Certainly not, my dear. But these are not my children, they are the children of Negroes; we can't quite forget that, can we?"

"No, I suppose not," Miss Taylor admitted, a little helplessly. "But—it seems to me—that's the modern idea of taking culture to the masses."

"Frankly, then, the modern idea is not my idea; it is too socialistic.

And as for culture applied to the masses, you utter a paradox. The masses and work is the truth one must face."

"And culture and work?"

"Quite incompatible, I assure you, my dear." She stretched her silken limbs, lazily, while Miss Taylor sat silently staring at the waters.

Just then Mrs. Grey drove up in her new red motor.

Up to the time of Mary Taylor's arrival the acquaintance of the Vanderpools and Mrs. Grey had been a matter chiefly of smiling bows. After Miss Taylor came there had been calls and casual intercourse, to Mrs. Grey's great gratification and Mrs. Vanderpool's mingled amusement and annoyance. Mrs. Grey announced the arrival of the Easterlys and John Taylor for the week-end. As Mrs. Vanderpool could think of nothing less boring, she consented to dine.

The atmosphere of Mrs. Grey's ornate cottage was different from that of the Vanderpools. The display of wealth and splendor had a touch of the barbaric. Mary Taylor liked it, although she found the Vanderpool atmosphere more subtly satisfying. There was a certain grim power beneath the Greys' mahogany and velvets that thrilled while it appalled. Precisely that side of the thing appealed to her brother. He would have seen little or nothing in the plain elegance yonder, while here he saw a Japanese vase that cost no cent less than a thousand dollars. He meant to be able to duplicate it some day. He knew that Grey was poor and less knowing than he sixty years ago.

The dead millionaire had begun his fortune by buying and selling cotton—travelling in the South in reconstruction times, and sending his agents. In this way he made his thousands. Then he took a step forward, and instead of following the prices induced the prices to follow him. Two or three small cotton corners brought him his tens of thousands. About this time Easterly joined him and pointed out a new road—the buying and selling of stock in various cotton-mills and other industrial enterprises. Grey hesitated, but Easterly pushed him on and he made his hundreds of thousands. Then Easterly proposed buying controlling interests in certain large mills and gradually consolidating them. The plan grew and succeeded, and Grey made his millions.

Then Grey stopped; he had money enough, and he would venture no farther. He "was going to retire and eat peanuts," he said with a chuckle.

Easterly was disgusted. He, too, had made millions—not as many as Grey, but a few. It was not, however, simply money that he wanted, but power. The lust of financial dominion had gripped his soul, and he had a vision of a vast trust of cotton manufacturing covering the land. He talked this incessantly into Grey, but Grey continued to shake his head; the thing was too big for his imagination. He was bent on retiring, and just as he had set the date a year hence he inadvertently died. On the whole, Mr. Easterly was glad of his partner's definite withdrawal, since he left his capital behind him, until he found his vast plans about to be circumvented by Mrs. Grey withdrawing this capital from his control. "To give to the niggers and Chinamen," he snorted to John Taylor, and strode up and down the veranda. John Taylor removed his coat, lighted a black cigar, and elevated his heels. The ladies were in the parlor, where the female Easterlys were prostrating themselves before Mrs. Vanderpool.

"Just what is your plan?" asked Taylor, quite as if he did not know.

"Why, man, the transfer of a hundred millions of stock would give me control of the cotton-mills of America. Think of it!—the biggest trust next to steel."

"Why not bigger?" asked Taylor, imperturbably puffing away. Mr. Easterly eyed him. He had regarded Taylor hitherto as a very valuable asset to the business—had relied on his knowledge of routine, his judgment and his honesty; but he detected tonight a new tone in his clerk, something almost authoritative and self-reliant. He paused and smiled at him.

"Bigger?"

But John Taylor was dead in earnest. He did not smile.

"First, there's England—and all Europe; why not bring them into the trust?"

"Possibly, later; but first, America. Of course, I've got my eyes on the European situation and feelers out; but such matters are more difficult and slower of adjustment over there—so damned much law and gospel."

"But there's another side."

"What's that?"

"You are planning to combine and control the manufacture of cotton—"

"Yes."

"But how about your raw material? The steel trust owns its iron mines."

"Of course—mines could be monopolized and hold the trust up; but our raw material is perfectly safe—farms growing smaller, farms isolated, and we fixing the price. It's a cinch."

"Are you sure?" Taylor surveyed him with a narrowed look.

"Certain."

"I'm not. I've been looking up things, and there are three points you'd better study: First, cotton farms are *not* getting smaller; they're getting bigger almighty fast, and there's a big cotton-land monopoly in sight. Second, the banks and wholesale houses in the South *can* control the cotton output if they work together. Third, watch the Southern 'Farmers' League' of big landlords."

Mr. Easterly threw away his cigar and sat down. Taylor straightened up, switched on the porch light, and took a bundle of papers from his coat pocket.

"Here are census figures," he said, "commercial reports and letters." They pored over them a half hour. Then Easterly arose.

"There's something in it," he admitted, "but what can we do? What do you propose?"

"Monopolize the growth as well as the manufacture of cotton, and use the first to club European manufacturers into submission."

Easterly stared at him.

"Good Lord!" he ejaculated; "you're crazy!"

But Taylor smiled a slow, thin smile, and put away his papers. Easterly continued to stare at his subordinate with a sort of fascination, with the awe that one feels when genius unexpectedly reveals itself from a source hitherto regarded as entirely ordinary. At last he drew a long breath, remarking indefinitely:

"I'll think it over."

A stir in the parlor indicated departure.

"Well, you watch the Farmers' League, and note its success and methods," counselled John Taylor, his tone and manner unchanged. "Then figure what it might do in the hands of—let us say, friends."

"Who's running it?"

"A Colonel Cresswell is its head, and happens also to be the force behind it. Aristocratic family—big planter—near where my sister teaches."

"H'm—well, we'll watch *him.*"

"And say," as Easterly was turning away, "you know Congressman Smith?"

"I should say I did."

"Well, Mrs. Grey seems to be depending on him for advice in distributing some of her charity funds."

Easterly appeared startled.

"She is, is she!" he exclaimed. "But here come the ladies." He went forward at once, but John Taylor drew back. He noted Mrs. Vanderpool, and thought her too thin and pale. The dashing young Miss Easterly was more to his taste. He intended to have a wife like that one of these days.

"Mary," said he to his sister as he finally rose to go, "tell me about the Cresswells."

Mary explained to him at length the impossibility of her knowing much about the local white aristocracy of Tooms County, and then told him all she had heard.

"Mrs. Grey talked to you much?"

"Yes."

"About darky schools?"

"Yes."

"What does she intend to do?"

"I think she will aid Miss Smith first."

"Did you suggest anything?"

"Well, I told her what I thought about coöperating with the local white people."

"The Cresswells?"

"Yes—you see Mrs. Vanderpool knows the Cresswells."

"Does, eh? Good! Say, that's a good point. You just bear heavy on it—coöperate with the Cresswells."

"Why, yes. But—you see, John, I don't just know whether one *could* coöperate with the Cresswells or not—one hears such contradictory stories of them. But there must be some other white people—"

"Stuff! It's the Cresswells we want."

"Well," Mary was very dubious, "they are—the most important."

Seven

THE PLACE OF DREAMS

When she went South late in September, Mary Taylor had two definite but allied objects: she was to get all possible business information concerning the Cresswells, and she was to induce Miss Smith to prepare for Mrs. Grey's benevolence by interesting the local whites in her work. The programme attracted Miss Taylor. She felt in touch, even if dimly and slightly, with great industrial movements, and she felt, too, like a discerning pioneer in philanthropy. Both roles she liked. Besides, they held, each, certain promises of social prestige, and society, Miss Taylor argued, one must have even in Alabama.

Bles Alwyn met her at the train. He was growing to be a big fine bronze giant, and Mary was glad to see him. She especially tried, in the first few weeks of opening school, to glean as much information as possible concerning the community, and particularly the Cresswells. She found the Negro youth quicker, surer, and more intelligent in his answers than those she questioned elsewhere, and she gained real enjoyment from her long talks with him.

"Isn't Bles developing splendidly?" she said to Miss Smith one afternoon. There was an unmistakable note of enthusiasm in her voice. Miss Smith slowly closed her letter-file but did not look up.

"Yes," she said crisply. "He's eighteen now—quite a man."

"And most interesting to talk with."

"H'm—very"—drily. Mary was busy with her own thoughts, and she did not notice the other woman's manner.

"Do you know," she pursued, "I'm a little afraid of one thing."

"So am I."

"Oh, you've noted it, too?—his friendship for that impossible girl, Zora?"

Miss Smith gave her a searching look.

"What of it?" she demanded.

"She is so far beneath him."

"How so?"

"She is a bold, godless thing; I don't understand her."

"The two are not quite the same."

"Of course not; but she is unnaturally forward."

"Too bright," Miss Smith amplified.

"Yes; she knows quite too much. You surely remember that awful scarlet dress? Well, all her clothes have arrived, or remained, at a simplicity and vividness that is—well—immodest."

"Does she think them immodest?"

"What she thinks is a problem."

"*The* problem, you mean?"

"Well, yes."

They paused a moment. Then Miss Smith said slowly: "What I don't understand, I don't judge."

"No, but you can't always help seeing and meeting it," laughed Miss Taylor.

"Certainly not. I don't try; I court the meeting and seeing. It is the only way."

"Well, perhaps, for us—but not for a boy like Bles, and a girl like Zora."

"True; men and women must exercise judgment in their intercourse and"—she glanced sharply at Miss Taylor—"my dear, you yourself must not forget that Bles Alwyn is a man."

Far up the road came a low, long, musical shouting; then with creaking and straining of wagons, four great black mules dashed into sight with twelve bursting bales of yellowish cotton looming and swaying behind. The drivers and helpers were lolling and laughing and singing, but Miss Taylor did not hear nor see. She had sat suddenly upright; her face had flamed crimson, and then went dead white.

"Miss—Miss Smith!" she gasped, overwhelmed with dismay, a picture of wounded pride and consternation.

Miss Smith turned around very methodically and took her hand; but while she spoke the girl merely stared at her in stony silence.

"Now, dear, don't mean more than I do. I'm an old woman, and I've seen many things. This is but a little corner of the world, and yet many people pass here in thirty years. The trouble with new teachers who come is, that like you, they cannot see black folk as human. All to them are either impossible Zoras, or else lovable Blessings. They forget that Zora is not to be annihilated, but studied and understood, and that Bles is a young man of eighteen and not a clod."

"But that he should dare—" Mary began breathlessly.

"He hasn't dared," Miss Smith went gently on. "No thought of you but as a teacher has yet entered his dear, simple head. But, my point is simply this: he's a man, and a human one, and if you keep on making much over him, and talking to him and petting him, he'll have the right to interpret your manner in his own way—the same that any young man would."

"But—but, he's a—a—"

"A Negro. To be sure, he is; and a man in addition. Now, dear, don't take this too much to heart; this is not a rebuke, but a clumsy warning. I am simply trying to make clear to you *why* you should be careful. Treat poor Zora a little more lovingly, and Bles a little less warmly. They are just human—but, oh! so human."

Mary Taylor rose up stiffly and mumbled a brief good-night. She went to her room, and sat down in the dark. The mere mention of the thing was to her so preposterous—no, loathsome, she kept repeating.

She slowly undressed in the dark, and heard the rumbling of the cotton wagons as they swayed toward town. The cry of the Naked was sweeping the world, and yonder in the night black men were answering the call. They knew not what or why they answered, but obeyed the irresistible call, with hearts light and song upon their lips—the Song of Service. They lashed their mules and drank their whiskey, and all night the piled fleece swept by Mary Taylor's window, flying—flying to that far cry. Miss Taylor turned uneasily in her bed and jerked the bed-clothes about her ears.

"Mrs. Vanderpool is right," she confided to the night, with something of the awe with which one suddenly comprehends a hidden oracle; "there must be a difference, always, always! That impudent Negro!"

All night she dreamed, and all day,—especially when trim and immaculate she sat in her chair and looked down upon fifty dark faces—and upon Zora.

Zora sat thinking. She saw neither Miss Taylor nor the long straight rows of desks and faces. She heard neither the drone of the spellers nor did she hear Miss Taylor say, "Zora!" She heard and saw none of this. She only heard the prattle of the birds in the wood, far down where the Silver Fleece would be planted.

For the time of cotton-planting was coming; the gray and drizzle of December was past and the hesitation of January. Already a certain warmth and glow had stolen into the air, and the Swamp was calling its child with low, seductive voice. She knew where the first leaves were bursting, where tiny flowers nestled, and where young living things looked upward to the light and cried and crawled. A wistful longing was stealing into her heart. She wanted to be free. She wanted to run and dance and sing, but Bles wanted—

"Zora!"

This time she heard the call, but did not heed it. Miss Taylor was very tiresome, and was forever doing and saying silly things. So Zora paid no attention, but sat still and thought. Yes, she would show Bles the place that very night; she had kept it secret from him until now, out of perverseness, out of her love of mystery and secrets. But tonight, after school, when he met her on the big road with the clothes, she would take him and show him the chosen spot.

Soon she was aware that school had been dismissed, and she leisurely gathered up her books and rose. Mary Taylor regarded her in perplexed despair. Oh, these people! Mrs. Vanderpool was right: culture and—some masses, at least—were not to be linked; and, too, culture and work—were they incompatible? At any rate, culture and *this* work were.

Now, there was Mrs. Vanderpool—she toiled not, neither did she spin, and yet! If all these folk were like poor, stupid, docile Jennie it would be simpler, but what earthly sense was there in trying do to anything with a girl like Zora, so stupid in some matters, so startlingly bright in others, and so stubborn in everything? Here, she was doing some work twice as well and twice as fast as the class, and other work she would not touch because she "didn't like it." Her classification in school was nearly as difficult as her classification in the world, and Miss Taylor reached up impatiently and removed the gold pin from her stock to adjust it more comfortably when Zora sauntered past unseeing, unheeding, with that curious gliding walk which Miss Taylor called stealthy. She laid the pin on the desk and on sudden impulse spoke again to the girl as she arranged her neck trimmings.

"Zora," she said evenly, "why didn't you come to class when I called?"

"I didn't hear you," said Zora, looking at her full-eyed and telling the half-truth easily.

Miss Taylor was sure Zora was lying, and she knew that she had lied to her on other occasions. Indeed, she had found lying customary in this community, and she had a New England horror of it. She looked at Zora disapprovingly, while Zora looked at her quite impersonally, but steadily. Then Miss Taylor braced herself, mentally, and took the war into Africa.

"Do you ever tell lies, Zora?"

"Yes."

"Don't you know that is a wicked, bad habit?"

"Why?"

"Because God hates them."

"How does *you* know He does?" Zora's tone was still impersonal.

"He hates all evil."

"But why is lies evil?"

"Because they make us deceive each other."

"Is that wrong?"

"Yes."

Zora bent forward and looked squarely into Miss Taylor's blue eyes. Miss Taylor looked into the velvet blackness of hers and wondered what they veiled.

"Is it wrong," asked Zora, "to make believe you likes people when you don't, when you'se afeared of them and thinks they may rub off and dirty you?"

"Why—why—yes, if you—if you, deceive."

"Then you lies sometimes, don't you?"

Miss Taylor stared helplessly at the solemn eyes that seemed to look so deeply into her.

"Perhaps—I do, Zora; I'm sure I don't mean to, and—I hope God will forgive me."

Zora softened.

"Oh, I reckon He will if He's a good God, because He'd know that lies like that are heaps better than blabbing the truth right out. Only," she added severely, "you mustn't keep saying it's wicked to lie 'cause it ain't. Sometimes I lies," she reflected pensively, "and sometimes I don't—it depends."

Miss Taylor forgot her collar, and fingered the pin on the desk. She felt at once a desperate desire to know this girl better and to establish her own authority. Yet how should she do it? She kept toying with the pin, and Zora watched her. Then Miss Taylor said, absently:

"Zora, what do you propose to do when you grow up?"

Zora considered.

"Think and walk—and rest," she concluded.

"I mean, what work?"

"Work? Oh, I sha'n't work. I don't like work—do you?"

Miss Taylor winced, wondering if the girl were lying again. She said quickly:

"Why, yes—that is, I like some kinds of work."

"What kinds?"

But Miss Taylor refused to have the matter made personal, as Zora had a disconcerting way of pointing all their discussions.

"Everybody likes some kinds of work," she insisted.

"If you likes it, it ain't work," declared Zora; but Mary Taylor proceeded around her circumscribed circle:

"You might make a good cook, or a maid."

"I hate cooking. What's a maid?"

"Why, a woman who helps others."

"Helps folks that they love? I'd like that."

"It is not a question of affection," said Miss Taylor, firmly: "one is paid for it."

"I wouldn't work for pay."

"But you'll have to, child; you'll have to earn a living."

"Do you work for pay?"

"I work to earn a living."

"Same thing, I reckon, and it ain't true. Living just comes free, like—like sunshine."

"Stuff! Zora, your people must learn to work and work steadily and work hard—" She stopped, for she was sure Zora was not listening; the far away look was in her eyes and they were shining. She was beautiful as she stood there—strangely, almost uncannily, but startlingly beautiful with her rich dark skin, softly moulded features, and wonderful eyes.

"My people?—my people?" she murmured, half to herself. "Do you know my people? They don't never work; they plays. They is all little, funny dark people. They flies and creeps and crawls, slippery-like; and they cries and calls. Ah, my people! my poor little people! they misses me these days, because they is shadowy things that sing and smell and bloom in dark and terrible nights—"

Miss Taylor started up. "Zora, I believe you're crazy!" she cried. But Zora was looking at her calmly again.

"We'se both crazy, ain't we?" she returned, with a simplicity that left the teacher helpless.

Miss Taylor hurried out, forgetting her pin. Zora looked it over leisurely, and tried it on. She decided that she liked it, and putting it in her pocket, went out too.

School was out but the sun was still high, as Bles hurried from the barn up the big road beside the soft shadows of the swamp. His head was busy with new thoughts and his lips were whistling merrily, for to-day Zora was to show him the long dreamed of spot for the planting of the Silver Fleece. He hastened toward the Cresswell mansion, and glanced anxiously up the road. At last he saw her coming, swinging down the road, lithe and dark, with the big white basket of clothes poised on her head.

"Zora," he yodled, and she waved her apron.

He eased her burden to the ground and they sat down together, he nervous and eager; she silent, passive, but her eyes restless. Bles was full of his plans.

"Zora," he said, "we'll make it the finest bale ever raised in Tooms; we'll just work it to the inch—just love it into life."

She considered the matter intently.

"But,"—presently,—"how can we sell it without the Cresswells knowing?"

"We won't try; we'll just take it to them and give them half, like the other tenants."

"But the swamp is mortal thick and hard to clear."

"We can do it."

Zora had sat still, listening; but now, suddenly, she leapt to her feet.

"Come," she said, "I'll take the clothes home, then we'll go"—she glanced at him—"down where the dreams are." And laughing, they hurried on.

Elspeth stood in the path that wound down to the cottage, and without a word Zora dropped the basket at her feet. She turned back; but Bles, struck by a thought, paused. The old woman was short, broad, black and wrinkled, with yellow fangs, red hanging lips, and wicked eyes. She leered at them; the boy shrank before it, but stood his ground.

"Aunt Elspeth," he began, "Zora and I are going to plant and tend some cotton to pay for her schooling—just the very best cotton we can find—and I heard"—he hesitated,—"I heard you had some wonderful seed."

"Yes," she mumbled, "I'se got the seed—I'se got it—wonder seed, sowed wid the three spells of Obi in the old land ten tousand moons ago. But you couldn't plant it," with a sudden shrillness, "it would kill you."

"But—" Bles tried to object, but she waved him away.

"Git the ground—git the ground; dig it—pet it, and we'll see what we'll see." And she disappeared.

Zora was not sure that it had been wise to tell their secret.

"I was going to steal the seed," she said. "I knows where it is, and I don't fear conjure."

"You mustn't steal, Zora," said Bles, gravely.

"Why?" Zora quickly asked.

But before he answered, they both forgot; for their faces were turned toward the wonder of the swamp. The golden sun was pouring floods of glory through the slim black trees, and the mystic sombre pools caught and tossed back the glow in darker, duller crimson. Long echoing cries leapt to and fro; silent footsteps crept hither and yonder; and the girl's eyes gleamed with a wild new joy.

"The dreams!" she cried. "The dreams!" And leaping ahead, she danced along the shadowed path. He hastened after her, but she flew fast and faster; he followed, laughing, calling, pleading. He saw her twinkling limbs a-dancing as once he saw them dance in a halo of firelight; but now the fire was the fire of the world. Her garments twined and flew in shadowy drapings about the perfect moulding of her young and dark half-naked figure. Her heavy hair had burst its fastenings and lay in stiffened, straggling masses, bending reluctantly to the breeze, like curled smoke; while all about, the mad, wild singing rose and fell and trembled, till his head whirled. He paused uncertainly at a parting of the paths, crying:

"Zora! Zora!" as for some lost soul. "Zora! Zora!" echoed the cry, faintly.

Abruptly the music fell; there came a long slow-growing silence; and then, with a flutter, she was beside him again, laughing in his ears and crying with mocking voice:

"Is you afeared, honey?"

He saw in her eyes sweet yearnings, but could speak nothing. He could only clasp her hand tightly, and again down they raced through the wood.

All at once the swamp changed and chilled to a dull grayness; tall, dull trees started down upon the murky waters; and long pendent streamings of moss-like tears dripped from tree to earth. Slowly and warily they threaded their way.

"Are you sure of the path, Zora?" he once inquired anxiously.

"I could find it asleep," she answered, skipping sure-footed onward. He continued to hold her hand tightly, and his own pace never slackened. Around them the gray and death-like wilderness darkened. They felt and saw the cold white mist rising slowly from the ground, and waters growing blacker and broader.

At last they came to what seemed the end. Silently and dismally the half-dead forest, with its ghostly moss, lowered and darkened, and the black waters spread into a great silent lake of slimy ooze. The dead trunk of a fallen tree lay straight in front, torn and twisted, its top hidden yonder and mingled with impenetrable undergrowth.

"Where now, Zora?" he cried.

In a moment she had slipped her hand away and was scrambling upon the tree trunk. The waters yawned murkily below.

"Careful! careful!" he warned, struggling after her until she disappeared amid the leaves. He followed eagerly, but cautiously; and all at once found himself confronting a paradise.

Before them lay a long island, opening to the south, on the black lake, but sheltered north and east by the dense undergrowth of the black swamp and the rampart of dead and living trees. The soil was virgin and black, thickly covered over with a tangle of bushes, vines, and smaller growth all brilliant with early leaves and wild flowers.

"A pretty tough proposition for clearing and ploughing," said Bles, with practised eye. But Zora eagerly surveyed the prospect.

"It's where the Dreams lives," she whispered.

Meantime Miss Taylor had missed her brooch and searched for it in vain. In the midst of this pursuit the truth occurred to her—Zora had stolen it. Negroes would steal, everybody said. Well, she must and would have the pin, and she started for Elspeth's cabin.

On the way she met the old woman in the path, but got little satisfaction. Elspeth merely grunted ungraciously while eyeing the white woman with suspicion.

Mary Taylor, again alone, sat down at a turn in the path, just out of sight of the house, and waited. Soon she saw, with a certain grim satisfaction, Zora and Bles emerging from the swamp engaged in earnest conversation. Here was an opportunity to overwhelm both with an unforgettable reprimand. She rose before them like a spectral vengeance.

"Zora, I want my pin."

Bles started and stared; but Zora eyed her calmly with something like disdain.

"What pin?" she returned, unmoved.

"Zora, don't deny that you took my pin from the desk this afternoon," the teacher commanded severely.

"I didn't say I didn't take no pin."

"Persons who will lie and steal will do anything."

"Why shouldn't people do anything they wants to?"

"And you knew the pin was mine."

"I saw you a-wearing of it," admitted Zora easily.

"Then you have stolen it, and you are a thief."

Still Zora appeared to be unimpressed with the heinousness of her fault.

"Did you make that pin?" she asked.

"No, but it is mine."

"Why is it yours?"

"Because it was given to me."

"But you don't need it; you've got four other prettier ones—I counted."

"That makes no difference."

"Yes it does—folks ain't got no right to things they don't need."

"That makes no difference, Zora, and you know it. The pin is mine. You stole it. If you had wanted a pin and asked me I might have given you—"

The girl blazed.

"I don't want your old gifts," she almost hissed. "You don't own what you don't need and can't use. God owns it and I'm going to send it back to Him."

With a swift motion she whipped the pin from her pocket and raised her arm to hurl it into the swamp. Bles caught her hand. He caught it lightly and smiled sorrowfully into her eyes. She wavered a moment, then the answering light sprang to her face. Dropping the brooch into his hand, she wheeled and fled toward the cabin.

Bles handed it silently to Miss Taylor. Mary Taylor was beside herself with impatient anger—and anger intensified by a conviction of utter helplessness to cope with any strained or unusual situations between herself and these two.

"Alwyn," she said sharply, "I shall report Zora for stealing. And you may report yourself to Miss Smith tonight for disrespect toward a teacher."

Eight

MR. HARRY CRESSWELL

The Cresswells, father and son, were at breakfast. The daughter was taking her coffee and rolls up stairs in bed.

"P'sh! I don't like it!" declared Harry Cresswell, tossing the letter back to his father. "I tell you, it is a damned Yankee trick."

He was a man of thirty-five, smooth and white, slight, well-bred and masterful. His father, St. John Cresswell, was sixty, white-haired, mustached and goateed; a stately, kindly old man with a temper and much family pride.

"Well, well," he said, his air half preoccupied, half unconcerned, "I suppose so—and yet"—he read the letter again, aloud: "'Approaching you as one of the most influential landowners of Alabama, on a confidential matter'—h'm—h'm—'a combination of capital and power, such as this nation has never seen'—'cotton manufacturers and cotton growers.' . . . Well, well! Of course, I suppose there's nothing in it. And yet, Harry, my boy, this cotton-growing business is getting in a pretty tight pinch. Unless relief comes somehow—well, we'll just have to quit. We simply can't keep the cost of cotton down to a remunerative figure with niggers getting scarcer and dearer. Every year I have to pinch 'em closer and closer. I had to pay Maxwell two hundred and fifty to get that old darky and his boys turned over to me, and one of the young ones has run away already."

Harry lighted a cigarette.

"We must drive them more. You're too easy, father; they understand that. By the way, what did that letter say about a 'sister'?"

"Says he's got a sister over at the nigger school whom perhaps we know. I suppose he thinks we dine there occasionally." The old man chuckled. "That reminds me, Elspeth is sending her girl there."

"What's that?" An angry gleam shot into the younger man's eye.

"Yes. She announced this morning, pert as you please, that she couldn't tote clothes any more—she had to study."

"Damn it! This thing is going too far. We can't keep a maid or a plough-boy on the place because of this devilish school. It's going to ruin the whole labor system. We've been too mild and decent. I'm going to put my foot down right here. I'll make Elspeth take that girl out of school if I have to horse-whip her, and I'll warn the school against further interference with our tenants. Here, in less than a week, go two plough-hands—and now this girl."

The old man smiled.

"You'll hardly miss any work Zora does," he said.

"I'll make her work. She's giving herself too many damned airs. I know who's back of this—it's that nigger we saw talking to the white woman in the field the other day."

"Well, don't work yourself up. The wench don't amount to much anyhow. By the way, though, if you do go to the school it won't hurt to see this Taylor's sister and size the family up."

"Pshaw! I'm going to give the Smith woman such a scare that she'll keep her hands off our niggers." And Harry Cresswell rode away.

Mary Taylor had charge of the office that morning, while Miss Smith, shut up in her bedroom, went laboriously over her accounts. Miss Mary suddenly sat up, threw a hasty glance into the glass and felt the back of her belt. It was—it couldn't be—surely, it was Mr. Harry Cresswell riding through the gateway on his beautiful white mare. He kicked the gate open rather viciously, did not stop to close it, and rode straight across the lawn. Miss Taylor noticed his riding breeches and leggings, his white linen and white, clean-cut, high-bred face. Such apparitions were few about the country lands. She felt inclined to flutter, but gripped herself.

"Good-morning," she said, a little stiffly.

Mr. Cresswell halted and stared; then lifting the hat which he had neglected to remove in crossing the hall, he bowed in stately grace. Miss Taylor was no ordinary picture. Her brown hair was almost golden; her dark eyes shone blue; her skin was clear and healthy, and her white dress—happy coincidence!—had been laundered that very morning. Her half-suppressed excitement at the sudden duty of welcoming the great aristocrat of the county, gave a piquancy to her prettiness.

"The—devil!" commented Mr. Harry Cresswell to himself. But to Miss Taylor:

"I beg pardon—er—Miss Smith?"

"No—I'm sorry. Miss Smith is engaged this morning. I am Miss Taylor."

"I cannot share Miss Taylor's sorrow," returned Mr. Cresswell gravely, "for I believe I have the honor of some correspondence with Miss Taylor's brother." Mr. Cresswell searched for the letter, but did not find it.

"Oh! Has John written you?" She beamed suddenly. "I'm so glad. It's more than he's done for me this three-month. I beg your pardon—

do sit down—I think you'll find this one easier. Our stock of chairs is limited."

It was delightful to have a casual meeting receive this social stamp; the girl was all at once transfigured—animated, glowing, lovely; all of which did not escape the caller's appraising inspection.

"There!" said Mr. Cresswell. "I've left your gate gaping."

"Oh, don't mind . . . I hope John's well?"

"The truth is," confessed Cresswell, "it was a business matter— cotton, you know."

"John is nothing but cotton; I tell him his soul is fibrous."

"He mentioned your being here and I thought I'd drop over and welcome you to the South."

"Thank you," returned Miss Taylor, reddening with pleasure despite herself. There was a real sincerity in the tone. All this confirmed so many convictions of hers.

"Of course, you know how it is in the South," Cresswell pursued, the opening having been so easily accomplished.

"I understand perfectly."

"My sister would be delighted to meet you, but—"

"Oh I realize the—difficulties."

"Perhaps you wouldn't mind riding by some day—it's embarrassing to suggest this, but, you know—"

Miss Taylor was perfectly self-possessed.

"Mr. Cresswell," she said seriously, "I know very well that it wouldn't do for your sister to call here, and I sha'n't mind a bit coming by to see her first. I don't believe in standing on stupid ceremony."

Cresswell thanked her with quiet cordiality, and suggested that when he was driving by he might pick her up in his gig some morning. Miss Taylor expressed her pleasure at the prospect. Then the talk wandered to general matters—the rain, the trees, the people round about, and, inevitably—the Negro.

"Oh, by the bye," said Mr. Cresswell, frowning and hesitating over the recollection of his errand's purpose, "there was one matter"—he paused. Miss Taylor leant forward, all interest. "I hardly know that I ought to mention it, but your school—"

This charming young lady disarmed his truculent spirit, and the usually collected and determined young man was at a loss how to proceed. The girl, however, was obviously impressed and pleased by his evidence of interest, whatever its nature; so in a manner vastly different from the one he had intended to assume, he continued:

"There is a way in which we may be of service to you, and that is by enlightening you upon points concerning which the nature of your position—both as teacher and socially—must keep you in the dark.

"For instance, all these Negroes are, as you know, of wretchedly low morals; but there are a few so depraved that it would be suicidal to take them into this school. We recognize the good you are doing, but we do not want it more than offset by utter lack of discrimination in choosing your material."

"Certainly not—have we—" Miss Mary faltered. This beginning was a bit ominous, wholly unexpected.

"There is a girl, Zora, who has just entered, who—I must speak candidly—who ought not to be here; I thought it but right to let you know."

"Thank you, so much. I'll tell Miss Smith." Mary Taylor suddenly felt herself a judge of character. "I suspected that she was—not what she ought to be. Believe me, we appreciate your interest."

A few more words, and Mr. Cresswell, after bending courteously over her hand with a deference no New Englander had ever shown, was riding away on his white mare.

For a while Mary Taylor sat very quietly. It was like a breath of air from the real world, this hour's chat with a well-bred gentleman. She wondered how she had done her part—had she been too eager and school-girlish? Had she met this stately ceremony with enough breeding to show that she too was somebody? She pounced upon Miss Smith the minute that lady entered the office.

"Miss Smith, who do you think has been here?" she burst out enthusiastically.

"I saw him on the lawn." There was a suspicious lack of warmth in this brief affirmation.

"He was so gracious and kindly, and he knows my brother. And oh, Miss Smith! we've got to send that Zora right away."

"Indeed"—the observation was not even interrogatory. The preceptress of the struggling school for Negro children merely evinced patience for the younger woman's fervency.

"Yes; he says she's utterly depraved."

"Said that, did he?" Miss Smith watched her with tranquil regard. Miss Taylor paused.

"Of course, we cannot think of keeping her."

Miss Smith pursed her lips, offering her first expression of opinion.

"I guess we'll worry along with her a little while anyhow," she said.

The girl stared at Miss Smith in honest, if unpardonable, amazement.

"Do you mean to say that you are going to keep in this school a girl who not only lies and steals but is positively—*immoral?*"

Miss Smith smiled, wholly unmoved.

"No; but I mean that *I* am here to learn from those whose ideas of right do not agree with mine, to discover *why* they differ, and to let them learn of me—so far as I am worthy."

Mary Taylor was not unappreciative of Miss Smith's stern high-mindedness, but her heart hardened at this, to her, misdirected zeal. Echo of the spirit of an older day, Miss Smith seemed, to her, to be cramped and paralyzed in an armor of prejudice and sectionalisms. Plain-speaking was the only course, and Mary, if a little complacent perhaps in her frankness, was sincere in her purpose.

"I think, Miss Smith, you are making a very grave mistake. I regard Zora as a very undesirable person from every point of view. I look upon Mr. Cresswell's visit today as almost providential. He came offering an olive branch from the white aristocracy to this work; to bespeak his appreciation and safeguard the future. Moreover," and Miss Taylor's voice gathered firmness despite Miss Smith's inscrutable eye, "moreover, I have reason to know that the disposition—indeed, the plan—in certain quarters to help this work materially depends very largely on your willingness to meet the advances of the Southern whites half way."

She paused for a reply or a question. Receiving neither, she walked with dignity up the stairs. From her window she could see Cresswell's straight shoulders, as he rode toward town, and beyond him a black speck in the road. But she could not see the smile on Mr. Cresswell's lips, nor did she hear him remark twice, with seeming irrelevance, "The devil!"

The rider, being closer to it, recognized in Mary Taylor's "black speck" Bles Alwyn walking toward him rapidly with axe and hoe on shoulder, whistling merrily. They saw each other almost at the same moment and whistle and smile faded. Mr. Cresswell knew the Negro by sight and disliked him. He belonged in his mind to that younger class of half-educated blacks who were impudent and disrespectful toward their superiors, not even touching his hat when he met a white man. Moreover, he was sure that it was Miss Taylor with whom this boy had been talking so long and familiarly in the cotton-field last Spring—an offence doubly heinous now that he had seen Miss Taylor.

His first impulse was to halt the Negro then and there and tell him a few plain truths. But he did not feel quarrelsome at the moment, and there was, after all, nothing very tangible to justify a berating. The fellow's impudence was sure to increase, and then! So he merely reined his horse to the better part of the foot-path and rode on.

Bles, too, was thinking. He knew the well-dressed man with his milk-white face and overbearing way. He would expect to be greeted with raised hat but Bles bit his lips and pulled down his cap firmly. The axe, too, in some indistinct way felt good in his hand. He saw the horse coming in his pathway and stepping aside in the dust continued on his way, neither looking nor speaking.

So they passed each other by, Mr. Cresswell to town, Bles to the swamp, apparently ignorant of each other's very existence. Yet, as the space widened between them, each felt a more vindictive anger for the other.

How dares the black puppy to ignore a Cresswell on the highway? If this went on, the day would surely come when Negroes felt no respect or fear whatever for whites? And then—my God! Mr. Cresswell struck his mare a vicious blow and dashed toward town.

The black boy, too, went his way in silent, burning rage. Why should he be elbowed into the roadside dust by an insolent bully? Why had he not stood his ground? Pshaw! All this fine frenzy was useless, and he knew it. The sweat oozed on his forehead. It wasn't man against man, or he would have dragged the pale puppy from his horse and rubbed his face in the earth. It wasn't even one against many, else how willingly, swinging his axe, would have stood his ground before a mob.

No, it was one against a world, a world of power, opinion, wealth, opportunity; and he, the one, must cringe and bear in silence lest the world crash about the ears of his people. He slowly plodded on in bitter silence toward the swamp. But the day was balmy, the way was beautiful; contempt slowly succeeded anger, and hope soon triumphed over all. For yonder was Zora, poised, waiting. And behind her lay the Field of Dreams.

Nine

___

THE PLANTING

Zora looked down upon Bles, where he stood to his knees in mud. The toil was beyond exhilaration—it was sickening weariness and panting despair. The great roots, twined in one unbroken snarl, clung frantically to the black soil. The vines and bushes fought back with thorn and bramble. Zora stood wiping the blood from her hands and staring at Bles. She saw the long gnarled fingers of the tough little trees and they looked like the fingers of Elspeth down there beneath the earth pulling against the boy. Slowly Zora forgot her blood and pain. Who would win—the witch, or Jason?

Bles looked up and saw the bleeding hands. With a bound he was beside her.

"Zora!" The cry seemed wrung from his heart by contrition. Why had he not known—not seen before! "Zora, come right out of this! Sit down here and rest."

She looked at him unwaveringly; there was no flinching of her spirit. "I sha'n't do it," she said. "You'se working, and I'se going to work."

"But—Zora—you're not used to such work, and I am. You're tired out."

"So is you," was her reply.

He looked himself over ruefully, and dropping his axe, sat down beside her on a great log. Silently they contemplated the land; it seemed indeed a hopeless task. Then they looked at each other in sudden, unspoken fear of failure.

"If we only had a mule!" he sighed. Immediately her face lighted and her lips parted, but she said nothing. He presently bounded to his feet.

"Never mind, Zora. To-morrow is Saturday, and I'll work all day. We just *will* get it done—sometime." His mouth closed with determination.

"We won't work any more today, then?" cried Zora, her eagerness betraying itself despite her efforts to hide it.

"*You* won't," affirmed Bles. "But I've got to do just a little—"

But Zora was adamant: he was tired; she was tired; they would rest. To-morrow with the rising sun they would begin again.

"There'll be a bright moon tonight," ventured Bles.

"Then I'll come too," Zora announced positively, and he had to promise for her sake to rest.

They went up the path together and parted diffidently, he watching her flit away with sorrowful eyes, a little disturbed and puzzled at the burden he had voluntarily assumed, but never dreaming of drawing back.

Zora did not go far. No sooner did she know herself well out of his sight than she dropped lightly down beside the path, listening intently until the last echo of his footsteps had died away. Then, leaving the cabin on her right, and the scene of their toil on her left, she cut straight through the swamp, skirted the big road, and in a half-hour was in the lower meadows of the Cresswell plantations, where the tired stock was being turned out to graze for the night. Here, in the shadow of the wood, she lingered. Slowly, but with infinite patience, she broke one strand after another of the barbed-wire fencing, watching, the while, the sun grow great and crimson, and die at last in mighty splendor behind the dimmer westward forests.

The voices of the hands and hostlers grew fainter and thinner in the distance of purple twilight until the last of them disappeared. Silence fell, deep and soft; the silence of a day sinking to sleep. Not until then did Zora steal forth from her hiding-place.

She had chosen her mule long before—a big, black beast, snorting over his pile of corn,—and gliding up to him, she gathered his supper into her skirt, found a stout halter, and fed him sparingly as he followed her. Quickly she unfastened the pieces of the fence, led the animal through, and spliced them again; and then, with fox-like caution, she guided her prize through the labyrinthine windings of the swamp. It was dark and haunting, and ever and again rose lonely night cries. The girl trembled a little, but plodded resolutely on until the dim silver disk of the half-moon began to glimmer through the trees. Then she pressed on more swiftly, and fed more scantily, until finally, with the moonlight pouring over them at the black lagoon, Zora attempted to drive the animal into the still waters; but he gave a loud protesting snort and balked. By subtle temptings she gave him to understand that plenty lay beyond the dark waters, and quickly swinging herself to his back she started to ride him up and down along the edge of the lagoon, petting and whispering to him of good things beyond. Slowly her eyes grew wide; she seemed to be riding out of dreamland on some hobgoblin beast.

Deeper and deeper they penetrated into the dark waters. Now they entered the slime; now they stumbled on hidden roots; but deeper and deeper they waded until at last, turning the animal's head with a jerk, and giving him a sharp stroke of the whip, she headed straight for the island. A moment the beast snorted and plunged; higher and higher the black still waters rose round the girl. They crept up her little limbs, swirled round her breasts and gleamed green and slimy along her shoulders. A wild terror gripped her. Maybe she *was* riding the devil's horse, and these were the yawning gates of hell, black and sombre beneath the cold, dead radiance of the moon. She saw again the gnarled and black and claw-like fingers of Elspeth gripping and dragging her down.

A scream struggled in her breast, her fingers relaxed, and the big beast, stretching his cramped neck, rose in one mighty plunge and planted his feet on the sand of the island.

Bles, hurrying down in the morning with new tools and new determination, stopped and stared in blank amazement. Zora was perched in a tree singing softly and beneath a fat black mule was finishing his breakfast.

"Zora—" he gasped, "how—how did you do it?"

She only smiled and sang a happier measure, pausing only to whisper:

"Dreams—dreams—it's all dreams here, I tells you."

Bles frowned and stood irresolute. The song proceeded with less assurance, slower and lower, till it stopped, and the singer dropped to the ground, watching him with wide eyes. He looked down at her, slight, tired, scratched, but undaunted, striving blindly toward the light with stanch, unfaltering faith. A pity surged in his heart. He put his arm about her shoulders and murmured:

"You poor, brave child."

And she shivered with joy.

All day Saturday and part of Sunday they worked feverishly. The trees crashed and the stumps groaned and crept up into the air, the brambles blazed and smoked; little frightened animals fled for shelter; and a wide black patch of rich loam broadened and broadened till it kissed, on every side but the sheltered east, the black waters of the lagoon. Late Sunday night the mule again swam the slimy lagoon, and disappeared toward the Cresswell fields. Then Bles sat down beside Zora, facing the fields, and gravely took her hand. She looked at him in quick, breathless fear.

"Zora," he said, "sometimes you tell lies, don't you?"

"Yes," she said slowly; "sometimes."

"And, Zora, sometimes you steal—you stole the pin from Miss Taylor, and we stole Mr. Cresswell's mule for two days."

"Yes," she said faintly, with a perplexed wrinkle in her brows, "*I* stole it."

"Well, Zora, I don't want you ever to tell another lie, or ever to take anything that doesn't belong to you."

She looked at him silently with the shadow of something like terror far back in the depths of her deep eyes.

"Always—tell—the truth?" she repeated slowly.

"Yes."

Her fingers worked nervously.

"All the truth?" she asked.

He thought a while.

"No," said he finally, "it is not necessary always to tell all the truth; but never tell anything that isn't the truth."

"Never?"

"Never."

"Even if it hurts me?"

"Even if it hurts. God is good, He will not let it hurt much."

"He's a fair God, ain't He?" she mused, scanning the evening sky.

"Yes—He's fair, He wouldn't take advantage of a little girl that did wrong, when she didn't know it was wrong."

Her face lightened and she held his hands in both hers, and said solemnly as though saying a prayer:

"I won't lie any more, and I won't steal—and—" she looked at him in startled wistfulness—he remembered it in after years; but he felt he had preached enough.

"And now for the seed!" he interrupted joyously. "And then—the Silver Fleece!"

That night, for the first time, Bles entered Zora's home. It was a single low, black room, smoke-shadowed and dirty, with two dingy beds and a gaping fire-place. On one side of the fire-place sat the yellow woman, young, with traces of beauty, holding the white child in her arms; on the other, hugging the blaze, huddled a formless heap, wreathed in coils of tobacco smoke—Elspeth, Zora's mother.

Zora said nothing, but glided in and stood in the shadows.

"Good-evening," said Bles cheerily. The woman with the baby alone responded.

"I came for the seed you promised us—the cotton-seed."

The hag wheeled and approached him swiftly, grasping his shoulders and twisting her face into his. She was a horrible thing—filthy of breath, dirty, with dribbling mouth and red eyes. Her few long black teeth hung loosely like tusks and the folds of fat on her chin curled down on her great neck. Bles shuddered and stepped back.

"Is you afeared, honey?" she whispered.

"No," he said sturdily.

She chuckled drily. "Yes, you is—everybody's 'feared of old Elspeth; but she won't hurt you—you's got the spell;" and wheeling again, she was back at the fire.

"But the seed?" he ventured.

She pointed impressively roofward. "The dark of the moon, boy, the dark of the moon—the first dark—at midnight." Bles could not wring another word from her; nor did the ancient witch, by word or look, again give the slightest indication that she was aware of his presence.

With reluctant farewell, Bles turned home. For a space Zora watched him, and once she started after him, but came slowly back, and sat by the fire-place.

Out of the night came voices and laughter, and the sound of wheels and galloping horses. It was not the soft, rollicking laughter of black men, but the keener, more metallic sound of white men's cries, and Bles Alwyn paused at the edge of the wood, looked back and hesitated, but decided after a moment to go home and to bed.

Zora, however, leapt to her feet and fled into the night, while the hag screamed after her and cursed. There was tramping of feet on the cabin floor, and loud voices and singing and cursing.

"Where's Zora?" some one yelled, with an oath. "Damn it! where is she? I haven't seen her for a year, you old devil."

The hag whimpered and snarled. Far down in the field of the Fleece, Zora lay curled beneath a tall dark tree asleep. All night there was coming and going in the cabin; the talk and laughter grew loud and boisterous, and the red fire glared in the night.

The days flew by and the moon darkened. In the swamp, the hidden island lay spaded and bedded, and Bles was throwing up a dyke around the edge; Zora helped him until he came to the black oak at the western edge. It was a large twisted thing with one low flying limb that curled out across another tree and made a mighty seat above the waters.

"Don't throw the dirt too high there," she begged; "it'll bring my seat too near the earth."

He looked up.

"Why, it's a throne," he laughed.

"It needs a roof," he whimsically told her when his day's work was done. Deftly twisting and intertwining the branches of tree and bush, he wove a canopy of living green that shadowed the curious nest and warded it snugly from wind and water.

Early next morning Bles slipped down and improved the nest; adding foot-rests to make the climbing easy, peep-holes east and west,

a bit of carpet over the bark, and on the rough main trunk, a little picture in blue and gold of Bougereau's Madonna. Zora sat hidden and
alone in silent ecstasy. Bles peeped in—there was not room to enter:
the girl was staring silently at the Madonna. She seemed to feel rather
than hear his presence, and she inquired softly:

"Who's it, Bles?"

"The mother of God," he answered reverently.

"And why does she hold a lily?"

"It stands for purity—she was a good woman."

"With a baby," Zora added slowly.

"Yes—" said Bles, and then more quickly—"It is the Christ
Child—God's baby."

"God is the father of all the little babies, ain't He, Bles?"

"Why, yes—yes, of course; only this little baby didn't have any
other father."

"Yes, I know one like that," she said,—and then she added softly:
"Poor little Christ-baby."

Bles hesitated, and before he found words Zora was saying:

"How white she is; she's as white as the lily, Bles; but—I'm sorry
she's white—Bles, what's purity—just whiteness?"

Bles glanced at her awkwardly but she was still staring wide-eyed at
the picture, and her voice was earnest. She was now so old and again so
much a child, an eager questioning child, that there seemed about her
innocence something holy.

"It means," he stammered, groping for meanings—"it means being
good—just as good as a woman knows how."

She wheeled quickly toward him and asked him eagerly:

"Not better—not better than she knows, but just as good, in—lying
and stealing and—and everything?"

Bles smiled.

"No—not better than she knows, but just as good."

She trembled happily.

"I'm—pure," she said, with a strange little breaking voice and gesture. A sob struggled in his throat.

"Of course you are," he whispered tenderly, hiding her little hands in his.

"I—I was so afraid—sometimes—that I wasn't," she whispered, lifting up to him her eyes streaming with tears. Silently he kissed her lips.

From that day on they walked together in a new world. No revealing word was spoken; no vows were given, none asked for; but a new bond held them. She grew older, quieter, taller, he humbler, more tender and reverent, as they toiled together.

So the days passed. The sun burned in the heavens; but the silvered glory of the moon grew fainter and fainter and each night it rose later than the night before. Then one day Zora whispered:

"tonight!"

Bles came to the cabin, and he and Zora and Elspeth sat silently around the fire-place with its meagre embers. The night was balmy and still; only occasionally a wandering breeze searching the hidden places of the swamp, or the call and song of night birds, jarred the stillness. Long they sat, until the silence crept into Bles's flesh, and stretching out his hand, he touched Zora's, clasping it.

After a time the old woman rose and hobbled to a big black chest. Out of it she brought an old bag of cotton seed—not the white-green seed which Bles had always known, but small, smooth black seeds, which she handled carefully, dipping her hands deep down and letting them drop through her gnarled fingers. And so again they sat and waited and waited, saying no word.

Not until the stars of midnight had swung to the zenith did they start down through the swamp. Bles sought to guide the old woman, but he found she knew the way better than he did. Her shadowy figure darting in and out among the trunks till they crossed the tree bridge, moved ever noiselessly ahead.

She motioned the boy and girl away to the thicket at the edge, and stood still and black in the midst of the cleared island. Bles slipped his arm protectingly around Zora, glancing fearfully about in the darkness. Slowly a great cry rose and swept the island. It struck madly and sharply, and then died away to uneasy murmuring. From afar there seemed to come the echo or the answer to the call. The form of Elspeth blurred the night dimly far off, almost disappearing, and then growing blacker and larger. They heard the whispering *"swish-swish"* of falling seed; they felt the heavy tread of a great coming body. The form of the old woman suddenly loomed black above them, hovering a moment formless and vast then fading again away, and the *"swish-swish"* of the falling seed alone rose in the silence of the night.

At last all was still. A long silence. Then again the air seemed suddenly filled with that great and awful cry; its echoing answer screamed afar and they heard the raucous voice of Elspeth beating in their ears:

"De seed done sowed! De seed done sowed!"

Ten

MR. TAYLOR CALLS

Thinking the matter over," said Harry Cresswell to his father, "I'm inclined to advise drawing this Taylor out a little further."

The Colonel puffed his cigar and one eye twinkled, the lid of the other being at the moment suggestively lowered.

"Was she pretty?" he asked; but his son ignored the remark, and the father continued:

"I had a telegram from Taylor this morning, after you left. He'll be passing through Montgomery the first of next month, and proposes calling."

"I'll wire him to come," said Harry, promptly.

At this juncture the door opened and a young lady entered. Helen Cresswell was twenty, small and pretty, with a slightly languid air. Outside herself there was little in which she took very great interest, and her interest in herself was not absorbing. Yet she had a curiously sweet way. Her servants liked her and the tenants could count on her spasmodic attentions in time of sickness and trouble.

"Good-morning," she said, with a soft drawl. She sauntered over to her father, kissed him, and hung over the back of his chair.

"Did you get that novel for me, Harry?"—expectantly regarding her brother.

"I forgot it, Sis. But I'll be going to town again soon."

The young lady showed that she was annoyed.

"By the bye, Sis, there's a young lady over at the Negro school whom I think you'd like."

"Black or white?"

"A young lady, I said. Don't be sarcastic."

"I heard you. I did not know whether you were using our language or others'."

"She's really unusual, and seems to understand things. She's planning to call some day—shall you be at home?"

"Certainly not, Harry; you're crazy." And she strolled out to the porch, exchanged some remarks with a passing servant, and then nestled comfortably into a hammock. She helped herself to a chocolate and called out musically:

"Pa, are you going to town today?"

"Yes, honey."

"Can I go?"

"I'm going in an hour or so, and business at the bank will keep me until after lunch."

"I don't care, I just must go. I'm clean out of anything to read. And I want to shop and call on Dolly's friend—she's going soon."

"All right. Can you be ready by eleven?"

She considered.

"Yes—I reckon," she drawled, prettily swinging her foot and watching the tree-tops above the distant swamp.

Harry Cresswell, left alone, rang the bell for the butler.

"Still thinking of going, are you, Sam?" asked Cresswell, carelessly, when the servant appeared. He was a young, light-brown boy, his manner obsequious.

"Why, yes, sir—if you can spare me."

"Spare you, you black rascal! You're going anyhow. Well, you'll repent it; the North is no place for niggers. See here, I want lunch for two at one o'clock." The directions that followed were explicit and given with a particularity that made Sam wonder. "Order my trap," he finally directed.

Cresswell went out on the high-pillared porch until the trap appeared.

"Oh, Harry! I wanted to go in the trap—take me?" coaxed his sister.

"Sorry, Sis, but I'm going the other way."

"I don't believe it," said Miss Cresswell, easily, as she settled down to another chocolate. Cresswell did not take the trouble to reply.

Miss Taylor was on her morning walk when she saw him spinning down the road, and both expressed surprise and pleasure at the meeting.

"What a delightful morning!" said the school-teacher, and the glow on her face said even more.

"I'm driving round through the old plantation," he explained; "won't you join me?"

"The invitation is tempting," she hesitated; "but I've got just oodles of work."

"What! on Saturday?"

"Saturday is my really busy day, don't you know. I guess I could get off; really, though, I suspect I ought to tell Miss Smith."

He looked a little perplexed; but the direction in which her inclinations lay was quite clear to him.

"It—it would be decidedly the proper thing," he murmured, "and we could, of course, invite Miss——"

She saw the difficulty and interrupted him:

"It's quite unnecessary; she'll think I have simply gone for a long walk." And soon they were speeding down the silent road, breathing the perfume of the pines.

Now a ride of an early spring morning, in Alabama, over a leisurely old plantation road and behind a spirited horse, is an event to be enjoyed. Add to this a man bred to be agreeable and outdoing his training, and a pretty girl gay with new-found companionship—all this is apt to make a morning worth remembering.

They turned off the highway and passed through long stretches of ploughed and tumbled fields, and other fields brown with the dead ghosts of past years' cotton standing straggling and weather-worn. Long, straight, or curling rows of ploughers passed by with steaming, struggling mules, with whips snapping and the yodle of workers or the sharp guttural growl of overseers as a constant accompaniment.

"They're beginning to plough up the land for the cotton-crop," he explained.

"What a wonderful crop it is!" Mary had fallen pensive.

"Yes, indeed—if only we could get decent returns for it."

"Why, I thought it was a most valuable crop." She turned to him inquiringly.

"It is—to Negroes and manufacturers, but not to planters."

"But why don't the planters do something?"

"What can be done with Negroes?" His tone was bitter. "We tried to combine against manufacturers in the Farmers' League of last winter. My father was president. The pastime cost him fifty thousand dollars."

Miss Taylor was perplexed, but eager. "You must correspond with my brother, Mr. Cresswell," she gravely observed. "I'm sure he—" Before she could finish, an overseer rode up. He began talking abruptly, with a quick side-glance at Mary, in which she might have caught a gleam of surprised curiosity.

"That old nigger, Jim Sykes, over on the lower place, sir, ain't showed up again this morning."

Cresswell nodded. "I'll drive by and see," he said carelessly.

The old man was discovered sitting before his cabin with his head in his hands. He was tall, black, and gaunt, partly bald, with tufted hair. One leg was swathed in rags, and his eyes, as he raised them, wore a cowed and furtive look.

"Well, Uncle Jim, why aren't you at work?" called Cresswell from the roadside. The old man rose painfully to his feet, swayed against the cabin, and clutched off his cap.

"It's my leg again, Master Harry—the leg what I hurt in the gin last fall," he answered, uneasily.

Cresswell frowned. "It's probably whiskey," he assured his companion, in an undertone; then to the man:

"You must get to the field to-morrow,"—his habitually calm, unfeeling positiveness left no ground for objection; "I cannot support you in idleness, you know."

"Yes, Master Harry," the other returned, with conciliatory eagerness; "I knows that—I knows it and I ain't shirking. But, Master Harry, they ain't doing me right 'bout my cabin—I just wants to show you." He got out some dirty papers, and started to hobble forward, wincing with pain. Mary Taylor stirred in her seat under an involuntary impulse to help, but Cresswell touched the horse.

"All right, Uncle Jim," he said; "we'll look it over to-morrow."

They turned presently to where they could see the Cresswell oaks waving lazily in the sunlight and the white gleam of the pillared "Big House."

A pause at the Cresswell store, where Mr. Cresswell entered, afforded Mary Taylor an opportunity further to extend her fund of information.

"Do you go to school?" she inquired of the black boy who held the horse, her mien sympathetic and interested.

"No, ma'am," he mumbled.

"What's your name?"

"Buddy—I'se one of Aunt Rachel's chilluns."

"And where do you live, Buddy?"

"I lives with granny, on de upper place."

"Well, I'll see Aunt Rachel and ask her to send you to school."

"Won't do no good—she done ast, and Mr. Cresswell, he say he ain't going to have no more of his niggers—"

But Mr. Cresswell came out just then, and with him a big, fat, and greasy black man, with little eyes and soft wheedling voice. He was following Cresswell at the side but just a little behind, hat in hand, head aslant, and talking deferentially. Cresswell strode carelessly on, answering him with good-natured tolerance.

The black man stopped with humility before the trap and swept a profound obeisance. Cresswell glanced up quizzically at Miss Taylor.

"This," he announced, "is Jones, the Baptist preacher—begging."

"Ah, lady,"—in mellow, unctuous tones—"I don't know what we poor black folks would do without Mr. Cresswell—the Lord bless him," said the minister, shoving his hand far down into his pocket.

Shortly afterward they were approaching the Cresswell Mansion, when the young man reined in the horse.

"If you wouldn't mind," he suggested, "I could introduce my sister to you."

"I should be delighted," answered Miss Taylor, readily.

When they rolled up to the homestead under its famous oaks the hour was past one. The house was a white oblong building of two stories. In front was the high pillared porch, semi-circular, extending to the roof with a balcony in the second story. On the right was a broad verandah looking toward a wide lawn, with the main road and the red swamp in the distance.

The butler met them, all obeisance.

"Ask Miss Helen to come down," said Mr. Cresswell.

Sam glanced at him.

"Miss Helen will be dreadful sorry, but she and the Colonel have just gone to town—I believe her Aunty ain't well."

Mr. Cresswell looked annoyed.

"Well, well! that's too bad," he said. "But at any rate, have a seat a moment out here on the verandah, Miss Taylor. And, Sam, can't you find us a sandwich and something cool? I could not be so inhospitable as to send you away hungry at this time of day."

Miss Taylor sat down in a comfortable low chair facing the refreshing breeze, and feasted her eyes on the scene. Oh, this was life: a smooth green lawn, and beds of flowers, a vista of brown fields, and the dark line of wood beyond. The deft, quiet butler brought out a little table, spread with the whitest of cloths and laid with the brightest of silver, and "found" a dainty lunch. There was a bit of fried chicken breast, some crisp bacon, browned potatoes, little round beaten biscuit, and rose-colored sherbet with a whiff of wine in it. Miss Taylor wondered a little at the bounty of Southern hospitality; but she was hungry, and she ate heartily, then leaned back dreamily and listened to Mr. Cresswell's smooth Southern r's, adding a word here and there that kept the conversation going and brought a grave smile to his pale lips. At last with a sigh she arose to her feet.

"I must go! What shall I tell Miss Smith! No, no—no carriage; I must walk." Of course, however, she could not refuse to let him go at least half-way, ostensibly to tell her of the coming of her brother. He expressed again his disappointment at his sister's absence.

Somewhat to Miss Taylor's surprise Miss Smith said nothing until they were parting for the night, then she asked:

"Was Miss Cresswell at home?"

Mary reddened.

"She had been called suddenly to town."

"Well, my dear, I wouldn't do it again."

The girl was angry.

"I'm not a school-girl, but a grown woman, and capable of caring for myself. Moreover, in matter of propriety I do not think you have usually found my ideas too lax—rather the opposite."

"There, there, dear; don't be angry. Only I think if your brother knew—"

"He will know in a very few weeks; he is coming to visit the Cresswells." And Miss Taylor sailed triumphantly up the stairs.

But John Taylor was not the man to wait weeks when a purpose could be accomplished in days or hours. No sooner was Harry Cresswell's telegram at hand than he hastened back from Savannah, struck across country, and the week after his sister's ride found him striding up the carriage-way of the Cresswell home.

John Taylor had prospered since summer. The cotton manufacturers' combine was all but a fact; Mr. Easterly had discovered that his chief clerk's sense and executive ability were invaluable, and John Taylor was slated for a salary in five figures when things should be finally settled, not to mention a generous slice of stock—watery at present, but warranted to ripen early.

While Mr. Easterly still regarded Taylor's larger trust as chimerical, some occurrences of the fall made him take a respectful attitude toward it. Just as the final clauses of the combine agreement were to be signed, there appeared a shortage in the cotton-crop, and prices began to soar. The cause was obviously the unexpected success of the new Farmers' League among the cotton-growers. Mr. Easterly found it comparatively easy to overthrow the corner, but the flurry made some of the manufacturers timid, and the trust agreement was postponed until a year later. This experience and the persistence of Mr. Taylor induced Mr. Easterly to take a step toward the larger project: he let in some eager outside capital to the safer manufacturing scheme, and withdrew a corresponding amount of Mrs. Grey's money. This he put into John Taylor's hands to invest in the South in bank stock and industries with the idea of playing a part in the financial situation there.

"It's a risk, Taylor, of course, and we'll let the old lady take the risk. At the worst it's safer than the damned foolishness she has in mind."

So it happened that John Taylor went South to look after large investments and, as Mr. Easterly expressed it, "to bring back facts, not dreams." His investment matters went quickly and well, and now he turned to his wider and bigger scheme. He wrote the Cresswells tentatively, expecting no reply, or an evasive one; planning to circle around them, drawing his nets closer, and trying them again later. To his surprise they responded quickly.

"Humph! Hard pressed," he decided, and hurried to them.

So it was the week after Mary Taylor's ride that found him at Cresswell's front door, thin, eagle-eyed, fairly well dressed and radiating confidence.

"John Taylor," he announced to Sam, jerkily, thrusting out a card. "Want to see Mr. Cresswell; soon as possible."

Sam made him wait a half-hour, for the sake of discipline, and then brought father and son.

"Good-morning, Mr. Cresswell, and Mr. Cresswell again," said Mr. Taylor, helping himself to a straight-backed chair. "Hope you'll pardon this unexpected visit. Found myself called through Montgomery, just after I got your wire; thought I'd better drop over."

At Harry's suggestion they moved to the verandah and sat down over whiskey and soda, which Taylor refused, and plunged into the subject without preliminaries.

"I'm assuming that you gentlemen are in the cotton business for making money. So am I. I see a way in which you and your friends can help me and mine, and clear up more millions than all of us can spend; for this reason I've hunted you up. This is my scheme.

"See here; there are a thousand cotton-mills in this country, half of them in the South, one-fourth in New England, and one-fourth in the Middle States. They are capitalized at six hundred million dollars. Now let me tell you: we control three hundred and fifty millions of that capitalization. The trust is going through capitalization at a billion. The only thing that threatens it is child-labor legislation in the South, the tariff, and the control of the supply of cotton. Pretty big hindrances, you say. That's so, but look here: we've got the stock so placed that nothing short of a popular upheaval can send any Child Labor bill through Congress in six years. See? After that we don't care. Same thing applies to the tariff. The last bill ran ten years. The present bill will last longer, or I lose my guess—'specially if Smith is in the Senate.

"Well, then, there remains raw cotton. The connection of cotton-raising and its raw material is too close to risk a manufacturing trust that does not include practical control of the raw material. For that reason we're planning a trust to include the raising and manufacturing of cotton in America. Then, too, cornering the cotton market here means the whip-hand of the industrial world. Gentlemen, it's the biggest idea of the century. It beats steel."

Colonel Cresswell chuckled.

"How do you spell that?" he asked.

But John Taylor was not to be diverted; his thin face was pale, but his gray eyes burned with the fire of a zealot. Harry Cresswell only smiled dimly and looked interested.

"Now, again," continued John Taylor. "There are a million cotton farms in the South, half run by colored people and half by whites. Leave the colored out of account as long as they are disfranchised. The half million white farms are owned or controlled by five thousand wholesale merchants and three thousand big landowners, of whom you, Colonel Cresswell, are among the biggest with your fifty thousand acres. Ten banks control these eight thousand people—one of these is the Jefferson National of Montgomery, of which you are a silent director."

Colonel Cresswell started; this man evidently had inside information. Did he know of the mortgage, too?

"Don't be alarmed. I'm safe," Taylor assured him. "Now, then, if we can get the banks, wholesale merchants, and biggest planters into line we can control the cotton crop."

"But," objected Harry Cresswell, "while the banks and the large merchants may be possibilities, do you know what it means to try to get planters into line?"

"Yes, I do. And what I don't know you and your father do. Colonel Cresswell is president of the Farmers' League. That's the reason I'm here. Your success last year made you indispensable to our plans."

"Our success?" laughed Colonel Cresswell, ruefully, thinking of the fifty thousand dollars lost and the mortgage to cover it.

"Yes, sir—success! You didn't know it; we were too careful to allow that; and I say frankly you wouldn't know it now if we weren't convinced you were too far involved and the League too discouraged to repeat the dose."

"Now, look here, sir," began Colonel Cresswell, flushing and drawing himself erect.

"There, there, Colonel Cresswell, don't misunderstand me. I'm a plain man. I'm playing a big game—a tremendous one. I need you, and I know you need me. I find out about you, and my sources of knowledge are wide and unerring. But the knowledge is safe, sir; it's buried. Last year when you people curtailed cotton acreage and warehoused a big chunk of the crop you gave the mill men the scare of their lives. We had a hasty conference and the result was that the bottom fell out of your credit."

Colonel Cresswell grew pale. There was a disquieting, relentless element in this unimpassioned man's tone.

"You failed," pursued John Taylor, "because you couldn't get the banks and the big merchants behind you. We've got 'em behind us—with big chunks of stock and a signed iron-clad agreement. You can wheel the planters into line—will you do it?" John Taylor bent forward tense but cool and steel-like. Harry Cresswell laid his hand on his father's arm and said quietly:

"And where do we come in?"

"That's business," affirmed John Taylor. "You and two hundred and fifty of the biggest planters come in on the ground-floor of the two-billion-dollar All-Cotton combine. It can easily mean two million to you in five years."

"And the other planters?"

"They come in for high-priced cotton until we get our grip."

"And then?"

The quiet question seemed to invoke a vision for John Taylor; the gray eyes took on the faraway look of a seer; the thin, bloodless lips formed a smile in which there was nothing pleasant.

"They keep their mouths shut or we squeeze 'em and buy the land. We propose to own the cotton belt of the South."

Colonel Cresswell started indignantly from his seat.

"Do you think—by God, sir!—that I'd betray Southern gentlemen to—"

But Harry's hand and impassive manner restrained him; he cooled as suddenly as he had flared up.

"Thank you very much, Mr. Taylor," he concluded; "we'll consider this matter carefully. You'll spend the night, of course."

"Can't possibly—must catch that next train back."

"But we must talk further," the Colonel insisted. "And then, there's your sister."

"By Jove! Forgot all about Mary." John Taylor after a little desultory talk, followed his host up-stairs.

The next afternoon John Taylor was sitting beside Helen Cresswell on the porch which overlooked the terrace, and was, on the whole, thinking less of cotton than he had for several years. To be sure, he was talking cotton; but he was doing it mechanically and from long habit, and was really thinking how charming a girl Helen Cresswell was. She fascinated him. For his sister Taylor had a feeling of superiority that was almost contempt. The idea of a woman trying to understand and argue about things men knew! He admired the dashing and handsome Miss Easterly, but she scared him and made him angrily awkward. This girl, on the other hand, just lounged and listened with an amused smile, or asked the most child-like questions. She required him to wait on her quite as a matter of course—to adjust her pillows, hand her the bon-bons, and hunt for her lost fan. Mr. Taylor, who had not waited on anybody since his mother died, and not much before, found a quite inexplicable pleasure in these little domesticities. Several times he took out his watch and frowned; yet he managed to stay with her quite happily.

On her part Miss Cresswell was vastly amused. Her acquaintance with men was not wide, but it was thorough so far as her own class was concerned. They were all well-dressed and leisurely, fairly good looking, and they said the same words and did the same things in the same way. They paid her compliments which she did not believe, and they did not expect her to believe. They were charmingly deferential in the matter of dropped handkerchiefs, but tyrannical of opinion. They were thoughtful about candy and flowers, but thoughtless about feelings and income. Altogether they were delightful, but cloying. This man was startlingly different; ungainly and always in a desperate, unaccountable hurry. He knew no pretty speeches, he certainly did not measure up to her standard of breeding, and yet somehow he was a gentleman. All this was new to Helen Cresswell, and she liked it.

Meanwhile the men above-stairs lingered in the Colonel's office— the older one perturbed and sputtering, the younger insistent and imperturbable.

"The fact is, father," he was saying, "as you yourself have said, one bad crop of cotton would almost ruin us."

"But the prospects are good."

"What are prospects in March? No, father, this is the situation— three good crops in succession will wipe off our indebtedness and leave us facing only low prices and a scarcity of niggers; on the other hand—" The father interrupted impatiently.

"Yes, on the other hand, if we plunge deeper in debt and betray our friends we may come out millionaires or—paupers."

"Precisely," said Harry Cresswell, calmly. "Now, our plan is to take no chances; I propose going North and looking into this matter thoroughly. If he represents money and has money, and if the trust has really got the grip he says it has, why, it's a case of crush or get crushed, and we'll have to join them on their own terms. If he's bluffing, or the thing looks weak, we'll wait."

It all ended as matters usually did end, in Harry's having his way. He came downstairs, expecting, indeed, rather hoping, to find Taylor impatiently striding to and fro, watch in hand; but here he was, ungainly, it might be, but quite docile, drawing the picture of a power-loom for Miss Cresswell, who seemed really interested. Harry silently surveyed them from the door, and his face lighted with a new thought.

Taylor, espying him, leapt to his feet and hauled out his watch.

"Well—I—" he began lamely.

"No, you weren't either," interrupted Harry, with a laugh that was unmistakably cordial and friendly. "You had quite forgotten what you were waiting for—isn't that so, Sis?"

Helen regarded her brother through her veiling lashes: what meant this sudden assumption of warmth and amiability?

"No, indeed; he was raging with impatience," she returned.

"Why, Miss Cresswell, I—I—" John Taylor forsook social amenities and pulled himself together. "Well," shortly, "now for that talk— ready?" And quite forgetting Miss Cresswell, he bolted into the parlor.

"The decision we have come to is this," said Harry Cresswell. "We are in debt, as you know."

"Forty-nine thousand, seven hundred and forty-two dollars and twelve cents," responded Taylor; "in three notes, due in twelve, twenty-four, and thirty-six months, interest at eight per cent, held by—"

The Colonel snorted his amazement, and Harry Cresswell cut in:

"Yes," he calmly admitted; "and with good crops for three years we'd be all right; good crops even for two years would leave us fairly well off."

"You mean it would relieve you of the present stringency and put you face to face with the falling price of cotton and rising wages," was John Taylor's dry addendum.

"Rising price of cotton, you mean," Harry corrected.

"Oh, temporarily," John Taylor admitted.

"Precisely, and thus postpone the decision."

"No, Mr. Cresswell. I'm offering to let you in on the ground floor—*now*—not next year, or year after."

"Mr. Taylor, have you any money in this?"

"Everything I've got."

"Well, the thing is this way: if you can prove to us that conditions are as you say, we're in for it."

"Good! Meet me in New York, say—let's see, this is March tenth— well, May third."

Young Cresswell was thinking rapidly. This man without doubt represented money. He was anxious for an alliance. Why? Was it all straight, or did the whole move conceal a trick?

His eyes strayed to the porch where his pretty sister sat languidly, and then toward the school where the other sister lived. John Taylor looked out on the porch, too. They glanced quickly at each other, and each wondered if the other had shared his thought. Harry Cresswell did not voice his mind for he was not wholly disposed to welcome what was there; but he could not refrain from saying in tones almost confidential:

"You could recommend this deal, then, could you—to your own friends?"

"To my own family," asserted John Taylor, looking at Harry Cresswell with sudden interest. But Mr. Cresswell was staring at the end of his cigar.

Eleven

THE FLOWERING OF
THE FLEECE

Z ora," observed Miss Smith, "it's a great blessing not to need spectacles, isn't it?"

Zora thought that it was; but she was wondering just what spectacles had to do with the complaint she had brought to the office from Miss Taylor.

"I'm always losing my glasses and they get dirty and—Oh, dear! now where is that paper?"

Zora pointed silently to the complaint.

"No, not that—another paper. It must be in my room. Don't you want to come up and help me look?"

They went up to the clean, bare room, with its white iron bed, its cool, spotless shades and shining windows. Zora walked about softly and looked, while Miss Smith quietly searched on desk and bureau, paying no attention to the girl. For the time being she was silent.

"I sometimes wish," she began at length, "I had a bright-eyed girl like you to help me find and place things."

Zora made no comment.

"Sometimes Bles helps me," added Miss Smith, guilefully.

Zora looked sharply at her. "Could I help?" she asked, almost timidly.

"Why, I don't know,"—the answer was deliberate. "There are one or two little things perhaps—"

Placing a hand gently upon Zora's shoulder, she pointed out a few odd tasks, and left the girl busily doing them; then she returned to the office, and threw Miss Taylor's complaint into the waste-basket.

For a week or more Zora slipped in every day and performed the little tasks that Miss Smith laid out: she sorted papers, dusted the bureau, hung a curtain; she did not do the things very well, and she broke some china, but she worked earnestly and quickly, and there was no thought of pay. Then, too, did not Bles praise her with a happy smile, as together, day after day, they stood and watched the black dirt where the Silver Fleece lay planted? She dreamed and sang over that dark field, and again and again appealed to him: "S'pose it shouldn't come up after all?" And he would laugh and say that of course it would come up.

One day, when Zora was helping Miss Smith in the bedroom, she paused with her arms full of clothes fresh from the laundry.

"Where shall I put these?"

Miss Smith looked around. "They might go in there," she said, pointing to a door. Zora opened it. A tiny bedroom was disclosed, with one broad window looking toward the swamp; white curtains adorned it, and white hangings draped the plain bureau and wash-stand and the little bed. There was a study table, and a small bookshelf holding a few books, all simple and clean. Zora paused uncertainly, and surveyed the room.

"Sometimes when you're tired and want to be alone you can come up here, Zora," said Miss Smith carelessly. "No one uses this room."

Zora caught her breath sharply, but said nothing. The next day Miss Smith said to her when she came in:

"I'm busy now, dear, but you go up to your little room and read and I'll call."

Zora quietly obeyed. An hour later Miss Smith looked in, then she closed the door lightly and left. Another hour flew by before Zora hurried down.

"I was reading, and I forgot," she said.

"It's all right," returned Miss Smith. "I didn't need you. And any day, after you get all your lessons, I think Miss Taylor will excuse you and let you go to your room and read." Miss Taylor, it transpired, was more than glad.

Day after day Bles and Zora visited the field; but ever the ground lay an unrelieved black beneath the bright sun, and they would go reluctantly home again. today there was much work to be done, and Zora labored steadily and eagerly, never pausing, and gaining in deftness and care.

In the afternoon Bles went to town with the school wagon. A light shower flew up from the south, lingered a while and fled, leaving a fragrance in the air. For a moment Zora paused, and her nostrils quivered; then without a word she slipped down-stairs, glided into the swamp, and sped away to the island. She swung across the tree and a low, delighted cry bubbled on her lips. All the rich, black ground was sprinkled with tender green. She bent above the verdant tenderness and kissed it; then she rushed back, bursting into the room.

"It's come! It's come!—the Silver Fleece!"

Miss Smith was startled.

"The Silver Fleece!" she echoed in bewilderment.

Zora hesitated. It came over her all at once that this one great all-absorbing thing meant nothing to the gaunt tired-look woman before her.

"Would Bles care if I told?" she asked doubtfully.

"No," Miss Smith ventured.

And then the girl crouched at her feet and told the dream and the story. Many factors were involved that were quite foreign to the older woman's nature and training. The recital brought to her New England mind many questions of policy and propriety. And yet, as she looked down upon the dark face, hot with enthusiasm, it all seemed somehow more than right. Slowly and lightly Miss Smith slipped her arm about Zora, and nodded and smiled a perfect understanding. They looked out together into the darkening twilight.

"It is so late and wet and you're tired tonight—don't you think you'd better sleep in your little room?"

Zora sat still. She thought of the noisy flaming cabin and the dark swamp; but a contrasting thought of the white bed made her timid, and slowly she shook her head. Nevertheless Miss Smith led her to the room.

"Here are things for you to wear," she pointed out, opening the bureau, "and here is the bath-room." She left the girl standing in the middle of the floor.

In time Zora came to stay often at Miss Smith's cottage, and to learn new and unknown ways of living and dressing. She still refused to board, for that would cost more than she could pay yet, and she would accept no charity. Gradually an undemonstrative friendship sprang up between the pale old gray-haired teacher and the dark young black-haired girl. Delicately, too, but gradually, the companionship of Bles and Zora was guided and regulated. Of mornings Zora would hurry through her lessons and get excused to fly to the swamp, to work and dream alone. At noon Bles would run down, and they would linger until he must hurry back to dinner. After school he would go again, working while she was busy in Miss Smith's office, and returning later, would linger awhile to tell Zora of his day while she busied herself with her little tasks. Saturday mornings they would go to the swamp and work together, and sometimes Miss Smith, stealing away from curious eyes, would come and sit and talk with them as they toiled.

In those days, for these two souls, earth came very near to heaven. Both were in the midst of that mighty change from youth to womanhood and manhood. Their manner toward each other by degrees grew shyer and more thoughtful. There was less of comradeship, but the little meant more. The rough good fellowship was silently put aside; they no longer lightly clasped hands; and each at times wondered, in painful self-consciousness, if the other cared.

Then began, too, that long and subtle change wherein a soul, until now unmindful of its wrappings, comes suddenly to consciousness of body and clothes; when it gropes and tries to adjust one with the other, and through them to give to the inner deeper self, finer and fuller expression. One saw it easily, almost suddenly, in Alwyn's Sunday suit, vivid neckties, and awkward fads.

Slower, subtler, but more striking was the change in Zora, as she began to earn bits of pin money in the office and to learn to sew. Dresses hung straighter; belts served a better purpose; stockings were smoother; underwear was daintier. Then her hair—that great dark mass of immovable infinitely curled hair—began to be subdued and twisted and combed until, with steady pains and study, it lay in thick twisted braids about her velvet forehead, like some shadowed halo. All this came much more slowly and spasmodically than one tells it. Few noticed the change much; none noticed all; and yet there came a night— a student's social—when with a certain suddenness the whole school, teachers and pupils, realized the newness of the girl, and even Bles was startled.

He had bought her in town, at Christmas time, a pair of white satin slippers, partly to test the smallness of her feet on which in younger days he had rallied her, and partly because she had mentioned a possible white dress. They were a cheap, plain pair but dainty, and they fitted well.

When the evening came and the students were marching and the teachers, save Miss Smith, were sitting rather primly apart and commenting, she entered the room. She was a little late, and a hush greeted her. One boy, with the inimitable drawl of the race, pushed back his ice-cream and addressed it with a mournful head-shake:

"Go way, honey, yo' los' yo' tas'e!"

The dress was plain and fitted every curving of a healthy girlish form. She paused a moment white-bodied and white-limbed but dark and velvet-armed, her full neck and oval head rising rich and almost black above, with its deep-lighted eyes and crown of silent darkling hair.

To some, such a revelation of grace and womanliness in this hoyden, the gentle swelling of lankness to beauty, of lowliness to shy self-poise, was a sudden joy, to others a mere blindness. Mary Taylor was perplexed and in some indefinite way amazed; and many of the other teachers saw no beauty, only a strangeness that brought a smile. They were such as know beauty by convention only, and find it lip-ringed, hoop-skirted, tattooed, or corsetted, as time and place decree.

The change in Zora, however, had been neither cataclysmic nor revolutionary and it was yet far—very far—from complete. She still ran and romped in the woods, and dreamed her dreams; she still was passionately independent and "queer." Tendencies merely had become manifest, some dominant. She would, unhindered, develop to a brilliant, sumptuous womanhood; proud, conquering, full-blooded, and deep bosomed—a passionate mother of men. Herein lay all her early wildness and strangeness. Herein lay, as yet half hidden, dimly sensed and all unspoken, the power of a mighty all-compelling love for one human soul, and, through it, for all the souls of men. All this lay growing and developing; but as yet she was still a girl, with a new shyness and comeliness and a bold, searching heart.

In the field of the Silver Fleece all her possibilities were beginning to find expression. These new-born green things hidden far down in the swamp, begotten in want and mystery, were to her a living wonderful fairy tale come true. All the latent mother in her brooded over them; all her brilliant fancy wove itself about them. They were her dream-children, and she tended them jealously; they were her Hope, and she worshipped them. When the rabbits tried the tender plants she watched hours to drive them off, and catching now and then a pulsing pink-eyed invader, she talked to it earnestly:

"Brer Rabbit—poor little Brer Rabbit, don't you know you mustn't eat Zora's cotton? Naughty, naughty Brer Rabbit." And then she would show it where she had gathered piles of fragrant weeds for it and its fellows.

The golden green of the first leaves darkened, and the plants sprang forward steadily. Never before was such a magnificent beginning, a full month ahead of other cotton. The rain swept down in laughing, bubbling showers, and laved their thirsty souls, and Zora held her beating breast day by day lest it rain too long or too heavily. The sun burned fiercely upon the young cotton plants as the spring hastened, and they lifted their heads in darker, wilder luxuriance; for the time of hoeing was at hand.

These days were days of alternate hope and doubt with Bles Alwyn. Strength and ambition and inarticulate love were fighting within him. He felt, in the dark thousands of his kind about him, a mighty calling to deeds. He was becoming conscious of the narrowness and straight-ness of his black world, and red anger flashed in him ever and again as he felt his bonds. His mental horizon was broadening as he prepared for the college of next year; he was faintly grasping the wider, fuller world, and its thoughts and aspirations.

But beside and around and above all this, like subtle, permeating ether, was—Zora. His feelings for her were not as yet definite, ex-pressed, or grasped; they were rather the atmosphere in which all things occurred and were felt and judged. From an amusing pastime she had come to be a companion and thought-mate; and now, beyond this, insensibly they were drifting to a silenter, mightier mingling of souls. But drifting, merely—not arrived; going gently, irresistibly, but not yet at the realized goal.

He felt all this as the stirring of a mighty force, but knew not what he felt. The teasing of his fellows, the common love-gossip of the school yard, seemed far different from his plight. He laughed at it and indignantly denied it. Yet he was uncomfortable, restless, unhappy. He fancied Zora cared less for his company, and he gave her less, and then was puzzled to find time hanging so empty, so wretchedly empty, on his hands. When they were together in these days they found less to talk about, and had it not been for the Silver Fleece which in magic wilfulness opened both their mouths, they would have found their companionship little more than a series of awkward silences. Yet in their silences, their walks, and their sittings there was a companionship, a glow, a satisfaction, as came to them nowhere else on earth, and they wondered at it.

They were both wondering at it this morning as they watched their cotton. It had seemingly bounded forward in a night and it must be hoed forthwith. Yet, hoeing was murder—the ruthless cutting away of tenderer plants that the sturdier might thrive the more and grow.

"I hate it, Bles, don't you?"

"Hate what?"

"Killing any of it; it's all so pretty."

"But it must be, so that what's left will be prettier, or at least more useful."

"But it shouldn't be so; everything ought to have a chance to be beautiful and useful."

"Perhaps it ought to be so," admitted Bles, "but it isn't."

"Isn't it so—anywhere?"

"I reckon not. Death and pain pay for all good things."

She hoed away silently, hesitating over the choice of the plants, pondering this world-old truth, saddened by its ruthless cruelty.

"Death and pain," she murmured; "what a price!"

Bles leaned on his hoe and considered. It had not occurred to him till now that Zora was speaking better and better English: the idioms and errors were dropping away; they had not utterly departed, however, but came crowding back in moments of excitement. At other times she clothed Miss Smith's clear-cut, correct speech in softer Southern accents. She was drifting away from him in some intangible way to an upper world of dress and language and deportment, and the new thought was pain to him.

So it was that the Fleece rose and spread and grew to its wonderful flowering; and so these two children grew with it into theirs. Zora never forgot how they found the first white flower in that green and billowing sea, nor her low cry of pleasure and his gay shout of joy. Slowly, wonderfully the flowers spread—white, blue, and purple bells, hiding timidly, blazing luxuriantly amid the velvet leaves; until one day—it was after a southern rain and the sunlight was twinkling through the morning—all the Fleece was in flower—a mighty swaying sea, darkling rich and waving, and upon it flecks and stars of white and purple foam. The joy of the two so madly craved expression that they burst into singing; not the wild light song of dancing feet, but a low, sweet melody of her fathers' fathers, whereunto Alwyn's own deep voice fell fitly in minor cadence.

Miss Smith and Miss Taylor, who were sorting the mail, heard them singing as they came up out of the swamp. Miss Taylor looked at them, then at Miss Smith.

But Miss Smith sat white and rigid with the first opened letter in her hand.

Twelve

THE PROMISE

M iss Smith sat with her face buried in her hands while the tears trickled silently through her thin fingers. Before her lay the letter, read a dozen times:

"Old Mrs. Grey has been to see me, and she has announced her intention of endowing five colored schools, yours being one. She asked if $500,000 would do it. She has plenty of money, so I told her $750,000 would be better—$150,000 apiece. She's arranging for a Board of Trust, etc. You'll probably hear from her soon. You've been so worried about expenses that I thought I'd send this word on; I knew you'd be glad."

Glad? Dear God, how flat the word fell! For thirty years she had sown the seed, planting her life-blood in this work, that had become the marrow of her soul.

Successful? No, it had not been successful; but it had been human.

Through yonder doorway had trooped an army of hundreds upon hundreds of bright and dull, light and dark, eager and sullen faces. There had been good and bad, honest and deceptive, frank and furtive. Some had caught, kindled and flashed to ambition and achievement; some, glowing dimly, had plodded on in a slow, dumb faithful work worth while; and yet others had suddenly exploded, hurtling human fragments to heaven and to hell. Around this school home, as around the centre of some little universe, had whirled the sorrowful, sordid, laughing, pulsing drama of a world: birth pains, and the stupor of death; hunger and pale murder; the riot of thirst and the orgies of such red and black cabins as Elspeth's, crouching in the swamp.

She groaned as she read of the extravagances of the world and saw her own vanishing revenues; but the funds continued to dwindle until Sarah Smith asked herself: "What will become of this school when I die?" With trembling fingers she had sat down to figure how many teachers must be dropped next year, when her brother's letter came, and she slipped to her knees and prayed.

Mrs. Grey's decision was due in no little way to Mary Taylor's reports. Slowly but surely the girl had begun to think that she had found herself in this new world. She would never be attuned to it thoroughly, for she was set for different music. The veil of color and race still hung thickly between her and her pupils; and yet she seemed to see some points of penetration. No one could meet daily a hundred or more of these light-hearted, good-natured children without feeling drawn to them. No one could cross the thresholds of the cabins and not see the old and well-known problems of life and striving. More and more, therefore, the work met Miss Taylor's approval and she told Mrs. Grey so.

At the same time Mary Taylor had come to some other definite conclusions: she believed it wrong to encourage the ambitions of these children to any great extent; she believed they should be servants and farmers, content to work under present conditions until those conditions could be changed; and she believed that the local white aristocracy, helped by Northern philanthropy, should take charge of such gradual changes.

These conclusions she did not pretend to have originated; but she adopted them from reading and conversation, after hesitating for a year before such puzzling contradictions as Bles Alwyn and Harry Cresswell. For her to conclude to treat Bles Alwyn as a man despite his color was as impossible as to think Mr. Cresswell a criminal. Some compromise was imperative which would save her the pleasure of Mr. Cresswell's company and at the same time leave open a way of fulfilling the world's duty to this black boy. She thought she had found this compromise and she wrote Mrs. Grey suggesting a chain of endowed Negro schools under the management of trustees composed of Northern business men and local Southern whites. Mrs. Grey acquiesced gladly and announced her plan, eventually writing Miss Smith of her decision "to second her noble efforts in helping the poor colored people," and she hoped to have the plan under way before next fall.

The sharpness of Miss Smith's joy did not let her dwell on the proposed "Board of Trust"; of course, it would be a board of friends of the school.

She sat in her office looking out across the land. School had closed for the year and Bles with the carryall was just taking Miss Taylor to the train with her trunk and bags. Far up the road she could see dotted here and there the little dirty cabins of Cresswell's tenants—the Cresswell domain that lay like a mighty hand around the school, ready at a word to squeeze its life out. Only yonder, to the eastward, lay the way out; the five hundred acres of the Tolliver plantation, which the school needed so sadly for its farm and community. But the owner was a hard and ignorant white man, hating "niggers" only a shade more than he hated white aristocrats of the Cresswell type. He had sold the school its first land to pique the Cresswells; but he would not sell any more, she was sure, even now when the promise of wealth faced the school.

She lay back and closed her eyes and fell lightly asleep. As she slept an old woman came toiling up the hill northward from the school, and out of the eastward spur of the Cresswell barony. She was fat and black, hooded and aproned, with great round head and massive bosom. Her face was dull and heavy and homely, her old eyes sorrowful. She moved swiftly, carrying a basket on her arm. Opposite her, to the southward, but too far for sight, an old man came out of the lower Cresswell place, skirting the swamp. He was tall, black, and gaunt, part bald with tufted hair, and a cowed and furtive look was in his eyes. One leg was crippled, and he hobbled painfully.

Up the road to the eastward that ran past the school, with the morning sun at his back, strode a young man, yellow, crisp-haired, strong-faced, with darkly knit brows. He greeted Bles and the teacher coldly, and moved on in nervous haste. A woman, hurrying out of the westward swamp up the path that led from Elspeth's, saw him and shrank back hastily. She turned quickly into the swamp and waited, looking toward the school. The old woman hurried into the back gate just as the old man appeared to the southward on the road. The young man greeted him cordially and they stopped a moment to talk, while the hiding woman watched.

"Howdy, Uncle Jim."

"Howdy, son. Hit's hot, ain't it? How is you?"

"Tolerable, how are you?"

"Poorly, son, poorly—and worser in mind. I'se goin' up to talk to old Miss."

"So am I, but I just see Aunt Rachel going in. We'd better wait."

Miss Smith started up at the timid knocking, and rubbed her eyes. It was long since she had slept in the daytime and she was annoyed at such laziness. She opened the back door and led the old woman to the office.

"Now, what have you got there?" she demanded, eyeing the basket.

"Just a little chicken fo' you and a few aigs."

"Oh, you are so thoughtful!" Sarah Smith's was a grateful heart.

"Go 'long now—hit ain't a thing."

Then came a pause, the old woman sliding into the proffered seat, while over her genial, dimpled smile there dropped a dull veil of care. Her eyes shifted uneasily. Miss Smith tried not to notice the change.

"Well, are you all moved, Aunt Rachel?" she inquired cheerfully.

"No'm, and we ain't gwine to move."

"But I thought it was all arranged."

"It was," gloomily, "but de ole Cunnel, he won't let us go."

The listener was instantly sympathetic. "Why not?" she asked.

"He says we owes him."

"But didn't you settle at Christmas?"

"Yas'm; but when he found we was goin' away, he looked up some more debts."

"How much?"

"I don't know 'zactly—more'n a hundred dollars. Den de boys done got in dat trouble, and he paid their fines."

"What was the trouble?"

"Well, one was a-gambling, and the other struck the overseer what was a-whippin' him."

"Whipping him!"—in horrified exclamation, quite as much at Aunt Rachel's matter-of-fact way of regarding the matter as at the deed itself.

"Yas'm. He didn't do his work right and he whipped him. I speck he needed it."

"But he's a grown man," Miss Smith urged earnestly.

"Yas'm; he's twenty now, and big."

"Whipped him!" Miss Smith repeated. "And so you can't leave?"

"No'm, he say he'll sell us out and put us in de chain-gang if we go. The boys is plumb mad, but I'se a-pleadin' with 'em not to do nothin' rash."

"But—but I thought they had already started to work a crop on the Tolliver place?"

"Yes'm, dey had; but, you see, dey were arrested, and then Cunnel Cresswell took 'em and 'lowed they couldn't leave his place. Ol' man Tolliver was powerful mad."

"Why, Aunt Rachel, it's slavery!" cried the lady in dismay. Aunt Rachel did not offer to dispute her declaration.

"Yas'm, hit's slavery," she agreed. "I hates it mighty bad, too, 'cause I wanted de little chillens in school; but—" The old woman broke down and sobbed.

A knocking came at the door; hastily wiping her eyes Aunt Rachel rose.

"I'll—I'll see what I can do, Aunt Rachel—I *must* do something," murmured Miss Smith hastily, as the woman departed, and an old black man came limping in. Miss Smith looked up in surprise.

"I begs pardon, Mistress—I begs pardon. Good-morning."

"Good-morning—" she hesitated.

"Sykes—Jim Sykes—that's me."

"Yes, I've heard of you, Mr. Sykes; you live over south of the swamp."

"Yes, ma'am, that's me; and I'se got a little shack dar and a bit of land what I'se trying to buy."

"Of Colonel Cresswell?"

"Yas'm, of de Cunnel."

"And how long have you been buying it?"

"Going on ten year now; and dat's what I comes to ask you about."

"Goodness me! And how much have you paid a year?"

"I gen'rally pays 'bout three bales of cotton a year."

"Does he furnish you rations?"

"Only sugar and coffee and a little meat now and then."

"What does it amount to a year?"

"I doesn't rightly know—but I'se got some papers here."

Miss Smith looked them over and sighed. It was the same old tale of blind receipts for money "on account"—no items, no balancing. By his help she made out that last year his total bill at Cresswell's store was perhaps forty dollars.

"An' last year's bill was bigger'n common 'cause I hurt my leg working at the gin and had to have some medicine."

"Why, as far as I can see, Mr. Sykes, you've paid Cresswell about a thousand dollars in the last ten years. How large is your place?"

"About twenty acres."

"And what were you to pay for it?"

"Four hundred."

"Have you got the deed?"

"Yes'm, but I ain't finished paying yet; de Cunnel say as how I owes him two hundred dollars still, and I can't see it. Dat's why I come over here to talk wid you."

"Where is the deed?"

He handed it to her and her heart sank. It was no deed, but a complicated contract binding the tenant hand and foot to the landlord. She sighed, he watching her eagerly.

"I'se getting old," he explained, "and I ain't got nobody to take care of me. I can't work as I once could, and de overseers dey drives me too hard. I wants a little home to die in."

Miss Smith's throat swelled. She couldn't tell him that he would never get one at the present rate; she only said:

"I'll—look this up. You come again next Saturday."

Then sadly she watched the ragged old slave hobble away with his cherished "papers." He greeted the young man at the gate and passed out, while the latter walked briskly up to the door and knocked.

"Why, how do you do, Robert?"

"How do you do, Miss Smith?"

"Well, are you getting things in shape so as to enter school early next year?"

Robert looked embarrassed.

"That's what I came to tell you, Miss Smith. Mr. Cresswell has offered me forty acres of good land."

Miss Smith looked disheartened.

"Robert, here you are almost finished, and my heart is set on your going to Atlanta University and finishing college. With your fine voice and talent for drawing—"

A dogged look settled on Robert's young bright face, and the speaker paused.

"What's the use, Miss Smith—what opening is there for a—a nigger with an education?"

Miss Smith was shocked.

"Why—why, every chance," she protested. "and where there's none *make* a chance!"

"Miss Taylor says"—Miss Smith's heart sank; how often had she heard that deadening phrase in the last year!—"that there's no use. That farming is the only thing we ought to try to do, and I reckon she thinks there ain't much chance even there."

"Robert, farming is a noble calling. Whether you're suited to it or not, I don't yet know, but I'd like nothing better than to see you settled here in a decent home with a family, running a farm. But, Robert, farming doesn't call for less intelligence than other things; it calls for more. It is because the world thinks any training good enough for a farmer that the Southern farmer is today practically at the mercy of his keener and more intelligent fellows. And of all people, Robert, your people need trained intelligence to cope with this problem of farming here. Without intelligence and training and some capital it is the wildest nonsense to think you can lead your people out of slavery. Look round you." She told him of the visitors. "Are they not hard working honest people?"

"Yes, ma'am."

"Yet they are slaves—dumb driven cattle."

"But they have no education."

"And you have a smattering; therefore are ready to pit yourself against the organized plantation system without capital or experience. Robert, you may succeed; you may find your landlord honest and the way clear; but my advice to you is—finish your education, develop your talents, and then come to your life work a full-fledged man and not a half-ignorant boy."

"I'll think of it," returned the boy soberly. "I reckon you're right. I know Miss Taylor don't think much of us. But I'm tired of waiting; I want to get to work."

Miss Smith laid a kindly hand upon his shoulder.

"I've been waiting thirty years, Robert," she said, with feeling, and he hung his head.

"I wanted to talk about it," he awkwardly responded, turning slowly away. But Miss Smith stopped him.

"Robert, where is the land Cresswell offers you?"

"It's on the Tolliver place."

"The Tolliver place?"

"Yes, he is going to buy it."

Miss Smith dismissed the boy absently and sat down. The crisis seemed drawing near. She had not dreamed the Tolliver place was for sale. The old man must be hard pressed to sell to the Cresswells.

She started up. Why not go see him? Perhaps a mortgage on the strength of the endowment? It was dangerous—but—

She threw a veil over her hair, and opened the door. A woman stood there, who shrank and cowered, as if used to blows. Miss Smith eyed her grimly, then slowly stepped back.

"Come in," she commanded briefly, motioning the woman to a chair.

But she stood, a pathetic figure, faded, worn, yet with unmistakable traces of beauty in her golden face and soft brown hair. Miss Smith contemplated her sadly. Here was her most haunting failure, this girl whom she first had seen twelve years ago in her wonderful girlish comeliness. She had struggled and fought for her, but the forces of the devil had triumphed. She caught glimpses of her now and then, but to-day was the first time she had spoken to her for ten years. She saw the tears that gathered but did not fall; then her hands quivered.

"Bertie," she began brokenly. The girl shivered, but stood aloof.

"Miss Smith," she said. "No—don't talk—I'm bad—but I've got a little girl, Miss Smith, ten years old, and—and—I'm afraid for her; I want you to take her."

"I have no place for one so young. And why are you afraid for her?"

"The men there are beginning to notice her."

"Where?"

"At Elspeth's."

"Do you stay there now?"

"Yes."

"Why?"

"*He* wants me to."

"Must you do as he wants?"

"Yes. But I want the child—different."

"Don't *you* want to be different?"

The woman quivered again but she answered steadily: "No." Miss Smith sank into a chair and moistened her dry lips.

"Elspeth's is an awful place," she affirmed solemnly.

"Yes."

"And Zora?"

"She is not there much now, she stays away."

"But if she escapes, why not you?"

"She wants to escape."

"And you?"

"I don't want to."

This stubborn depravity was so distressing that Sarah Smith was at an utter loss what to say or do.

"I can do nothing——" she began.

"For me," the woman quickly replied; "I don't ask anything; but for the child,—*she* isn't to blame."

The older woman wavered.

"Won't you try?" pleaded the younger.

"Yes—I'll try, I'll try; I am trying all the time, but there are more things than my weak strength can do. Good-bye."

Miss Smith stood a long time in the doorway, watching the fading figure and vaguely trying to remember what it was that she had started to do, when the sharp staccato step of a mule drew her attention to a rider who stopped at the gate. It was her neighbor, Tolliver—a gaunt, yellow-faced white man, ragged, rough, and unkempt; one of the poor whites who had struggled up and failed. He spent no courtesy on the "nigger" teacher, but sat in his saddle and called her to the gate, and she went.

"Say," he roughly opened up, "I've got to sell some land and them damn Cresswells are after it. You can have it for five thousand dollars if you git the cash in a week." With a muttered oath he rode abruptly off; but not before she had seen the tears in his eyes.

All night Sarah Smith lay thinking, and all day she thought and dreamed. Toward dark she walked slowly out the gate and up the high-way toward the Cresswell oaks. She had never been within the gates before, and she looked about thoughtfully. The great trees in their regular curving rows must have been planted more than half a century ago. The lawn was well tended and the flowers. Yes, there were signs of taste and wealth. "But it was built on a moan," cried Miss Smith to herself, passionately, and she would not look round any more, but stared straight ahead where she saw old Colonel Cresswell smoking and reading on the verandah.

The Colonel saw her, too, and was uneasy, for he knew that Miss Smith had a sharp tongue and a most disconcerting method of argument, which he, as a Southern gentleman, courteous to all white females, even if they did eat with "niggers," could not properly answer.

He received her with courtesy, offered a chair, laid aside his cigar, and essayed some general remarks on cotton weather. But Miss Smith plunged into her subject:

"Colonel Cresswell, I'm thinking of raising some money from a mortgage on our school property."

The Colonel's face involuntarily lighted up. He thought he saw the beginning of the end of an institution which had been a thorn in his flesh ever since Tolliver, in a fit of rage, had sold land for a Negro school.

"H'm," he reflected deprecatingly, wiping his brow.

"I need some ready money," she continued, "to keep from curtailing our work."

"Indeed?"

"I have good prospects in a year or so"—the Colonel looked up sharply, but said nothing—"and so I thought of a mortgage."

"Money is pretty tight," was the Colonel's first objection.

"The land is worth, you know, at least fifty dollars an acre."

"Not more than twenty-five dollars, I fear."

"Why, you wanted seventy-five dollars for poorer land last year! We have two hundred acres." It was not for nothing that this lady had been born in New England.

"I wouldn't reckon it as worth more than five thousand dollars," insisted the Colonel.

"And ten thousand dollars for improvements."

But the Colonel arose. "You had better talk to the directors of the Jefferson Bank," he said politely. "They may accommodate you—how much would you want?"

"Five thousand dollars," Miss Smith replied. Then she hesitated. That would buy the land, to be sure; but money was needed to develop and run it; to install tenants; and then, too, for new teachers. But she said nothing more, and, nodding to his polite bow, departed. Colonel Cresswell had noticed her hesitation, and thought of it as he settled to his cigar again.

Bles Alwyn arose next morning and examined the sky critically. He feared rain. The season had been quite wet enough, particularly down on the swamp land, and but yesterday Bles had viewed his dykes with apprehension for the black pool scowled about them. He dared not think what a long heavy rain might do to the wonderful island of cotton which now stood fully five feet high, with flowers and squares and budding bolls. It might not rain, but the safest thing would be to work at those dykes, so he started for spade and hoe. He heard Miss Smith calling, however.

"Bles—hitch up!"

He was vexed. "Are you—in a hurry, Miss Smith?" he asked.

"Yes, I am," she replied, with unmistakable positiveness.

He started off, and hesitated. "Miss Smith, would Jim do to drive?"

"No," sharply. "I want you particularly." At another time she might have observed his anxiety, but today she was agitated. She knew she was taking a critical step.

Slowly Bles hitched up. After all it might not rain, he argued as they jogged toward town. In silence they rode on. Bles kept looking at the skies. The south was getting darker and darker. It might rain. It might rain only an hour or so, but, suppose it should rain a day—two days— a week?

Miss Smith was looking at her own skies and despite the promised sunrise they loomed darkly. Five thousand was needed for the land and at least another thousand for repairs. Two thousand would "buy" a half dozen desirable tenants by paying their debts to their present landlords. Then two thousand would be wanted for new teachers and a carpenter shop—ten thousand dollars!

It was a great temptation. And yet, once in the hands of these past-masters of debt-manipulation, would her school be safe? Suppose, after all, this Grey gift—but she caught her breath sharply just as a wet splash of rain struck upon her forehead. No. God could not be so cruel. She pushed her bonnet back: how good and cool the water felt! But on Bles as he raised the buggy top it felt hot and fiery.

He felt the coming of some great calamity, the end of a dream. This rain might stay for days; it looked like such a downpour; and that would mean the end of the Silver Fleece; the end of Zora's hopes; the end of everything. He gulped in despairing anger and hit the staid old horse the smartest tap she had known all summer.

"Why, Bles, what's the matter?" called Miss Smith, as the horse started forward. He murmured something about getting wet and drew up at the Toombsville bank.

Miss Smith was invited politely into the private parlor. She explained her business. The President was there and Colonel Cresswell and one other local director.

"I have come for a mortgage. Our land is, as you know, gentlemen, worth at least ten thousand dollars; the buildings cost fifteen thousand dollars; our property is, therefore, conservatively valued at twenty-five thousand dollars. Now I want to mortgage it for"—she hesitated—"five thousand dollars."

Colonel Cresswell was silent, but the president said:

"Money is rather scarce just now, Miss Smith; but it happens that I have ten thousand dollars on hand, which we prefer, however, to loan in one lump sum. Now, if the security were ample, I think perhaps you might get this ten thousand dollars."

Miss Smith grew white; it was the sum she wanted. She tried to escape the temptation, yet the larger amount was more than twice as desirable to her as the smaller, and she knew that they knew it. They were trying to tempt her; they wanted as firm a hold on the school property as possible. And yet, why should she hesitate? It was a risk, but the returns would be enormous—she must do it. Besides, there was the endowment; it was certain; yes—she felt forced to close the bargain.

"Very well," she declared her decision, and they handed her the preliminary papers. She took the pen and glanced at Mr. Cresswell; he was smiling slightly, but nevertheless she signed her name grimly, in a large round hand, "Sarah Smith."

Thirteen

MRS. GREY
GIVES A DINNER

The Hon. Charles Smith, Miss Sarah's brother, was walking swiftly uptown from Mr. Easterly's Wall Street office and his face was pale. At last the Cotton Combine was to all appearances an assured fact and he was slated for the Senate. The price he had paid was high: he was to represent the interests of the new trust and sundry favorable measures were already drafted and reposing in the safe of the combine's legal department. Among others was one relating to child labor, another that would effect certain changes in the tariff, and a proposed law providing for a cotton bale of a shape and dimensions different from the customary—the last constituting a particularly clever artifice which, under the guise of convenience in handling, would necessitate the installation of entirely new gin and compress machinery, to be supplied, of course, by the trust.

As Mr. Smith drew near Mrs. Grey's Murray Hill residence his face had melted to a cynical smile. After all why should he care? He had tried independence and philanthropy and failed. Why should he not be as other men? He had seen many others that very day swallow the golden bait and promise everything. They were gentlemen. Why should he pose as better than his fellows? There was young Cresswell. Did his aristocratic air prevent his succumbing to the lure of millions and promising the influence of his father and the whole Farmer's League to the new project? Mr. Smith snapped his fingers and rang the bell. The door opened softly. The dark woodwork of the old English wainscoting glowed with the crimson flaming of logs in the wide fireplace. There was just the touch of early autumn chill in the air without, that made both the fire and the table with its soft linen, gold and silver plate, and twinkling glasses a warming, satisfying sight.

Mrs. Grey was a portly woman, inclined to think much of her dinner and her clothes, both of which were always rich and costly. She was not herself a notably intelligent woman; she greatly admired intelligence or whatever looked to her like intelligence in others. Her money, too, was to her an ever worrying mystery and surprise, which she found herself always scheming to husband shrewdly and spend philanthropically—a difficult combination.

As she awaited her guests she surveyed the table with both satisfaction and disquietude, for her social functions were few. tonight there were—she checked them off on her fingers—Sir James Creighton, the rich English manufacturer, and Lady Creighton, Mr. and Mrs. Vanderpool, Mr. Harry Cresswell and his sister, John Taylor and his sister, and Mr. Charles Smith, whom the evening papers mentioned as likely to be United States Senator from New Jersey—a selection of guests that had been determined, unknown to the hostess, by the meeting of cotton interests earlier in the day.

Mrs. Grey's chef was high-priced and efficient, and her butler was the envy of many; consequently, she knew the dinner would be good. To her intense satisfaction, it was far more than this. It was a most agreeable couple of hours; all save perhaps Mr. Smith unbent, the Englishman especially, and the Vanderpools were most gracious; but if the general pleasure was owing to any one person particularly it was to Mr. Harry Cresswell. Mrs. Grey had met Southerners before, but not intimately, and she always had in mind vividly their cruelty to "poor Negroes," a subject she made a point of introducing forthwith. She was therefore most agreeably surprised to hear Mr. Cresswell express himself so cordially as approving of Negro education.

"Why, I thought," said Mrs. Grey, "that you Southerners rather disapproved—or at least—"

Mr. Cresswell inclined his head courteously.

"We Southerners, my dear Mrs. Grey, are responsible for a variety of reputations." And he told an anecdote that set the table laughing. "Seriously, though," he continued, "we are not as black as the blacks paint us, although on the whole I *prefer* that Helen should marry—a white man."

They all glanced at Miss Cresswell, who lay softly back in her chair like a white lily, gleaming and bejewelled, her pale face flushing under the scrutiny; Mrs. Grey was horrified.

"Why—why the idea!" she sputtered. "Why, Mr. Cresswell, how can you conceive of anything else—no Northerner dreams—"

Mr. Cresswell sipped his wine slowly.

"No—no—I do not think you do *mean* that—" He paused and the Englishman bent forward.

"Really, now, you do not mean to say that there is a danger of—of amalgamation, do you?" he sang.

Mr. Cresswell explained. No, of course there was no immediate danger; but when people were suddenly thrust beyond their natural station, filled with wild ideas and impossible ambitions, it meant terrible danger to Southern white women.

"But you believe in some education?" asked Mary Taylor.

"I believe in the training of people to their highest capacity." The Englishman here heartily seconded him.

"But," Cresswell added significantly, "capacity differs enormously between races."

The Vanderpools were sure of this and the Englishman, instancing India, became quite eloquent. Mrs. Grey was mystified, but hardly dared admit it. The general trend of the conversation seemed to be that most individuals needed to be submitted to the sharpest scrutiny before being allowed much education, and as for the "lower races" it was simply criminal to open such useless opportunities to them.

"Why, I had a colored servant-girl once," laughed Mrs. Vanderpool by way of climax, "who spent half her wages in piano lessons."

Then Mary Taylor, whose conscience was uncomfortable, said:

"But, Mr. Cresswell, you surely believe in schools like Miss Smith's?"

"Decidedly," returned Mr. Cresswell, with enthusiasm, "it has done great good."

Mrs. Grey was gratified and murmured something of Miss Smith's "sacrifice."

"Positively heroic," added Cresswell, avoiding his sister's eyes.

"Of course," Mary Taylor hastened to encourage this turn of the conversation, "there are many points on which Miss Smith and I disagree, but I think everybody admires her work."

Mrs. Grey wanted particulars. "What did you disagree about?" she asked bluntly.

"I may be responsible for some of the disagreement," interrupted Mr. Cresswell, hesitatingly; "I'm afraid Miss Smith does not approve of us white Southerners."

"But you mean to say you can't even advise her?"

"Oh, no; we can. But—we're not—er—exactly welcomed. In fact," said Cresswell gravely, "the chief criticism I have against your Northerners' schools for Negroes is, that they not only fail to enlist the sympathy and aid of the *best* Southerners, but even repel it."

"That is very wrong—very wrong," commented the Englishman warmly, a sentiment in which Mrs. Grey hastened to agree.

"Of course," continued Cresswell, "I am free to confess that I have no personal desire to dabble in philanthropy, or conduct schools of any kind; my hands are full of other matters."

"But it's precisely the advice of such disinterested men that philanthropic work needs," Mr. Vanderpool urged.

"Well, I volunteered advice once in this case and I sha'n't repeat the experiment soon," said Cresswell laughing. Mrs. Grey wanted to hear the incident, but the young man was politely reluctant. Mary Taylor, however, related the tale of Zora to Mrs. Grey's private ear later.

"Fortunately," said Mr. Vanderpool, "Northerners and Southerners are arriving at a better mutual understanding on most of these matters."

"Yes, indeed," Cresswell agreed. "After all, they never were far apart, even in slavery days; both sides were honest and sincere."

All through the dinner Mr. Smith had been preoccupied and taciturn. Now he abruptly shot a glance at Cresswell.

"I suppose that one was right and one was wrong."

"No," said Cresswell, "both were right."

"I thought the only excuse for fighting was a great Right; if Right is on neither side or simultaneously on both, then War is not only Hell but Damnation."

Mrs. Grey looked shocked and Mrs. Vanderpool smiled.

"How about fighting for exercise?" she suggested.

"At any rate," said Cresswell, "we can all agree on helping these poor victims of our quarrel as far as their limited capacity will allow— and no farther, for that is impossible."

Very soon after dinner Charles Smith excused himself. He was not yet inured to the ways of high finance, and the programme of the cotton barons, as unfolded that day, lay heavy on his mind, despite all his philosophy.

"I have had a—full day," he explained to Mrs. Grey.

Fourteen

LOVE

The rain was sweeping down in great thick winding sheets. The wind screamed in the ancient Cresswell oaks and swirled across the swamp in loud, wild gusts. The waters roared and gurgled in the streams, and along the roadside. Then, when the wind fell murmuring away, the clouds grew blacker and blacker and rain in long slim columns fell straight from Heaven to earth digging itself into the land and throwing back the red mud in angry flashes.

So it rained for one long week, and so for seven endless days Bles watched it with leaden heart. He knew the Silver Fleece—his and Zora's—must be ruined. It was the first great sorrow of his life; it was not so much the loss of the cotton itself—but the fantasy, the hopes, the dreams built around it. If it failed, would not they fail? Was not this angry beating rain, this dull spiritless drizzle, this wild war of air and earth, but foretaste and prophecy of ruin and discouragement, of the utter futility of striving? But if his own despair was great his pain at the plight of Zora made it almost unbearable. He did not see her in these seven days. He pictured her huddled there in the swamp in the cheerless leaky cabin with worse than no companions. Ah! the swamp, the cruel swamp! It was a fearful place in the rain. Its oozing mud and fetid vapors, its clinging slimy draperies,—how they twined about the bones of its victims and chilled their hearts. Yet here his Zora,—his poor disappointed child—was imprisoned.

Child? He had always called her child—but now in the inward illumination of these dark days he knew her as neither child nor sister nor friend, but as the One Woman. The revelation of his love lighted and brightened slowly till it flamed like a sunrise over him and left him in burning wonder. He panted to know if she, too, knew, or knew and cared not, or cared and knew not. She was so strange and human a creature. To her all things meant something—nothing was aimless, nothing merely happened. Was this rain beating down and back her love for him, or had she never loved? He walked his room, gripping his hands, peering through the misty windows toward the swamp—rain, rain, rain, nothing but rain. The world was water veiled in mists.

Then of a sudden, at midday, the sun shot out, hot and still; no breath of air stirred; the sky was like blue steel; the earth steamed. Bles rushed to the edge of the swamp and stood there irresolute. Perhaps—if the water had but drained from the cotton!—it was so strong and tall! But, pshaw! Where was the use of imagining? The lagoon had been level with the dykes a week ago; and now? He could almost see the beautiful Silver Fleece, bedraggled, drowned, and rolling beneath the black lake of slime. He went back to his work, but early in the morning the thought of it lured him again. He must at least see the grave of his hope and Zora's, and out of it resurrect new love and strength.

Perhaps she, too, might be there, waiting, weeping. He started at the thought. He hurried forth sadly. The rain-drops were still dripping and gleaming from the trees, flashing back the heavy yellow sunlight.

He splashed and stamped along, farther and farther onward until he neared the rampart of the clearing, and put foot upon the tree-bridge. Then he looked down. The lagoon was dry. He stood a moment bewildered, then turned and rushed upon the island. A great sheet of dazzling sunlight swept the place, and beneath lay a mighty mass of olive green, thick, tall, wet, and willowy. The squares of cotton, sharp-edged, heavy, were just about to burst to bolls! And underneath, the land lay carefully drained and black! For one long moment he paused, stupid, agape with utter amazement, then leaned dizzily against a tree.

The swamp, the eternal swamp, had been drained in its deepest fastness; but, how?—how? He gazed about, perplexed, astonished. What a field of cotton! what a marvellous field! But how had it been saved?

He skirted the island slowly, stopping near Zora's oak. Here lay the reading of the riddle: with infinite work and pain, some one had dug a canal from the lagoon to the creek, into which the former had drained by a long and crooked way, thus allowing it to empty directly. The canal went straight, a hundred yards through stubborn soil, and it was oozing now with slimy waters.

He sat down weak, bewildered, and one thought was uppermost—Zora! And with the thought came a low moan of pain. He wheeled and leapt toward the dripping shelter in the tree. There she lay—wet, bedraggled, motionless, gray-pallid beneath her dark-drawn skin, her burning eyes searching restlessly for some lost thing, her lips a-moaning.

In dumb despair he dropped beside her and gathered her in his arms. The earth staggered beneath him as he stumbled on; the mud splashed and sunlight glistened; he saw long snakes slithering across his path and fear-struck beasts fleeing before his coming. He paused for neither path nor way but went straight for the school, running in mighty strides, yet gently, listening to the moans that struck death upon his heart. Once he fell headlong, but with a great wrench held her from harm, and minded not the pain that shot through his ribs. The yellow sunshine beat fiercely around and upon him, as he stumbled into the highway, lurched across the mud-strewn road, and panted up the porch.

"Miss Smith—!" he gasped, and then—darkness.

The years of the days of her dying were ten. The boy that entered the darkness and the shadow of death emerged a man, a silent man and grave, working furiously and haunting, day and night, the little window above the door. At last, of one gray morning when the earth was stillest, they came and told him, "She will live!" And he went out under the stars, lifted his long arms and sobbed: "Curse me, O God, if I let me lose her again!" And God remembered this in after years.

The hope and dream of harvest was upon the land. The cotton crop was short and poor because of the great rain; but the sun had saved the best, and the price had soared. So the world was happy, and the face of the black-belt green and luxuriant with thickening flecks of the coming foam of the cotton.

Up in the sick room Zora lay on the little white bed. The net and web of endless things had been crawling and creeping around her; she had struggled in dumb, speechless terror against some mighty grasping that strove for her life, with gnarled and creeping fingers; but now at last, weakly, she opened her eyes and questioned.

Bles, where was he? The Silver Fleece, how was it? The Sun, the Swamp? Then finding all well, she closed her eyes and slept. After some days they let her sit by the window, and she saw Bles pass, but drew back timidly when he looked; and he saw only the flutter of her gown, and waved.

At last there came a day when they let her walk down to the porch, and she felt the flickering of her strength again. Yet she looked different; her buxom comeliness was spiritualized; her face looked smaller, and her masses of hair, brought low about her ears, heightened her ghostly beauty; her skin was darkly transparent, and her eyes looked out from velvet veils of gloom. For a while she lay in her chair, in happy, dreamy pleasure at sun and bird and tree. Bles did not know yet that she was down; but soon he would come searching, for he came each hour, and she pressed her little hands against her breast to still the beating of her heart and the bursting wonder of her love.

Then suddenly a panic seized her. He must not find her here—not here; there was but one place in all the earth for them to meet, and that was yonder in the Silver Fleece. She rose with a fleeting glance, gathered the shawl round her, then gliding forward, wavering, tremulous, slipped across the road and into the swamp. The dark mystery of the Swamp swept over her; the place was hers. She had been born within its borders; within its borders she had lived and grown, and within its borders she had met her love. On she hurried until, sweeping down to the lagoon and the island, lo! the cotton lay before her! A great white foam was spread upon its brown and green; the whole field was waving and shivering in the sunlight. A low cry of pleasure burst from her lips; she forgot her weakness, and picking her way across the bridge, stood still amid the cotton that nestled about her shoulders, clasping it lovingly in her hands.

He heard that she was down-stairs and ran to meet her with beating heart. The chair was empty; but he knew. There was but one place then for these two souls to meet. Yet it was far, and he feared, and ran with startled eyes.

She stood on the island, ethereal, splendid, like some tall, dark, and gorgeous flower of the storied East. The green and white of the cotton billowed and foamed about her breasts; the red scarf burned upon her neck; the dark brown velvet of her skin pulsed warm and tremulous with the uprushing blood, and in the midnight depths of her great eyes flamed the mighty fires of long-concealed and new-born love.

He darted through the trees and paused, a tall man strongly but slimly made. He threw up his hands in the old way and hallooed; happily she crooned back a low mother-melody, and waited. He came down to her slowly, with fixed, hungry eyes, threading his way amid the Fleece. She did not move, but lifted both her dark hands, white with cotton; and then, as he came, casting it suddenly to the winds, in tears and laughter she swayed and dropped quivering in his arms. And all the world was sunshine and peace.

Fifteen

REVELATION

Harry Cresswell was scowling over his breakfast. It was not because his apartment in the New York hotel was not satisfactory, or his breakfast unpalatable; possibly a rather bewildering night in Broadway was expressing its influence; but he was satisfied that his ill-temper was due to a paragraph in the morning paper:

"It is stated on good authority that the widow of the late multimillionaire, Job Grey, will announce a large and carefully planned scheme of Negro education in the South, and will richly endow schools in South Carolina, Georgia, Alabama, Louisiana, and Texas."

Cresswell finally thrust his food away. He knew that Mrs. Grey helped Miss Smith's school, and supposed she would continue to do so; with that in mind he had striven to impress her, hoping that she might trust his judgment in later years. He had no idea, however, that she meant to endow the school, or entertained wholesale plans for

Negro education. The knowledge made him suspicious. Why had neither Mary nor John Taylor mentioned this? Was there, after all, some "nigger-loving" conspiracy back of the cotton combine? He took his hat and started down-town.

Once in John Taylor's Broadway office, he opened the subject abruptly—the more so perhaps because he felt a resentment against Taylor for certain unnamed or partially voiced assumptions. Here was a place, however, for speech, and he spoke almost roughly.

"Taylor, what does this mean?" He thrust the clipping at him.

"Mean? That Mrs. Grey is going to get rid of some of her surplus cash—is going to endow some nigger schools," Taylor drily retorted.

"It must be stopped," declared Cresswell.

The other's brows drew up.

"Why?" in a surprised tone.

"Why? Why? Do you think the plantation system can be maintained without laborers? Do you think there's the slightest chance of cornering cotton and buying the Black Belt if the niggers are unwilling to work under present conditions? Do you know the man that stands ready to gobble up every inch of cotton land in this country at a price which no trust can hope to rival?"

John Taylor's interest quickened.

"Why, no," he returned sharply. "Who?"

"The Black Man, whose woolly head is filled with ideas of rising. We're striving by main force to prevent this, and here come your damned Northern philanthropists to plant schools. Why, Taylor, it'll knock the cotton trust to hell."

"Don't get excited," said Taylor, judicially. "We've got things in our hands; it's the Grey money, you know, that is back of us."

"That's just what confounds me," declared the perplexed young man. "Are you men fools, or rascals? Don't you see the two schemes can't mix? They're dead opposite, mutually contradictory, absolutely—"

Taylor checked him; it was odd to behold Harry Cresswell so disturbed.

"Well, wait a moment. Let's see. Sit down. Wish I had a cigar for you, but I don't smoke."

"Do you happen to have any whiskey handy?"

"No, I don't drink."

"Well, what the devil—Oh, well, fire away."

"Now, see here. We control the Grey millions. Of course, we've got to let her play with her income, and that's considerable. Her favorite game just now is Negro education, and she's planning to go in heavy. Her adviser in this line, however, is Smith, and he belongs to us."

"What Smith?"

"Why, the man who's going to be Senator from New Jersey. He has a sister teaching in the South—you know, of course; it's at your home where my sister Mary taught."

"Great Scott! Is that woman's brother going to spend this money? Why, are you daft? See here! American cotton-spinning supremacy is built on cheap cotton; cheap cotton is built on cheap niggers. Educating, or rather *trying* to educate niggers, will make them restless and discontented—that is, scarce and dear as workers. Don't you see you're planning to cut off your noses? This Smith School, particularly, has nearly ruined our plantation. It's stuck almost in our front yard; *you* are planning to put our plough-hands all to studying Greek, and at the same time to corner the cotton crop—rot!"

John Taylor caressed his lean jaw.

"New point of view to me; I sort of thought education would improve things in the South," he commented, unmoved.

"It would if we ran it."

"We?"

"Yes—we Southerners."

"Um!—I see—there's light. See here, let's talk to Easterly about this." They went into the next office, and after a while got audience with the trust magnate. Mr. Easterly heard the matter carefully and waved it aside.

"Oh, that doesn't concern us, Taylor; let Cresswell take care of the whole thing. We'll see that Smith does what Cresswell wants."

But Taylor shook his head.

"Smith would kick. Mrs. Grey would get suspicious, and the devil be to pay. This is better. Form a big committee of Northern business men like yourself—philanthropists like Vanderpool, and Southerners like Cresswell; let them be a sort of Negro Education steering-committee. We'll see that on such committee you Southerners get what you want—control of Negro education."

"That sounds fair. But how about the Smith School? My father writes me that they are showing signs of expecting money right off—is that true? If it is, I want it stopped; it will ruin our campaign for the Farmers' League."

John Taylor looked at Cresswell. He thought he saw something more than general policy, or even racial prejudice—something personal—in his vehemence. The Smith School was evidently a severe thorn in the flesh of this man. All the more reason for mollifying him. Then, too, there was something in his argument. It was not wise to start educating these Negroes and getting them discontented just now. Ignorant labor was not ideal, but it was worth too much to employers to lose it now. Educated Negro labor might be worth more to Negroes, but not to the cotton combine. "H'm—well, then—" and John Taylor went into a brown study, while Cresswell puffed impatiently at a cigarette.

"I have it," said Taylor. Cresswell sat up. "First, let Mr. Easterly get Smith." Easterly turned to the telephone.

"Is that you, Smith?"

"Well, this is Easterly . . . Yes—how about Mrs. Grey's education schemes? . . . Yes . . . h'm—well,—see here Smith, we must go a little easy there . . . Oh, no, no,—but to advertise just now a big scheme of Negro Education would drive the Cresswells, the Farmers' League, and the whole business South dead against us. . . . Yes, yes indeed;

they believe in education all right, but they ain't in for training lawyers and professors just yet . . . No, I don't suppose her school is . . . Well, then; see here. She'll be reasonable, won't she, and placate the Cresswells? . . . No, I mean run the school to suit their ideas. . . . No, no, but in general along the lines which they could approve . . . Yes, I thought so . . . of course . . . good-bye."

"Inclined to be a little nasty?" asked Taylor.

"A little sharp—but tractable. Now, Mr. Cresswell, the thing is in your hands. We'll get this committee which Taylor suggests appointed, and send it on a junket to Alabama; you do the rest—see?"

"Who'll be the committee?" asked Cresswell.

"Name it."

Mr. Cresswell smiled and left.

The winter started in severely, and it was easy to fill two private cars with members of the new Negro Education Board right after Thanksgiving. Cresswell had worked carefully and with caution. There was Mrs. Grey, comfortable and beaming, Mr. Easterly, who thought this a good business opportunity, and his family. Mrs. Vanderpool liked the South and was amused at the trip, and had induced Mr. Vanderpool to come by stories of shooting.

"Ah!" said Mr. Vanderpool.

Mr. Charles Smith and John Taylor were both too busy to go, but bronchial trouble induced the Rev. Dr. Boldish of St. Faith's rich parish to be one of the party, and at the last moment Temple Bocombe, the sociologist, consented to join.

"Awfully busy," he said, "but I've been reading up on the Negro problem since you mentioned the matter to me last week, Mr. Cresswell, and I think I understand it thoroughly. I may be able to help out."

The necessary spice of young womanhood was added to the party by Miss Taylor and Miss Cresswell, together with the silent Miss Boldish. They were a comfortable and sometimes merry party. Dr. Boldish pointed out the loafers at the stations, especially the black ones; Mr. Bocombe counted them and estimated the number of hours of work lost at ten cents an hour.

"Do they get that—ten cents an hour?" asked Miss Taylor.

"Oh, I don't know," replied Mr. Bocombe; "but suppose they do, for instance. That is an average wage today."

"They look lazy," said Mrs. Grey.

"They are lazy," said Mr. Cresswell.

"So am I," added Mrs. Vanderpool, suppressing a yawn.

"It is uninteresting," murmured her husband, preparing for a nap.

On the whole the members of the party enjoyed themselves from the moment they drew out of Jersey City to the afternoon when, in four carriages, they rolled beneath the curious eyes of all Toomsville and swept under the shadowed rampart of the swamp.

"The Christmas" was coming and all the Southern world was busy. Few people were busier than Bles and Zora. Slowly, wonderfully for them, heaven bent in these dying days of the year and kissed the earth, and the tremor thrilled all lands and seas. Everything was good, all things were happy, and these two were happiest of all. Out of the shadows and hesitations of childhood they had stepped suddenly into manhood and womanhood, with firm feet and uplifted heads. All the day that was theirs they worked, picking the Silver Fleece—picking it tenderly and lovingly from off the brown and spent bodies which had so utterly yielded life and beauty to the full fruition of this long and silken tendril, this white beauty of the cotton. November came and flew, and still the unexhausted field yielded its frothing fruit.

today seemed doubly glorious, for Bles had spoken of their marriage; with twined hands and arms, and lips ever and again seeking their mates, they walked the leafy way.

Unconscious, rapt, they stepped out into the Big Road skirting the edge of the swamp. Why not? Was it not the King's Highway? And Love was King. So they talked on, unknowing that far up the road the Cresswell coaches were wheeling along with precious burdens. In the first carriage were Mrs. Grey and Mrs. Vanderpool, Mr. Cresswell and Miss Taylor. Mrs. Vanderpool was lolling luxuriously, but Mrs. Grey was a little stiff from long travel and sat upright. Mr. Cresswell looked clean-cut and handsome, and Miss Taylor seemed complacent and responsible. The dying of the day soothed them all insensibly. Groups of dark little children passed them as they neared the school, staring with wide eyes and greeting timidly.

"There seems to be marrying and giving in marriage," laughed Mrs. Vanderpool.

"Not very much," said Mr. Cresswell drily.

"Well, at least plenty of children."

"Plenty."

"But where are the houses?" asked Mrs. Grey.

"Perhaps in the swamp," said Mrs. Vanderpool lightly, looking up at the sombre trees that lined the left.

"They live where they please and do as they please," Cresswell explained; to which Mrs. Vanderpool added: "Like other animals."

Mary Taylor opened her lips to rebuke this levity when suddenly the coachman called out and the horses swerved, and the carriage's four occupants faced a young man and a young woman embracing heartily.

Out through the wood Bles and Zora had come to the broad red road; playfully he celebrated all her beauty unconscious of time and place.

"You are tall and bend like grasses on the swamp," he said.

"And yet look up to you," she murmured.

"Your eyes are darkness dressed in night."

"To see you brighter, dear," she said.

"Your little hands are much too frail for work."

"They must grow larger, then, and soon."

"Your feet are far too small to travel on."

"They'll travel on to you—that's far enough."

"Your lips—your full and purple lips—were made alone for kissing, not for words."

"They'll do for both."

He laughed in utter joy and touched her hair with light caressing hands.

"It does not fly with sunlight," she said quickly, with an upward glance.

"No," he answered. "It sits and listens to the night."

But even as she nestled to him happily there came the harsh thunder of horses' hoofs, beating on their ears. He drew her quickly to him in fear, and the coach lurched and turned, and left them facing four pairs of eyes. Miss Taylor reddened; Mrs. Grey looked surprised; Mrs. Vanderpool smiled; but Mr. Cresswell darkened with anger. The couple unclasped shamefacedly, and the young man, lifting his hat, started to stammer an apology; but Cresswell interrupted him:

"Keep your—your philandering to the woods, or I shall have you arrested," he said slowly, his face colorless, his lips twitching with anger. "Drive on, John."

Miss Taylor felt that her worst suspicions had been confirmed; but Mrs. Vanderpool was curious as to the cause of Cresswell's anger. It was so genuine that it needed explanation.

"Are kisses illegal here?" she asked before the horses started, turning the battery of her eyes full upon him. But Cresswell had himself well in hand.

"No," he said. "But the girl is—notorious."

On the lovers the words fell like a blow. Zora shivered, and a grayish horror mottled the dark burning of her face. Bles started in anger, then paused in shivering doubt. What had happened? They knew not; yet involuntarily their hands fell apart; they avoided each other's eyes.

"I—I must go now," gasped Zora, as the carriage swept away.

He did not hold her, he did not offer the farewell kiss, but stood staring at the road as she walked into the swamp. A moment she paused and looked back; then slowly, almost painfully, she took the path back to the field of the Fleece, and reaching it after long, long minutes, began mechanically to pick the cotton. But the cotton glowed crimson in the failing sun.

Bles walked toward the school. What had happened? he kept asking. And yet he dared not question the awful shape that sat somewhere, cold and still, behind his soul. He heard the hoofs of horses again. It was Miss Taylor being brought back to the school to greet Miss Smith and break the news of the coming of the party. He raised his hat. She did not return the greeting, but he found her pausing at the gate. It seemed to her too awful for this foolish fellow thus to throw himself away. She faced him and he flinched as from some descending blow.

"Bles," she said primly, "have you absolutely no shame?"

He braced himself and raised his head proudly.

"I am going to marry her; it is no crime." Then he noted the expression on her face, and paused.

She stepped back, scandalized.

"Can it be, Bles Alwyn," she said, "that you don't know the sort of girl she is?"

He raised his hands and warded off her words, dumbly, as she turned to go, almost frightened at the havoc she saw. The heavens flamed scarlet in his eyes and he screamed.

"It's a lie! It's a damned lie!" He wheeled about and tore into the swamp.

"It's a damned lie!" he shouted to the trees. *"Is it?—is it?"* chirped the birds. "It's a cruel falsehood!" he moaned. *"Is it?—is it?"* whispered the devils within.

It seemed to him as though suddenly the world was staggering and faltering about him. The trees bent curiously and strange breathings were upon the breezes. He unbuttoned his collar that he might get more air. A thousand things he had forgotten surged suddenly to life. Slower and slower he ran, more and more the thoughts crowded his head. He thought of that first red night and the yelling and singing and wild dancing; he thought of Cresswell's bitter words; he thought of Zora telling how she stayed out nights; he thought of the little bower that he had built her in the cotton field. A wild fear struggled with his anger, but he kept repeating, "No, no," and then, "At any rate, she will tell me the truth." She had never lied to him; she would not dare; he clenched his hands, murder in his heart.

Slowly and more slowly he ran. He knew where she was—where she must be, waiting. And yet as he drew near huge hands held him back, and heavy weights clogged his feet. His heart said: "On! quick! She will tell the truth, and all will be well." His mind said: "Slow, slow; this is the end." He hurled the thought aside, and crashed through the barrier.

She was standing still and listening, with a huge basket of the piled froth of the field upon her head. One long brown arm, tender with curvings, balanced the cotton; the other, poised, balanced the slim swaying body. Bending she listened, her eyes shining, her lips apart, her bosom fluttering at the well-known step.

He burst into her view with the fury of a beast, rending the wood away and trampling the underbrush, reeling and muttering until he saw her. She looked at him. Her hands dropped, she stood very still with drawn face, grayish-brown, both hands unconsciously out-stretched, and the cotton swaying, while deep down in her eyes, dimly, slowly, a horror lit and grew. He paused a moment, then came slowly onward doggedly, drunkenly, with torn clothes, flying collar, and red eyes. Then he paused again, still beyond arm's-length, looking at her with fear-struck eyes. The cotton on her head shivered and dropped in a pure mass of white and silvery snow about her limbs. Her hands fell limply and the horror flamed in her wet eyes. He struggled with his voice but it grated and came hoarse and hard from his quivering throat.

"Zora!"

"Yes, Bles."

"You—you told me—you were—pure."

She was silent, but her body went all a-tremble. He stepped forward until she could almost touch him; there standing straight and tall he glared down upon her.

"Answer me," he whispered in a voice hard with its tight held sobs. A misery darkened her face and the light died from her eyes, yet she looked at him bravely and her voice came low and full as from afar.

"I asked you what it meant to be pure, Bles, and—and you told—and I told you the truth."

"What it meant!—what it meant!" he repeated in the low, tense anguish.

"But—but, Bles—" She faltered; there came an awful pleading in her eyes; her hand groped toward him; but he stepped slowly back—"But, Bles—you said—willingly—you said—if—if she knew—"

He thundered back in livid anger:

"Knew! All women know! You should have *died!*"

Sobs were rising and shaking her from head to foot, but she drove them back and gripped her breasts with her hands.

"No, Bles—no—all girls do not know. I was a child. Not since I knew you, Bles—never, never since I saw you."

"Since—since," he groaned—"Christ! But before?"

"Yes, before."

"My God!"

She knew the end had come. Yet she babbled on tremblingly:

"He was our master, and all the other girls that gathered there did his will; I—I—" she choked and faltered, and he drew farther away—"I began running away, and they hunted me through the swamps. And then—then I reckon I'd have gone back and been—as they all are—but *you* came, Bles—*you* came, and you—you were a new great thing in my life, and—and—yet, I was afraid I was not worthy until you—you said the words. I thought you knew, and I thought that—that purity was just *wanting* to be pure."

He ground his teeth in fury. Oh, he was an innocent—a blind baby—the joke and laughing-stock of the country around, with yokels grinning at him and pale-faced devils laughing aloud. The teachers knew; the girls knew; God knew; everybody but he knew—poor blind, deaf mole, stupid jackass that he was. He must run—run away from this world, and far off in some free land beat back this pain.

Then in sheer weariness the anger died within his soul, leaving but ashes and despair. Slowly he turned away, but with a quick motion she stood in his path.

"Bles," she cried, "how can I grow pure?"

He looked at her listlessly.

"Never—never again," he slowly answered her.

Dark fear swept her drawn face.

"Never?" she gasped.

Pity surged and fought in his breast; but one thought held and burned him. He bent to her fiercely:

"Who?" he demanded.

She pointed toward the Cresswell Oaks, and he turned away. She did not attempt to stop him again, but dropped her hands and stared drearily up into the clear sky with its shining worlds.

"Good-bye, Bles," she said slowly. "I thank God he gave you to me—just a little time." She hesitated and waited. There came no word as the man moved slowly away. She stood motionless. Then slowly he turned and came back. He laid his hand a moment, lightly, upon her head.

"Good-bye—Zora," he sobbed, and was gone.

She did not look up, but knelt there silent, dry-eyed, till the last rustle of his going died in the night. And then, like a waiting storm, the torrent of her grief swept down upon her; she stretched herself upon the black and fleece-strewn earth, and writhed.

Sixteen

THE GREAT REFUSAL

All night Miss Smith lay holding the quivering form of Zora close to her breast, staring wide-eyed into the darkness— thinking, thinking. In the morning the party would come. There would be Mrs. Grey and Mary Taylor, Mrs. Vanderpool, who had left her so coldly in the lurch before, and some of the Cresswells. They would come well fed and impressed with the charming hospitality of their hosts, and rather more than willing to see through those host's eyes. They would be in a hurry to return to some social function, and would give her work but casual attention.

It seemed so dark an ending to so bright a dream. Never for her had a fall opened as gloriously. The love of this boy and girl, blossoming as it had beneath her tender care, had been a sacred, wonderful history that revived within her memories of long-forgotten days. But above lay the vision of her school, redeemed and enlarged, its future safe, its usefulness broadened—small wonder that to Sarah Smith the future had seemed in November almost golden.

Then things began to go wrong. The transfer of the Tolliver land had not yet been effected; the money was ready, but Mr. Tolliver seemed busy or hesitating. Next came this news of Mrs. Grey's probable conditions. So here it was Christmas time, and Sarah Smith's castles lay almost in ruins about her.

The girl moaned in her fitful sleep and Miss Smith soothed her. Poor child! here too was work—a strange strong soul cruelly stricken in her youth. Could she be brought back to a useful life? How she needed such a strong, clear-eyed helper in this crisis of her work! Would Zora make one or would this blow send her to perdition? Not if Sarah Smith could save her, she resolved, and stared out the window where the pale red dawn was sending its first rays on the white-pillared mansion of the Cresswells.

Mrs. Grey saw the light on the columns, too, as she lay lazily in her soft white bed. There was a certain delicious languor in the late lingering fall of Alabama that suited her perfectly. Then, too, she liked the house and its appointments; there was not, to be sure, all the luxury that she was used to in her New York mansion, but there was a certain finish about it, an elegance and staid old-fashioned hospitality that appealed to her tremendously. Mrs. Grey's heart warmed to the sight of Helen in her moments of spasmodic caring for the sick and afflicted on the estate. No better guardian of her philanthropies could be found than these same Cresswells. She must, of course, go over and see dear Sarah Smith; but really there was not much to say or to look at.

The prospects seemed most alluring. Later, Mr. Easterly talked a while on routine business, saying, as he turned away:

"I am more and more impressed, Mrs. Grey, with your wisdom in placing large investments in the South. With peaceful social conditions the returns will be large."

Mrs. Grey heard this delicate flattery complacently. She had her streak of thrift, and wanted her business capacity recognized. She listened attentively.

"For this reason, I trust you will handle your Negro philanthropies judicially, as I know you will. There's dynamite in this race problem for amateur reformers, but fortunately you have at hand wise and sympathetic advisers in the Cresswells."

Mrs. Grey agreed entirely.

Mary Taylor, alone of the committee, took her commission so seriously as to be anxious to begin work.

"We are to visit the school this morning, you know," she reminded the others, looking at her watch; "I'm afraid we're late already."

The remark created mild consternation. It seemed that Mr. Vanderpool had gone hunting and his wife had not yet arisen. Dr. Boldish was very hoarse, Mr. Easterly was going to look over some plantations with Colonel Cresswell, and Mr. Bocombe was engrossed in a novel.

"Clever, but not true to life," he said.

Finally the clergyman and Mr. Bocombe, Mrs. Grey and Mrs. Vanderpool and Miss Taylor started for the school, with Harry Cresswell, about an hour after lunch. The delay and suppressed excitement among the little folks had upset things considerably there, but at the sight of the visitors at the gate Miss Smith rang the bell.

The party came in, laughing and chatting. They greeted Miss Smith cordially. Dr. Boldish was beginning to tell a good story when a silence fell.

The children had gathered, quietly, almost timidly, and before the distinguished company realized it, they turned to meet that battery of four hundred eyes. A human eye is a wonderful thing when it simply waits and watches. Not one of these little things alone would have been worth more than a glance, but together, they became mighty, portentous. Mr. Bocombe got out his note-book and wrote furiously therein. Dr. Boldish, naturally the appointed spokesman, looked helplessly about and whispered to Mrs. Vanderpool:

"What on earth shall I talk about?"

"The brotherhood of man?" suggested the lady.

"Hardly advisable," returned Dr. Boldish, seriously, "in our friend's presence,"—with a glance toward Cresswell. Then he arose.

"My friends," he said, touching his finger-tips and using blank verse in A minor. "This is an auspicious day. You should be thankful for the gifts of the Lord. His bounty surrounds you—the trees, the fields, the glorious sun. He gives cotton to clothe you, corn to eat, devoted friends to teach you. Be joyful. Be good. Above all, be thrifty and save your money, and do not complain and whine at your apparent disadvantages. Remember that God did not create men equal but unequal, and set metes and bounds. It is not for us to question the wisdom of the Almighty, but to bow humbly to His will.

"Remember that the slavery of your people was not necessarily a crime. It was a school of work and love. It gave you noble friends, like Mr. Cresswell here." A restless stirring, and the battery of eyes was turned upon that imperturbable gentleman, as if he were some strange animal. "Love and serve them. Remember that we get, after all, little education from books; rather in the fields, at the plough and in the kitchen. Let your ambition be to serve rather than rule, to be humble followers of the lowly Jesus."

With an upward glance the Rev. Dr. Boldish sat down amid a silence a shade more intense than that which had greeted him. Then slowly from the far corner rose a thin voice, tremulously. It wavered on the air and almost broke, then swelled in sweet, low music. Other and stronger voices gathered themselves to it, until two hundred were singing a soft minor wail that gripped the hearts and tingled in the ears of the hearers. Mr. Bocombe groped with a puzzled expression to find the pocket for his note-book; Harry Cresswell dropped his eyes, and on Mrs. Vanderpool's lips the smile died. Mary Taylor flushed, and Mrs. Grey cried frankly:

"Poor things!" she whispered.

"Now," said Mrs. Grey, turning about, "we haven't but just a moment and we want to take a little look at your work." She smiled graciously upon Miss Smith.

Mrs. Grey thought the cooking-school very nice.

"I suppose," she said, "that you furnish cooks for the county."

"Largely," said Miss Smith. Mrs. Vanderpool looked surprised, but Miss Smith added: "This county, you know, is mostly black." Mrs. Grey did not catch the point.

The dormitories were neat and the ladies expressed great pleasure in them.

"It is certainly nice for them to know what a clean place is," commented Mrs. Grey. Mr. Cresswell, however, looked at a bath-room and smiled.

"How practical!" he said.

"Can you not stop and see some of the classes?" Sarah Smith knew in her heart that the visit was a failure, still she would do her part to the end.

"I doubt if we shall have time," Mrs. Grey returned, as they walked on. "Mr. Cresswell expects friends to dinner."

"What a magnificent intelligence office," remarked Mr. Bocombe, "for furnishing servants to the nation. I saw splendid material for cooks and maids."

"And plough-boys," added Cresswell.

"And singers," said Mary Taylor.

"Well, now that's just my idea," said Mrs. Grey, "that these schools should furnish trained servants and laborers for the South. Isn't that your idea, Miss Smith?"

"Not exactly," the lady replied, "or at least I shouldn't put it just that way. My idea is that this school should furnish men and women who can work and earn an honest living, train up families aright, and perform their duties as fathers, mothers, and citizens."

"Yes—yes, precisely," said Mrs. Grey, "that's what I meant."

"I think the whites can attend to the duties of citizenship without help," observed Mr. Cresswell.

"Don't let the blacks meddle in politics," said Dr. Boldish.

"I want to make these children full-fledged men and women, strong, self-reliant, honest, without any 'ifs' and 'ands' to their development," insisted Miss Smith.

"Of course, and that is just what Mr. Cresswell wants. Isn't it, Mr. Cresswell?" asked Mrs. Grey.

"I think I may say yes," Mr. Cresswell agreed. "I certainly want these people to develop as far as they can, although Miss Smith and I would differ as to their possibilities. But it is not so much in the general theory of Negro education as in its particular applications where our chief differences would lie. I may agree that a boy should learn higher arithmetic, yet object to his loafing in plough-time. I might want to educate some girls but not girls like Zora."

Mrs. Vanderpool glanced at Mr. Cresswell, smiling to herself.

Mrs. Grey broke in, beaming:

"That's just it, dear Miss Smith,—just it. Your heart is good, but you need strong practical advice. You know we weak women are so impractical, as my poor Job so often said. Now, I'm going to arrange to endow this school with at least—at least a hundred and fifty thousand dollars. One condition is that my friend, Mr. Cresswell here, and these other gentlemen, including sound Northern business men like Mr. Easterly, shall hold this money in trust, and expend it for your school as they think best."

"Mr. Cresswell would be their local representative?" asked Miss Smith slowly with white face.

"Why yes—yes, of course."

There was a long, tense silence. Then the firm reply,

"Mrs. Grey, I thank you, but I cannot accept your offer."

Sarah Smith's voice was strong, the tremor had left her hands. She had expected something like this, of course; yet when it came—somehow it failed to stun. She would not turn over the direction of the school, or the direction of the education of these people, to those who were most opposed to their education. Therefore, there was no need to hesitate; there was no need to think the thing over—she had thought it over—and she looked into Mrs. Grey's eyes and with gathering tears in her own said:

"Again, I thank you very much, Mrs. Grey."

Mrs. Grey was a picture of the most emphatic surprise, and Mr. Cresswell moved to the window. Mrs. Grey looked helplessly at her companions.

"But—I don't understand, Miss Smith—why can't you accept my offer?"

"Because you ask me to put my school in control of those who do not wish for the best interests of black folk, and in particular I object to Mr. Cresswell," said Miss Smith, slowly but very distinctly, "because his relation to the forces of evil in this community has been such that he can direct no school of mine." Mrs. Vanderpool moved toward the door and Mr. Cresswell bowing slightly followed. Dr. Boldish looked indignant and Mr. Bocombe dove after his note-book. Mary Taylor, her head in a whirl, came forward. She felt that in some way she was responsible for this dreadful situation and she wanted desperately to save matters from final disaster.

"Come," she said, "Mrs. Grey, we'll talk this matter over again later. I am sure Miss Smith does not mean quite all she says—she is tired and nervous. You join the others and don't wait for me and I will be along directly."

Mrs. Grey was only too glad to escape and Mr. Bocombe got a chance to talk. He drew out his note-book.

"Awfully interesting," he said, "awfully. Now—er—let's see—oh, yes. Did you notice how unhealthy the children looked? Race is undoubtedly dying out; fact. No hope. Weak. No spontaneity either—rather languid, did you notice? Yes, and their heads—small and narrow—no brain capacity. They can't concentrate; notice how some slept when Dr. Boldish was speaking? Mr. Cresswell says they own almost no land here; think of it? This land was worth only ten dollars an acre a decade ago, he says. Negroes might have bought all and been rich. Very shiftless—and that singing. Now, I wonder where they got the music? Imitation, of course." And so he rattled on, noting not the silence of the others.

As the carriage drove off Mary turned to Miss Smith.

"Now, Miss Smith," she began—but Miss Smith looked at her, and said sternly, "Sit down."

Mary Taylor sat down. She had been so used to lecturing the older woman that the sudden summoning of her well known sternness against herself took her breath, and she sat awkwardly like the school girl that she was waiting for Miss Smith to speak. She felt suddenly very young and very helpless—she who had so jauntily set out to solve this mighty problem by a waving of her wand. She saw with a swelling of pity the drawn and stricken face of her old friend and she started up.

"Sit down," repeated Miss Smith harshly. "Mary Taylor, you are a fool. You are not foolish, for the foolish learn; you are simply a fool. You will never learn; you have blundered into this life work of mine and well nigh ruined it. Whether I can yet save it God alone knows. You have blundered into the lives of two loving children, and sent one wandering aimless on the face of the earth and the other moaning in yonder chamber with death in her heart. You are going to marry the man that sought Zora's ruin when she was yet a child because you think of his aristocratic pose and pretensions built on the poverty, crime, and exploitation of six generations of serfs. You'll marry him and—"

But Miss Taylor leapt to her feet with blazing cheeks.

"How dare you?" she screamed, beside herself.

"But God in heaven help you if you do," finished Miss Smith, calmly.

Seventeen

THE RAPE OF THE FLEECE

When slowly from the torpor of ether, one wakens to the misty sense of eternal loss, and there comes the exquisite prick of pain, then one feels in part the horror of the ache when Zora wakened to the world again. The awakening was the work of days and weeks. At first in sheer exhaustion, physical and mental, she lay and moaned. The sense of loss—of utter loss—lay heavy upon her. Something of herself, something dearer than self, was gone from her forever, and an infinite loneliness and silence, as of endless years, settled on her soul. She wished neither food nor words, only to be alone. Then gradually the pain of injury stung her when the blood flowed fuller. As Miss Smith knelt beside her one night to make her simple prayer Zora sat suddenly upright, white-swathed, dishevelled, with fury in her midnight eyes.

"I want no prayers!" she cried, "I will not pray! He is no God of mine. He isn't fair. He knows and won't tell. He takes advantage of us—He works and fools us." All night Miss Smith heard mutterings of this bitterness, and the next day the girl walked her room like a tigress,—to and fro, to and fro, all the long day. Toward night a dumb despair settled upon her. Miss Smith found her sitting by the window gazing blankly toward the swamp. She came to Miss Smith, slowly, and put her hands upon her shoulders with almost a caress.

"You must forgive me," she pleaded plaintively. "I reckon I've been mighty bad with you, and you always so good to me; but—but, you see—it hurts so."

"I know it hurts, dear; I know it does. But men and women must learn to bear hurts in this world."

"Not hurts like this; they couldn't."

"Yes, even hurts like this. Bear and stand straight; be brave. After all, Zora, no man is quite worth a woman's soul; no love is worth a whole life."

Zora turned away with a gesture of impatience.

"You were born in ice," she retorted, adding a bit more tenderly, "in clear strong ice; but I was born in fire. I live—I love; that's all." And she sat down again, despairingly, and stared at the dull swamp. Miss Smith stood for a moment and closed her eyes upon a vision.

"Ice!" she whispered. "My God!"

Then, at length, she said to Zora:

"Zora, there's only one way: do something; if you sit thus brooding you'll go crazy."

"Do crazy folks forget?"

"Nonsense, Zora!" Miss Smith ridiculed the girl's fantastic vagaries; her sound common sense rallied to her aid. "They are the people who remember; sane folk forget. Work is the only cure for such pain."

"But there's nothing to do—nothing I want to do—nothing worth doing—now."

"The Silver Fleece?"

The girl sat upright.

"The Silver Fleece," she murmured. Without further word, slowly she arose and walked down the stairs, and out into the swamp. Miss Smith watched her go; she knew that every step must be the keen prickle of awakening flesh. Yet the girl walked steadily on.

It was the Christmas—not Christmas-tide of the North and West, but Christmas of the Southern South. It was not the festival of the Christ Child, but a time of noise and frolic and license, the great Pay-Day of the year when black men lifted their heads from a year's toiling in the earth, and, hat in hand, asked anxiously: "Master, what have I earned? Have I paid my old debts to you? Have I made my clothes and food? Have I got a little of the year's wage coming to me?" Or, more carelessly and cringingly: "Master, gimme a Christmas gift."

The lords of the soil stood round, gauging their cotton, measuring their men. Their stores were crowded, their scales groaned, their gins sang. In the long run public opinion determines all wage, but in more primitive times and places, private opinion, personal judgment of some man in power, determines. The Black Belt is primitive and the landlord wields the power.

"What about Johnson?" calls the head clerk.

"Well, he's a faithful nigger and needs encouragement; cancel his debt and give him ten dollars for Christmas." Colonel Cresswell glowed, as if he were full of the season's spirit.

"And Sanders?"

"How's his cotton?"

"Good, and a lot of it."

"He's trying to get away. Keep him in debt, but let him draw what he wants."

"Aunt Rachel?"

"H'm, they're way behind, aren't they? Give her a couple of dollars—not a cent more."

"Jim Sykes?"

"Say, Harry, how about that darky, Sykes?" called out the Colonel.

Excusing himself from his guests, Harry Cresswell came into the office.

To them this peculiar spectacle of the market place was of unusual interest. They saw its humor and its crowding, its bizarre effects and unwonted pageantry. Black giants and pigmies were there; kerchiefed aunties, giggling black girls, saffron beauties, and loafing white men. There were mules and horses and oxen, wagons and buggies and carts; but above all and in all, rushing through, piled and flying, bound and baled—was cotton. Cotton was currency; cotton was merchandise; cotton was conversation.

All this was "beautiful" to Mrs. Grey and "unusually interesting" to Mrs. Vanderpool. To Mary Taylor it had the fascination of a puzzle whose other side she had already been partially studying. She was particularly impressed with the joy and abandon of the scene—light laughter, huge guffaws, handshakes, and gossipings.

"At all events," she concluded, "this is no oppressed people." And sauntering away from the rest she noted the smiles of an undersized smirking yellow man who hurried by with a handful of dollar bills. At a side entrance liquor was evidently on sale—men were drinking and women, too; some were staggering, others cursing, and yet others singing. Then suddenly a man swung around the corner swearing in bitter rage:

"The damned thieves, they'se stole a year's work—the white—" But some one called, "Hush up, Sanders! There's a white woman." And he threw a startled look at Mary and hurried by. She was perplexed and upset and stood hesitating a moment when she heard a well-known voice:

"Why, Miss Taylor, I was alarmed for you; you really must be careful about trusting yourself with these half drunken Negroes."

"Wouldn't it be better not to give them drink, Mr. Cresswell?"

"And let your neighbor sell them poison at all hours? No, Miss Taylor." They joined the others, and all were turning toward the carriage when a figure coming down the road attracted them.

"Quite picturesque," observed Mrs. Vanderpool, looking at the tall, slim girl swaying toward them with a piled basket of white cotton poised lightly on her head. "Why," in abrupt recognition, "it is our Venus of the Roadside, is it not?"

Mary saw it was Zora. Just then, too, Zora caught sight of them, and for a moment hesitated, then came on; the carriage was in front of the store, and she was bound for the store. A moment Mary hesitated, too, and then turned resolutely to greet her. But Zora's eyes did not see her. After one look at that sorrow-stricken face, Mary turned away.

Colonel Cresswell stood by the door, his hat on, his hands in his pockets.

"Well, Zora, what have you there?" he asked.

"Cotton, sir."

Harry Cresswell bent over it.

"Great heavens! Look at this cotton!" he ejaculated. His father approached. The cotton lay in silken handfuls, clean and shimmering, with threads full two inches long. The idlers, black and white, clustered round, gazing at it, and fingering it with repeated exclamations of astonishment.

"Where did this come from?" asked the Colonel sharply. He and Harry were both eying the girl intently.

"I raised it in the swamp," Zora replied quietly, in a dead voice. There was no pride of achievement in her manner, no gladness; all that had flown.

"Is that all?"

"No, sir; I think there's two bales."

"Two bales! Where is it? How the devil—" The Colonel was forgetting his guests, but Harry intervened.

"You'll need to get it picked right off," he suggested.

"It's all picked, sir."

"But where is it?"

"If you'll send a wagon, sir—"

But the Colonel hardly waited.

"Here you, Jim, take the big mules and drive like—Where's that wench?"

But Zora was already striding on ahead, and was far up the red road when the great mules galloped into sight and the long whip snapped above their backs. The Colonel was still excited.

"That cotton must be ours, Harry—all of it. And see that none is stolen. We've got no contract with the wench, so don't dally with her." But Harry said firmly, quietly:

"It's fine cotton, and she raised it; she must be paid well for it." Colonel Cresswell glanced at him with something between contempt and astonishment on his face.

"You go along with the ladies," Harry added; "I'll see to this cotton." Mary Taylor's smile had rewarded him; now he must get rid of his company—before Zora returned.

It was dark when the cotton came; such a load as Cresswell's store had never seen before. Zora watched it weighed, received the cotton checks, and entered the store. Only the clerk was there, and he was closing. He pointed her carelessly to the office in the back part. She went into the small dim room, and laying the cotton-check on the desk, stood waiting. Slowly the hopelessness and bitterness of it all came back in a great whelming flood. What was the use of trying for anything? She was lost forever. The world was against her, and again she saw the fingers of Elspeth—the long black claw-like talons that clutched and dragged her down—down. She did not struggle—she dropped her hands listlessly, wearily, and stood but half conscious as the door opened and Mr. Harry Cresswell entered the dimly lighted room. She opened her eyes. She had expected his father. Somewhere way down in the depths of her nature the primal tiger awoke and snarled. She was suddenly alive from hair to finger tip. Harry Cresswell paused a second and swept her full length with his eye—her profile, the long supple line of bosom and hip, the little foot. Then he closed the door softly and walked slowly toward her. She stood like stone, without a quiver; only her eye followed the crooked line of the Cresswell blue blood on his marble forehead as she looked down from her greater height; her hand closed almost caressingly on a rusty poker lying on the stove nearby; and as she sensed the hot breath of him she felt herself purring in a half heard whisper.

"I should not like—to kill you."

He looked at her long and steadily as he passed to his desk. Slowly he lighted a cigarette, opened the great ledger, and compared the cotton-check with it.

"Three thousand pounds," he announced in a careless tone. "Yes, that will make about two bales of lint. It's extra cotton—say fifteen cents a pound—one hundred fifty dollars—seventy-five dollars to you—h'm." He took a note-book out of his pocket, pushed his hat back on his head, and paused to relight his cigarette.

"Let's see—your rent and rations—"

"Elspeth pays no rent," she said slowly, but he did not seem to hear.

"Your rent and rations with the five years' back debt,"—he made a hasty calculation—"will be one hundred dollars. That leaves you twenty-five in our debt. Here's your receipt."

The blow had fallen. She did not wince nor cry out. She took the receipt, calmly, and walked out into the darkness.

They had stolen the Silver Fleece.

What should she do? She never thought of appeal to courts, for

Colonel Cresswell was Justice of the Peace and his son was bailiff. Why had they stolen from her? She knew. She was now penniless, and in a sense helpless. She was now a peon bound to a master's bidding. If Elspeth chose to sign a contract of work for her to-morrow, it would mean slavery, jail, or hounded running away. What would Elspeth do? One never knew. Zora walked on. An hour ago it seemed that this last blow must have killed her. But now it was different. Into her first despair had crept, in one fierce moment, grim determination. Somewhere in the world sat a great dim Injustice which had veiled the light before her young eyes, just as she raised them to the morning. With the veiling, death had come into her heart.

And yet, they should not kill her; they should not enslave her. A desperate resolve to find some way up toward the light, if not to it, formed itself within her. She would not fall into the pit opening before her. Somehow, somewhere lay The Way. She must never fall lower; never be utterly despicable in the eyes of the man she had loved. There was no dream of forgiveness, of purification, of re-kindled love; all these she placed sadly and gently into the dead past. But in awful earnestness, she turned toward the future; struggling blindly, groping in half formed plans for a way.

She came thus into the room where sat Miss Smith, strangely pallid beneath her dusky skin. But there lay a light in her eyes.

Eighteen

THE COTTON CORNER

All over the land the cotton had foamed in great white flakes under the winter sun. The Silver Fleece lay like a mighty mantle across the earth. Black men and mules had staggered beneath its burden, while deep songs welled in the hearts of men; for the Fleece was goodly and gleaming and soft, and men dreamed of the gold it would buy. All the roads in the country had been lined with wagons—a million wagons speeding to and fro with straining mules and laughing black men, bearing bubbling masses of piled white Fleece. The gins were still roaring and spitting flames and smoke—fifty thousand of them in town and vale. Then hoarse iron throats were filled with fifteen billion pounds of white-fleeced, black-specked cotton, for the whirling saws to tear out the seed and fling five thousand million pounds of the silken fibre to the press.

And there again the black men sang, like dark earth-spirits flitting in twilight; the presses creaked and groaned; closer and closer they pressed the silken fleece. It quivered, trembled, and then lay cramped, dead, and still, in massive, hard, square bundles, tied with iron strings. Out fell the heavy bales, thousand upon thousand, million upon million, until they settled over the South like some vast dull-white swarm of birds. Colonel Cresswell and his son, in these days, had a long and earnest conversation perforated here and there by explosions of the Colonel's wrath. The Colonel could not understand some things.

"They want us to revive the Farmers' League?" he fiercely demanded.

"Yes," Harry calmly replied.

"And throw the rest of our capital after the fifty thousand dollars we've already lost?"

"Yes."

"And you were fool enough to consent—"

"Wait, Father—and don't get excited. Listen. Cotton is going up—"

"Of course it's going up! Short crop and big demand—"

"Cotton is going up, and then it's going to fall."

"I don't believe it."

"I know it; the trust has got money and credit enough to force it down."

"Well, what then?" The Colonel glared.

"Then somebody will corner it."

"The Farmers' League won't stand—"

"Precisely. The Farmers' League can do the cornering and hold it for higher prices."

"Lord, son! if we only could!" groaned the Colonel.

"We can; we'll have unlimited credit."

"But—but—" stuttered the bewildered Colonel, "I don't understand. Why should the trust—"

"Nonsense, Father—what's the use of understanding. Our advantage is plain, and John Taylor guarantees the thing."

"Who's John Taylor?" snorted the Colonel. "Why should we trust him?"

"Well," said Harry slowly, "he wants to marry Helen—"

His father grew apopletic.

"I'm not saying he will, Father; I'm only saying that he wants to," Harry made haste to placate the rising tide of wrath.

"No Southern gentleman—" began the Colonel. But Harry shrugged his shoulders.

"Which is better, to be crushed by the trust or to escape at their expense, even if that escape involves unwarranted assumptions on the part of one of them? I tell you, Father, the code of the Southern gentleman won't work in Wall Street."

"And I'll tell you why—there *are* no Southern gentlemen," growled his father.

The Silver Fleece was golden, for its prices were flying aloft. Mr. Caldwell told Colonel Cresswell that he confidently expected twelve-cent cotton.

"The crop is excellent and small, scarcely ten million bales," he declared. "The price is bound to go up."

Colonel Cresswell was hesitant, even doubtful; the demand for cotton at high prices usually fell off rapidly and he had heard rumors of curtailed mill production. While, then, he hoped for high prices he advised the Farmers' League to be on guard.

Mr. Caldwell seemed to be right, for cotton rose to ten cents a pound—ten and a half—eleven—and then the South began to see visions and to dream dreams.

"Yes, my dear," said Mr. Maxwell, whose lands lay next to the Cresswells' on the northwest, "yes, if cotton goes to twelve or thirteen cents as seems probable, I think we can begin the New House"—for Mrs. Maxwell's cherished dream was a pillared mansion like the Cresswells'.

Mr. Tolliver looked at his house and barns. "Well, daughter, if this crop sells at twelve cents, I'll be on my feet again, and I won't have to sell that land to the nigger school after all. Once out of the clutch of the Cresswells—well, I think we can have a coat of paint." And he laughed as he had not laughed in ten years.

Down in the bottoms west of the swamp a man and woman were figuring painfully on an old slate. He was light brown and she was yellow.

"Honey," he said tremblingly, "I b'lieve we can do it—if cotton goes to twelve cents, we can pay the mortgage."

Two miles north of the school an old black woman was shouting and waving her arms. "If cotton goes to twelve cents we can pay out and be free!" and she threw her apron over her head and wept, gathering her children in her arms.

But even as she cried a flash and tremor shook the South. Far away to the north a great spider sat weaving his web. The office looked down from the clouds on lower Broadway, and was soft with velvet and leather. Swift, silent messengers hurried in and out, and Mr. Easterly, deciding the time was ripe, called his henchman to him.

"Taylor, we're ready—go South."

And John Taylor rose, shook hands silently, and went.

As he entered Cresswell's plantation store three days later, a colored woman with a little boy turned sadly away from the counter.

"No, aunty," the clerk was telling her, "calico is too high; can't let you have any till we see how your cotton comes out."

"I just wanted a bit; I promised the boy—"

"Go on, go on—Why, Mr. Taylor!" And the little boy burst into tears while he was hurried out.

"Tightening up on the tenants?" asked Taylor.

"Yes; these niggers are mighty extravagant. Besides, cotton fell a little today—eleven to ten and three-fourths; just a flurry, I reckon. Had you heard?"

Mr. Taylor said he had heard, and he hurried on. Next morning the long shining wires of that great Broadway web trembled and flashed again and cotton went to ten cents.

"No house this year, I fear," quoth Mr. Maxwell, bitterly.

The next day nine and a half was the quotation, and men began to look at each other and asked questions.

"Paper says the crop is larger than the government estimate," said Tolliver, and added, "There'll be no painting this year." He looked toward the Smith School and thought of the five thousand dollars waiting; but he hesitated. John Taylor had carefully mentioned seven thousand dollars as a price he was willing to pay and "perhaps more." Was Cresswell back of Taylor? Tolliver was suspicious and moved to delay matters.

"It's manipulation and speculation in New York," said Colonel Cresswell, "and the Farmers' League must begin operations."

The local paper soon had an editorial on "our distinguished fellow citizen, Colonel Cresswell," and his efforts to revive the Farmers' League. It was understood that Colonel Cresswell was risking his whole private fortune to hold the price of cotton, and some effort seemed to be needed, for cotton dropped to nine cents within a week. Swift negotiations ensued, and a meeting of the executive committee of the Farmers' League was held in Montgomery. A system of warehouses and warehouse certificates was proposed.

"But that will cost money," responded each of the dozen big landlords who composed the committee; whereupon Harry Cresswell introduced John Taylor, who represented thirty millions of Southern bank stock.

"I promise you credit to any reasonable amount," said Mr. Taylor, "I believe in cotton—the present price is abnormal." And Mr. Taylor knew whereof he spoke, for when he sent a cipher despatch North, cotton dropped to eight and a half. The Farmers' League leased three warehouses at Savannah, Montgomery, and New Orleans.

Then silently the South gripped itself and prepared for battle. Men stopped spending, business grew dull, and millions of eyes were glued to the blackboards of the cotton-exchange. Tighter and tighter the reins grew on the backs of the black tenants.

"Miss Smith, is yo' got just a drap of coffee to lend me? Mr. Cresswell won't give me none at the store and I'se just starving for some," said Aunt Rachel from over the hill. "We won't git free this year, Miss Smith, not this year," she concluded plaintively.

Cotton fell to seven and a half cents and the muttered protest became angry denunciation. Why was it? Who was doing it?

Harry Cresswell went to Montgomery. He was getting nervous. The thing was too vast. He could not grasp it. It set his head in a whirl. Harry Cresswell was not a bad man—are there any bad men? He was a man who from the day he first wheedled his black mammy into submission, down to his thirty-sixth year, had seldom known what it was voluntarily to deny himself or curb a desire. To rise when he would, eat what he craved, and do what the passing fancy suggested had long been his day's programme. Such emptiness of life and aim had to be filled, and it was filled; he helped his father sometimes with the plantations, but he helped spasmodically and played at work.

The unregulated fire of energy and delicacy of nervous poise within him continually hounded him to the verge of excess and sometimes beyond. Cool, quiet, and gentlemanly as he was by rule of his clan, the ice was thin and underneath raged unappeased fires. He craved the madness of alcohol in his veins till his delicate hands trembled of mornings. The women whom he bent above in languid, veiled-eyed homage, feared lest they love him, and what work was to others gambling was to him.

The Cotton Combine, then, appealed to him overpoweringly—to his passion for wealth, to his passion for gambling. But once entered upon the game it drove him to fear and frenzy: first, it was a long game and Harry Cresswell was not trained to waiting, and, secondly, it was a game whose intricacies he did not know. In vain did he try to study the matter through. He ordered books from the North, he subscribed for financial journals, he received special telegraphic reports only to toss them away, curse his valet, and call for another brandy. After all, he kept saying to himself, what guarantee, what knowledge had he that this was not a "damned Yankee trick"?

Now that the web was weaving its last mesh in early January he haunted Montgomery, and on this day when it seemed that things must culminate or he would go mad, he hastened again down to the Planters' Hotel and was quickly ushered to John Taylor's room. The place was filled with tobacco smoke. An electric ticker was drumming away in one corner, a telephone ringing on the desk, and messenger boys hovered outside the door and raced to and fro.

"Well," asked Cresswell, maintaining his composure by an effort, "how are things?"

"Great!" returned Taylor. "League holds three million bales and controls five. It's the biggest corner in years."

"But how's cotton?"

"Ticker says six and three-fourths."

Cresswell sat down abruptly opposite Taylor, looking at him fixedly.

"That last drop means liabilities of a hundred thousand to us," he said slowly.

"Exactly," Taylor blandly admitted.

Beads of sweat gathered on Cresswell's forehead. He looked at the scrawny iron man opposite, who had already forgotten his presence. He ordered whiskey, and taking paper and pencil began to figure, drinking as he figured. Slowly the blood crept out of his white face leaving it whiter, and went surging and pounding in his heart. Poverty—that was what those figures spelled. Poverty—unclothed, wineless poverty, to dig and toil like a "nigger" from morning until night, and to give up horses and carriages and women; that was what they spelled.

"How much—farther will it drop?" he asked harshly.

Taylor did not look up.

"Can't tell," he said, " 'fraid not much though." He glanced through a telegram. "No—damn it!—outside mills are low; they'll stampede soon. Meantime we'll buy."

"But, Taylor—"

"Here are one hundred thousand offered at six and three-fourths."

"I tell you, Taylor—" Cresswell half arose.

"Done!" cried Taylor. "Six and one-half," clicked the machine.

Cresswell arose from his chair by the window and came slowly to the wide flat desk where Taylor was working feverishly. He sat down heavily in the chair opposite and tried quietly to regain his self-control. The liabilities of the Cresswells already amounted to half the value of their property, at a fair market valuation. The cotton for which they had made debts was still falling in value. Every fourth of a cent fall meant—he figured it again tremblingly—meant one hundred thousand more of liabilities. If cotton fell to six he hadn't a cent on earth. If it stayed there—"My God!" He felt a faintness stealing over him but he beat it back and gulped down another glass of fiery liquor.

Then the one protecting instinct of his clan gripped him. Slowly, quietly his hand moved back until it grasped the hilt of the big Colt's revolver that was ever with him—his thin white hand became suddenly steady as it slipped the weapon beneath the shadow of the desk.

"If it goes to six," he kept murmuring, "we're ruined—if it goes to six—if—"

"Tick," sounded the wheel and the sound reverberated like sudden thunder in his ears. His hand was iron, and he raised it slightly. "Six," said the wheel—his finger quivered—"and a half."

"Hell!" yelled Taylor. "She's turned—there'll be the devil to pay now." A messenger burst in and Taylor scowled.

"She's loose in New York—a regular mob in New Orleans—and—hark!—By God! there's something doing here. Damn it—I wish we'd got another million bales. Let's see, we've got—" He figured while the wheel whirred—"7—7½—8—8½."

Cresswell listened, staggered to his feet, his face crimson and his hair wild.

"My God, Taylor," he gasped. "I'm—I'm a half a million ahead—great heavens!"

The ticker whirred, "8¾—9—9½—10." Then it stopped dead.

"Exchange closed," said Taylor. "We've cornered the market all right—cornered it—d'ye hear, Cresswell? We got over half the crop and we can send prices to the North Star—you—why, I figure it you Cresswells are worth at least seven hundred and fifty thousand above liabilities this minute," and John Taylor leaned back and lighted a big black cigar.

"I've made a million or so myself," he added reflectively.

Cresswell leaned back in his chair, his face had gone white again, and he spoke slowly to still the tremor in his voice.

"I've gambled—before; I've gambled on cards and on horses; I've gambled—for money—and—women—but—"

"But not on cotton, hey? Well, I don't know about cards and such; but they can't beat cotton."

"And say, John Taylor, you're my friend." Cresswell stretched his hand across the desk, and as he bent forward the pistol crashed to the floor.

Nineteen

THE DYING OF ELSPETH

Rich! This was the thought that awakened Harry Cresswell to a sense of endless well-being. Rich! No longer the mirage and semblance of wealth, the memory of opulence, the shadow of homage without the substance of power—no; now the wealth was real, cold hard dollars, and in piles. How much? He laughed aloud as he turned on his pillow. What did he care? Enough—enough. Not less than half a million; perhaps three-quarters of a million; perhaps—was not cotton still rising?—a whole round million! That would mean from twenty-five to fifty thousand a year. Great heavens! and he'd been starving on a bare couple of thousand and trying to keep up appearances! today the Cresswells were almost millionaires; aye, and he might be married to more millions.

He sat up with a start. Today Mary was going North. He had quite forgotten it in the wild excitement of the cotton corner. He had neglected her. Of course, there was always the hovering doubt as to whether he really wanted her or not. She had the form and carriage; her beauty, while not startling, was young and fresh and firm. On the other hand there was about her a certain independence that he did not like to associate with women. She had thoughts and notions of the world which were, to his Southern training, hardly feminine. And yet even they piqued him and spurred him like the sight of an untrained colt. He had not seen her falter yet beneath his glances or tremble at his touch. All this he desired—ardently desired. But did he desire her as a wife? He rather thought that he did. And if so he must speak today.

There was his father, too, to reckon with. Colonel Cresswell, with the perversity of the simple-minded, had taken the sudden bettering of their fortunes as his own doing. He had foreseen; he had stuck it out; his credit had pulled the thing through; and the trust had learned a thing or two about Southern gentlemen.

Toward John Taylor he perceptibly warmed. His business methods were such as a Cresswell could never stoop to; but he was a man of his word, and Colonel Cresswell's correspondence with Mr. Easterly opened his eyes to the beneficent ideals of Northern capital. At the same time he could not consider the Easterlys and the Taylors and such folk as the social equals of the Cresswells, and his prejudice on this score must still be reckoned with.

Below, Mary Taylor lingered on the porch in strange uncertainty. Harry Cresswell would soon be coming downstairs. Did she want him to find her? She liked him frankly, undisguisedly; but from the love she knew to be so near her heart she recoiled in perturbation. He wooed her—whether consciously or not, she was always uncertain—with every quiet attention and subtle deference, with a devotion seemingly quite too delicate for words; he not only fetched her flowers, but flowers that chimed with day and gown and season—almost with mood. He had a woman's premonitions in fulfilling her wishes. His hands, if they touched her, were soft and tender, and yet he gave a curious impression of strength and poise and will.

Indeed, in all things he was in her eyes a gentleman in the fine old-fashioned aristocracy of the term; her own heart voiced all he did not say, and pleaded for him to her own confusion.

And yet, in her heart, lay the awful doubt—and the words kept ringing in her ears! "You will marry this man—but heaven help you if you do!"

So it was that on this day when she somehow felt he would speak, his footsteps on the stairs filled her with sudden panic. Without a word she slipped behind the pillars and ran down among the oaks and sauntered out upon the big road. He caught the white flutter of her dress, and smiled indulgently as he watched and waited and lightly puffed his cigarette.

The morning was splendid with that first delicious languor of the spring which breathes over the Southland in February. Mary Taylor filled her lungs, lifted her arms aloft, and turning, stepped into the deep shadow of the swamp.

Abruptly the air, the day, the scene about her subtly changed. She felt a closeness and a tremor, a certain brooding terror in the languid sombre winds. The gold of the sunlight faded to a sickly green, and the earth was black and burned. A moment she paused and looked back; she caught the man's silhouette against the tall white pillars of the mansion and she fled deeper into the forest with the hush of death about her, and the silence which is one great Voice. Slowly, and mysteriously it loomed before her—that squat and darksome cabin which seemed to fitly set in the centre of the wilderness, beside its crawling slime.

She paused in sudden certainty that there lay the answer to her doubts and mistrust. She felt impelled to go forward and ask—what? She did not know, but something to still this war in her bosom. She had seldom seen Elspeth; she had never been in her cabin. She had felt an inconquerable aversion for the evil hag; she felt it now, and shivered in the warm breeze.

As she came in full view of the door, she paused. On the step of the cabin, framed in the black doorway, stood Zora. Measured by the squat cabin she seemed in height colossal; slim, straight as a pine, motionless, with one long outstretched arm pointing to where the path swept onward toward the town.

It was too far for words but the scene lay strangely clear and sharp-cut in the green mystery of the sunlight. Before that motionless, fateful figure crouched a slighter, smaller woman, dishevelled, clutching her breast; she bent and rose—hesitated—seemed to plead; then turning, clasped in passionate embrace the child whose head was hid in Zora's gown. Next instant she was staggering along the path whither Zora pointed.

Slowly the sun was darkened, and plaintive murmurings pulsed through the wood. The oppression and fear of the swamp redoubled in Mary Taylor.

Zora gave no sign of having seen her. She stood tall and still, and the little golden-haired girl still sobbed in her gown. Mary Taylor looked up into Zora's face, then paused in awe. It was a face she did not know; it was neither the beautifully mischievous face of the girl, nor the pain-stricken face of the woman. It was a face cold and mask-like, regular and comely; clothed in a mighty calm, yet subtly, masterfully veiling behind itself depths of unfathomed misery and wild revolt. All this lay in its darkness.

"Good-morning, Miss Taylor."

Mary, who was wont to teach this woman—so lately a child—searched in vain for words to address her now. She stood bare-haired and hesitating in the pale green light of the darkened morning. It seemed fit that a deep groan of pain should gather itself from the mysterious depths of the swamp, and drop like a pall on the black portal of the cabin. But it brought Mary Taylor back to a sense of things, and under a sudden impulse she spoke.

"Is—is anything the matter?" she asked nervously.

"Elspeth is sick," replied Zora.

"Is she very sick?"

"Yes—she has been called," solemnly returned the dark young woman.

Mary was puzzled. "Called?" she repeated vaguely.

"We heard the great cry in the night, and Elspeth says it is the End."

It did not occur to Mary Taylor to question this mysticism; she all at once understood—perhaps read the riddle in the dark, melancholy eyes that so steadily regarded her.

"Then you can leave the place, Zora?" she exclaimed gladly.

"Yes, I could leave."

"And you will."

"I don't know."

"But the place looks—evil."

"It is evil."

"And yet you will stay?"

Zora's eyes were now fixed far above the woman's head, and she saw a human face forming itself in the vast rafters of the forest. Its eyes were wet with pain and anger.

"Perhaps," she answered.

The child furtively uncovered her face and looked at the stranger. She was blue-eyed and golden-haired.

"Whose child is this?" queried Mary, curiously.

Zora looked coldly down upon the child.

"It is Bertie's. Her mother is bad. She is gone. I sent her. She and the others like her."

"But where have you sent them?"

"To Hell!"

Mary Taylor started under the shock. Impulsively she moved forward with hands that wanted to stretch themselves in appeal.

"Zora! Zora! *You* mustn't go, too!"

But the black girl drew proudly back.

"I *am* there," she returned, with unmistakable simplicity of absolute conviction.

The white woman shrank back. Her heart was wrung; she wanted to say more—to explain, to ask to help; there came welling to her lips a flood of things that she would know. But Zora's face again was masked.

"I must go," she said, before Mary could speak. "Good-bye." And the dark groaning depths of the cabin swallowed her.

With a satisfied smile, Harry Cresswell had seen the Northern girl disappear toward the swamp; for it is significant when maidens run from lovers. But maidens should also come back, and when, after the lapse of many minutes, Mary did not reappear, he followed her footsteps to the swamp.

He frowned as he noted the footprints pointing to Elspeth's—what did Mary Taylor want there? A fear started within him, and something else. He was suddenly aware that he wanted this woman, intensely; at the moment he would have turned Heaven and earth to get her. He strode forward and the wood rose darkly green above him. A long, low, distant moan seemed to sound upon the breeze, and after it came Mary Taylor.

He met her with tender solicitude, and she was glad to feel his arm beneath hers.

"I've been searching for you," he said after a silence. "You should not wander here alone—it is dangerous."

"Why, dangerous?" she asked.

"Wandering Negroes, and even wild beasts, in the forest depths— and malaria—see, you tremble now."

"But not from malaria," she slowly returned.

He caught an unfamiliar note in his voice, and a wild desire to justify himself before this woman clamored in his heart. With it, too, came a cooler calculating intuition that frankness alone would win her now. At all hazards he must win, and he cast the die.

"Miss Taylor," he said, "I want to talk to you—I have wanted to for—a year." He glanced at her: she was white and silent, but she did not tremble. He went on:

"I have hesitated because I do not know that I have a right to speak or explain to—to—a good woman."

He felt her arm tighten on his and he continued:

"You have been to Elspeth's cabin; it is an evil place, and has meant evil for this community, and for me. Elspeth was my mother's favorite servant and my own mammy. My mother died when I was ten and left me to her tender mercies. She let me have my way and encouraged the bad in me. It's a wonder I escaped total ruin. Her cabin became a rendezvous for drinking and carousing. I told my father, but he, in lazy indifference, declared the place no worse than all Negro cabins, and did nothing. I ceased my visits. Still she tried every lure and set false stories going among the Negroes, even when I sought to rescue Zora. I tell you this because I know you have heard evil rumors. I have not been a good man—Mary; but I love you, and you can make me good."

Perhaps no other appeal would have stirred Mary Taylor. She was in many respects an inexperienced girl. But she thought she knew the world; she knew that Harry Cresswell was not all he should be, and she knew too that many other men were not. Moreover, she argued he had not had a fair chance. All the school-ma'am in her leaped to his teaching. What he needed was a superior person like herself. She loved him, and she deliberately put her arms about his neck and lifted her face to be kissed.

Back by the place of the Silver Fleece they wandered, across the Big Road, up to the mansion. On the steps stood John Taylor and Helen Cresswell hand in hand and they all smiled at each other. The Colonel came out, smiling too, with the paper in his hands.

"Easterly's right," he beamed, "the stock of the Cotton Combine—" he paused at the silence and looked up. The smile faded slowly and the red blood mounted to his forehead. Anger struggled back of surprise, but before it burst forth silently the Colonel turned, and muttering some unintelligible word, went slowly into the house and slammed the door.

So for Harry Cresswell the day burst, flamed, and waned, and then suddenly went out, leaving him dull and gray; for Mary and her brother had gone North, Helen had gone to bed, and the Colonel was in town. Outside the weather was gusty and lowering with a chill in the air. He paced the room fitfully.

Well, he was happy. Or, *was* he happy?

He gnawed his mustache, for already his quick, changeable nature was feeling the rebound from glory to misery. He was a little ashamed of his exaltation; a bit doubtful and uncertain. He had stooped low to this Yankee school-ma'am, lower than he had ever stooped to a woman. Usually, while he played at loving, women grovelled; for was he not a Cresswell? Would this woman recognize that fact and respect him accordingly?

Then there was Zora; what had she said and hinted to Mary? The wench was always eluding and mocking him, the black devil! But, pshaw!—he poured himself a glass of brandy—was he not rich and young? The world was his.

His valet knocked.

"Gentleman is asking if you forgits it's Saturday night, sir?" said Sam.

Cresswell walked thoughtfully to the window, swept back the curtain, and looked toward the darkness and the swamp. It lowered threateningly; behind it the night sky was tinged with blood.

"No," he said; "I'm not going." And he shut out the glow.

Yet he grew more and more restless. The devil danced in his veins and burned in his forehead. His hands shook. He heard a rustle of departing feet beneath his window, then a pause and a faint halloo.

"All right," he called, and in a moment went downstairs and out into the night. As he closed the front door there seemed to come faintly up from the swamp a low ululation, like the prolonged cry of some wild bird, or the wail of one's mourning for his dead.

Within the cabin, Elspeth heard. Tremblingly, she swayed to her feet, a haggard, awful sight. She motioned Zora away, and stretching her hands palms upward to the sky, cried with dry and fear-struck gasp:

"I'se called! I'se called!"

On the bed the child smiled in its dreaming; the red flame of the fire-light set the gold to dancing in her hair. Zora shrank back into the shadows and listened. Then it came. She heard the heavy footsteps crashing through the underbrush—coming, coming, as from the end of the world. She shrank still farther back, and a shadow swept the door.

He was a mighty man, black and white-haired, and his eyes were the eyes of death. He bent to enter the door, and then uplifting himself and stretching his great arms, his palms touched the blackened rafters.

Zora started forward. Thick memories of some forgotten past came piling in upon her. Where had she known him? What was he to her?

Slowly Elspeth, with quivering hands, unwound the black and snake-like object that always guarded her breast. Without a word, he took it, and again his hands flew heavenward. With a low and fearful moan the old woman lurched sideways, then crashed, like a fallen pine, upon the hearthstone. She lay still—dead.

Three times the man passed his hands, wave-like, above the dead. Three times he murmured, and his eyes burned into the shadows, where the girl trembled. Then he turned and went as he had come, his heavy feet crashing through the underbrush, on and on, fainter and fainter, as to the end of the world.

Zora shook herself from the trance-like horror and passed her hands across her eyes to drive out the nightmare. But, no! there lay the dead upon the hearth with the firelight flashing over her, a bloated, hideous, twisted thing, distorted in the rigor of death. A moment Zora looked down upon her mother. She felt the cold body whence the wandering, wrecked soul had passed. She sat down and stared death in the face for the first time. A mighty questioning arose within, a questioning and a yearning.

Was Elspeth now at peace? Was Death the Way—the wide, dark Way? She had never thought of it before, and as she thought she crept forward and looked into the fearful face pityingly.

"Mammy!" she whispered—with bated breath—"Mammy Elspeth!" Out of the night came a whispered answer: *"Elspeth! Elspeth!"*

Zora sprang to her feet, alert, fearful. With a swing of her arm, she pulled the great oaken door to and dropped the bar into its place. Over the dead she spread a clean white sheet. Into the fire she thrust pine-knots. They glared in vague red, and shadowy brilliance, waving and quivering and throwing up thin swirling columns of black smoke. Then standing beside the fireplace with the white, still corpse between her and the door, she took up her awful vigil.

There came a low knocking at the door; then silence and footsteps wandering furtively about. The night seemed all footsteps and whispers. There came a louder knocking, and a voice:

"Elspeth! Elspeth! Open the door; it's me."

Then muttering and wandering noises, and silence again.

The child on the bed turned itself, murmuring uneasily in its dreams. And then *they* came. Zora froze, watching the door, wide-eyed, while the fire flamed redder. A loud quick knock at the door—a pause—an oath and a cry.

"Elspeth! Open this door, damn you!"

A moment of waiting and then the knocking came again, furious and long continued. Outside there was much trampling and swearing. Zora did not move; the child slept on. A tugging and dragging, a dull blow that set the cabin quivering; then,—

"*Bang! Crack! Crash!*"—the door wavered, splintered, and dropped upon the floor.

With a snarl, a crowd of some half-dozen white faces rushed forward, wavered and stopped. The awakened child sat up and stared with wide blue eyes. Slowly, with no word, the intruders turned and went silently away, leaving but one late comer who pressed forward.

"What damned mummery is this?" he cried, and snatching at the sheet, dragged it from the black distorted countenance of the corpse. He shuddered but for a moment he could not stir. He felt the midnight eyes of the girl—he saw the twisted, oozing mouth of the hag, blue-black and hideous.

Suddenly back behind there in the darkness a shriek split the night like a sudden flash of flame—a great ringing scream that cracked and swelled and stopped. With one wild effort the man hurled himself out the door and plunged through the darkness. Panting and cursing, he flashed his huge revolver—"*bang! bang! bang!*" it cracked into the night. The sweat poured from his forehead; the terror of the swamp was upon him. With a struggling and tearing in his throat, he tripped and fell fainting under the silent oaks.

Twenty

THE WEAVING OF THE
SILVER FLEECE

The Silver Fleece, darkly cloaked and girded, lay in the cotton
warehouse of the Cresswells, near the store. Its silken fibres,
cramped and close, shone yellow-white in the sunlight; sadly soiled,
yet beautiful. Many came to see Zora's twin bales, as they lay, handling
them and questioning, while Colonel Cresswell grew proud of his pos-
session.

The world was going well with the Colonel. Freed from money
cares, praised for his generalship in the cotton corner, able to entertain
sumptuously, he was again a Southern gentleman of the older school,
and so in his envied element. Yet today he frowned as he stood poking
absently with his cane at the baled Fleece.

This marriage—or, rather, these marriages—were not to his liking.
It was a *mesalliance* of a sort that pricked him tenderly; it savored
grossly of bargain and sale. His neighbors regarded it with disconcert-

ing equanimity. They seemed to think an alliance with Northern millions an honor for Cresswell blood, and the Colonel thumped the nearer bale vigorously. His cane slipped along the iron bands suddenly, and the old man lurching forward, clutched in space to save himself and touched a human hand.

Zora, sitting shadowed on the farther bale, drew back her hand quickly at the contact, and started to move away.

"Who's that?" thundered the Colonel, more angry at his involuntary fright than at the intrusion. "Here, boys!"

But Zora had come forward into the space where the sunlight of the wide front doors poured in upon the cotton bales.

"It's me, Colonel," she said.

He glared at her. She was taller and thinner than formerly, darkly transparent of skin, and her dark eyes shone in strange and dusky brilliance. Still indignant and surprised, the Colonel lifted his voice sharply.

"What the devil are you doing here?—sleeping when you ought to be at work! Get out! And see here, next week cotton chopping begins—you'll go to the fields or to the chain-gang. I'll have no more of your loafing about my place."

Awaiting no reply, the Colonel, already half ashamed of his vehemence, stormed out into the sunlight and climbed upon his bay mare.

But Zora still stood silent in the shadow of the Silver Fleece, hearing and yet not hearing. She was searching for the Way, groping for the threads of life, seeking almost wildly to understand the foundations of understanding, piteously asking for answer to the puzzle of life. All the while the walls rose straight about her and narrow. To continue in school meant charity, yet she had nowhere to go and nothing to go with. To refuse to work for the Cresswells meant trouble for the school and perhaps arrest for herself. To work in the fields meant endless toil and a vista that opened upon death.

Like a hunted thing the girl turned and twisted in thought and faced everywhere the blank Impossible. Cold and dreamlike without, her shut teeth held back seething fires within, and a spirit of revolt that gathered wildness as it grew. Above all flew the dream, the phantasy, the memory of the past, the vision of the future. Over and over she whispered to herself: "This is not the End; this can not be the End."

Somehow, somewhere, would come salvation. Yet what it would be and what she expected she did not know. She sought the Way, but what way and whither she did not know, she dared not dream.

One thing alone lay in her wild fancy like a great and wonderful fact dragging the dream to earth and anchoring it there. That was the Silver Fleece. Like a brooding mother, Zora had watched it. She knew how the gin had been cleaned for its pressing and how it had been baled apart and carefully covered. She knew how proud Colonel Cresswell was of it and how daily he had visitors to see it and finger the wide white wound in its side.

"Yes, sir, grown on my place, by my niggers, sir!" he assured them; and they marvelled.

To Zora's mind, this beautiful baled fibre was hers; it typified happiness; it was an holy thing which profane hands had stolen. When it came back to her (as come it must, she cried with clenched hands) it would bring happiness; not the great Happiness—that was gone forever—but illumination, atonement, and something of the power and the glory. So, involuntarily almost, she haunted the cotton storehouse, flitting like a dark and silent ghost in among the workmen, greeting them with her low musical voice, warding them with the cold majesty of her eyes; each day afraid of some last parting, each night triumphant—it was still there!

The Colonel—Zora already forgotten—rode up to the Cresswell Oaks, pondering darkly. It was bad enough to contemplate Helen's marriage in distant prospect, but the sudden, almost peremptory desire for marrying at Eastertide, a little less than two months away, was absurd. There were "business reasons arising from the presidential campaign in the fall," John Taylor had telegraphed; but there was already too much business in the arrangement to suit the Colonel. With Harry it was different. Indeed it was his own quiet suggestion that made John Taylor hurry matters.

Harry trusted to the novelty of his father's new wealth to make the latter complacent; he himself felt an impatient longing for the haven of a home. He had been too long untethered. He distrusted himself. The devil within was too fond of taking the bit in his teeth. He would remember to his dying day one awful shriek in the night, as of a soul tormenting and tormented. He wanted the protection of a good woman, and sometimes against the clear whiteness of her letters so joyous and generous, even if a bit prim and didactic, he saw a vision of himself reflected as he was, and he feared.

It was distinctively disconcerting to Colonel Cresswell to find Harry quite in favor of early nuptials, and to learn that the sole objection even in Helen's mind was the improbability of getting a wedding-gown in time. Helen had all a child's naive love for beautiful and dainty things, and a wedding-gown from Paris had been her life dream. On this point, therefore, there ensued spirited arguments and much correspondence, and both her brother and her lover evinced characteristic interest in the planning.

Said Harry: "Sis, I'll cable to Paris today. They can easily hurry the thing along."

Helen was delighted; she handed over a telegram just received from John Taylor. "Send me, express, two bales best cotton you can get."

The Colonel read the message. "I don't see the connection between this and hurrying up a wedding-gown," he growled. None of them discerned the handwriting of Destiny.

"Neither do I," said Harry, who detected yielding in his father's tone. "But we'd better send him the two prize bales; it will be a fine advertisement of our plantation, and evidently he has a surprise in store for us."

The Colonel affected to hesitate, but next morning the Silver Fleece went to town.

Zora watched it go, and her heart swelled and died within her. She walked to town, to the station. She did not see Mrs. Vanderpool arriving from New Orleans; but Mrs. Vanderpool saw her, and looked curiously at the tall, tragic figure that leaned so dolorously beside the freight car. The bales were loaded into the express car; the train pulled away, its hoarse snorting waking vague echoes in the forest beyond. But to the girl who stood at the End, looking outward to darkness, those echoes roared like the crack of doom. A passing band of contract hands called to her mockingly, and one black giant, laughing loudly, gripped her hand.

"Come, honey," he shouted, "you'se a'dreaming! Come on, honey!"

She turned abruptly and gripped his hand, as one drowning grips anything offered—gripped till he winced. She laughed a loud mirthless laugh, that came pouring like a sob from her deep lungs.

"Come on!" she mocked, and joined them.

They were a motley crowd, ragged, swaggering, jolly. There were husky, big-limbed youths, and bold-faced, loud-tongued girls. Tomorrow they would start up-country to some backwoods barony in the kingdom of cotton, and work till Christmas time. today was the last in town; there was craftily advanced money in their pockets and riot in their hearts. In the gathering twilight they marched noisily through the streets; in their midst, wide-eyed and laughing almost hysterically, marched Zora.

Mrs. Vanderpool meantime rode thoughtfully out of town toward Cresswell Oaks. She was returning from witnessing the Mardi Gras festivities at New Orleans and at the urgent invitation of the Cresswells had stopped off. She might even stay to the wedding if the new plans matured.

Mrs. Vanderpool was quite upset. Her French maid, on whom she had depended absolutely for five years or more, had left her.

"I think I want to try a colored maid," she told the Cresswells, laughingly, as they drove home. "They have sweet voices and they can't doff their uniform. Helene without her cap and apron was often mistaken for a lady, and while I was in New Orleans a French confectioner married her under some such delusion. Now, haven't you a girl about here who would do?"

"No," declared Harry decisively, but his sister suggested that she might ask Miss Smith at the colored school.

Again Mrs. Vanderpool laughed, but after tea she wandered idly down the road. The sun behind the swamp was crimsoning the world. Mrs. Vanderpool strolled alone to the school, and saw Sarah Smith. There was no cordiality in the latter's greeting, but when she heard the caller's errand her attention was at once arrested and held. The interests of her charges were always uppermost in her mind.

"Can't I have the girl Zora?" Mrs. Vanderpool at last inquired.

Miss Smith started, for she was thinking of Zora at that very instant. The girl was later than usual, and she was momentarily expecting to see her tall form moving languidly up the walk.

She gave Mrs. Vanderpool a searching look. Mrs. Vanderpool glanced involuntarily at her gown and smiled as she did it.

"Could I trust you with a human soul?" asked Miss Smith abruptly.

Mrs. Vanderpool looked up quickly. The half mocking answer that rose involuntarily to her lips was checked. Within, Mrs. Vanderpool was a little puzzled at herself. Why had she asked for this girl? She had felt a strange interest in her—a peculiar human interest since she first saw her and as she saw her again this afternoon. But would she make a satisfactory maid? Was it not a rather dangerous experiment? Why had she asked for her? She certainly had not intended to when she entered the house.

In the silence Miss Smith continued: "Here is a child in whom the fountains of the great deep are suddenly broken up. With peace and care she would find herself, for she is strong. But here there is no peace.

Slavery of soul and body awaits her and I am powerless to protect her. She must go away. That going away may make or ruin her. She knows nothing of working for wages and she has not the servant's humility; but she has loyalty and pluck. For one she loves there is nothing she would not do; but she cannot be driven. Or rather, if she is driven, it may rouse in her the devil incarnate. She needs not exactly affection— she would almost resent that—but intelligent interest and care. In return for this she will gradually learn to serve and serve loyally. Frankly, Mrs. Vanderpool, I would not have chosen you for this task of human education. Indeed, you would have been my last thought—you seem to me—I speak plainly—a worldly woman. Yet, perhaps—who can tell?—God has especially set you to this task. At any rate, I have little choice. I am at my wits' end. Elspeth, the mother of this child, is not long dead; and here is the girl, beautiful, unprotected; and here am I, almost helpless. She is in debt to the Cresswells, and they are pressing the claim to her service. Take her if you can get her—it is, I fear, her only chance. Mind you—if you can persuade her; and that may be impossible."

"Where is she now?"

Miss Smith glanced out at the darkening landscape, and then at her watch.

"I do not know; she's very late. She's given to wandering, but usually she is here before this time."

"I saw her in town this afternoon," said Mrs. Vanderpool.

"Zora? In town?" Miss Smith rose. "I'll send her to you tomorrow," she said quietly. Mrs. Vanderpool had hardly reached the Oaks before Miss Smith was driving toward town.

A small cabin on the town's ragged fringe was crowded to suffocation. Within arose noisy shouts, loud songs, and raucous laughter; the scraping of a fiddle and whine of an accordion. Liquor began to appear and happy faces grew red-eyed and sodden as the dances whirled. At the edge of the orgy stood Zora, wild-eyed and bewildered, mad with the pain that gripped her heart and hammered in her head, crying in tune with the frenzied music—"the End—the End!"

Abruptly she recognized a face despite the wreck and ruin of its beauty.

"Bertie!" she cried as she seized the mother of little Emma by the arm.

The woman staggered and offered her glass.

"Drink," she cried, "drink and forget."

In a moment Zora sprang forward and seized the burning liquid in both hands. A dozen hands clapped a devil's tattoo. A score of voices yelled and laughed. The shriek of the music was drowned beneath the thunder of stamping feet. Men reeled to singing women's arms, but above the roar rose the song of the voice of Zora—she glided to the middle of the room, standing tip-toed with skirts that curled and turned; she threw back her head, raised the liquor to her lips, paused— and looked into the face of Miss Smith.

A silence fell like a lightning flash on the room as that white face peered in at the door. Slowly Zora's hands fell and her eyes blinked as though waking from some awful dream. She staggered toward the woman's outstretched arms. . . .

Late that night the girl lay close in Miss Smith's motherly embrace.

"I was going to hell!" she whispered, trembling.

"Why, Zora?" asked Miss Smith calmly.

"I couldn't find the Way—and I wanted to forget."

"People in hell don't forget," was the matter-of-fact comment. "And, Zora, what way do you seek? The way where?"

Zora sat up in bed, and lifted a gray and stricken face.

"It's a lie," she cried, with hoarse earnestness, "the way nowhere. There is no Way! You know—I want *him*—I want nothing on earth but him—and him I can't ever have."

The older woman drew her down tenderly.

"No, Zora," she said, "there's something you want more than him and something you can have!"

"What?" asked the wondering girl.

"His respect," said Sarah Smith, "and I know the Way."

Twenty-one

THE MARRIAGE MORNING

Mrs. Vanderpool watched Zora as she came up the path beneath the oaks. "She walks well," she observed. And laying aside her book, she waited with a marked curiosity.

The girl's greeting was brief, almost curt, but unintentionally so, as one could easily see, for back in her eyes lurked an impatient hunger; she was not thinking of greetings. She murmured a quick word, and stood straight and tall with her eyes squarely on the lady.

In the depths of Mrs. Vanderpool's heart something strange—not new, but very old—stirred. Before her stood this tall black girl, quietly returning her look. Mrs. Vanderpool had a most uncomfortable sense of being judged, of being weighed,—and there arose within her an impulse to self-justification.

She smiled and said sweetly, "Won't you sit?" But despite all this, her mind seemed leaping backward a thousand years; back to a simpler, primal day when she herself, white, frail, and fettered, stood before the dusky magnificence of some bejewelled barbarian queen and sought to justify herself. She shook off the phantasy,—and yet how well the girl stood. It was not every one that could stand still and well.

"Please sit down," she repeated with her softest charm, not dreaming that outside the school white persons did not ask this girl to sit in their presence. But even this did not move Zora. She sat down. There was in her, walking, standing, sitting, a simple directness which Mrs. Vanderpool sensed and met.

"Zora, I need some one to help me—to do my hair and serve my coffee, and dress and take care of me. The work will not be hard, and you can travel and see the world and live well. Would you like it?"

"But I do not know how to do all these things," returned Zora, slowly. She was thinking rapidly—Was this the Way? It sounded wonderful. The World, the great mysterious World, that stretched beyond the swamp and into which Bles and the Silver Fleece had gone—did it lead to the Way? But if she went there what would she see and do, and would it be possible to become such a woman as Miss Smith pictured?

"What is the world like?" asked Zora.

Mrs. Vanderpool smiled. "Oh, I meant great active cities and buildings, myriads of people and wonderful sights."

"Yes—but back of it all, what is it really? What does it look like?"

"Heavens, child! Don't ask. Really, it isn't worth while peering back of things. One is sure to be disappointed."

"Then what's the use of seeing the world?"

"Why, one must live; and why not be happy?" answered Mrs. Vanderpool, amused, baffled, spurred for the time being from her chronic *ennui*.

"Are you happy?" retorted Zora, looking her over carefully, from silken stockings to garden hat. Mrs. Vanderpool laid aside her little mockery and met the situation bravely.

"No," she replied simply. Her eyes grew old and tired.

Involuntarily Zora's hand crept out protectingly and lay a moment over the white jewelled fingers. Then quickly recovering herself, she started hastily to withdraw it, but the woman's fingers closed around the darker ones, and Mrs. Vanderpool's eyes became dim,

"I need you, Zora," she said; and then, seeing the half-formed question, "Yes, and you need me; we need each other. In the world lies opportunity, and I will help you."

Zora rose abruptly, and Mrs. Vanderpool feared, with a tightening of heart, that she had lost this strangely alluring girl.

"I will come to-morrow," said Zora.

As Mrs. Vanderpool went in to lunch, reaction and lingering doubts came trouping back. To replace the daintiest of trained experts with the most baffling semi-barbarian, well!

"Have you hired a maid?" asked Helen.

"I've engaged Zora," laughed Mrs. Vanderpool, lightly; "and now I'm wondering whether I have a jewel or—a white elephant."

"Probably neither," remarked Harry Cresswell, drily; but he avoided the lady's inquiring eyes.

Next morning Zora came easily into Mrs. Vanderpool's life. There was little she knew of her duties, but little, too, that she could not learn with a deftness and divination almost startling. Her quietness, her quickness, her young strength, were like a soothing balm to the tired woman of fashion, and within a week she had sunk back contentedly into Zora's strong arms.

"It's a jewel," she decided.

With this verdict, the house agreed. The servants waited on "Miss Zora" gladly; the men scarcely saw her, and the ladies ran to her for help in all sorts. Harry Cresswell looked upon this transformation with an amused smile, but the Colonel saw in it simply evidence of dangerous obstinacy in a black girl who hitherto had refused to work.

Zora had been in the house but a week when a large express package was received from John Taylor. Its unwrapping brought a cry of pleasure from the ladies. There lay a bolt of silken-like cambric of wondrous fineness and lustre, marked: "For the wedding-dress." The explanation accompanied the package, that Mary Taylor had a similar piece in the North.

Helen and Harry said nothing of the cablegram to the Paris tailor, and Helen took no steps toward having the cambric dress made, not even when the wedding invitations appeared.

"A Cresswell married in cotton!" Helen was almost in tears lest the Paris gown be delayed, and sure enough a cablegram came at last saying that there was little likelihood of the gown being ready by Easter. It would be shipped at the earliest convenience, but it could hardly catch the necessary boat. Helen had a good cry, and then came a wild rush to get John Taylor's cloth ready. Still, Helen was querulous. She decided that silk embroidery must embellish the skirt. The dressmaker was in despair.

"I haven't a single spare worker," she declared.

Helen was appealing to Mrs. Vanderpool.

"I can do it," said Zora, who was in the room.

"Do you know how?" asked the dressmaker.

"No, but I want to know."

Mrs. Vanderpool gave a satisfied nod. "Show her," she said. The dressmaker was on the edge of rebellion. "Zora sews beautifully," added Mrs. Vanderpool.

Thus the beautiful cloth came to Zora's room, and was spread in a glossy cloud over her bed. She trembled at its beauty and felt a vague inner yearning, as if some subtle magic of the woven web were trying to tell her its story.

She worked over it faithfully and lovingly in every spare hour and in long nights of dreaming. Wilfully she departed from the set pattern and sewed into the cloth something of the beauty in her heart. In new and intricate ways, with soft shadowings and coverings, she wove in that white veil her own strange soul, and Mrs. Vanderpool watched her curiously, but in silence.

Meantime all things were arranged for a double wedding at Cresswell Oaks. As John and Mary Taylor had no suitable home, they were to come down and the two brides to go forth from the Cresswell mansion. Accordingly the Taylors arrived a week before the wedding and the home took on a festive air. Even Colonel Cresswell expanded under the genial influences, and while his head still protested his heart was glad. He had to respect John Taylor's undoubted ability; and Mary Taylor was certainly lovely, in spite of that assumption of cleverness of which the Colonel could not approve.

Mary returned to the old scenes with mingled feelings. Especially was she startled at seeing Zora a member of the household and apparently high in favor. It brought back something of the old uneasiness and suspicion.

All this she soon forgot under the cadence of Harry Cresswell's pleasant voice and the caressing touch of his arm. He seemed handsomer than ever; and he was, for sleep and temperance and the wooing of a woman had put a tinge in his marble face, smoothed the puffs beneath his eyes, and given him a more distinguished bearing and a firmer hand. And Mary Taylor was very happy. So was her brother, only differently; he was making money; he was planning to make more, and he had something to pet which seemed to him extraordinarily precious and valuable.

Taylor eagerly inquired after the cloth, and followed the ladies to Zora's room, adjoining Mrs. Vanderpool's, to see it. It lay uncut and shimmering, covered with dim silken tracery of a delicacy and beauty which brought an exclamation to all lips.

"That's what we can do with Alabama cotton," cried John Taylor in triumph.

They turned to him incredulously.

"But—"

"No 'buts' about it; these are the two bales you sent me, woven with a silk woof." No one particularly noticed that Zora had hastily left the room. "I had it done in Easterly's New Jersey mills according to an old plan of mine. I'm going to make cloth like that right in this county some day," and he chuckled gayly.

But Zora was striding up and down the halls, the blood surging in her ears. After they were gone she came back and closed the doors. She dropped on her knees and buried her face in the filmy folds of the Silver Fleece.

"I knew it! I knew it!" she whispered in mingled tears and joy. "It called and I did not understand."

It was her talisman new-found; her love come back, her stolen dream come true. Now she could face the world; God had turned it straight again. She would go into the world and find—not Love, but the thing greater than Love. Outside the door came voices—the dressmaker's tones, Helen's soft drawl, and Mrs. Vanderpool's finished accents. Her face went suddenly gray. The Silver Fleece was not hers! It belonged— She rose hastily. The door opened and they came in. The cutting must begin at once, they all agreed.

"Is it ready, Zora?" inquired Helen.

"No," Zora quietly answered, "not quite, but tomorrow morning, early." As soon as she was alone again, she sat down and considered. By and by, while the family was at lunch, she folded the Silver Fleece carefully and locked it in her new trunk. She would hide it in the swamp. During the afternoon she sent to town for oil-cloth, and bade the black carpenter at Miss Smith's make a cedar box, tight and tarred. In the morning she prepared Mrs. Vanderpool's breakfast with unusual care. She was sorry for Mrs. Vanderpool, and sorry for Miss Smith. They would not, they could not, understand. What would happen to her? She did not know; she did not care. The Silver Fleece had returned to her. Soon it would be buried in the swamp whence it came. She had no alternative; she must keep it and wait.

She heard the dressmaker's voice, and then her step upon the stair. She heard the sound of Harry Cresswell's buggy, and a scurrying at the front door. On came the dressmaker's footsteps—then her door was unceremoniously burst open.

Helen Cresswell stood there radiant; the dressmaker, too, was wreathed in smiles. She carried a big red-sealed bundle.

"Zora!" cried Helen in ecstasy. "It's come!" Zora regarded her coldly, and stood at bay. The dressmaker was ripping and snipping, and soon there lay revealed before them—the Paris gown!

Helen was in raptures, but her conscience pricked her. She appealed to them. "Ought I to tell? You see, Mary's gown will look miserably common beside it."

The dressmaker was voluble. There was really nothing to tell; and besides, Helen was a Cresswell and it was to be expected, and so forth. Helen pursed her lips and petulantly tapped the floor with her foot.

"But the other gown?"

"Where is it?" asked the dressmaker, looking about. "It would make a pretty morning-dress—"

But Helen had taken a sudden dislike to the thought of it.

"I don't want it," she declared. "And besides, I haven't room for it in my trunks."

Of a sudden she leaned down and whispered to Zora: "Zora, hide it and keep it if you want it. Come," to the dressmaker, "I'm dying to try this on—now. . . . Remember, Zora—not a word." And all this to Zora seemed no surprise; it was the Way, and it was opening before her because the talisman lay in her trunk.

So at last it came to Easter morning. The world was golden with jasmine, and crimson with azalea; down in the darker places gleamed the misty glory of the dogwood; new cotton shook, glimmered, and blossomed in the black fields, and over all the soft Southern sun poured its awakening light of life. There was happiness and hope again in the cabins, and hope and—if not happiness, ambition, in the mansions.

Zora, almost forgetting the wedding, stood before the mirror. Laying aside her dress, she draped her shimmering cloth about her, dragging her hair down in a heavy mass over ears and neck until she seemed herself a bride. And as she stood there, awed with the mystical union of a dead love and a living new born self, there came drifting in at the window, faintly, the soft sound of far-off marriage music.

"'Tis thy marriage morning, shining in the sun!"

Two white and white-swathed brides were coming slowly down the great staircase of Cresswell Oaks, and two white and black-clothed bridegrooms awaited them. Either bridegroom looked gladly at the flow of his sister's garments and almost darkly at his bride's. For Helen was decked in Parisian splendor, while Mary was gowned in the Fleece.

"'Tis thy marriage morning, shining in the sun!"

Up floated the song of the little dark-faced children, and Zora listened.

Twenty-two

MISS CAROLINE WYNN

B les Alwyn was seated in the anteroom of Senator Smith's office in Washington. The Senator had not come in yet, and there were others waiting, too.

The young man sat in a corner, dreaming. Washington was his first great city, and it seemed a never-ending delight—the streets, the buildings, the crowds; the shops, and lights, and noise; the kaleidoscopic panorama of a world's doing, the myriad forms and faces, the talk and laughter of men. It was all wonderful magic to the country boy, and he stretched his arms and filled his lungs and cried: "Here I shall live!"

Especially was he attracted by his own people. They seemed transformed, revivified, changed. Some might be mistaken for field hands on a holiday—but not many. Others he did not recognize—they seemed strange and alien—sharper, quicker, and at once more overbearing and more unscrupulous.

There were yet others—and at the sight of these Bles stood straighter and breathed like a man. They were well dressed, and well appearing men and women, who walked upright and looked one in the eye, and seemed like persons of affairs and money. They had arrived—they were men—they filled his mind's ideal—he felt like going up to them and grasping their hands and saying, "At last, brother!" Ah, it was good to find one's dreams, walking in the light, in flesh and blood. Continually such thoughts were surging through his brain, and they were rioting through it again as he sat waiting in Senator Smith's office.

The Senator was late this morning; when he came in he glanced at the morning paper before looking over his mail and the list of his callers. "Do fools like the American people deserve salvation?" he sneered, holding off the headlines and glancing at them.

"'League Beats Trust.' . . . 'Farmers of South Smash Effort to Bear Market . . . Send Cotton to Twelve Cents . . . Common People Triumph.'

"A man is induced to bite off his own nose and then to sing a pæan of victory. It's nauseating—senseless. There is no earthly use striving for such blockheads; they'd crucify any Saviour." Thus half consciously Senator Smith salved his conscience, while he extracted a certificate of deposit for fifty thousand dollars from his New York mail. He thrust it aside from his secretary's view and looked at his list as he rang the bell: there was Representative Todd, and somebody named Alwyn—nobody of importance. Easterly was due in a half-hour. He would get rid of Todd meantime.

"Poor Todd," he mused; "a lamb for the slaughter."

But he patiently listened to him plead for party support and influence for his bill to prohibit gambling in futures.

"I was warned that it was useless to see you, Senator Smith, but I would come. I believe in you. Frankly, there is a strong group of your old friends and followers forming against you; they met only last night, but I did not go. Won't you take a stand on some of these progressive matters—this bill, or the Child Labor movement, or Low Tariff legislation?"

Mr. Smith listened but shook his head.

"When the time comes," he announced deliberately, "I shall have something to say on several of these matters. At present I can only say that I cannot support this bill," and Mr. Todd was ushered out. He met Mr. Easterly coming in and greeted him effusively. He knew him only as a rich philanthropist, who had helped the Neighborhood Guild in Washington—one of Todd's hobbies.

Easterly greeted Smith quietly.

"Got my letter?"

"Yes."

"Here are the three bills. You will go on the Finance Committee to-morrow; Sumdrich is chairman by courtesy, but you'll have the real power. Put the Child Labor Bill first, and we'll work the press. The Tariff will take most of the session, of course. We'll put the cotton inspection bill through in the last days of the session—see? I'm manœuvring to get the Southern Congressmen into line. . . . Oh, one thing. Thompson says he's a little worried about the Negroes; says there's something more than froth in the talk of a bolt in the Northern Negro vote. We may have to give them a little extra money and a few more minor offices than usual. Talk with Thompson; the Negroes are sweet on you and he's going to be the new chairman of the campaign, you know. Ever met him?"

"Yes."

"Well—so long."

"Just a moment," the statesman stayed the financier.

"Todd just let fall something of a combination against us in Congress—know anything of it?"

"Not definitely; I heard some rumors. Better see if you can run it down. Well, I must hurry—good day."

While Bles Alwyn in the outer office was waiting and musing, a lady came in. Out of the corner of his eye he caught the curve of her gown, and as she seated herself beside him, the suggestion of a faint perfume. A vague resentment rose in him. Colored women would look as well as that, he argued, with the clothes and wealth and training. He paused, however, in his thought: he did not want them like the whites—so cold and formal and precise, without heart or marrow. He started up, for the secretary was speaking to him.

"Are you the—er—the man who had a letter to the Senator?"

"Yes, sir."

"Let me see it. Oh, yes—he will see you in a moment."

Bles was returning the letter to his pocket when he heard a voice almost at his ear.

"I beg your pardon—"

He turned and started. It was the lady next to him, and she was colored! Not extremely colored, but undoubtedly colored, with waving black hair, light brown skin, and the fuller facial curving of the darker world. And yet Bles was surprised, for everything else about her—her voice, her bearing, the set of her gown, her gloves and shoes, the whole impression was—Bles hesitated for a word—well, "white."

"Yes—yes, ma'am," he stammered, becoming suddenly conscious that the lady had now a second time asked him if he was acquainted with Senator Smith. "That is, ma'am,"—why was he saying "ma'am," like a child or a servant?—"I know his sister and have a letter for him."

"Do you live in Washington?" she inquired.

"No—but I want to. I've been trying to get in as a clerk, and I haven't succeeded yet. That's what I'm going to see Senator Smith about."

"Have you had the civil-service examinations?"

"Yes. I made ninety-three in the examination for a treasury clerkship."

"And no appointment? I see—they are not partial to us there."

Bles was glad to hear her say "us."

She continued after a pause:

"May I venture to ask a favor of you?"

"Certainly," he responded.

"My name is Wynn," lowering her voice slightly and leaning toward him. "There are so many ahead of me and I am in a hurry to get to my school; but I must see the Senator—couldn't I go in with you? I think I might be of service in this matter of the examination, and then perhaps I'd get a chance to say a word for myself."

"I'd be very glad to have you come," said Bles, cordially.

The secretary hesitated a little when the two started in, but Miss Wynn's air was so quietly assured that he yielded.

Senator Smith looked at the tall, straight black man with his smooth skin and frank eyes. And for a second time that morning a vision of his own youth dimmed his eyes. But he spoke coldly:

"Mr. Alwyn, I believe."

"Yes, sir."

"And—"

"My friend, Miss Wynn."

The Senator glanced at Miss Wynn and she bowed demurely. Then he turned to Alwyn.

"Well, Mr. Alwyn, Washington is a bad place to start in the world."

Bles looked surprised and incredulous. He could conceive of no finer starting-place, but he said nothing.

"It is a grave," continued the Senator, "of ambitions and ideals. You would far better go back to Alabama"—pausing and looking at the young man keenly—"but you won't—you won't—not yet, at any rate." And Bles shook his head slowly.

"No—well, what can I do for you?"

"I want work—I'll do anything."

"No, you'll do one thing—be a clerk, and then if you have the right stuff in you you will throw up that job in a year and start again."

"I'd like at least to try it, sir."

"Well, I can't help you much there; that's in civil-service, and you must take the examination."

"I have, sir."

"So? Where, and what mark?"

"In the Treasury Department; I got a mark of ninety-three."

"What!—and no appointment?" The Senator was incredulous.

"No, sir; not yet."

Here Miss Wynn interposed.

"You see, Senator," she said, "civil-service rules are not always impervious to race prejudice."

The Senator frowned.

"Do you mean to intimate that Mr. Alwyn's appointment is held up because he is colored?"

"I do."

"Well—well!" The Senator rang for a clerk.

"Get me the Treasury on the telephone."

In a moment the bell rang.

"I want Mr. Cole. Is that you, Mr. Cole? Good-morning. Have you a young man named Alwyn on your eligible list? What? Yes?" A pause. "Indeed? Well, why has he no appointment? Of course, I know, he's a Negro. Yes, I desire it very much—thank you."

"You'll get an appointment to-morrow morning," and the Senator rose. "How is my sister?" he asked absently.

"She was looking worried, but hopeful of the new endowment when I left." The Senator held out his hand; Bles took it and then remembered.

"Oh, I beg pardon, but Miss Wynn wanted a word on another matter."

The Senator turned to Miss Wynn.

"I am a school-teacher, Senator Smith, and like all the rest of us I am deeply interested in the appointment of the new school-board."

"But you know the district committee attends to those things," said the Senator hastily. "And then, too, I believe there is talk of abolishing the school-board and concentrating power in the hands of the superintendent."

"Precisely," said Miss Wynn. "And I came to tell you, Senator Smith, that the interests which are back of this attack upon the schools are no friends of yours." Miss Wynn extracted from her reticule a typewritten paper.

He took the paper and read it intently. Then he keenly scrutinized the young woman, and she steadily returned his regard.

"How am I to know this is true?"

"Follow it up and see."

He mused.

"Where did you get these facts?" he asked suddenly.

She smiled.

"It is hardly necessary to say."

"And yet," he persisted, "if I were sure of its source I would know my ground better and—my obligation to you would be greater."

She laughed and glanced toward Alwyn. He had moved out of earshot and was waiting by the window.

"I am a teacher in the M Street High School," she said, "and we have some intelligent boys there who work their way through."

"Yes," said the Senator.

"Some," continued Miss Wynn, tapping her boot on the carpet, "some—wait on table."

The Senator slowly put the paper in his pocket.

"And now," he said, "Miss Wynn, what can I do for you?"

She looked at him.

"If Judge Haynes is reappointed to the school-board I shall probably continue to teach in the M Street High School," she said slowly.

The Senator made a memorandum and said:

"I shall not forget Miss Wynn—nor her friends." And he bowed, glancing at Alwyn.

The woman contemplated Bles in momentary perplexity, then bowing in turn, left. Bles followed, debating just what he ought to say, how far he might venture to accompany her, what—but she easily settled it all.

"I thank you—good-bye," she said briefly at the door, and was gone. Bles did not know whether to feel relieved or provoked, or disappointed, and by way of compromise felt something of all three.

The next morning he received notice of his appointment to a clerkship in the Treasury Department, at a salary of nine hundred dollars. The sum seemed fabulous and he was in the seventh heaven. For many days the consciousness of wealth, the new duties, the street scenes, and the city life kept him more than busy. He planned to study, and arranged with a professor at Howard University to guide him. He bought an armful of books and a desk, and plunged desperately to work.

Gradually as he became used to the office routine, and in the hours when he was weary of study, he began to find time hanging a little heavily on his hands; indeed—although he would not acknowledge it—he was getting lonesome, homesick, amid the myriad men of a busy city. He argued to himself that this was absurd, and yet he knew that he was longing for human companionship. When he looked about him for fellowship he found himself in a strange dilemma: those black folk in whom he recognized the old sweet-tempered Negro traits, had also looser, uglier manners than he was accustomed to, from which he shrank. The upper classes of Negroes, on the other hand, he still observed from afar; they were strangers not only in acquaintance but because of a curious coldness and aloofness that made them cease to seem his own kind; they seemed almost at times like black white people—strangers in way and thought.

He tried to shake off this feeling but it clung, and at last in sheer desperation, he promised to go out of a night with a fellow clerk who rather boasted of the "people" he knew. He was soon tired of the strange company, and had turned to go home, when he met a new-comer in the doorway.

"Why, hello, Sam! Sam Stillings!" he exclaimed delightedly, and was soon grasping the hand of a slim, well-dressed man of perhaps thirty, with yellow face, curling hair, and shifting eyes.

"Well, of all things, Bles—er—ah—Mr. Alwyn! Thought you were hoeing cotton."

Bles laughed and continued shaking his head. He was foolishly glad to see the former Cresswell butler, whom he had known but slightly. His face brought back unuttered things that made his heart beat faster and a yearning surge within him.

"I thought you went to Chicago," cried Bles.

"I did, but goin' into politics—having entered the political field, I came here. And you graduated, I suppose, and all that?"

"No," Bless admitted a little sadly, as he told of his coming north, and of Senator Smith's influence. "But—but how are—all?"

Abruptly Sam hooked his arm into Alwyn's and pulled him with him down the street. Stillings was a type. Up from servility and menial service he was struggling to climb to money and power. He was shrewd, willing to stoop to anything in order to win. The very slights and humiliations of prejudice he turned to his advantage. When he learned all the particulars of Alwyn's visit to Senator Smith and his cordial reception he judged it best to keep in touch with this young man, and he forthwith invited Bles to accompany him the next night to the Fifteenth Street Presbyterian Church.

"You'll find the best people there," he said; "the aristocracy. The Treble Clef gives a concert, and everybody that's anybody will be there."

They met again the following evening and proceeded to the church. It was a simple but pleasant auditorium, nearly filled with well-dressed people. During the programme Bles applauded vociferously every number that pleased him, which is to say, every one—and stamped his feet, until he realized that he was attracting considerable attention to himself. Then the entertainment straightway lost all its charm; he grew painfully embarrassed, and for the remainder of the evening was awkwardly self-conscious. When all was over, the audience rose leisurely and stood in little knots and eddies, laughing and talking; many moved forward to say a word to the singers and players. Stillings stepped aside to a group of men, and Bles was left miserably alone. A man came to him, a white-faced man, with slightly curling close gray hair, and high-bred ascetic countenance.

"You are a stranger?" he asked pleasantly, and Bles liked him.

"Yes, sir," he answered, and they fell to talking. He discovered that this was the pastor of the church.

"Do you know no one in town?"

"One or two of my fellow clerks and Mr. Stillings. Oh, yes, I've met Miss Wynn."

"Why, here is Miss Wynn now."

Bles turned. She was right behind him, the centre of a group. She turned, slowly, and smiled.

"Oh!" she uttered twice, but with difference cadence. Then something like amusement lurked a moment in her eye, and she quietly presented Bles to her friends, while Stillings hovered unnoticed in the offing:

"Miss Jones—Mr. Alwyn of—" she paused a second—"Alabama. Miss Taylor—Mr. Alwyn—and," with a backward curving of her neck, "Mr. Teerswell," and so on. Mr. Teerswell was handsome and indolent, with indecision in his face and a cynical voice. In a moment Bles felt the subtle antagonism of the group. He was an intruder. Mr. Teerswell nodded easily and turned away, continuing his conversation with the ladies.

But Miss Wynn was perverse and interrupted. "I saw you enjoyed the concert, Mr. Alwyn," she said, and one of the young ladies rippled audibly. Bles darkened painfully, realizing that these people must have been just behind him. But he answered frankly:

"Yes, I did immensely—I hope I didn't disturb you; you see, I'm not used to hearing such singing."

Mr. Teerswell, compelled to listen, laughed drily.

"Plantation melodies, I suppose, are more your specialty," he said with a slight cadence.

"Yes," said Bles simply. A slight pause ensued.

Then came the surprise of the evening for Bles Alwyn. Even his inexperienced eye could discern that Miss Wynn was very popular, and that most of the men were rivals for her attentions.

"Mr. Alwyn," she said graciously, rising. "I'm going to trouble you to see me to my door; it's only a block. Good-night, all!" she called, but she bowed to Mr. Teerswell.

Miss Wynn placed her hand lightly on Bles's arm, and for a moment he paused. A thrill ran through him as he felt again the weight of a little hand and saw beside him the dark beautiful eyes of a girl. He felt again the warm quiver of her body. Then he awoke to the lighted church and the moving, well-dressed throng. The hand on his arm was not so small; but it was well-gloved, and somehow the fancy struck him that it was a cold hand and not always sympathetic in its touch.

Twenty-three

THE TRAINING OF ZORA

I did not know the world was so large," remarked Zora as she and Mrs. Vanderpool flew east and northward on the New York–New Orleans limited. For a long time the girl had given herself up to the sheer delight of motion. Gazing from the window, she compared the lands she passed with the lands she knew: noting the formation of the cotton; the kind and growth of the trees; the state of the roads. Then the comparisons became infinite, endless; the world stretched on and on until it seemed mere distance, and she suddenly realized how vast a thing it was and spoke.

Mrs. Vanderpool was amused. "It's much smaller than one would think," she responded.

When they came to Atlanta Zora stared and wrinkled her brows. It was her first large city. The other towns were replicas of Toomsville; strange in number, not in kind; but this was different, and she could not understand it. It seemed senseless and unreasonable, and yet so strangely so that she was at a loss to ask questions. She was very solemn as they rode on and night came down with dreams.

She awoke in Washington to new fairylands and wonders; the endless going and coming of men; great piles that challenged heaven, and homes crowded on homes till one could not believe that they were full of living things. They rolled by Baltimore and Philadelphia, and she talked of every-day matters: of the sky which alone stood steadfast amid whirling change; of bits of empty earth that shook themselves here and there loose from their burden of men, and lay naked in the cold shining sunlight.

All the while the greater questions were beating and curling and building themselves back in her brain, and above all she was wondering why no one had told her before of all this mighty world. Mrs. Vanderpool, to whom it seemed too familiar for comment, had said no word; or, if she had spoken, Zora's ears had not been tuned to understand; and as they flew toward the towering ramparts of New York, she sat up big with the terror of a new thought: suppose this world were full yet of things she did not know nor dream of? How could she find out? She must know.

When finally they were settled in New York and sat high up on the Fifth Avenue front of the hotel, gradually the inarticulate questioning found words, albeit strange ones.

"It reminds me of the swamp," she said.

Mrs. Vanderpool, just returned from a shopping tour, burst into laughter.

"It is—but I marvel at your penetration."

"I mean, it is moving—always moving."

"The swamp seemed to me unearthly still."

"Yes—yes," cried Zora, eagerly, brushing back the rumpled hair; "and so did the city, at first, to me."

"Still! New York?"

"Yes. You see, I saw the buildings and forgot the men; and the buildings were so tall and silent against Heaven. And then I came to see the people, and suddenly I knew the city was like the swamp, always restless and changing."

"And more beautiful?" suggested Mrs. Vanderpool, slipping her arms into her lounging-robe.

"Oh, no; not nearly so beautiful. And yet—more interesting." Then with a puzzled look: "I wonder why?"

"Perhaps because it's people and not things."

"It's people in the swamp," asserted Zora, dreamily, smoothing out the pillows of the couch, " 'little people,' I call them. The difference is, I think, that there I know how the story will come out; everything is changing, but I know how and why and from what and to what. Now here, *every*thing seems to be happening; but what is it that *is* happening?"

"You must know what has happened, to know what may happen," said Mrs. Vanderpool.

"But how *can* I know?"

"I'll get you some books to-morrow."

"I'd like to know what it means," wistfully.

"It is meaningless." The woman's cynicism was lost upon Zora, of course, but it possessed the salutary effect of stimulating the girl's thoughts, encouraging her to discover for herself.

"I think not; so much must mean something," she protested.

Zora gathered up the clothes and things and shaded the windows, glancing the while down on the street.

"Everybody is going, going," she murmured. "I wonder where. Don't they ever get there?"

"Few arrive," said Mrs. Vanderpool. Zora softly bent and passed her cool soft hand over her forehead.

"Then why do they go?"

"The zest of the search, perhaps."

"No," said Zora as she noiselessly left the room and closed the door; "no, they are searching for something they have lost. Perhaps they, too, are searching for the Way," and the tears blinded her eyes.

Mrs. Vanderpool lay in the quiet darkened room with a puzzled smile on her lips. A month ago she had not dreamed that human interest in anybody would take so strong a hold upon her as her liking for Zora had done. She was a woman of unusual personal charm, but her own interest and affections were seldom stirred. Had she been compelled to earn a living she would have made a successful teacher or manipulator of men. As it was, she viewed the human scene with detached and cynical interest. She had no children, few near relations, a husband who went his way and still was a gentleman.

Essentially Mrs. Vanderpool was unmoral. She held the code of her social set with sportsmanlike honor; but even beyond this she stooped to no intrigue, because none interested her. She had all the elements of power save the motive for doing anything in particular. For the first time, perhaps, Zora gave her life a peculiar human interest. She did not love the girl, but she was intensely interested in her; some of the interest was selfish, for Zora was going to be a perfect maid. The girl's language came to be more and more like Mrs. Vanderpool's; her dress and taste in adornment had been Mrs. Vanderpool's first care, and it led to a curious training in art and sense of beauty until the lady now and then found herself learner before the quick suggestiveness of Zora's mind.

When Mrs. Harry Cresswell called a month or so later the talk naturally included mention of Zora. Mary was happy and vivacious, and noted the girl's rapid development.

"I wonder what I shall make out of her?" queried Mrs. Vanderpool. "Do you know, I believe I could mould her into a lady if she were not black."

Mary Cresswell laughed. "With that hair?"

"It has artistic possibilities. You should have seen my hair-dresser's face when I told her to do it up. Her face and Zora's were a pantomime for the gods. Yet it was done. It lay in some great twisted cloud and in that black net gown of mine Zora was simply magnificent. Her form is perfect, her height is regal, her skin is satin, and my jewels found a resting place at last. Jewels, you know, dear, were never meant for white folk. I was tempted to take her to the box at the opera and let New York break its impudent neck."

Mary was shocked.

"But, Mrs. Vanderpool," she protested, "is it right? Is it fair? Why should you spoil this black girl and put impossible ideas into her head? You can make her a perfect maid, but she can never be much more in America."

"She is a perfect maid now; that's the miracle of it—she's that deft and quick and quiet and thoughtful! The hotel employees think her perfect; my friends rave—really, I'm the most blessed of women. But do you know I like the girl? I—well, I think of her future."

"It's wrong to treat her as you do. You make her an equal. Her room is one of the best and filled with books and bric-a-brac. She sometimes eats with you—is your companion, in fact."

"What of it? She loves to read, and I guide her while she keeps me up on the latest stuff. She can talk much better than many of my friends and then she piques my curiosity: she's a sort of intellectual sauce that stirs my rapidly failing mental appetite. I think that as soon as I can make up my mind to spare her, I'll take her to France and marry her off in the colonies."

"Well, that's possible; but one doesn't easily give up good servants. By the way, I learn from Miss Smith that the boy, Bles Alwyn, in whom Zora was so interested, is a clerk in the Treasury Department at Washington."

"Indeed! I'm going to Washington this winter; I'll look him over and see if he's worth Zora—which I greatly doubt."

Mrs. Cresswell pursed her lips and changed the subject.

"Have you seen the Easterlys?"

"The ladies left their cards—they are quite impossible. Mr. Easterly calls this afternoon. I can't imagine why, but he asked for an appointment. Will you go South with Mr. Cresswell? I'm glad to hear he's entering politics."

"No, I shall do some early house hunting in Washington," said Mrs. Cresswell, rising as Mr. Easterly was announced.

Mr. Easterly was not at home in Mrs. Vanderpool's presence. She spoke a language different from his, and she had shown a disconcerting way, in the few times when he had spoken with her, of letting the weight of the conversation rest on him. He felt very distinctly that Mrs. Vanderpool was not particularly desirous of his company, nor that of his family. Nevertheless, he needed Mrs. Vanderpool's influence just now, and he was willing to pay considerable for it. Once under obligation to him her services would be very valuable. He was glad to find Mrs. Cresswell there. It showed that the Cresswells were still intimate, and the Cresswells were bound to him and his interests by strong ties. He bowed as Mrs. Cresswell left, and then did not beat around the bush because, in this case, he did not know how.

"Mrs. Vanderpool, I need your aid."

Mrs. Vanderpool smiled politely, and murmured something.

"We are, you know, in the midst of a rather warm presidential campaign," continued Mr. Easterly.

"Yes?" with polite interest.

"We are going to win easily, but our majority in Congress for certain matters will depend on the attitude of Southerners and you usually spend the winters in Washington. If, now, you could drop a word here and there—"

"But why should I?" asked Mrs. Vanderpool.

"Mrs. Vanderpool, to be frank, I know some excellent investments that your influence in this line would help. I take it you're not so rich but that—"

Mrs. Vanderpool smiled faintly.

"Really, Mr. Easterly, I know little about such matters and care less. I have food and clothes. Why worry with more?"

Mr. Easterly half expected this and he determined to deliver his last shot on the run. He arose with a disappointed air.

"Of course, Mrs. Vanderpool, I see how it is: you have plenty and one can't expect your services or influence for nothing. It had occurred to me that your husband might like something political; but I presume not."

"Something political?"

"Yes. You see, it's barely possible, for instance, that there will be a change in the French ambassadorship. The present ambassador is old and—well, I don't know, but as I say, it's possible. Of course though, that may not appeal to you, and I can only beg your good offices in charity if—if you see your way to help us. Well, I must be going."

"What is—I thought the President appointed ambassadors."

"To be sure, but we appoint Presidents," laughed Mr. Easterly. "Good-day. I shall hope to see you in Washington."

"Good-day," Mrs. Vanderpool returned absently.

After he had gone she walked slowly to Zora's room and opened the door. For a long time she stood quietly looking in. Zora was curled in a chair with a book. She was in dreamland; in a world of books builded thoughtfully for her by Mrs. Vanderpool, and before that by Miss Smith. Her work took but little of her time and left hours for reading and thinking. In that thought-life, more and more her real living centred.

Hour after hour, day after day, she lay buried, deaf and dumb to all else. Her heart cried, up on the World's four corners of the Way, and to it came the Vision Splendid. She gossiped with old Herodotus across the earth to the black and blameless Ethiopians; she saw the sculptured glories of Phidias marbled amid the splendor of the swamp; she listened to Demosthenes and walked the Appian Way with Cornelia—while all New York streamed beneath her window.

She saw the drunken Goths reel upon Rome and heard the careless Negroes yodle as they galloped to Toomsville. Paris, she knew,—wonderful, haunting Paris: the Paris of Clovis, and St. Louis; of Louis the Great, and Napoleon III; of Balzac, and her own Dumas. She tasted the mud and comfort of thick old London, and the while wept with Jeremiah and sang with Deborah, Semiramis, and Atala. Mary of Scotland and Joan of Arc held her dark hands in theirs, and Kings lifted up their sceptres.

She walked on worlds, and worlds of worlds, and heard there in her little room the tread of armies, the paeans of victory, the breaking of hearts, and the music of the spheres.

Mrs. Vanderpool watched her a while.

"Zora," she presently broke into the girl's absorption, "how would you like to be Ambassador to France?"

Twenty-four

THE EDUCATION OF ALWYN

Miss Caroline Wynn of Washington had little faith in the world and its people. Nor was this wholly her fault. The world had dealt cruelly with the young dreams and youthful ambitions of the girl; partly with its usual heartlessness, partly with that cynical and deadening reserve fund which it has today for its darker peoples. The girl had bitterly resented her experiences at first: she was brilliant and well-trained; she had a real talent for sculpture, and had studied considerably; she was sprung from at least three generations of respectable mulattoes, who had left a little competence which yielded her three or four hundred dollars a year. Furthermore, while not precisely pretty, she was good-looking and interesting, and she had acquired the marks and insignia of good breeding. Perhaps she wore her manners just a trifle consciously; perhaps she was a little morbid that she would fail of recognition as a lady. Nor was this unnatural: her brown skin invited a different assumption. Despite this almost unconscious mental aggressiveness, she was unusually presentable and always well-groomed and pleasant of speech. Yet she found nearly all careers closed to her. At first it seemed accidental, the luck of life. Then she attributed it to her sex; but at last she was sure that, beyond chance and womanhood, it was the colorline that was hemming her in. Once convinced of this, she let her imagination play and saw the line even where it did not exist.

With her bit of property and brilliant parts she had had many suitors but they had been refused one after another for reasons she could hardly have explained. For years now Tom Teerswell had been her escort. Whether or not Caroline Wynn would every marry him was a perennial subject of speculation among their friends and it usually ended in the verdict that she could not afford it—that it was financially impossible.

Nevertheless, the two were usually seen in public together, and although she often showed her quiet mastery of the situation, seldom had she snubbed him so openly as at the Treble Clef concert.

Teerswell was furious and began to plot vengeance; but Miss Wynn was attracted by the personality of Bles Alwyn. Southern country Negroes were rare in her set, but here was a man of intelligence and keenness coupled with an amazing frankness and modesty, and perceptibly shadowed by sorrow. The combination was, so far as she had observed, both rare and temporary and she was disposed to watch it in this case purely as a matter of intellectual curiosity. At the door of her home, therefore, after a walk of unusual interest, she said:

"I'm going to have a few friends in next Tuesday night; won't you come, Mr. Alwyn?" And Mr. Alwyn said that he would.

Next morning Miss Wynn rather repented her hasty invitation, but of course nothing could be done now. Nothing? Well, there was one thing; and she went to the telephone. A suggestion to Bles that he might profitably extend his acquaintance sent him to a certain tailor shop kept by a friend of hers; a word to the tailor guarded against the least suspicion of intrigue entering Bles's head.

It turned out quite as Miss Wynn had designed; Mr. Grey, the tailor, gave Bles some points on dressing, and made him, Southern fashion, a frock-coat for dress wear that set off his fine figure. On the night of the gathering at Miss Wynn's Bles dressed with care, hesitating long over a necktie, but at last choosing one which he had recently purchased and which pleased him particularly. He was prompt to the minute and was consequently the first guest; but Miss Wynn's greeting was so quietly cordial that his embarrassment soon fled. She looked him over at leisure and sighed at his tie; otherwise he was thoroughly presentable according to the strictest Washington standard.

They sat down and talked of generalities. Then an idea occurring to her, she conducted the conversation by devious paths to ties and asked Alwyn if he had heard of the fad of collecting ties. He had not, and she showed him a sofa pillow.

"Your tie quite attracted me," she said; "it would make just the dash of color I need in my new pillow."

"You may have it and welcome. I'll send—"

"Oh, no! A bird in the hand, you know. I'll trade with you now for another I have."

"Done!"

The exchange was soon made, Miss Wynn tying the new one herself and sticking a small carved pin in it. Bles slowly sat down again, and after a pause said, "Thank you."

She looked up quickly, but he seemed quite serious and good-natured.

"You see," he explained, "in the country we don't know much about ties."

The well-balanced Miss Wynn for a moment lost her aplomb, but only for a moment.

"We must all learn," she replied with penetration, and so their friendship was established.

The company now began to gather, and soon the double parlor held an assemblage of twenty-five or thirty persons. They formed a picturesque group: conventional but graceful in dress; animated in movement; full of good-natured laughter, but quite un-American in the beautiful modulation of their speaking tones; chiefly noticeable, however, to a stranger, in the vast variety of color in skin, which imparted to the throng a piquant and unusual interest. Every color was here; from the dark brown of Alwyn, who was customarily accounted black, to the pale pink-white of Miss Jones, who could "pass for white" when she would, and found her greatest difficulties when she was trying to "pass" for black. Midway between these two extremes lay the sallow pastor of the church, the creamy Miss Williams, the golden yellow of Mr. Teerswell, the golden brown of Miss Johnson, and the velvet brown of Mr. Grey. The guest themselves did not notice this; they were used to asking one's color as one asks of height and weight; it was simply an extra dimension in their world whereby to classify men.

Beyond this and their hair, there was little to distinguish them from a modern group of men and women. The speech was a softened English, purely and, on the whole, correctly spoken—so much so that it seemed at first almost unfamiliar to Bles, and he experienced again the uncomfortable feeling of being among strangers. Then, too, he missed the loud but hearty good-nature of what he had always called "his people." To be sure, a more experienced observer might have noted a lively, excitable tropical temperament set and cast in a cold Northern mould, and yet flashing fire now and then in a sudden anomalous outbursting. But Bles missed this; he seemed to have slipped and lost his bearings, and the characteristics of his simple world were rolling curiously about. Here stood a black man with a white man's voice, and yonder a white woman with a Negro's musical cadences; and yet again, a brown girl with exactly Miss Cresswell's air, and yonder, Miss Williams, with Zora's wistful willfulness.

Bles was bewildered and silent, and his great undying sorrow sank on his heart with sickening hopeless weight. His hands got in the way, and he found no natural nook in all those wide and tastefully furnished rooms. Once he discovered himself standing by a marble statue of a nude woman, and he edged away; then he stumbled over a rug and saved himself only to step on Miss Jones's silken train. Miss Jones's smile of pardon was wintry. When he did approach a group and listen, they seemed speaking of things foreign to him—usually of people he did not know, their homes, their doings, their daughters and their fathers. They seemed to know people intimately who lived far away.

"You mean the Smiths of Boston?" asked Miss Jones.

"No, of Cleveland. They're not related."

"I heard that McGhee of St. Paul will be in the city next week with his daughter."

"Yes, and the Bentleys of Chicago."

Bles passed on. He was disappointed. He was full of things to say, of mighty matters to discuss; he felt like stopping these people and crying: "Ho! What of the morning? How goes the great battle for black men's rights? I have came with messages from the host, to you who guard the mountain tops."

Apparently they were not discussing or caring about "the Problem." He grew disgusted and was edging toward the door when he encountered his hostess.

"Is all well with you, Mr. Alwyn?" she asked lightly.

"No, I'm not enjoying myself," said Bles, truthfully.

"Delicious! And why not?"

He regarded her earnestly.

"There are so many things to talk about," he said; "earnest things; things of importance. I—I think when our people—" he hesitated.

Our?—was *our* right? But he went on: "When our people meet we ought to talk of our situation, and what to do and—"

Miss Wynn continued to smile.

"We're all talking of it all the time," she said.

He looked incredulous.

"Yes, we are," she insisted. "We veil it a little, and laugh as lightly as we can; but there is only one thought in this room, and that's grave and serious enough to suit even you, and quite your daily topic."

"But I don't understand."

"Ah, there's the rub. You haven't learned our language yet. We don't just blurt into the Negro Problem; that's voted bad form. We leave that to our white friends. We saunter to it sideways, touch it delicately because"—her face became a little graver—"because, you see, it hurts."

Bles stood thoughtful and abashed.

"I—I think I understand," he gravely said at last.

"Come here," she said with a sudden turn, and they joined an absorbed group in the midst of a conversation.

"—Thinking of sending Jessie to Bryn Mawr," Bles heard Miss Jones saying.

"Could she pass?"

"Oh, they might think her Spanish."

"But it's a snobbish place and she would have to give up all her friends."

"Yes, Freddie could scarcely visit—" the rest was lost.

"Which, being interpreted," whispered Miss Wynn, "means that Bryn Mawr draws the color line while we at times surmount it."

They moved on to another group.

"—Splendid draughtsman," a man was saying, "and passed at the head of the crowd; but, of course, he has no chance."

"Why, it's civil-service, isn't it?"

"It is. But what of that? There was Watson—"

Miss Wynn did not pause. She whispered: "This is the tale of Civil

Service Reform, and how this mighty government gets rid of black men who know too much."

"But—" Bles tried to protest.

"Hush," Miss Wynn commanded and they joined the group about the piano. Teerswell, who was speaking, affected not to notice them, and continued:

"—I tell you, it's got to come. We must act independently and not be bought by a few offices."

"That's all well enough for you to talk, Teerswell; you have no wife and babies dependant on you. Why should we who have sacrifice the substance for the shadow?"

"You see, the Judge has got the substance," laughed Teerswell. "Still I insist: divide and conquer."

"Nonsense! Unite, and keep."

Bles was puzzled.

"They're talking of the coming campaign," said Miss Wynn.

"What!" exclaimed Bles aloud. "You don't mean that any one can advise a black man to vote the Democratic ticket?"

An elderly man turned to them.

"Thank you, sir," he said; "that is just my attitude; I fought for my freedom. I know what slavery is; may I forget God when I vote for traitors and slave-holders."

The discussion waxed warm and Miss Wynn turned away and sought Miss Jones.

"Come, my dear," she said, "it's 'The Problem' again." They sauntered away toward a ring of laughter.

The discussion thus begun at Miss Wynn's did not end there. It was on the eve of the great party conventions, and the next night Sam Stillings came around to get some crumbs from this assembly of the inner circle, into which Alwyn had been so unaccountably snatched, and outside of which, despite his endeavors, Stillings lingered and seemed destined to linger. But Stillings was a patient, resolute man beneath his deferential exterior, and he saw in Bles a stepping stone. So he began to drop in at his lodgings and tonight invited him to the Bethel Literary.

"What's that?" asked Bles.

"A debating club—oldest in the city; the best people all attend."

Bles hesitated. He had half made up his mind that this was the proper time to call on Miss Wynn. He told Stillings so, and told him also of the evening and the discussion.

"Why, that's the subject up tonight," Stillings declared, "and Miss Wynn will be sure to be there. You can make your call later. Perhaps you wouldn't mind taking me when you call." Alwyn reached for his hat.

When they arrived, the basement of the great church was filling with a throng of men and women. Soon the officers and the speaker of the evening appeared. The president was a brown woman who spoke easily and well, and introduced the main speaker. He was a tall, thin, hatchet-faced black man, clean shaven and well dressed, a lawyer by profession. His theme was "The Democratic Party and the Negro." His argument was cool, carefully reasoned, and plausible. He was evidently feeling for the sympathy of his audience, and while they were not enthusiastic, they warmed to him gradually and he certainly was strongly impressing them.

Bles was thinking. He sat in the back of the hall, tense, alert, nervous. As the speaker progressed a white man came in and sat down beside him. He was spectacled, with bushy eyebrows and a sleepy look. But he did not sleep. He was very observant.

"Who's speaking?" he asked Bles, and Bles told him. Then he inquired about one or two other persons. Bles could not inform him, but Stillings could and did. Stillings seemed willing to devote considerable time to him.

Bles forgot the man. He was almost crouching for a spring, and no sooner had the speaker, with a really fine apostrophe to independence and reason in voting, sat down, than Bles was on his feet, walking forward. His form was commanding, his voice deep and musical, and his earnestness terribly evident. He hardly waited for recognition from the slightly astonished president, but fairly burst into speech.

"I am from Alabama," he began earnestly, "and I know the Democratic Party." Then he told of government and conditions in the Black Belt, of the lying, oppression, and helplessness of the sodden black masses; then, turning, he reminded them of the history of slavery. Finally, he pointed to Lincoln's picture and to Sumner's and mentioned other white friends.

"And, my brothers, they are not all dead yet. The gentleman spoke of Senator Smith and blamed and ridiculed him. I know Senator Smith but slightly, but I do know his sister well."

Dropping to simple narrative, he told of Miss Smith and of his coming to school; and if his audience felt that great depth of emotion that welled beneath his quiet, almost hesitating, address, it was not simply because of what he did say, but because, too, of the unspoken story that lay too deep for words. He spoke for nearly an hour, and when he stopped, for a moment his hearers sighed and then sprang into a whirlwind of applause. They shouted, clapped, and waved while he sat in blank amazement, and was with difficulty forced to the rostrum to bow again and again. The spectacled white man leaned over to Stillings.

"Who is he?" he asked. Stillings told him. The man noted the name and went quietly out.

Miss Wynn sat lost in thought, and Teerswell beside her fumed. She was not easily moved, but that speech had moved her. If he could thus stir men and not be himself swayed, she mused, he would be— invincible. But tonight he was moved as greatly as his hearers had been, and that was dangerous. If his intense belief happened to be popular, all right; but if not? She frowned. He was worth watching, she concluded; quite worth watching, and perhaps worth guiding.

When Alwyn accompanied her home that night, Miss Wynn set

herself to know him better for she suspected that he might be a coming man. The best preliminary to her purpose was, she knew, to speak frankly of herself, and that she did. She told him of her youth and training, her ambitions, her disappointments. Quite unconsciously her cynicism crept to the fore, until in word and tone she had almost scoffed at many things that Alwyn held true and dear. The touch was too light, the meaning too elusive, for Alwyn to grasp always the point of attack; but somehow he got the distant impression that Miss Wynn had little faith in Truth and Goodness and Love. Vaguely shocked he grew so silent that she noticed it and concluded she had said too much. But he pursued the subject.

"Surely there must be many friends of our race willing to stand for the right and sacrifice for it?"

She laughed unpleasantly, almost mockingly.

"Where?"

"Well—there's Miss Smith."

"She gets a salary, doesn't she?"

"A very small one."

"About as large as she could earn. North, I don't doubt."

"But the unselfish work she does—the utter sacrifice?"

"Oh, well, we'll omit Alabama, and admit the exception."

"Well, here, in Washington—there's your friend, the Judge, who has befriended you so, as you admit."

She laughed again.

"You remember our visit to Senator Smith?"

"Yes."

"Well, it got the Judge his reappointment to the school board."

"He deserved it, didn't he?"

"I deserved it," she said luxuriously, hugging her knee and smiling; "you see, his appointment meant mine."

"Well, what of it—didn't—"

"Listen," she cut in a little sharply. "Once a young brown girl, with boundless faith in white folks, went to a Judge's office to ask for an appointment which she deserved. There was no one there. The benign old Judge with his saintly face and white hair suggested that she lay aside her wraps and spend the afternoon."

Bles arose to his feet.

"What—what did you do?" he asked.

"Sit down—there's a good boy." I said: 'Judge, a friend is expecting me at two,' it was then half-past one, 'would I not best telephone?'"

"'Step right into the booth,' said the Judge, quite indulgently." Miss Wynn leaned back, and Bles felt his heart sinking; but he said nothing. "And then," she continued, "I telephoned the Judge's wife that he was anxious to see her on a matter of urgent business; namely, my appointment." She gazed reflectively out of the window. "You should have seen his face when I told him," she concluded. "I was appointed."

But Bles asked coldly:

"Why didn't you have him arrested?"

"For what? And suppose I had?"

Bles threw out his arms helplessly.

"Oh! it isn't as bad as that all over the world, is it?"

"It's worse," affirmed Miss Wynn, quietly positive.

"And you are still friendly with him?"

"What would you have? I use the world; I did not make it; I did not choose it. He is the world. Through him I earn my bread and butter. I have shown him his place. Shall I try in addition to reform? Shall I make him an enemy? I have neither time nor inclination. Shall I resign and beg, or go tilting at windmills? If he were the only one it would be different; but they're all alike." Her face grew hard. "Have I shocked you?" she said as they went toward the door.

"No," he answered slowly. "But I still—believe in the world."

"You are young yet, my friend," she lightly replied. "And besides, that good Miss Smith has gone and grafted a New England con-science on a tropical heart, and—dear me!—but it's a gorgeous misfit. Good-bye—come again." She bowed him graciously out, and paused to take the mail from the box. There was, among many others, a letter from Senator Smith.

Twenty-five

THE CAMPAIGN

Mr. Easterly sat in Mrs. Vanderpool's apartments in the New Willard, Washington, drinking tea. His hostess was saying rather carelessly:

"Do you know, Mr. Vanderpool has developed a quite unaccountable liking for the idea of being Ambassador to France?"

"Dear me!" mildly exclaimed Mr. Easterly, helping himself liberally to cakes. "I do hope the thing can be managed, but—"

"What are the difficulties?" Mrs. Vanderpool interrupted.

"Well, first and foremost, the difficulty of electing our man."

"I thought that a foregone conclusion."

"It was. But do you know that we're encountering opposition from the most unexpected source?"

The lady was receptive, and the speaker concluded:

"The Negroes."

"The Negroes!"

"Yes. There are five hundred thousand or more black voters in pivotal Northern States, you know, and they're in revolt. In a close election the Negroes of New York, Ohio, Indiana, and Illinois choose the President."

"What's the matter?"

"Well, business interests have driven our party to make friends with the South. The South has disfranchised Negroes and lynched a few. The darkies say we've deserted them."

Mrs. Vanderpool laughed.

"What extraordinary penetration," she cried.

"At any rate," said Mr. Easterly, drily, "Mr. Vanderpool's first step toward Paris lies in getting the Northern Negroes to vote the Republican ticket. After that the way is clear."

Mrs. Vanderpool mused.

"I don't suppose you know any one who is acquainted with any number of these Northern darkies?" continued Mr. Easterly.

"Not on my calling-list," said Mrs. Vanderpool, and then she added more thoughtfully:

"There's a young clerk in the Treasury Department named Alwyn who has brains. He's just from the South, and I happened to read of him this morning—see here."

Mr. Easterly read an account of the speech at the Bethel Literary.

"We'll look this young man up," he decided; "he may help. Of course, Mrs. Vanderpool, we'll probably win; we can buy these Negroes off with a little money and a few small offices; then if you will use your influence for the part with the Southerners, I can confidently predict from four to eight years' sojourn in Paris."

Mrs. Vanderpool smiled and called her maid as Mr. Easterly went.

"Zora!" She had to call twice, for Zora, with widened eyes, was reading the *Washington Post*.

Meantime in the office of Senator Smith, toward which Mr. Easterly was making his way, several members of the National Republican campaign committee had been closeted the day before.

"Now, about the niggers," the chairman had asked; "how much more boodle do they want?"

"That's what's bothering us," announced a member; "it isn't the boodle crowd that's hollering, but a new set, and I don't understand them; I don't know what they represent, nor just how influential they are."

"What can I do to help you?" asked Senator Smith.

"This. You are here at Washington with these Negro office-holders at your back. Find out for us just what this revolt is, how far it goes, and what good men we can get to swing the darkies into line—see?"

"Very good," the Senator acquiesced. He called in a spectacled man with bushy eyebrows and a sleepy look.

"I want you to work the Negro political situation," directed the Senator, "and bring me all the data you can get. Personally, I'm at sea. I don't understand the Negro of today at all; he puzzles me; he doesn't fit any of my categories, and I suspect that I don't fit his. See what you can find out."

The man went out, and the Senator turned to his desk, then paused and smiled. One day, not long since, he had met a colored person who personified his perplexity concerning Negroes; she was a lady, yet she was black—that is, brown; she was educated, even cultured, yet she taught Negroes; she was quiet, astute, quick and diplomatic—everything, in fact, that "Negroes" were not supposed to be; and yet she was a "Negro." She had given him valuable information which he had sought in vain elsewhere, and the event proved it correct. Suppose he asked Caroline Wynn to help him in this case? It would certainly do no harm and it might elect a Republican president. He wrote a short letter with his own hand and sent it to post.

Miss Wynn read the letter after Alwyn's departure with a distinct thrill which was something of a luxury for her. Evidently she was coming to her kingdom. The Republican boss was turning to her for confidential information.

"What do the colored people want, and who can best influence them in this campaign?"

She curled up on the ottoman and considered. The first part of the query did not bother her.

"Whatever they want they won't get," she said decisively.

But as to the man or men who could influence them to believe that they were getting, or about to get, what they wanted—there was a question. One by one she considered the men she knew, and, by a process of elimination, finally arrived at Bles Alwyn.

Why not take this young man in hand and make a Negro leader of him—a protagonist of ten millions? It would not be unpleasant. But could she do it? Would he be amenable to her training and become worldly wise? She flattered herself that he would, and yet—there was a certain steadfast look in the depths of his eyes that might prove to be sheer stubbornness. At any rate, who was better? There was a fellow, Stillings, whom Alwyn had introduced and whom she had heard of. Now he was a politician—but nothing else. She dismissed him. Of course, there was the older set of office-holders and rounders. But she was determined to pick a new man. He was worth trying, at any rate; she knew none other with the same build, the brains, the gifts, the adorable youth. Very good. She wrote two letters, and then curled up to her novel and candy.

Next day Senator Smith held Miss Wynn's letter unopened in his hand when Mr. Easterly entered. They talked of the campaign and various matters, until at last Easterly said:

"Say, there's a Negro clerk in the Treasury named Alwyn."

"I know him—I had him appointed."

"Good. He may help us. Have you seen this?"

The Senator read the clipping.

"I hadn't noticed it—but here's my agent."

The spectacled man entered with a mass of documents. He had papers, posters, programmes, and letters.

"The situation is this," he said. "A small group of educated Negroes are trying to induce the rest to punish the Republican Party for not protecting them. These men are not politicians, nor popular leaders, but they have influence and are using it. The old-style Negro politicians are no match for them, and the crowd of office-holders are rather bewildered. Strong measures are needed. Educated men of earnestness and ability might stem the tide. And I believe I know one such man. He spoke at a big meeting last night at the Metropolitan church. His name is Alwyn."

Senator Smith listened as he opened the letter from Caroline Wynn. Then he started.

"Well!" he ejaculated, looking quickly up at Easterly. "This is positively uncanny. From three separate sources the name of Alwyn pops up. Looks like a mascot. Call up the Treasury. Let's have him up when the sub-committee meets to-morrow."

Bles Alwyn hurried up to Senator Smith's office, hoping to hear something about the school; perhaps even about—but he stopped with a sigh, and sat down in the ante-room. He was kept waiting a few moments while Senator Smith, the chairman, and one other member of the sub-committee had a word.

"Now, I don't know the young man, mind you," said the Senator; "but he's strongly recommended."

"What shall we offer him?" asked the chairman.

"Try him at twenty-five dollars a speech. If he balks, raise to fifty dollars, but no more."

They summoned the young man. The chairman produced cigars.

"I don't smoke," said Bles apologetically.

"Well, we haven't anything to drink," said the chairman. But Senator Smith broke in, taking up at once the paramount interest.

"Mr. Alwyn, as you know, the Democrats are making an effort to get the Negro vote in this campaign. Now, I know the disadvantages and wrongs which black men in this land are suffering. I believe the Republicans ought to do more to defend them, and I'm satisfied they will; but I doubt if the way to get Negro rights is to vote for those who took them away."

"I agree with you perfectly," said Bles.

"I understand you do, and that you made an unusually fine speech on the subject the other night."

"Thank you, sir." This was a good deal more than Bles had expected, and he was embarrassed.

"Well, now, we think you're just the man to take the stump during September and October and convince the colored people of their real interests."

"I doubt if I could, sir; I'm not a speaker. In fact, that was my first public speech."

"So much the better. Are you willing to try?"

"Why, yes, sir; but I could hardly afford to give up my position."

"We'll arrange for a leave of absence."

"Then I'll try, sir."

"What would you expect as pay?"

"I suppose my salary would stop?"

"I mean in addition to that."

"Oh, nothing, sir; I'd be glad to do the work."

The chairman nearly choked; sitting back, he eyed the young man. Either they were dealing with a fool, or else a very astute politician. If the former, how far could they trust him; if the latter, what was his game?

"Of course, there'll be considerable travelling," the chairman ventured, looking reflectively out of the window.

"Yes, sir, I suppose so."

"We might pay the railroad fare."

"Thank you, sir. When shall I begin?"

The chairman consulted his calendar.

"Suppose you hold yourself in readiness for one week from today."

"All right," and Bles rose. "Good-day, gentlemen."

But the chairman was still puzzled.

"Now, what's his game?" he asked helplessly.

"He may be honest," offered Senator Smith, contemplating the door almost wistfully.

The campaign progressed. The National Republican Committee said little about the Negro revolt and affected to ignore it. The papers were silent. Underneath this calm, however, the activity was redoubled. The prominent Negroes were carefully catalogued, written to, and put under personal influence. The Negro papers were quietly subsidized, and they began to ridicule and reproach the new leaders.

As the Fall progressed, mass-meetings were held in Washington and the small towns. Larger and larger ones were projected, and more and more Alwyn was pushed to the front. He was developing into a most effective speaker. He had the voice, the presence, the ideas, and above all he was intensely in earnest. There were other colored orators with voice, presence, and eloquence; but their people knew their record and discounted them. Alwyn was new, clear, and sincere, and the black folk hung on his words. Large and larger crowds greeted him until he was the central figure in a half dozen great negro mass-meetings in the chief cities of the country, culminating in New York the night before election. Perhaps the secret newspaper work, the personal advice of employers and friends, and the liberal distribution of cash, would have delivered a large part of the Negro vote to the Republican candidate. Perhaps—but there was a doubt. With the work of Alwyn, however, all doubt disappeared, and there was little reason for denying that the new President walked into the White House through the instrumentality of an unknown Georgia Negro, little past his majority. This is what Senator Smith said to Mr. Easterly; what Miss Wynn said to herself; and it was what Mrs. Vanderpool remarked to Zora as Zora was combing her hair on the Wednesday after election.

Zora murmured an indistinct response. As already something of the beauty of the world had found question and answer in her soul, and as she began to realize how the world had waxed old in thought and stature, so now in their last days a sense of the power of men, as set over against the immensity and force of their surroundings, became real to her. She had begun to read of the lives and doing of those called great, and in her mind a plan was forming. She saw herself standing dim within the shadows, directing the growing power of a man: a man who would be great as the world counted greatness, rich, high in position, powerful—wonderful because his face was black. He would never see her; never know how she worked and planned, save perhaps at last, in that supreme moment as she passed, her soul would cry to his, "Redeemed!" And he would understand.

All this she was thinking and weaving; not clearly and definitely, but in great blurred clouds of thought of things as she said slowly:

"He should have a great position for this."

"Why, certainly," Mrs. Vanderpool agreed, and then curiously: "What?"

Zora considered. "Negroes," she said, "have been Registers of the Treasury, and Recorders of Deeds here in Washington, and Douglas was Marshal; but I want Bles—" she paused and started again. "Those are not great enough for Mr. Alwyn; he should have an office so important that Negroes would not think of leaving their party again."

Mrs. Vanderpool took pains to repeat Zora's words to Mr. Easterly. He considered the matter.

"In one sense, it's good advice," he admitted; "but there's the South to reckon with. I'll think it over and speak to the President. Oh, yes; I'm going to mention France at the same time."

Mrs. Vanderpool smiled and leaned back in her carriage. She noted with considerable interest the young colored woman who was watching her from the sidewalk: a brown, well-appearing young woman of notable self-possession. Caroline Wynn scrutinized Mrs. Vanderpool because she had been speaking with Mr. Easterly, and Mr. Easterly was a figure of political importance. That very morning Miss Wynn had telegraphed Bles Alwyn. Alwyn arrived at Washington just as the morning papers heralded the sweeping Republican victory. All about he met new deference and new friends; strangers greeted him familiarly on the street; Sam Stillings became his shadow; and when he reported for work his chief and fellow clerks took unusual interest in him.

"Have you seen Senator Smith yet?" Miss Wynn asked after a few words of congratulation.

"No. What for?"

"What for?" she answered. "Go to him today; don't fail. I shall be at home at eight tonight."

It seemed to Bles an exceedingly silly thing to do—calling on a busy man with no errand; but he went. He decided that he would just thank the Senator for his interest, and get out; or, if the Senator was busy, he would merely send in his card. Evidently the Senator was busy, for his waiting-room was full. Bles handed the card to the secretary with a word of apology, but the secretary detained him.

"Ah, Mr. Alwyn," he said affably; "glad to see you. The Senator will want to see you, I know. Wait just a minute." And soon Bles was shaking Senator Smith's hand.

"Well, Mr. Alwyn," said the Senator heartily, "you delivered the goods."

"Thank you, sir. I tried to."

Senator Smith thoughtfully looked him over and drew out the letters.

"Your friends, Mr. Alwyn," he said, adjusting his glasses, "have a rather high opinion of you. Here now is Stillings, who helped on the campaign. He suggests an eighteen-hundred-dollar clerkship for you." The Senator glanced up keenly and omitted to state what Stillings suggested for himself. Alwyn was visibly grateful as well as surprised.

"I—I hoped," he began hesitatingly, "that perhaps I might get a promotion, but I had not thought of a first-class clerkship."

"H'm." Senator Smith leaned back and twiddled his thumbs, staring at Alwyn until the hot blood darkened his cheeks. Then Bles sat up and stared politely but steadily back. The Senator's eyes dropped and he put out his hand for the second note.

"Now, your friend, Miss Wynn"—Alwyn started—"is even more ambitious. He handed her letter to the young man, and pointed out the words.

"Of course, Senator," Bles read, "we expect Mr. Alwyn to be the next Register of the Treasury."

Bles looked up in amazement, but the Senator reached for a third letter. The room was very still. At last he found it. "This," he announced quietly, "is from a man of great power and influence, who has the ear of the new President." He smoothed out the letter, paused briefly, then read aloud:

"'It has been suggested to me by'"—the Senator did not read the name; if he had "Mrs. Vanderpool" would have meant little to Alwyn—"'It has been suggested to me by *blank* that the future allegiance of the Negro vote to the Republican Party might be insured by giving to some prominent Negro a high political position—for instance, Treasurer of the United States'—salary, six thousand dollars," interpolated Senator Smith—"'and that Alwyn would be a popular and safe appointment for that position.'"

The Senator did not read the concluding sentence, which ran: "Think this over; we can't touch political conditions in the South; perhaps this sop will do."

For a long time Alwyn sat motionless, while the Senator said nothing. Then the young man rose unsteadily.

"I don't think I quite grasp all this," he said as he shook hands. "I'll think it over," and he went out.

When Caroline Wynn heard of that extraordinary conversation her amazement knew no bounds. Yet Alwyn ventured to voice doubts:

"I'm not fitted for either of those high offices; there are many others who deserve more, and I don't somehow like the idea of seeming to have worked hard in the campaign simply for money or fortune. You see, I talked against that very thing."

Miss Wynn's eyes widened.

"Well, what else—" she began and then changed. "Mr. Alwyn, the line between virtue and foolishness is dim and wavering, and I should hate to see you lost in that marshy borderland. By a streak of extraordinary luck you have gained the political leadership of Negroes in America. Here's your chance to lead your people, and here you stand blinking and hesitating. Be a man!"

Alwyn straightened up and felt his doubts going. The evening passed very pleasantly.

"I'm going to have a little dinner for you," said Miss Wynn finally, and Alwyn grew hot with pleasure. He turned to her suddenly and said:

"Why, I'm rather—black." She expressed no surprise but said reflectively:

"You *are* dark."

"And I've been given to understand that Miss Wynn and her set rather—well, preferred the lighter shades of colored folk."

Miss Wynn laughed lightly.

"My parents did," she said simply. "No dark man ever entered their house; they were simply copying the white world. Now I, as a matter of aesthetic beauty, prefer your brown-velvet color to a jaundiced yellow, or even an uncertain cream; but the world doesn't."

"The world?"

"Yes, the world; and especially America. One may be Chinese, Spaniard, even Indian—anything white or dirty white in this land, and demand decent treatment; but to be Negro or darkening toward it unmistakably means perpetual handicap and crucifixion."

"Why not, then, admit that you draw the color-line?"

"Because I don't; but the world does. I am not prejudiced as my parents were, but I am foresighted. Indeed, it is a deep ethical query, is it not, how far one has the right to bear black children to the world in the Land of the Free and the home of the brave. Is it fair—to the children?"

"Yes, it is!" he cried vehemently. "The more to take up the fight, the surer the victory."

She laughed at his earnestness.

"You are refreshing," she said. "Well, we'll dine next Tuesday, and we'll have the cream of our world to meet you."

He knew that this was a great triumph. It flattered his vanity. After all, he was entering this higher dark world whose existence had piqued and puzzled him so long. He glanced at Miss Wynn beside him there in the dimly lighted parlor: she looked so aloof and unapproachable, so handsome and so elegant. He thought how she would complete a house—such a home as his prospective four or six thousand dollars a year could easily purchase. She saw him surveying her, and she smiled at him.

"I find but one fault with you," she said.

He stammered for a pretty speech, but did not find it before she continued:

"Yes—you are so delightfully primitive; you will not use the world as it is but insist on acting as if it were something else."

"I am not sure I understand."

"Well, there is the wife of my Judge: she is a fact in my world; in yours she is a problem to be stated, straightened, and solved. If she had come to you, as she did to me yesterday, with her theory that all that Southern Negroes needed was to learn how to make good servants and lay brick—"

"I should have shown her—" Bles tried to interject.

"Nothing of the sort. You would have *tried* to show her and would have failed miserably. She hasn't learned anything in twenty years."

"But surely you didn't join her in advocating that ten million people be menials?"

"Oh, no; I simply listened."

"Well, there was no harm in that; I believe in silence at times."

"Ah! but I did not listen like a log, but positively and eloquently; with a nod, a half-formed word, a comment begun, which she finished."

Bles frowned.

"As a result," continued Miss Wynn, "I have a check for five hundred dollars to finish our cooking-school and buy a cast of Minerva for the assembly-room. More than that, I have now a wealthy friend. She thinks me an unusually clever person who, by a process of thought not unlike her own, has arrived at very similar conclusions."

"But—but," objected Bles, "if the time spent cajoling fools were used in convincing the honest and upright, think how much we would gain."

"Very little. The honest and upright are a sad minority. Most of these white folk—believe me, boy," she said caressingly,—"are fools and knaves: they don't want truth or progress; they want to keep niggers down."

"I don't believe it; there are scores, thousands, perhaps millions such, I admit; but the average American loves justice and right, and he is the one to whom I appeal with frankness and truth. Great heavens! don't you love to be frank and open?"

She narrowed her eyelids.

"Yes, sometimes I do; once I was; but it's a luxury few of us Negroes can afford. Then, too, I insist that it's jolly to fool them."

"Don't you hate the deception?"

She chuckled and put her head to one side.

"At first I did; but, do you know, now I believe I prefer it."

He looked so horrified that she burst out laughing. He laughed too.

She was a puzzle to him. He kept thinking what a mistress of a mansion she would make.

"Why do you say these things?" he asked suddenly.

"Because I want you to do well here in Washington."

"General philanthropy?"

"No, special." Her eyes were bright with meaning.

"Then you care—for me?"

"Yes."

He bent forward and cast the die.

"Enough to marry me?"

She answered very calmly and certainly:

"Yes."

He leaned toward her. And then between him and her lips a dark and shadowy face; two great storm-swept eyes looked into his out of a world of infinite pain, and he dropped his head in hesitation and shame, and kissed her hand. Miss Wynn thought him delightfully bashful.

Twenty-six

CONGRESSMAN CRESSWELL

The election of Harry Cresswell to Congress was a very simple matter. The Colonel and his son drove to town and consulted the Judge; together they summoned the sheriff and the local member of the State legislature.

"I think it's about time that we Cresswells asked for a little of the political pie," the Colonel smilingly opened.

"Well, what do you want?" asked the Judge.

"Harry wants to go to Congress."

The Judge hesitated. "We'd half promised that to Caldwell," he objected.

"It will be a little costly this year, too," suggested the sheriff, tentatively.

"About how much?" asked the Colonel.

"At least five thousand," said the Legislator.

The Colonel said nothing. He simply wrote a check and the matter was settled. In the Fall Harry Cresswell was declared elected. There were four hundred and seventy-two votes cast but the sheriff added a cipher. He said it would look better.

Early December found the Cresswells domiciled in a small house in Du Pont Circle, Washington. They had an automobile and four servants, and the house was furnished luxuriously. Mary Taylor Cresswell, standing in her morning room and looking out on the flowers of the square, told herself that few people in the world had cause to be as happy as she. She was tastefully gowned, in a way to set off her blonde beauty and her delicate rounded figure. She was surrounded with wealth, and above all, she was in that atmosphere of aristocracy for which she had always yearned; and already she was acquiring that poise of the head, and a manner of directing the servants, which showed her born to the purple.

She had cause to be extremely happy, she told herself this morning, and yet she was puzzled to understand why she was not. Why was she restless and vaguely ill at ease so often these days?

One matter, indeed, did worry her; but that would right itself in time, she was sure. She had always pictured herself as directing her husband's work. She did not plan to step in and demand a share; she knew from experience with her brother that a woman must prove her usefulness to a man before he will admit it, and even then he may be silent. She intended gradually and tactfully to relieve her husband of care connected with his public life so that, before he realized it, she would be his guiding spirit and his inspiration. She had dreamed the details of doing this so long that it seemed already done, and she could imagine no obstacle to its realization. And yet she found herself today no nearer her goal than when first she married. Not because Mr. Cresswell did not share his work, but because, apparently, he had no work, no duties, no cares. At first, in the dim glories of the honeymoon, this seemed but part of his delicate courtesy toward her, and it pleased her despite her thrifty New England nature; but now that they were settled in Washington, the election over and Congress in session, it really seemed time for Work and Life to begin in dead earnest, and New England Mary was dreaming mighty dreams and golden futures.

But Harry apparently was as content as ever with doing nothing. He arose at ten, dined at seven, and went to bed between midnight and sunrise. There was some committee meetings and much mail, but Mary was admitted to knowledge of none of these. The obvious step, of course, would be to set him at work; but from this undertaking Mary unconsciously recoiled. She had already recognized that while her tastes and her husband's were mostly alike, they were also strikingly different in many respects. They agreed in the daintiness of things, the elegance of detail; but they did not agree always as to the things themselves. Given the picture, they would choose the same frame— but they would not choose the same picture. They liked the same voice, but not the same song; the same company, but not the same conversation. Of course, Mary reflected, frowning at the flowers—of course, this must always be so when two human beings are thrown into new and intimate association. In time they would grow to sweet communion; only, she hoped the communion would be on tastes nearer hers than those he sometimes manifested.

She turned impatiently from the window with a feeling of loneliness. But why lonely? She idly fingered a new book on the table and then put it down sharply. There had been several attempts at reading aloud between them some evenings ago, and this book reminded her of them. She had bought Jane Addams' "Newer Ideals of Peace," and he had yawned over it undisguisedly. Then he had brought this novel, and—well, she had balked at the second chapter, and he had kissed her and called her his "little prude." She did not want to be a prude; she hated to seem so, and had for some time prided herself on emancipation from narrow New England prejudices. For example, she had not

objected to wine at dinner; it had seemed indeed rather fine, impart-
ing, as it did, an old-fashioned flavor; but she did not like the whiskey,
and Harry at times appeared to become just a bit too lively—nothing
excessive, of course, but his eyes and the smell and the color were a little too suggestive. And yet he was so kind and good, and when he came
in at evening he bent so gallantly for his kiss, and laid fresh flowers before her: could anything have been more thoughtful and knightly?

Just here again she was puzzled; with her folk, hard work and inflexible duty were of prime importance; they were the rock foundation;
and she somehow had always counted on the courtesies of life as added
to them, making them sweet and beautiful. But in this world, not perhaps so much with Harry as with others of his set, the depths beneath
the gravely inclined head, the deferential smile and ceremonious action, the light clever converse, had sounded strangely hollow once or
twice when she had essayed to sound them, and a certain fear to look
and see possessed her.

The bell rang, and she was a little startled at the fright that struck
her heart. She did not analyze it. In reality—pride forbade her to admit
it—she feared it was a call of some of Harry's friends: some languid,
assured Southern ladies, perilously gowned, with veiled disdain for
this interloping Northerner and her strong mind. Especially was there
one from New Orleans, tall and dark—

But it was no caller. It was simply some one named Stillings to see
Mr. Cresswell. She went down to see him—he might be a constituent—
and found a smirky brown man, very apologetic.

"You don't know me—does you, Mrs. Cresswell?" said Stillings. He
knew when it was diplomatic to forget his grammar and assume his
dialect.

"Why—no."

"You remember I worked for Mr. Harry and served you-all lunch
one day."

"Oh, yes—why, yes! I remember now very well."

"Well, I wants to see Mr. Harry very much; could I wait in the back hall?"

Mary started to have him wait in the front hall, but she thought better of it and had him shown back. Less than an hour later her husband entered and she went quickly to him. He looked worn and white and tired, but he laughed her concern lightly off.

"I'll be in earlier tonight," he declared.

"Is the Congressional business very heavy?"

He laughed so hilariously that she felt uncomfortable, which he observed.

"Oh, no," he answered deftly; "not very." And as they moved toward the dining-room Mary changed the subject.

"Oh," she exclaimed, suddenly remembering. "There is a man—a colored man—waiting to see you in the back hall, but I guess he can wait until after lunch."

They ate leisurely.

"There's going to be racing out at the park this evening," said Harry. "Want to go?"

"I was going to hear an art lecture at the Club," Mary returned, and grew thoughtful; for here walked her ghost again. Of course, the Club was an affair with more of gossip than of intellectual effort, but today, largely through her own suggestion, an art teacher of European reputation was going to lecture, and Mary preferred it to the company of the race track. And—just as certainly—her husband didn't.

"Don't forget the man, dear," she reminded him; but he was buried in his paper, frowning.

"Look at that," he said finally. She glanced at the head-lines— "Prominent Negro Politician Candidate for High Office at Hands of New Administration. B. Alwyn of Alabama."

"Why, it's Bles!" she said, her face lighting as his darkened.

"An impudent Negro," he voiced his disgust. "If they must appoint darkies why can't they get tractable ones like my nigger Stillings."

"Stillings?" she repeated. "Why, he's the man that's waiting."

"Sam, is it? Used to be one of our servants—you remember? Wants to borrow more money, I presume." He went down-stairs, after first helping himself to a glass of whiskey, and then gallantly kissing his wife. Mrs. Cresswell was more unsatisfied than usual. She could not help feeling that Mr. Cresswell was treating her about as he treated his wine—as an indulgence; a loved one, a regular one, but somehow not as the reality and prose of life, unless—she started at the thought—his life was all indulgence. Having nothing else to do, she went out and paraded the streets, watching the people who were happy enough to be busy.

Cresswell and Stillings had a long conference, and when Stillings hastened away he could not forbear cutting a discreet pigeon-wing as he rounded the corner. He had been promised the backing of the whole Southern delegation in his schemes.

That night Teerswell called on him in his modest lodgings, where over hot whiskey and water they talked.

"The damned Southern upstart," growled Teerswell, forgetting Stillings' birth-place. "Do you mean to say he's actually slated for the place?"

"He's sure of it, unless something turns up."

"Well, who'd have dreamed it?" Teerswell mixed another stiff dram.

"And that isn't all," came Sam Stillings' unctuous voice.

Teerswell glanced at him. "What else?" he asked, pausing with the steaming drink poised aloft.

"If I'm not mistaken, Alwyn intends to marry Miss Wynn."

"You lie!" the other suddenly yelled with an oath, overturning his tumbler and striding across the floor. "Do you suppose she'd look at that black—"

"Well, see here," said the astute Stillings, checking the details upon his fingers. "They visit Senator Smith's together; he takes her home from the Treble Clef; they say he talked to nobody else at her party; she recommends him for the campaign—"

"What!" Teerswell again exploded. But Stillings continued smoothly:

"Oh, I have ways of finding things out. She corresponds with him during the campaign; she asks Smith to make him Register; and he calls on her every night."

Teerswell sat down limply.

"I see," he groaned. "It's all up. She's jilted me—and I—and I—"

"I don't see as it's all up yet," Stillings tried to reassure him.

"But didn't you say they were engaged?"

"I think they are; but—well, you know Carrie Wynn better than I do: suppose, now—suppose he should lose the appointment?"

"But you say that's sure."

"Unless something turns up."

"But what *can* turn up?"

"We might turn something."

"What—what—I tell you man, I'd—I'd do anything to down that nigger. I hate him. If you'll help me I'll do anything for you."

Stillings arose and carefully opening the hall door peered out. Then he came back and, seating himself close to Teerswell, pushed aside the whiskey.

"Teerswell," he whispered, "you know I was working to be Register of the Treasury. Well, now, when the scheme of making Alwyn Treasurer came up they determined to appoint a Southern white Republican and give me a place under Alwyn. Now, if Alwyn fails to land I've got no chance for the bigger place, but I've got a good chance to be Register according to the first plan. I helped in the campaign; I've got the Negro secret societies backing me and—I don't mind telling you— the solid Southern Congressional delegation. I'm trying now ostensibly for a chief-clerkship under Bles, and I'm pretty sure of it: it pays twenty-five hundred. See here: if we can make Bles do some fool talking and get it into the papers, he'll be ditched, and I'll be Register."

"Great!" shouted Teerswell.

"Wait—wait. Now, if I get the job, how would you like to be my assistant?"

"Like it? Why, great Jehoshaphat! I'd marry Carrie—but how can I help you?"

"This way. I want to be better known among influential Negroes. You introduce me and let me make myself solid. Especially I must get in Miss Wynn's set so that both of us can watch her and Alwyn, and make her friends ours."

"I'll do it—shake!" And Stillings put his oily hand into Teerswell's nervous grip.

"Now, here," Stillings went on, "you stow all that jealousy and heavy tragedy. Treat Alwyn well and call on Miss Wynn as usual—see?"

"It's a hard pill—but all right."

"Leave the rest to me; I'm hand in glove with Alwyn. I'll put stuff into him that'll make him wave the bloody shirt at the next meeting of the Bethel Literary—see? Then I'll go to Cresswell and say, 'Dangerous nigger—, just as I told you.' He'll begin to move things. You see? Cresswell is in with Smith—both directors in the big Cotton Combine—and Smith will call Alwyn down. Then we'll think further."

"Stillings, you look like a fool, but you're a genius." And Teerswell fairly hugged him. A few more details settled, and some more whiskey consumed, and Teerswell went home at midnight in high spirits. Stillings looked into the glass and scowled.

"Look like a fool, do I?" he mused. "Well, I ain't!"

Congressman Cresswell was stirred to his first political activity by the hint given him through Stillings. He not only had a strong personal dislike for Alwyn, but he regarded the promise to him of a high office as a menace to the South.

The second speech which Alwyn made at the Bethel Literary was, as Stillings foresaw, a reply to the stinging criticisms of certain colored papers engineered by Teerswell, who said that Alwyn had been bribed to remain loyal to the Republicans by a six thousand dollar office. Alwyn had been cut to the quick, and his reply was a straight out defence of Negro rights and a call to the Republican Party to redeem its pledges.

Caroline Wynn, seeing the rocks for which her political craft was headed, adroitly steered several newspaper reports into the waste basket, but Stillings saw to it that a circumstantial account was in the *Colored American,* and that a copy of this paper was in Congressman Cresswell's hands. Cresswell lost no time in calling on Senator Smith and pointing out to him that Bles Alwyn was a dangerous Negro: seeking social equality, hating white people, and scheming to make trouble. He was too young and heady. It would be fatal to give such a man office and influence; fatal for the development of the South, and bad for the Cotton Combine.

Senator Smith was unconvinced. Alwyn struck him as a well-balanced fellow, and he thought he deserved the office. He would, however, warn him to make no further speeches like that of last night. Cresswell mentioned Stillings as a good, inoffensive Negro who knew his place and could be kept track of.

"Stillings is a good man," admitted Smith; "but Alwyn is better. However, I'll bear what you say in mind."

Cresswell found Mr. Easterly in Mrs. Vanderpool's parlor, and that gentleman was annoyed at the news.

"I especially picked out this Alwyn because he was Southern and tractable, and seemed to have sense enough to know how to say well what we wanted to say."

"When, as a matter of fact," drawled Mrs. Vanderpool, "he was simply honest."

"The South won't stand it," Cresswell decisively affirmed.

"Well—" began Mr. Easterly.

"See here," interrupted Mrs. Vanderpool. "I'm interested in Alwyn; in fact, an honest man in politics, even if he is black, piques my curiosity. Give him a chance and I'll warrant he'll develop all the desirable traits of a first class office-holder."

Easterly hesitated. "We must not offend the South, and we must placate the Negroes," he said.

"The right sort of Negro—one like Stillings—appointed to a reasonable position, would do both," opined Cresswell.

"It evidently didn't," Mrs. Vanderpool interjected.

Cresswell arose. "I tell you, Mr. Easterly, I object—it mustn't go through." He took his leave.

Mrs. Vanderpool did not readily give up her plea for Alwyn, and bade Zora get Mr. Smith on the telephone for discussion.

"Well," reported Easterly, hanging up the receiver, "we may land him. It seems that he is engaged to a Washington school-teacher, and Smith says she has him well in hand. She's a pretty shrewd proposition, and understands that Alwyn's only chance now lies in keeping his mouth shut. We may land him," he repeated.

"Engaged!" gasped Mrs. Vanderpool.

Zora quietly closed the door.

Twenty-seven

THE VISION OF ZORA

How Zora found the little church she never knew; but somehow, in the long dark wanderings which she had fallen into the habit of taking at nightfall, she stood one evening before it. It looked warm, and she was cold. It was full of her people, and she was very, very lonely. She sat in a back seat, and saw with unseeing eyes. She said again, as she had said to herself a hundred times, that it was all right and just what she had expected. What else could she have dreamed? That he should ever marry her was beyond possibility; that had been settled long since—there where the tall, dark pines, wan with the shades of evening, cast their haunting shadows across the Silver Fleece and half hid the blood-washed west. After *that* he would marry some one else, of course; some good and pure woman who would help and uplift and serve him.

She had dreamed that she would help—unknown, unseen—and

perhaps she had helped a little through Mrs. Vanderpool. It was all right, and yet why so suddenly had the threads of life let go? Why was she drifting in vast waters; in uncharted wastes of sea? Why was the puzzle of life suddenly so intricate when but a little week ago she was reading it, and its beauty and wisdom and power were thrilling her delighted hands? Could it be possible that all unconsciously she had dared dream a forbidden dream? No, she had always rejected it. When no one else had the right; when no one thought; when no one cared, she had hovered over his soul as some dark guardian angel; but now, now somebody else was receiving his gratitude. It was all right, she supposed; but she, the outcast child of the swamp, what was there for her to do in the great world—her, the burden of whose sin—

But then came the voice of the preacher: *"Behold the Lamb of God, that taketh away the sin of the world."*

She found herself all at once intently listening. She had been to church many times before, but under the sermons and ceremonies she had always sat coldly inert. In the South the cries, contortions, and religious frenzy left her mind untouched; she did not laugh or mock, she simply sat and watched and wondered. At the North, in the white churches, she enjoyed the beauty of wall, windows, and hymn, liked the voice and surplice of the preacher; but his words had no reference to anything in which she was interested. Here suddenly came an earnest voice addressed, by singular chance, to her of all the world.

She listened, bending forward, her eyes glued to the speaker's lips and letting no word drop. He had the build and look of the fanatic: thin to emancipation; brown; brilliant-eyed; his words snapped in nervous energy and rang in awful earnestness.

"Life is sin, and sin is sorrow. Sorrow is born of selfishness and self-seeking—our own good, our own happiness, our own glory. As if any one of us were worth a life! No, never. A single self as an end is, and ought to be, disappointment; it is too low; it is nothing. Only in a whole world of selves, infinite, endless, eternal world on worlds of selves—only in their vast good is true salvation. The good of others is our true good; work for others; not for *your* salvation, but the salvation of the world." The audience gave a low uneasy groan and the minister in whose pulpit the stranger preached stirred uneasily. But he went on tensely, with flying words:

"Unselfishness is sacrifice—Jesus was supreme sacrifice." ("Amen," screamed a voice.) "In your dark lives," he cried, "*who* is the King of Glory? Sacrifice. Lift up your heads, then, ye gates of prejudice and hate, and let the King of Glory come in. Forget yourselves and your petty wants, and behold your starving people. The wail of black millions sweeps the air—east and west they cry, Help! Help! Are you dumb? Are you blind? Do you dance and laugh, and hear and see not? The cry of death is in the air; they murder, burn, and maim us!" ("Oh—oh—" moaned the people swaying in their seats.) "When we cry they mock us; they ruin our women and debauch our children—what shall we do?

"Behold the Lamb of God that taketh away sin. Behold the Supreme Sacrifice that makes us clean. Give up your pleasures; give up your wants; give up all to the weak and wretched of our people. Go down to Pharaoh and smite him in God's name. Go down to the South where we writhe. Strive—work—build—hew—lead—inspire! God calls. Will you hear? Come to Jesus. The harvest is waiting. Who will cry: 'Here am I, send me!'"

Zora rose and walked up the aisle; she knelt before the altar and answered the call: "Here am I—send me."

And then she walked out. Above her sailed the same great stars; around her hummed the same hoarse city; but within her soul sang some new song of peace.

"What is the matter, Zora?" Mrs. Vanderpool inquired, for she seemed to see in the girl's face and carriage some subtle change; something that seemed to tell how out of the dream had stepped the dreamer into the realness of things; how suddenly the seeker saw; how to the wanderer, the Way was opened.

Just how she sensed this Mrs. Vanderpool could not have explained, nor could Zora. Was there a change, sudden, cataclysmic? No. There were to come in future days all the old doubts and shiverings, the old restless cry: "It is all right—all right!" But more and more, above the doubt and beyond the unrest, rose the great end, the mighty ideal, that flickered and wavered, but ever grew and waxed strong, until it became possible, and through it all things else were possible. Thus from the grave of youth and love, amid the soft, low singing of dark and bowed worshippers, the Angel of the Resurrection rolled away the stone.

"What is the matter, Zora?" Mrs. Vanderpool repeated.

Zora looked up, almost happily—standing poised on her feet as if to tell of strength and purpose.

"I have found the Way," she cried joyously.

Mrs. Vanderpool gave her a long searching look.

"Where have you been?" she asked. "I've been waiting."

"I'm sorry—but I've been—converted." And she told her story.

"Pshaw, Zora!" Mrs. Vanderpool uttered impatiently. "He's a fakir."

"Maybe," said Zora serenely and quietly; "but he brought the Word."

"Zora, don't talk cant; it isn't worthy of your intelligence."

"It was more than intelligent—it was true."

"Zora—listen, child! You were wrought up tonight, nervous—wild. You were happy to meet your people, and where he said one word you supplied two. What you attribute to him is the voice of your own soul."

But Zora merely smiled. "All you say may be true. But what does it matter? I know one thing, like the man in the Bible: 'Whereas I was blind now I see.'"

Mrs. Vanderpool gave a little helpless gesture. "And what shall you do?" she asked.

"I'm going back South to work for my people."

"When?" The old careworn look stole across Mrs. Vanderpool's features.

Zora came gently forward and slipped her arms lovingly about the other woman's neck.

"Not right off," she said gently; "not until I learn more. I hate to leave you, but—it calls!"

Mrs. Vanderpool held the dark girl close and began craftily:

"You see, Zora, the more you know the more you can do."

"Yes."

"And if you are determined I will see that you are taught. You must know settlement-work and reform movements; not simply here but—" she hesitated—"in England—in France."

"Will it take long?" Zora asked, smoothing the lady's hair.

Mrs. Vanderpool considered. "No—five years is not long; it is all too short."

"Five years: it is very long; but there is a great deal to learn. Must I study five years?"

Mrs. Vanderpool threw back her head.

"Zora, I am selfish I know, but five years truly is none too long. Then, too, Zora, we have work to do in that time."

"What?"

"There is Alwyn's career," and Mrs. Vanderpool looked into Zora's eyes.

The girl did not shrink, but she paused.

"Yes," she said slowly, "we must help him."

"And after he rises—"

"He will marry."

"Whom?"

"The woman he loves," returned Zora, quietly.

"Yes—that is best," sighed Mrs. Vanderpool. "But how shall we help him?"

"Make him Treasurer of the United States without sacrificing his manhood or betraying his people."

"I can do that," said Mrs. Vanderpool slowly.

"It will cost something," said Zora.

"I will do it," was the lady's firm assurance. Zora kissed her.

The next afternoon Mrs. Cresswell went down to a white social settlement of which Congressman Todd had spoken, where a meeting of the Civic Club was to be held. She had come painfully to realize that if she was to have a career she must make it for herself. The plain, unwelcome truth was that her husband had no great interests in life in which she could find permanent pleasure. Companionship and love there was and, she told herself, always would be; but in some respects their lives must flow in two streams. Last night, for the second time, she had irritated him; he had spoken almost harshly to her, and she knew she must brood or work today. And so she hunted work, eagerly.

She felt the atmosphere the moment she entered. There were carelessly gowned women and men smart and shabby, but none of them were thinking of clothes nor even of one another. They had great deeds in mind; they were scanning the earth; they were toiling for men. The same grim excitement that sends smaller souls hunting for birds and rabbits and lions, had sent them hunting the enemies of mankind: they were bent to the chase, scenting the game, knowing the infinite meaning of their hunt and the glory of victory. Mary Cresswell had listened but a half hour before her world seemed so small and sordid and narrow, so trivial, that a sense of shame spread over her. These people were not only earnest, but expert. They acknowledged the need of Mr. Todd's educational bill.

"But the Republicans are going to side-track it; I have that on the best authority," said one.

"True; but can't we force them to it?"

"Only by political power, and they've just won a campaign."

"They won it by Negro votes, and the Negro who secured the votes is eager for this bill; he's a fine, honest fellow."

"Very well; work with him; and when we can be of real service let us know. Meantime, this Child Labor bill is different. It's bound to pass. Both parties are back of it, and public opinion is aroused. Now our work is to force amendments enough to make the bill effective."

Discussion followed; not flamboyant and declamatory, but tense, staccato, pointed. Mrs. Cresswell found herself taking part. Someone mentioned her name, and one or two glances of interest and even curiosity were thrown her way. Congressmen's wives were rare at the Civic Club.

Congressmen Todd urged Mrs. Cresswell to stay after the discussion and attend a meeting of the managers and workers of the Washington social settlements.

"Have you many settlements?" she inquired.

"Three in all—two white and one colored."

"And will they all be represented?"

"Yes, of course, Mrs. Cresswell. If you object to meeting the colored people—"

Mrs. Cresswell blushed.

"No, indeed," she answered; "I used to teach colored people."

She watched this new group gather: a business man, two fashionable ladies, three college girls, a gray-haired colored woman, and a young spectacled brown man, and then, to her surprise, Mrs. Vanderpool and Zora.

Zora was scarcely seated when that strange sixth sense of hers told her that something had happened, and it needed but a side-glance from Mrs. Vanderpool to indicate what it was. She sat with folded hands and the old dreamy look in her eyes. In one moment she lived it all again—the red cabin, the moving oak, the sowing of the Fleece, and its fearful reaping. And now, when she turned her head, she would see the woman who was to marry Bles Alwyn. She had often dreamed of her, and had set a high ideal. She wanted her to be handsome, well dressed, earnest and good. She felt a sort of person proprietorship in her, and when at last the quickened pulse died to its regular healthy beat, she turned and looked and knew.

Caroline Wynn deemed it a part of the white world's education to participate in meetings like this; doing so was not pleasant, but it appealed to her cynicism and mocking sense of pleasure. She always roused hostility as she entered: her gown was too handsome, her gloves too spotless, her air had hauteur enough to be almost impudent in the opinion of most white people. Then gradually her intelligence, her cool wit and self-possession, would conquer and she would go gracefully out leaving a rather bewildered audience behind. She sat today with her dark gold profile toward Zora, and the girl looked and was glad. She was such a woman she would have Bles marry. She was glad, and she choked back the sob that struggled and fought in her throat.

The meeting never got beyond a certain constraint. The Congressman made an excellent speech; there were various sets of figures read by the workers; and Miss Wynn added a touch of spice by several pertinent questions and comments. Then, as the meeting broke up and Mrs. Cresswell came forward to speak to Zora, Mrs. Vanderpool managed to find herself near Miss Wynn and to be introduced. They exchanged a few polite phrases, fencing delicately to test the other's wrist and interest. They touched on the weather, and settlement work; but Miss Wynn did not propose to be stranded on the Negro problem.

"I suppose the next bit of excitement will be in the inauguration," she said to Mrs. Vanderpool.

"I understand it will be unusually elaborate," returned Mrs. Vanderpool, a little surprised at the turn. Then she added pleasantly: "I think I shall see it through, from speech to ball."

"Yes, I do usually," Miss Wynn asserted, adjusting her furs.

Mrs. Vanderpool was further surprised. Did colored people attend the ball?

"We sorely need a national ball-room," she said. "Isn't the census building wretched?"

"I do not know," smiled Miss Wynn.

"Oh, I thought you said—"

"I meant *our* ball."

"Oh!" said Mrs. Vanderpool in turn. "Oh!" Here a thought came. Of course, the colored people had their own ball; she remembered having heard about it. Why not send Zora? She plunged in:

"Miss Wynn, I have a maid—such an intelligent girl; I do wish she could attend your ball—" seeing her blunder, she paused. Miss Wynn was coolly buttoning her glove.

"Yes," she acknowledged politely, "few of us can afford maids, and therefore we do not usually arrange for them; but I think we can have your *protégée* look on from the gallery. Good-afternoon."

As Mrs. Vanderpool drove home she related the talk to Zora. Zora was silent at first. Then she said deliberately:

"Miss Wynn was right."

"Why, Zora!"

"Did Helene attend the ball four years ago?"

"But, Zora, must you folk ape our nonsense as well as our sense?"

"You force us to," said Zora.

Twenty-eight

THE ANNUNCIATION

The new President had been inaugurated. Beneath the creamy pile of the old Capitol, and facing the new library, he had stood aloft and looked down on a waving sea of faces—black-coated, jostling, eager-eyed fellow creatures. They had watched his lips move, had scanned eagerly his dress and the gowned and decorated dignitaries beside him; and then, with blare of band and prancing of horses, he had been whirled down the dip and curve of that long avenue, with its medley of meanness and thrift and hurry and wealth, until, swinging sharply, the dim walls of the White House rose before him. He entered with a sigh.

Then the vast welter of humanity dissolved and streamed hither and thither, gaping and laughing until night, when thousands poured into the red barn of the census shack and entered the artificial fairyland within. The President walked through, smiling; the senators protected their friends in the crush; and Harry Cresswell led his wife to a little oasis of Southern ladies and gentlemen.

"This is democracy for you," said he, wiping his brow.

From a whirling eddy Mrs. Vanderpool waved at them, and they rescued her.

"I think I am ready to go," she gasped. "Did you ever!"

"Come," Cresswell invited. But just then the crowd pushed them apart and shot them along, and Mrs. Cresswell found herself clinging to her husband amid two great whirling variegated throngs of driving, white-faced people. The band crashed and blared; the people laughed and pushed; and with rhythmic sound and swing the mighty throng was dancing.

It took much effort, but at last the Cresswell party escaped and rolled off in their carriages. They swept into the avenue and out again, then up 14th Street, where, turning for some street obstruction, they passed a throng of carriages on a cross street.

"It's the other ball," cried Mrs. Vanderpool, and amid laughter she added, "Let's go!"

It was—the other ball. For Washington is itself, and something else besides. Along beside it ever runs that dark and haunting echo; that shadowy world-in-world with its accusing silence, its emphatic self-sufficiency. Mrs. Cresswell at first demurred. She thought of Elspeth's cabin: the dirt, the smell, the squalor: of course, this would be different; but—well, Mrs. Cresswell had little inclination for slumming. She was interested in the under-world, but intellectually, not by personal contact. She did not know that this was a side-world, not an under-world. Yet the imposing building did not look sordid.

"Hired?" asked some one.

"No, owned."

"Indeed!"

Then there was a hitch.

"Tickets?"

"Where can we buy them?"

"Not on sale," was the curt reply.

"Actually exclusive!" sneered Cresswell, for he could not imagine any one unwelcome at a Negro ball. Then he bethought himself of Sam Stillings and sent for him. In a few minutes he had a dozen complimentary tickets in his hand.

They entered the balcony and sat down. Mary Cresswell leaned forward. It was interesting. Beneath her was an ordinary pretty ball—flowered, silked, and ribboned; with swaying whirling figures, music, and laughter, and all the human fun of gayety and converse.

And then she was impressed with the fact that this was no ordinary scene; it was, on the contrary, most extraordinary.

There was a black man waltzing with a white woman—no, she was not white, for Mary caught the cream and curl of the girl as she swept past: but there was a white man (was he white?) and a black woman. The color of the scene was wonderful. The hard human white seemed to glow and live and run a mad gamut of the spectrum, from morn till night, from white to black; through red and sombre browns, pale and brilliant yellows, dead and living blacks. Through her opera-glasses Mary scanned their hair; she noted everything from the infinitely twisted, crackled, dead, and grayish-black to the piled mass of red golden sunlight. Her eyes went dreaming; there below was the gathering of the worlds. She saw types of all nations and all lands swirling beneath her in human brotherhood, and a great wonder shook her. They seemed so happy. Surely, this was no nether world; it was upper earth, and—her husband beckoned; he had been laughing incontinently. He saw nothing but a crowd of queer looking people doing things they were not made to do and appearing absurdly happy over it. It irritated him unreasonably.

"See the washer-woman in red," he whispered. "Look at the monkey. Come, let's go."

They trooped noisily down-stairs, and Cresswell walked unceremoniously between a black man and his partner. Mrs. Vanderpool recognized and greeted the girl as Miss Wynn. Mrs. Cresswell did not notice her, but she paused with a start of recognition at the sight of the man.

"Why, Bles!" she exclaimed impetuously, starting to hold out her hand. She was sincerely pleased at seeing him. Then she remembered. She bowed and smiled, looking at him with interest and surprise. He was correctly dressed, and the white shirt set off the comeliness of his black face in compelling contrast. He carried himself like a man, and bowed with gravity and dignity. She passed on and heard her husband's petulant voice in her ear.

"Mary—Mary! for Heaven's sake, come on; don't shake hands with niggers."

It was recurring flashes of temper like this, together with evidences of dubious company and a growing fondness for liquor, that drove Mary Cresswell more and more to find solace in the work of Congressman Todd's Civic Club. She collected statistics for several of the Committee, wrote letters, interviewed a few persons, and felt herself growing in usefulness and importance. She did not mention these things to her husband; she knew he would not object, but she shrank from his ridicule.

The various causes advocated by the Civic Club felt the impetus of the aggressive work of the organization. This was especially the case with the National Education Bill and the amendment to the Child Labor Bill. The movement became strong enough to call Mr. Easterly down from New York. He and the inner circle went over matters carefully.

"We need the political strength of the South," said Easterly; "not only in framing national legislation in our own interests, but always in State laws. Particularly, we must get them into line to offset Todd's foolishness. The Child Labor Bill must either go through unamended or be killed. The Cotton Inspection Bill—our chief measure—must be slipped through quietly by Southern votes, while in the Tariff mix-up we must take good care of cotton.

"Now, on the other hand, we are offending the Southerners in three ways: Todd's revived Blair Bill is too good a thing for niggers; the South is clamoring for a first classy embassy appointment; and the President's nomination of Alwyn as Treasurer will raise a howl from Virginia to Texas."

"There is some strong influence back of Alwyn," said Senator Smith; "not only are the Negroes enthused, but the President has daily letters from prominent whites."

"The strong influence is named Vanderpool," Easterly drily remarked. "She's playing a bigger political game than I laid out for her. That's the devil with women: they can't concentrate: they get too damned many side issues. Now, I offered her husband the French ambassadorship provided she'd keep the Southerners feeling good toward us. She's hand in glove with the Southerners, all right; but she wants not only her husband's appointment but this darkey's too."

"But that's been decided, hasn't it?" put in Smith.

"Yes," grumbled Easterly; "but it makes it hard already. At any rate, the Educational Bill must be killed right off. No more talk; no more consideration—kill it, and kill it now. Now about this Child Labor Bill: Todd's Civic Club is raising the mischief. Who's responsible?"

The silent Jackson spoke up. "Congressman Cresswell's wife has been very active, and Todd thinks they've got the South with them."

"Congressman Cresswell's wife!" Easterly's face was one great exclamation point. "Now what the devil does this mean?"

"I'm afraid," said Senator Smith, "that it may mean an attempt on the part of Cresswell's friends to boost him for the French ambassadorship. He's the only Southerner with money enough to support the position, and there's been a good deal of quiet talk, I understand, in Southern circles."

"But it's treason!" Easterly shouted. "It will ruin the plans of the Combine to put this amended Child Labor Bill through. John Taylor has just written me that he's starting mills at Toomsville, and that he depends on unrestricted labor conditions, as we must throughout the South. Doesn't Cresswell know this?"

"Of course. I think it's just a bluff. If he gets the appointment he'll let the bill drop."

"I see—everybody is raising his price, is he? Pretty soon the darky will be holding us up. Well, see Cresswell, and put it to him strong. I must go. Wire me."

Senator Smith presented the matter bluntly to Cresswell as soon as he saw him. "Which would the South prefer—Todd's Education Bill, or Alwyn's appointment?"

It was characteristic of Cresswell that the smaller matter of Stillings' intrigue should interest him more than Todd's measure, of which he knew nothing.

"What is Todd's bill?" asked Harry Cresswell, darkening.

Smith, surprised, got out a copy and explained. Cresswell interrupted before he was half through.

"Don't you see," he said angrily, "that that will ruin our plans for the Cotton Combine?"

"Yes, I do," replied Smith; "but it will not do the immediate harm that the amended Child Labor Bill will do."

"What's that?" demanded Cresswell, frowning again.

Senator Smith regarded him again: was Cresswell playing a shrewd game?

"Why," he said at length, "aren't you promoting it?"

"No," was the reply. "Never heard of it."

"But," Senator Smith began, and paused. He turned and took up a circular issued by the Civic Club, giving a careful account of their endeavors to amend and pass the Child Labor Bill. Cresswell read it, then threw it aside.

"Nonsense!" he indignantly repudiated the measure. "That will never do; it's as bad as the Education Bill."

"But your wife is encouraging it and we thought you were back of it."

Cresswell stared in blank amazement.

"My wife!" he gasped. Then he bethought himself. "It's a mistake," he supplemented; "Mrs. Cresswell gave them no authority to sign her name."

"She's been very active," Smith persisted, "and naturally we were all anxious."

Cresswell bit his lip. "I shall speak to her; she does not realize what use they are making of her passing interest."

He hurried away, and Senator Smith felt a bit sorry for Mrs. Cresswell when he recalled the expression on her husband's face.

Mary Cresswell did not get home until nearly dinner time; then she came in glowing with enthusiasm. Her work had received special commendation that afternoon, and she had been asked to take the chairmanship of the committee on publicity. Finding that her husband was at home, she determined to tell him—it was so good to be doing something worth while. Perhaps, too, he might be made to show some interest. She thought of Mr. and Mrs. Todd and the old dream glowed faintly again.

Cresswell looked at her as she entered the library where he was waiting and smoking. She was rumpled and muddy, with flying hair and thick walking shoes and the air of bustle and vigor which had crept into her blood this last month. Truly, her cheeks were glowing and her eyes bright, but he disapproved. Softness and daintiness, silk and lace and glimmering flesh, belonged to women in his mind, and he despised Amazons and "business" women. He received her kiss coldly, and Mary's heart sank. She essayed some gay greeting, but he interrupted her.

"What's this stuff about the Civic Club?" he began sharply.

"Stuff?" she queried, blankly.

"That's what I said."

"I'm sure I don't know," she answered stiffly. "I belong to the Civic Club, and have been working with it."

"Why didn't you tell me?" His resentment grew as he proceeded.

"I did not think you were interested."

"Didn't you know that this Child Labor business was opposed to my interests?"

"Dear, I did not dream it. It's a Republican bill, to be sure; but you seemed very friendly with Senator Smith, who introduced it. We were simply trying to improve it."

"Suppose we didn't want it improved."

"That's what some said; but I did not believe such—deception."

The blood rushed to Cresswell's face.

"Well, you will drop this bill and the Civic Club from now on."

"Why?"

"Because I say so," he retorted explosively, too angry to explain further.

She looked at him—a long, fixed, penetrating look which revealed more than she had ever seen before, then turned away and went slowly up-stairs. She did not come down to dinner, and in the evening the doctor was called.

Cresswell drooped a bit after eating, hesitated, and reflected. He had acted too cavalierly in this Civic Club mess, he concluded, and yet he would not back down. He'd go see her and pet her a bit, but be firm.

He opened her boudoir door gently, and she stood before him radiant, clothed in silk and lace, her hair loosened. He paused, astonished. But she threw herself upon his neck, with a joyful, half hysterical cry.

"I will give it all up—everything! Willingly, willingly!" Her voice dropped abruptly to a tremulous whisper. "Oh, Harry! I—I am to be the mother of a child!"

Twenty-nine

A MASTER OF FATE

There is not the slightest doubt, Miss Wynn," Senator Smith was saying, "but that the schools of the District will be reorganized."

"And the Board of Education abolished?" she added.

"Yes. The power will be delegated to a single white superintendent."

The vertical line in Caroline Wynn's forehead became pronounced.

"Whose work is this, Senator?" she asked.

"Well, there are, of course, various parties back of the change: the 'outs,' the reformers, the whole tendency to concentrate responsibility, and so on. But, frankly, the deciding factor was the demand of the South."

"Is there anything in Washington that the South does not already own?"

Senator Smith smiled thinly.

"Not much," drily; "but we own the South."

"And part of the price is putting the colored schools of the District in the hands of a Southern man and depriving us of all voice in their control?"

"Precisely, Miss Wynn. But you'd be surprised to know that it was the Negroes themselves who stirred the South to this demand."

"Not at all; you mean the colored newspapers, I presume."

"The same, with Teerswell's clever articles; then his partner Stillings worked the 'impudent Negro teacher' argument on Cresswell until Cresswell was wild to get the South in control of the schools."

"But what do Teerswell and Stillings want?"

"They want Bles Alwyn to make a fool of himself."

"That is a trifle cryptic," Miss Wynn mused. The Senator amplified.

"We are giving the South the Washington schools and killing the Education Bill in return for this support of some of our measures and their assent to Alwyn's appointment. You see I speak frankly."

"I can stand it, Senator."

"I believe you can. Well, now, if Alwyn should act unwisely and offend the South, somebody else stands in line for the appointment."

"As Treasurer?" she asked in surprise.

"Oh, no, they are too shrewd to ask that; it would offend their backers, or shall I say their tools, the Southerners. No, they ask only to be Register and Assistant Register of the Treasury. This is an office colored men have held for years, and it is quite ambitious enough for them; so Stillings assures Cresswell and his friends."

"I see," Miss Wynn slowly acknowledged. "But how do they hope to make Mr. Alwyn blunder?"

"Too easily, I fear—unless *you* are very careful. Alwyn has been working like a beaver for the National Education Bill. He's been in to see me several times, as you probably know. His heart is set on it. He regards its passage as a sort of vindication of his defence of the party."

"Yes."

"Now, the party has dropped the bill for good, and Alwyn doesn't like it. If he should attack the party—"

"But he wouldn't," cried Miss Wynn with a start that belied her conviction.

"Did you know that he is to be invited to make the principal address to the graduates of the colored high-school?"

"But," she objected. "They have selected Bishop Johnson; I—"

"I know you did," laughed the Senator, "but the Judge got orders from higher up."

"Shrewd Mr. Teerswell," remarked Miss Wynn, sagely.

"Shrewd Mr. Stillings," the Senator corrected; "but perhaps too shrewd. Suppose Mr. Alwyn should take this occasion to make a thorough defence of the party?"

"But—will he?"

"That's where you come in," Senator Smith pointed out, rising, "and the real reason of this interview. We're depending on you to pull the party out of an awkward hole," and he shook hands with his caller.

Miss Wynn walked slowly up Pennsylvania Avenue with a smile on her face.

"I did not give him the credit," she declared, repeating it; "I did not give him the credit. Here I was, playing an alluring game on the side, and my dear Tom transforms it into a struggle for bread and butter; for of course, if the Board of Education goes, I lose my place." She lifted her head and stared along the avenue.

A bitterness dawned in her eyes. The whole street was a living insult to her. Here she was, an American girl by birth and breeding, a daughter of citizens who had fought and bled and worked for a dozen generations on this soil; yet if she stepped into this hotel to rest, even with full purse, she would be politely refused accommodation. Should she attempt to go into this picture show she would be denied entrance. She was thirsty with the walk; but at yonder fountain the clerk would roughly refuse to serve her. It was lunch time; there was no place within a mile where she was allowed to eat. The revolt deepened within her. Beyond these known and definite discriminations lay the unknown and hovering. In yonder store nothing hindered the clerk from being exceptionally pert; on yonder street-car the conductor might reserve his politeness for white folk; this policeman's business was to keep black and brown people in their places. All this Caroline Wynn thought of, and then smiled.

This was the thing poor blind Bles was trying to attack by "appeals" for "justice." Nonsense! Does one "appeal" to the red-eyed beast that throttles him? No. He composes himself, looks death in the eye, and speaks softly, on the chance. Whereupon Miss Wynn composed herself, waved gayly at a passing acquaintance, and matched some ribbons in a department store. The clerk was new and anxious to sell.

Meantime her brain was busy. She had a hard task before her. Alwyn's absurd conscience and Quixotic ideas were difficult to cope with. After his last indiscreet talk she had ventured deftly to remonstrate, and she well remembered the conversation.

"Wasn't what I said true?" he had asked.

"Perfectly. Is that an excuse for saying it?"

"The facts ought to be known."

"Yes, but ought you to tell them?"

"If not I, who?"

"Some one who is less useful elsewhere, and whom I like less."

"Carrie," he had been intensely earnest. "I want to do the best thing, but I'm puzzled. I wonder if I'm selling my birthright for six thousand dollars?"

"In case of doubt, do it."

"But there's the doubt: I may convert; I may open the eyes of the blind; I may start a crusade for Negro rights."

"Don't believe it; it's useless; we'll never get our rights in this land."

"You don't believe that!" he had ejaculated, shocked.

Well, she must begin again. As she had hoped, he was waiting for her when she reached home. She welcomed him cordially, made a little music for him, and served tea.

"Bles," she said, "the Opposition has been laying a pretty shrewd trap for you."

"What?" he asked absently.

"They are going to have you chosen as High School commencement orator."

"Me? Stuff!"

"You—and not stuff, but 'Education' will be your natural theme. Indeed, they have so engineered it that the party chiefs expect from you a defence of their dropping of the Educational Bill."

"What!"

"Yes, and probably your nomination will come before the speech and confirmation after."

Bles walked the floor excitedly for a while and then sat down and smiled.

"It was a shrewd move," he said; "but I think I thank them for it."

"I don't. But still,

> "'T is the sport to see the engineer hoist
>   by his own petar.'"

Bles mused and she watched him covertly. Suddenly she leaned over.

"Moreover," she said, "about that same date I'm liable to lose my position as teacher."

He looked at her quickly, and she explained the coming revolution in school management.

He did not discuss the matter, and she was equally reticent; but when he entered the doors of his lodging-place and, gathering his mail, slowly mounted the stairs, there came the battle of his life.

He knew it and he tried to wage it coolly and with method. He arrayed the arguments side by side: on this side lay success; the greatest office ever held by a Negro in America—greater than Douglass or Bruce or Lynch had held—a landmark, a living example and inspiration. A man owed the world success; there were plenty who could fail and stumble and give multiple excuses. Should he be one? He viewed the other side. What must he pay for success? Aye, face it boldly—what? Mechanically he searched for his mail and undid the latest number of the *Colored American.* He was sure the answer stood there in Teerswell's biting vulgar English. And there it was, with a cartoon:

His Master's Voice

Alwyn is Ordered to Eat His Words or Get Out
Watch Him Do It Gracefully
The Republican Leaders, etc.

He threw down his paper, and the hot blood sang in his ears. The sickening thought was that it was true. If he did make the speech demanded it would be like a dog obedient to his master's voice.

The cold sweat oozed on his face; throwing up the window, he drank in the Spring breeze, and stared at the city he once had thought so alluring. Somehow it looked like the swamp, only less beautiful; he stretched his arms and his lips breathed—"Zora!"

He turned hastily to his desk and looked at the other piece of mail—a single sealed note carefully written on heavy paper. He did not recognize the handwriting. Then his mind flew off again. What would they say if he failed to get the office? How they would silently hoot and jeer at the upstart who suddenly climbed so high and fell. And Carrie Wynn—poor Carrie, with her pride and position dragged down in his ruin: how would she take it? He writhed in soul. And yet, to be a man;

to say calmly, "No"; to stand in that great audience and say, "My people first and last"; to take Carrie's hand and together face the world and struggle again to newer finer triumphs—all this would be very close to attainment of the ideal. He found himself staring at the little letter. Would she go? Would she, could she, lay aside her pride and cynicism, her dainty ways and little extravagances? An odd fancy came to him: perhaps the answer to the riddle lay sealed within the envelope he fingered.

He opened it. Within lay four lines of writing—no more—no address, no signature; simply the words:

> "It matters now how strait the gate,
>   How charged with punishment the scroll;
> I am the master of my fate,
>   I am the captain of my soul."

He stared at the lines. Eleven o'clock—twelve—one—chimed the deep-voiced clock without, before Alwyn went to bed.

Miss Wynn had kept a vigil almost as long. She knew that Bles had influential friends who had urged his preferment; it might be wise to enlist them. Before she fell asleep she had determined to have a talk with Mrs. Vanderpool. She had learned from Senator Smith that the lady took special interest in Alwyn.

Mrs. Vanderpool heard Miss Wynn's story next day with some inward dismay. Really the breadth and depth of intrigue in this city almost frightened her as she walked deeper into the mire. She had promised Zora that Bles should receive his reward on terms which would not wound his manhood. It seemed an easy, almost an obvious thing, to promise at the time. Yet here was this rather unusual young woman asking Mrs. Vanderpool to use her influence in making Alwyn bow to the yoke. She fenced for time.

"But I do not know Mr. Alwyn."

"I thought you did; you recommended him highly."

"I knew of him slightly in the South and I have watched his career here."

"It would be too bad to have that career spoiled now."

"But is it necessary? Suppose he should defend the Education Bill."

"And criticise the party?" asked Miss Wynn. "It would take strong influence to pull him through."

"And if that strong influence were found?" said Mrs. Vanderpool thoughtfully.

"It would surely involve some other important concession to the South."

Mrs. Vanderpool looked up, and an interjection hovered on her lips. Was it possible that the price of Alwyn's manhood would be her husband's appointment to Paris? And if it were?

"I'll do what I can," she said graciously; "but I am afraid that will not be much."

Miss Wynn hesitated. She had not succeeded even in guessing the source of Mrs. Vanderpool's interest in Alwyn, and without that her appeal was but blind groping. She stopped on her way to the door to admire a bronze statuette and find time to think.

"You are interested in bronzes?" asked Mrs. Vanderpool.

"Oh, no; I'm far too poor. But I've dabbled a bit in sculpture."

"Indeed?" Mrs. Vanderpool revealed a mild interest, and Miss Wynn was compelled to depart with little enlightenment.

On the way up town she concluded that there was but one chance of success: she must write Alwyn's speech. With characteristic decision she began her plans at once.

"What will you say in your speech?" she asked him that night as he rose to go.

He looked at her and she wavered slightly under his black eyes. The fight was becoming a little too desperate even for her steady nerves.

"You would not like me to act dishonestly, would you?" he asked.

"No," she involuntarily replied, regretting the word the moment she had uttered it. He gave her one of his rare sweet smiles, and, rising, before she realized his intent, he had kissed her hands and was gone.

She asked herself why she had been so foolish; and yet, somehow, sitting there alone in the firelight, she felt glad for once that she had risen above intrigue. Then she sighed and smiled, and began to plot anew. Teerswell dropped in later and brought his friend, Stillings. They found their hostess gay and entertaining.

Miss Wynn gathered books about her, and in the days of April and May she and Alwyn read up on education. He marvelled at the subtlety of her mind, and she at the relentlessness of his. They were very near each other during these days, and yet there was ever something between them: a vision to him of dark and pleading eyes that he constantly saw beside her cool, keen glance. And he to her was always two men: one man above men, whom she could respect but would not marry, and one man like all men, whom she would marry but could not respect. His devotion to an ideal which she thought so utterly unpractical, aroused keen curiosity and admiration. She was sure he would fail in the end, and she wanted him to fail; and somehow, somewhere back beyond herself, her better self longed to find herself defeated; to see this mind stand firm on principle, under circumstances where she believed men never stood. Deep within her she discovered at times a passionate longing to believe in somebody; yet she found herself bending every energy to pull this man down to the level of time-servers, and even as she failed, feeling something like contempt for his stubbornness.

The great day came. He had her notes, her suggestions, her hints, but she had no intimation of what he would finally say.

"Will you come to hear me?" he asked.

"No," she murmured.

"That is best," he said, and then he added slowly, "I would not like you ever to despise me."

She answered sharply: "I want to despise you!"

Did he understand? She was not sure. She was sorry she had said it; but she meant it fiercely. Then he left her, for it was already four in the afternoon and he spoke at eight.

In the morning she came down early, despite some dawdling over her toilet. She brought the morning paper into the dining-room and sat down with it, sipping her coffee. She leaned back and looked leisurely at the headings. There was nothing on the front page but a divorce, a revolution, and a new Trust. She took another sip of her coffee, and turned the page. There it was, "Colored High Schools Close—Vicious Attack on Republican Party by Negro Orator."

She laid the paper aside and slowly finished her coffee. A few minutes later she went to her desk and sat there so long that she started at hearing the clock strike nine.

The day passed. When she came home from school she bought an evening paper. She was not surprised to learn that the Senate had rejected Alwyn's nomination; that Samuel Stillings had been nominated and confirmed as Register of the Treasury, and that Mr. Tom Teerswell was to be his assistant. Also the bill reorganizing the school board had passed. She wrote two notes and posted them as she went out to walk.

When she reached home Stillings was there, and they talked earnestly. The bell rang violently. Teerswell rushed in.

"Well, Carrie!" he cried eagerly.

"Well, Tom," she responded, giving him a languid hand. Stillings rose and departed. Teerswell nodded and said:

"Well, what do you think of last night?"

"A great speech, I hear."

"A fool speech—that speech cost him, I calculate, between twenty-four and forty-eight thousand dollars."

"Possibly he's satisfied with his bargain."

"Possibly. Are you?"

"With his bargain?" quickly. "Yes."

"No," he pressed her, "with your bargain?"

"What bargain?" she parried.

"To marry him."

"Oh, no; that's off."

"Is it off?" cried Teerswell delightedly. "Good! It was foolish from the first—that black country—"

"Gently," Miss Wynn checked him. "I'm not yet over the habit."

"Come. See what I've bought. You know I have a salary now." He produced a ring with a small diamond cluster.

"How pretty!" she said, taking it and looking at it. Then she handed it back.

He laughed gayly. "It's yours, Carrie. You're going to marry me."

She looked at him queerly.

"Am I? But I've got another ring already," she said.

"Oh, send Alwyn's back."

"I have. This is still another." And uncovering her hand she showed a ring with a large and beautiful diamond.

He rose. "Whose is that?" he demanded apprehensively.

"Mine—" her eyes met his.

"But who gave it to you?"

"Mr. Stillings," was the soft reply.

He stared at her helplessly. "I—I—don't understand!" he stammered.

"Well, to be brief, I'm engaged to Mr. Stillings."

"What! To that flat-headed—"

"No," she coolly interrupted, "to the Register of the Treasury."

The man was too dumbfounded, too overwhelmed for coherent speech.

"But—but—come; why in God's name—will you throw yourself away on—on such a—you're joking—you—"

She motioned him to a chair. He obeyed like one in a trance.

"Now, Tom, be calm. When I was a baby I loved you, but that is long ago. today, Tom, you're an insufferable cad and I—well, I'm too much like you to have two of us in the same family."

"But, Stillings!" he burst forth, almost in tears. "The snake—what is he?"

"Nearly as bad as you, I'll admit; but he has four thousand a year and sense enough to keep it. In truth, I need it; for, thanks to your political activity, my own position is gone."

"But he's a—a damned rascal!" Wounded self-conceit was now getting the upper hand.

She laughed.

"I think he is. But he's such an exceptional rascal; he appeals to me. You know, Tom, we're all more or less rascally—except one."

"Except who?" he asked quickly.

"Bles Alwyn."

"The fool!"

"Yes," she slowly agreed. "Bles Alwyn, the Fool—and the Man. But by grace of the Negro Problem, I cannot afford to marry a man—Hark! Some one is on the steps. I'm sure it's Bles. You'd better go now. Don't attempt to fight with him; he's very strong. Good-night."

Alwyn entered. He didn't notice Teerswell as he passed out. He went straight to Miss Wynn holding a crumpled note, and his voice faltered a little.

"Do you mean it?"

"Yes, Bles."

"Why?"

"Because I am selfish and—small."

"No, you are not. You want to be; but give it up, Carrie; it isn't worth the cost. Come, let's be honest and poor—and free."

She regarded him a moment, searchingly, then a look half quizzical, half sorrowful came into her eyes. She put both her hands on his shoulders and said as she kissed his lips:

"Bles, almost thou persuadest me—to be a fool. Now go."

Thirty

THE RETURN OF ZORA

I never realized before just what a lie meant," said Zora.

The paper in Mrs. Vanderpool's hands fell quickly to her lap, and she gazed across the toilet-table.

As she gazed that odd mirage of other days haunted her again. She did not seem to see her maid, nor the white and satin morning-room. She saw, with some long inner sight, a vast hall with mighty pillars; a smooth, marbled floor and a great throng whose silent eyes looked curiously upon her. Strange carven beasts gazed on from a setting of rich, barbaric splendor and she herself—the Liar—lay in rags before the gold and ivory of that lofty throne whereon sat Zora.

The foolish phantasy passed with the second of time that brought it, and Mrs. Vanderpool's eyes dropped again to her paper, to those lines,—

"The President has sent the following nominations to the Senate . . . To be ambassador to France, John Vanderpool, Esq."

The first feeling of triumph thrilled faintly again until the low voice of Zora startled her. It was so low and calm, it came as though journeying from great distances and weary with travel.

"I used to think a lie a little thing, a convenience; but now I see. It is a great No and it kills things. You remember that day when Mr. Easterly called?"

"Yes," replied Mrs. Vanderpool, faintly.

"I heard all he said. I could not help it; my transom was open. And then, too, after he mentioned—Mr. Alwyn's name, I wanted to hear. I knew that his appointment would cost you the embassy—unless Bles was tempted and should fall. So I came to you to say—to say you mustn't pay the price."

"And I lied," said Mrs. Vanderpool. "I told you that he should be appointed and remain a man. I meant to make him see that he could yield without great cost. But I let you think I was giving up the embassy when I never intended to."

She spoke coldly, yet Zora knew. She reached out and took the white, still hands in hers, and over the lady's face again flitted that stricken look of age.

"I do not blame you," said Zora gently. "I blame the world."

"I am the world," Mrs. Vanderpool uttered harshly, then suddenly laughed. But Zora went on:

"It bewildered me when I first read the news early this morning; the world—everything—seemed wrong. You see, my plan was all so splendid. Just as I turned away from him, back to my people, I was to help him to the highest. I was so afraid he would miss it and think that Right didn't win in Life, that I wrote him—"

"You wrote him? So did I."

Zora glanced at her quickly.

"Yes," said Mrs. Vanderpool. "I thought I knew him. He seemed an ordinary, rather priggish, opinionated country boy, and I wrote and said—Oh, I said that the world is the world; take it as it is. You wrote differently, and he obeyed you."

"No; he did not know it was I. I was just a Voice from nowhere calling to him. I thought I was right. I wrote each day, sometimes twice, sending bits of verse, quotations, references, all saying the same thing: Right always triumphs. But it doesn't, does it?"

"No. It never does save by accident."

"I do not think that is quite so," Zora pondered aloud, "and I am a little puzzled. I do not belong in this world where Right and Wrong get so mixed. With us yonder there is wrong, but we call it wrong— mostly. Oh, I don't know; even there things are mixed." She looked sadly at Mrs. Vanderpool, and the fear that had been hovering behind her mistress's eyes became visible.

"It was so beautiful," said Zora. "I expected a great thing of you—a sacrifice. I do not blame you because you could not do it; and yet—yet, after this,—don't you see?—I cannot stay here."

Mrs. Vanderpool arose and walked over to her. She stood above her, in her silken morning-gown, her brown and gray sprinkled hair rising above the pale, strong-lined face.

"Zora," she faltered, "will you leave me?"

Zora answered, "Yes." It was a soft "yes," a "yes" full of pity and regret, but a "yes" that Mrs. Vanderpool knew in her soul to be final.

She sat down again on the lounge and her fingers crept along the cushions.

"Ambassadorships come—high," she said with a catch in her voice. Then after a pause: "When will you go, Zora?"

"When you leave for the summer."

Mrs. Vanderpool looked out upon the beautiful city. She was a little surprised at herself. She had found herself willing to sacrifice almost anything for Zora. No living soul had ever raised in her so deep an affection, and yet she knew now that, although the cost was great, she was willing to sacrifice Zora for Paris. After all, it was not too late; a rapid ride even now might secure high office for Alwyn and make Cresswell ambassador. It would be difficult but possible. But she had not the slightest inclination to attempt it, and she said aloud, half mockingly:

"You are right, Zora. I promised—and—I lied. Liars have no place in heaven and heaven is doubtless a beautiful place—but oh, Zora! you haven't seen Paris!"

Two months later they parted simply, knowing well it was forever. Mrs. Vanderpool wrote a check.

"Use this in your work," she said. "Miss Smith asked for it long ago. It is—my campaign contribution."

Zora smiled and thanked her. As she put the sealed envelope in her trunk her hand came in contact with a long untouched package. Zora took it out silently and opened it and the beauty of it lightened the room.

"It is the Silver Fleece," said Zora, and Mrs. Vanderpool kissed her and went.

Zora walked alone to the vaulted station. She did not try to buy a Pullman ticket, although the journey was thirty-six hours. She knew it would be difficult if not impossible and she preferred to share the lot of her people. Once on the foremost car, she leaned back and looked. The car seemed clean and comfortable but strangely short. Then she realized that half of it was cut off for the white smokers and as the door swung whiffs of the smoke came in. But she was content for she was almost alone.

It was eighteen little months ago that she had ridden up to the world with widening eyes. In that time what had happened? Everything. How well she remembered her coming, the first reflection of yonder gilded dome and the soaring of the capitol; the swelling of her heart, with inarticulate wonder; the pain of the thirst to know and understand. She did not know much now but she had learned how to find things out. She did not understand all, but some things she—

"Ticket"—the tone was harsh and abrupt. Zora started. She had always noted how polite conductors were to her and Mrs. Vanderpool—was it simply because Mrs. Vanderpool was evidently a great and rich lady? She held up her ticket and he snatched it from her muttering some direction.

"I beg your pardon?" she said.

"Change at Charlotte," he snapped as he went on.

It seemed to Zora that his discourtesy was almost forced: that he was afraid he might be betrayed into some show of consideration for a black woman. She felt no anger, she simply wondered what he feared. The increasing smell of tobacco smoke started her coughing. She turned. To be sure. Not only was the door to the smoker standing open, but a white passenger was in her car, sitting by the conductor and puffing heartily. As the black porter passed her she said gently:

"Is smoking allowed in here?"

"It ain't non o' my business," he flung back at her and moved away. All day white men passed back and forward through the car as through a thoroughfare. They talked loudly and laughed and joked, and if they did not smoke they carried their lighted cigars. At her they stared and made comments, and one of them came and lounged almost over her seat, inquiring where she was going.

She did not reply; she neither looked nor stirred, but kept whispering to herself with something like awe: "This is what they must endure—my poor people!"

At Lynchburg a newsboy boarded the train with his wares. The conductor had already appropriated two seats for himself, and the newsboy routed out two colored passengers, and usurped two other seats. Then he began to be especially annoying. He joked and wrestled with the porter, and on every occasion pushed his wares at Zora, insisting on her buying.

"Ain't you got no money?" he asked. "Where you going?"

"Say," he whispered another time, "don't you want to buy these gold spectacles? I found 'em and I dassen't sell 'em open, see? They're worth ten dollars—take 'em for a dollar."

Zora sat still, keeping her eyes on the window; but her hands worked nervously, and when he threw a book with a picture of a man and half-dressed woman directly under her eyes, she took it and dropped it out the window.

The boy started to storm and demanded pay, while the conductor glared at her; but a white man in the conductor's seat whispered something, and the row suddenly stopped.

A gang of colored section hands got on, dirty and loud. They sprawled about and smoked, drank, and bought candy and cheap gew-gaws. They eyed her respectfully, and with one of them she talked a little as he awkwardly fingered his cap.

As the day wore on Zora found herself strangely weary. It was not simply the unpleasant things that kept happening, but the continued apprehension of unknown possibilities. Then, too, she began to realize that she had had nothing to eat. Travelling with Mrs. Vanderpool there was always a dainty lunch to be had at call. She did not expect this, but she asked the porter:

"Do you know where I can get a lunch?"

"Search me," he answered, lounging into a seat. "Ain't no chance betwixt here and Danville as I knows on."

Zora viewed her plight with a certain dismay—twelve hours without food! How foolish of her not to have thought of this. The hours passed. She turned desperately to the gruff conductor.

"Could I buy a lunch from the dining-car?" she inquired.

"No," was the curt reply.

She made herself as comfortable as she could, and tried to put the matter from her mind. She remembered how, forgotten years ago, she had often gone a day without eating and thought little of it. Night came slowly, and she fell to dreaming until the cry came, "Charlotte! Change cars!" She scrambled out. There was no step to the platform, her bag was heavy, and the porter was busy helping the white folks to alight. She saw a dingy lunchroom marked "Colored," but she had no time to go to it for her train was ready.

There was another colored porter on this, and he was very polite and affable.

"Yes, Miss; certainly I'll fetch you a lunch—plenty of time." And he did. It did not look clean but Zora was ravenous.

The white smoker now had few occupants, but the white train crew proceeded to use the colored coach as a lounging-room and sleeping-car. There was no passenger except Zora. They took off their coats, stretched themselves on the seats, and exchanged jokes; but Zora was too tired to notice much, and she was dozing wearily when she felt a touch on the arm and found the porter in the seat beside her with his arm thrown familiarly behind her along the top of the back. She rose abruptly to her feet and he started up.

"I beg pardon," he said, grinning.

Zora sat slowly down as he got up and left. She determined to sleep no more. Yet a vast vision sank on her weary spirit—the vision of a dark cloud that dropped and dropped upon her, and lay as lead along her straining shoulders. She must lift it, she knew, though it were big as a world, and she put her strength to it and groaned as the porter cried in the ghostly morning light:

"Atlanta! All change!"

Away yonder at the school near Toomsville, Miss Smith sat waiting for the coming of Zora, absently attending the duties of the office. Dark little heads and hands bobbed by and soft voices called:

"Miss Smith, I wants a penny pencil."

"Miss Smith, is yo' got a speller fo' ten cents?"

"Miss Smith, mammy say *please* lemme come to school this week and she'll sho' pay Sata'day."

Yet the little voices that summoned her back to earth were less clamorous than in other years, for the school was far from full, and Miss

Smith observed the falling off with grave eyes. This condition was patently the result of the cotton corner and the subsequent manipulation. When cotton rose, the tenants had already sold their cotton; when cotton fell the landlords squeezed the rations and lowered the wages. When cotton rose again, up went the new Spring rent contracts. So it was that the bewildered black serf dawdled in listless inability to understand. The Cresswells in their new wealth, the Maxwells and Tollivers in the new pinch of poverty, stretched long arms to gather in the tenants and their children. Excuse after excuse came to the school.

"I can't send the chilluns dis term, Miss Smith; dey has to work."

"Mr. Cresswell won't allow Will to go to school this term."

"Mr. Tolliver done put Sam in the field."

And so Miss Smith contemplated many empty desks.

Slowly a sort of fatal inaction seized her. The school went on; daily the dark little cloud of scholars rose up from hill and vale and settled in the white buildings; the hum of voices and the busy movements of industrious teachers filled the day; the office work went on methodically; but back of it all Miss Smith sat half hopeless. It cost five thousand a year to run the school, and this sum she raised with increasingly greater difficulty. Extra and heart-straining effort had been needed to raise the eight hundred dollars additional for interest money on the mortgage last year. Next year it might have to come out of the regular income and thus cut off two teachers. Beyond all this the raising of ten thousand dollars to satisfy the mortgage seemed simply impossible, and Miss Smith sat in fatal resignation, awaiting the coming day.

"It's the Lord's work. I've done what I could. I guess if He wants it to go on, He'll find a way. And if He doesn't—" She looked off across the swamp and was silent.

Then came Zora's letter, simple and brief, but breathing youth and strength of purpose. Miss Smith seized upon it as an omen of salvation. In vain her shrewd New England reason asked: "What can a half-taught black girl do in this wilderness?" Her heart answered back:

"What is impossible to youth and resolution?" Let the shabbiness increase; let the debts pile up; let the boarders complain and the teachers gossip—Zora was coming. And somehow she and Zora would find a way.

And Zora came just as the sun threw its last crimson through the black swamp; came and gathered the frail and white-haired woman in her arms; and they wept together. Long and low they talked, far into the soft Southern night; sitting shaded beneath the stars, while nearby blinked the drowsy lights of the girls' dormitory. At last Miss Smith said, rising stiffly:

"I forgot to ask about Mrs. Vanderpool. How is she, and where?"

Zora murmured some answer; but as she went to bed in her little white room she sat wondering sadly. Where was the poor spoiled woman? Who was putting her to bed and smoothing the pillow? Who was caring for her, and what was she doing? And Zora strained her eyes Northward through the night.

At this moment, Mrs. Vanderpool, rising from a gala dinner in the brilliant drawing-room of her Lake George mansion, was reading the evening paper which her husband had put into her hands. With startled eyes she caught the impudent headlines:

VANDERPOOL DROPPED

Senate Refuses to Confirm
Todd Insurgents Muster Enough Votes to Defeat
Confirmation of President's Nominee
Rumored Revenge for Machine's Defeat of Child Labor
Bill Amendment.

The paper trembled in her jewelled hands. She glanced down the column.

"Todd asks: Who is Vanderpool, anyhow? What did he ever do? He is known only as a selfish millionaire who thinks more of horses than of men."

Carelessly Mrs. Vanderpool threw the paper to the floor and bit her lips as the angry blood dyed her face.

"They *shall* confirm him," she whispered, "if I have to mortgage my immortal soul!" And she rang up long distance on the telephone.

Thirty-one

A PARTING OF WAYS

"Was the child born dead?"

"Worse than dead!"

Somehow, somewhere, Mary Cresswell had heard these words; long, long, ago, down there in the great pain-swept shadows of utter agony, where Earth seemed slipping its moorings; and now, today, she lay repeating them mechanically, grasping vaguely at their meaning. Long she had wrestled with them as they twisted and turned and knotted themselves, and she worked and toiled so hard as she lay there to make the thing clear—to understand.

"Was the child born dead?"

"Worse than dead!"

Then faint and fainter whisperings: what could be worse than death? She had tried to ask the grey old doctor, but he soothed her like a child each day and left her lying there. today she was stronger, and for the first time sitting up, looking listlessly out across the world—a queer world. Why had they not let her see the child—just one look at its little dead face? That would have been something. And again, as the doctor cheerily turned to go, she sought to repeat the old question. He looked at her sharply, then interrupted, saying kindly:

"There, now; you've been dreaming. You must rest quietly now." And with a nod he passed into the other room to talk with her husband.

She was not satisfied. She had not been dreaming. She would tell Harry to ask him—she did not often see her husband, but she must ask him now and she arose unsteadily and swayed noiselessly across the floor. A moment she leaned against the door, then opened it slightly. From the other side the words came distinctly and clearly:

"—other children, doctor?"

"You must have no other children, Mr. Cresswell."

"Why?"

"Because the sins of the fathers are visited upon the children unto the third and fourth generation."

Slowly, softly, she crept away. Her mind seemed very clear. And she began a long journey to reach her window and chair—a long, long journey; but at last she sank into the chair again and sat dry-eyed, wondering who had conceived this world and made it, and why.

A long time afterward she found herself lying in bed, awake, conscious, clear-minded. Yet she thought as little as possible, for that was pain; but she listened gladly, for without she heard the solemn beating of the sea, the mighty rhythmic beating of the sea. Long days she lay, and sat and walked beside those vast and speaking waters, till at last she knew their voice and they spoke to her and the sea-calm soothed her soul.

For one brief moment of her life she saw herself clearly: a well-meaning woman, ambitious, but curiously narrow; not willing to work long for the Vision, but leaping at it rashly, blindly, with a deep-seated sense of duty which she made a source of offence by preening and parading it, and forcing it to ill-timed notice. She saw that she had looked on her husband as a means not an end. She had wished to absorb him and his work for her own glory. She had idealized for her own uses a very human man whose life had been full of sin and fault. She must atone.

No sooner, in this brief moment, did she see herself honestly than her old habits swept her on tumultuously. No ordinary atonement would do. The sacrifice must be vast; the world must stand in wonder before this clever woman sinking her soul in another and raising him by sheer will to the highest.

So after six endless months Mary Cresswell walked into her Washington home again. She knew she had changed in appearance, but she had forgotten to note how much until she saw the stare—almost the recoil—of her husband, the muttered exclamation, the studied, almost overdone welcome. Then she went up to her mirror and looked long, and knew.

She was strong; she felt well; but she was slight, almost scrawny, and her beauty was gone forever. It had been of that blonde white-and-pink type that fades in a flash, and its going left her body flattened and angular, her skin drawn and dead white, her eyes sunken. From the radiant girl whom Cresswell had met three years earlier the change was startling, and yet the contrast seemed even greater than it was, for her glory then had been her abundant and almost golden hair. Now that hair was faded, and falling so fast that at last the doctor advised her to cut it short. This left her ill-shaped head exposed and emphasized the sunken hollows of her face. She knew that she was changed but she did not quite realize how changed, until now as she stood and gazed.

Yet she did not hesitate but from that moment set herself to her new life task. Characteristically, she started dramatically and largely. She was to make her life an endless sacrifice; she was to revivify the manhood in Harry Cresswell, and all this for no return, no partnership of soul—all was to be complete sacrifice and sinking soul in soul.

If Mary Cresswell had attempted less she would have accomplished more. As it was, she began well; she went to work tactfully, seeming to note no change in his manner toward her; but his manner had changed. He was studiously, scrupulously polite in private, and in public devoted; but there was no feeling, no passion, no love. The polished shell of his clan reflected conventional light even more carefully than formerly because the shell was cold and empty. There were no little flashes of anger now, no poutings nor sweet reconciliations. Life ran very smoothly and courteously; and while she did not try to regain the affection, she strove to enthrall his intellect. She supplied a subcommittee upon which he was serving—not directly, but through him—with figures, with reports, books, and papers, so that he received special commendations; a praise that piqued as well as pleased him, because it implied a certain surprise that he was able to do it.

"The damned Yankees!" he sneered. "They think they've got the brains of the nation."

"Why not make a speech on the subject?" she suggested.

He laughed. The matter under discussion was the cotton-goods schedule of the new tariff bill, about which really he knew a little; his wife placed every temptation to knowledge before him, even inspiring Senator Smith to ask him to defend that schedule against the low-tariff advocate. Mary Cresswell worked with redoubled energy, and for nearly a week Harry staid at home nights and studied. Thanks to his wife the speech was unusually informing and well put, and the fact that a prominent free-trader spoke the same afternoon gave it publicity, while Mr. Easterly saw to the press despatches.

Cresswell subscribed to a clipping-bureau and tasted the sweets of dawning notoriety, and Mrs. Cresswell arranged a select dinner-party which included a cabinet officer, a foreign ambassador, two millionaires, and the leading Southern Congressmen. The talk came around to the failure of the Senate to confirm Mr. Vanderpool, and it was generally assumed that the President would not force the issue.

Who, then, should be nominated? There were several suggestions, but the knot of Southern Congressmen about Mrs. Cresswell declared emphatically that it must be a Southerner. Not since the war had a prominent Southerner represented America at a first-class foreign court; it was shameful; the time was ripe for change. But who? Here opinions differed widely. Nearly every one mentioned a candidate, and those who did not seemed to refrain from motives of personal modesty.

Mary Cresswell sped her departing guests with a distinct purpose in mind. She must make herself leader of the Southern set in Washington and concentrate its whole force on the appointment of Harry Cresswell as ambassador to France. Quick reward and promotion were essential to Harry's success. He was not one to keep up the strain of effort a long time. Unless, then, tangible results came and came quickly, he was liable to relapse into old habits. Therefore he must succeed and succeed at once. She would have preferred a less ornamental position than the ambassadorship, but there were no other openings. The Alabama senators were firmly seated for at least four years and the Governorship had been carefully arranged for. A term of four years abroad, however, might bring Harry Cresswell back in time for greater advancement. At any rate, it was the only tangible offering, and Mary Cresswell silently determined to work for it.

Here it was that she made her mistake. It was one thing for her to be a tactful hostess, pleasing her husband and his guests; it was another for her to aim openly at social leadership and political influence. She had at first all the insignia of success. Her dinners became of real political significance and her husband figured more and more as a leading Southerner. The result was two-fold. Cresswell, on the one hand, with his usual selfishness, took his rising popularity as a matter of course and as the fruits of his own work; he was rising, he was making valuable speeches, he was becoming a social power, and his only handicap was his plain and over-ambitious wife. But on the other hand Mrs. Cresswell forgot two pitfalls: the cleft between the old Southern aristocracy and the pushing new Southerners; and above all, her own Northern birth and presumably pro-Negro sympathies.

What Mrs. Cresswell forgot Mrs. Vanderpool sensed unerringly. She had heard with uneasiness of Cresswell's renewed candidacy for the Paris ambassadorship, and she set herself to block it. She had worked hard. The President stood ready to send her husband's appointment again to the Senate whenever Easterly could assure him of favorable action. Easterly had long and satisfactory interviews with several senators, while the Todd insurgents were losing heart at the prospect of choosing between Vanderpool and Cresswell. At present four Southern votes were needed to confirm Vanderpool; but if they could not be had, Easterly declared it would be good politics to nominate Cresswell and give him Republican support. Manifestly, then, Mrs. Vanderpool's task was to discredit the Cresswells with the Southerners. It was not a work to her liking, but the die was cast and she refused to contemplate defeat.

The result was that while Mrs. Cresswell was giving large and brilliant parties to the whole Southern contingent, Mrs. Vanderpool was engineering exclusive dinners where old New York met stately Charleston and gossiped interestingly. On such occasions it was hinted not once, but many times, that the Cresswells were well enough, but who was that upstart wife who presumed to take social precedence?

It was not, however, until Mrs. Cresswell's plan for an all-Southern art exhibit in Washington that Mrs. Vanderpool, in a flash of inspiration, saw her chance. In the annual exhibit of the Corcoran Art Gallery, a Southern girl had nearly won first prize over a Western man. The concensus of Southern opinion was that the judgment had been unfair, and Mrs. Cresswell was convinced of this. With quick intuition she suggested a Southern exhibit with such social prestige back of it as to impress the country.

The proposal caught the imagination of the Southern set. None suspected a possible intrusion of the eternal race issue for no Negroes were allowed in the Corcoran exhibit or school. This Mrs. Vanderpool easily ascertained and a certain sense of justice combined in a curious way with her political intrigue to bring about the undoing of Mary Cresswell.

Mrs. Vanderpool's very first cautious inquiries by way of the back stairs brought gratifying response—for did not all black Washington know well of the work in sculpture done by Mrs. Samuel Stillings, *nee* Wynn? Mrs. Vanderpool remembered Mrs. Stillings perfectly, and she walked, that evening, through unobtrusive thoroughfares and called on Mrs. Stillings. Had Mrs. Stillings heard of the new art movement? Did she intend to exhibit? Mrs. Stillings did not intend to exhibit as she was sure she would not be welcome. She had had a bust accepted by the Corcoran Art Gallery once, and when they found she was colored they returned it. But if she were especially invited? That would make a difference, although even then the line would be drawn somehow.

"Would it not be worth a fight?" suggested Mrs. Vanderpool with a little heightening of color in her pale cheek.

"Perhaps," said Mrs. Stillings, as she brought out some specimens of her work.

Mrs. Vanderpool was both ashamed and grateful. With money and leisure Mrs. Stillings had been able to get in New York and Boston the training she had been denied in Washington on account of her color. The things she exhibited really had merit and one curiously original group appealed to Mrs. Vanderpool tremendously.

"Send it," she counseled with strangely contradictory feelings of enthusiasm, and added: "Enter it under the name of Wynn."

In addition to the general invitations to the art exhibit numbers of special ones were issued to promising Southern amateurs who had never exhibited. For these a prize of a long-term scholarship and other smaller prizes were offered. When Mrs. Vanderpool suggested the name of "Miss Wynn" to Mrs. Cresswell among a dozen others, for special invitation, there was nothing in its sound to distinguish it from the rest of the names, and the invitation went duly. As a result there came to the exhibit a little group called "The Outcasts," which was really a masterly thing and sent the director, Signor Alberni, into hysterical commendation.

In the private view and award of prizes which preceded the larger social function the jury hesitated long between "The Outcasts" and a painting from Georgia. Mrs. Cresswell was enthusiastic and voluble for the bit of sculpture, and it finally won the vote for the first prize.

All was ready for the great day. The President was coming and most of the diplomatic corps, high officers of the army, and all the social leaders. Congress would be well represented, and the boom for Cresswell as ambassador to France was almost visible in the air.

Mary Cresswell paused a moment in triumph looking back at the darkened hall, when a little woman fluttered up to her and whispered:

"Mrs. Cresswell, have you heard the gossip?"

"No—what?"

"That Wynn woman they say is a nigger. Some are whispering that you brought her in purposely to force social equality. They say you used to teach darkies. Of course, I don't believe all their talk, but I thought you ought to know." She talked a while longer, then fluttered furtively away.

Mrs. Cresswell sat down limply. She saw ruin ahead—to think of a black girl taking a prize at an all-Southern art exhibit! But there was still a chance, and she leaped to action. This colored woman was doubtless some poor deserving creature. She would call on her immediately, and by an offer of abundant help induce her to withdraw quietly.

Entering her motor, she drove near the address and then proceeded on foot. The street was a prominent one, the block one of the best, the house almost pretentious. She glanced at her memorandum again to see if she was mistaken. Perhaps the woman was a domestic; probably she was, for the name on the door was Stillings. It occurred to her that she had heard that name before—but where? She looked again at her memorandum and at the house.

She rang the bell, asking the trim black maid: "Is there a person named Caroline Wynn living in this house?"

The girl smiled and hesitated.

"Yes, ma'am," she finally replied. "Won't you come in?" She was shown into the parlor, where she sat down. The room was most interesting, furnished in unimpeachable taste. A few good pictures were on the walls, and Mrs. Cresswell was examining one when she heard the swish of silken skirts. A lady with gold brown face and straight hair stood before her with pleasant smile. Where had Mrs. Cresswell seen her before? She tried to remember, but could not.

"You wished to see—Caroline Wynn?"

"Yes."

"What can I do for you?"

Mrs. Cresswell groped for her proper cue, but the brown lady merely offered a chair and sat down silently. Mrs. Cresswell's perplexity increased. She had been planning to descend graciously but authoritatively upon some shrinking girl, but this woman not only seemed to assume equality but actually looked it. From a rapid survey, Mrs. Cresswell saw a black silk stocking, a bit of lace, a tailor-made gown, and a head with two full black eyes that waited in calmly polite expectancy.

Something had to be said.

"I—er—came; that is, I believe you sent a group to the art exhibit?"

"Yes."

"It was good—very good."

Miss Wynn said nothing, but sat calmly looking at her visitor. Mrs. Cresswell felt irritated.

"Of course," she managed to continue, "we are very sorry that we cannot receive it."

"Indeed? I understood it had taken the first prize."

Mrs. Cresswell was aghast. Who had rushed the news to this woman? She realized that there were depths to this matter that she did not understand and her irritation increased.

"You know that we could not give the prize to a—Negro."

"Why not?"

"That is quite immaterial. Social equality cannot be forced. At the same time I recognize the injustice, and I have come to say that if you will withdraw your exhibit you will be given a scholarship in a Boston school."

"I do not wish it."

"Well, what do you want?"

"I was not aware that I had asked for anything."

Mrs. Cresswell felt herself getting angry.

"Why did you send your exhibit when you knew it was not wanted?"

"Because you asked me to."

"We did not ask for colored people."

"You asked all Southern-born persons. I am a person and I am Southern born. Moreover, you sent me a personal letter."

Mrs. Cresswell was sure that this was a lie and was thoroughly incensed.

"You cannot have the prize," she almost snapped. "If you will withdraw I will pay you any reasonable sum."

"Thank you. I do not want money; I want justice."

Mrs. Cresswell arose and her face was white.

"That is the trouble with you Negroes: you wish to get above your places and force yourselves where you are not wanted. It does no good, it only makes trouble and enemies." Mrs. Cresswell stopped, for the colored woman had gone quietly out of the room and in a moment the maid entered and stood ready. Mrs. Cresswell walked slowly to the door and stepped out. Then she turned.

"What does Miss Wynn do for a living?"

The girl tittered.

"She used to teach school but she don't do nothing now. She's just married; her husband is Mr. Stillings, Register of the Treasury."

Mrs. Cresswell saw light as she turned to go down the steps. There was but one resource—she must keep the matter out of the newspapers, and see Stillings, whom she now remembered well.

"I beg pardon, does the Miss Wynn live here who got the prize in the art exhibition?"

Mrs. Cresswell turned in amazement. It was evidently a reporter, and the maid was admitting him. The news would reach the papers and be blazoned to-morrow. Slowly she caught her motor and fell wearily back on its cushions.

"Where to, Madame?" asked the chauffeur.

"I don't care," returned Madame; so the chauffeur took her home.

She walked slowly up the stairs. All her carefully laid plans seemed about to be thwarted and her castles were leaning toward ruin.

Yet all was not lost, if her husband continued to believe in her. If, as she feared, he should suspect her on account of this Negro woman, and quarrel with her—

But he must not. This very night, before the morning papers came out, she must explain. He must see; he must appreciate her efforts.

She rushed into her dressing-room and called her maid. Contrary to her Puritan notions, she frankly sought to beautify herself. She remembered that it was the anniversary of her coming to this house. She got out her wedding-dress, and although it hung loosely, the maid draped the Silver Fleece beautifully about her.

She heard her husband enter and come up-stairs. Quickly finishing her toilet, she hurried down to arrange the flowers, for they were alone that night. The telephone rang. She knew it would ring up-stairs in his room, but she usually answered it for he disliked to. She raised the receiver and started to speak when she realized that she had broken into the midst of a conversation.

"—committee won't meet tonight, Harry."

"So? All right. Anything on?"

"Yes—big spree at Nell's. Will you go?"

"Sure thing; you know me! What time?"

"Meet us at the Willard by nine. S'long."

"Good-bye."

She slowly, half guiltily, replaced the receiver. She had not meant to listen, but now to her desperate longing to keep him home was added a new motive. Where was "Nell's"? What was "Nell's"? What was— and there was fear in her heart. At dinner she tried all her powers on him. She had his favorite dishes; she mixed his salad and selected his wine; she talked interestingly, and listened sympathetically, to him. He looked at her with more attention. Her cheeks were more brilliant, for she had touched them with rouge. Her eyes flashed; but he glanced furtively at her short hair. She saw the act; but still she strove until he was content and laughing; then coming round back of his chair, she placed her arms about his neck.

"Harry, will you do me a favor?"

"Why, yes—if—"

"It is something I want very, very much."

"Well, all right, if—"

"Harry, I feel a little—hysterical, tonight, and—you will not refuse me, will you, Harry?"

Standing there, she saw the tableau in her own mind, and it looked strange. She was afraid of herself. She knew that she would do something foolish if she did not win this battle. She felt that overpowering fanaticism back within her raging restlessly. If she was not careful—

"But what is it you want?" asked her husband.

"I don't want you to go out tonight."

He laughed awkwardly.

"Nonsense, girl! The sub-committee on the cotton schedule meets tonight—very important; otherwise—"

She shuddered at the smooth lie and clasped him closer, putting her cheek to his.

"Harry," she pleaded, "just this once—for me."

He disengaged himself, half impatiently, and rose, glancing at the clock. It was nearly nine. A feeling of desperation came over her.

"Harry," she asked again as he slipped on his coat.

"Don't be foolish," he growled.

"Just this once—Harry—I—" But the door banged to, and he was gone.

She stood looking at the closed door a moment. Something in her head was ready to snap. She went to the rack and taking his long heavy overcoat slipped it on. It nearly touched the floor. She seized a soft broad-brimmed hat and umbrella and walked out. Just what she meant to do she did not know, but somehow she must save her husband and herself from evil. She hurried to the Willard Hotel and watched, walking up and down the opposite sidewalk. A woman brushed by her and looked her in the face.

"Hell! I thought you was a man," she said. "Is this a new gag?"

Mrs. Cresswell looked down at herself involuntarily and smiled wanly. She did look like a man, with her hat and coat and short hair. The woman peered at her doubtingly. She was, as Mrs. Cresswell noticed, a young woman, once pretty, perhaps, and a little over-dressed.

"Are you walking?" she asked.

"What do you mean?" asked Mrs. Cresswell, and then in a moment it flashed upon her. She took the woman's arm and walked with her. Suddenly she stopped.

"Where's—Nell's?"

The woman frowned. "Oh, that's a swell place," she said. "Senators and millionaires. Too high for us to fly."

Mrs. Cresswell winced. "But where is it?" she asked.

"We'll walk by it if you want to."

And Mary Cresswell walked in another world. Up from the ground of the drowsy city rose pale gray forms; pale, flushed, and brilliant, in silken rags. Up and down they passed, to and fro, looking and gliding like sheeted ghosts; now dodging policemen, now accosting them familiarly.

"Hello, Elise," growled one big blue-coat.

"Hello, Jack."

"What's this?" and he peered at Mrs. Cresswell, who shrank back.

"Friend of mine. All right."

A horror crept over Mary Cresswell: where had she lived that she had seen so little before? What was Washington, and what was this fine, tall, quiet residence? Was this—"Nell's"?

"Yes, this is it—good-bye—I must—"

"Wait—what is your name?"

"I haven't any name," answered the woman suspiciously.

"Well—pardon me! Here!" and she thrust a bill into the woman's hand.

The girl stared. "Well, you're a queer one! Thanks. Guess I'll turn in."

Mary Cresswell turned to see her husband and his companions ascending the steps of the quiet mansion. She stood uncertainly and looked at the opening and closing door. Then a policeman came by and looked at her.

"Come, move on," he brusquely ordered. Her vacillation promptly vanished, and she resolutely mounted the steps. She put out her hand to ring, but the door flew silently open and a man-servant stood looking at her.

"I have some friends here," she said, speaking coarsely.

"You will have to be introduced," said the man. She hesitated and started to turn away. Thrusting her hand in her pocket it closed upon her husband's card-case. She presented a card. It worked a rapid transformation in the servant's manner, which did not escape her.

"Come in," he invited her.

She did not stop at the outstretched arm of the cloakman, but glided quickly up the stairs toward a vision of handsome women and strains of music. Harry Cresswell was sitting opposite and bending over an impudent blue-and-blonde beauty. Mary slipped straight across to him and leaned across the table. The hat fell off, but she let it go.

"Harry!" she tried to say as he looked up.

Then the table swayed gently to and fro; the room bowed and whirled about; the voices grew fainter and fainter—all the world receded suddenly far away. She extended her hands languidly, then, feeling so utterly tired, let her eyelids drop and fell asleep.

She awoke with a start, in her own bed. She was physically exhausted but her mind was clear. She must go down and meet him at breakfast and talk frankly with him. She would let bygones be bygones. She would explain that she had followed him to save him, not to betray him. She would point out the greater career before him if only he would be a man; she would show him that they had not failed. For herself she asked nothing, only his word, his confidence, his promise to try.

After his first start of surprise at seeing her at the table, Cresswell uttered nothing immediately save the commonplaces of greeting. He mentioned one or two bits of news from the paper, upon which she commented while dawdling over her egg. When the servant went out and closed the door, she paused a moment considering whether to open by appeal or explanation. His smooth tones startled her:

"Of course, after your art exhibit and the scene of last night, Mary, it will be impossible for us to live longer together."

She stared at him, utterly aghast—voiceless and numb.

"I have seen the crisis approaching for some time, and the Negro business settles it," he continued. "I have now decided to send you to my home in Alabama, to my father or your brother. I am sure you will be happier there."

He rose. Bowing courteously, he waited, coldly and calmly, for her to go.

All at once she hated him and hated his aristocratic repression; this cold calm that hid hell and its fires. She looked at him, wide-eyed, and said in a voice hoarse with horror and loathing:

"You brute! You nasty brute!"

Thirty-two

___

ZORA'S WAY

Zora was looking on her world with the keener vision of one who, blind from very seeing, closes the eyes a space and looks again with wider clearer vision. Out of a nebulous cloudland she seemed to step; a land where all things floated in strange confusion, but where one thing stood steadfast, and that was love. When love was shaken all things moved, but now, at last, for the first time she seemed to know the real and mighty world that stood behind that old and shaken dream.

So she looked on the world about her with new eyes. These men and women of her childhood had hitherto walked by her like shadows; to-day they lived for her in flesh and blood. She saw hundreds and thousands of black men and women: crushed, half-spirited, and blind. She saw how high and clear a light Sarah Smith, for thirty years and more, had carried before them. She saw, too, how that the light had not simply shone in darkness, but had lighted answering beacons here and there in these dull souls.

There were thoughts and vague stirrings of unrest in this mass of black folk. They talked long about their firesides, and here Zora began to sit and listen, often speaking a word herself. All through the coutryside she flitted, till gradually the black folk came to know her and, in silent deference to some subtle difference, they gave her the title of white folk, calling her "Miss" Zora.

today, more than ever before, Zora sensed the vast unorganized power in this mass, and her mind was leaping here and there, scheming and testing, when voices arrested her.

It was a desolate bit of the Cresswell manor, a tiny cabin, new-boarded and bare, in front of it a blazing bonfire. A white man was tossing into the flames different household articles—a feather bed, a bedstead, two rickety chairs. A young, boyish fellow, golden-faced and curly, stood with clenched fists, while a woman with tear-stained eyes clung to him. The white man raised a cradle to dash it into the flames; the woman cried, and the yellow man raised his arm threateningly. But Zora's hand was on his shoulder.

"What's the matter, Rob?" she asked.

"They're selling us out," he muttered savagely. "Millie's been sick since the last baby died, and I had to neglect my crop to tend her and the other little ones—I didn't make much. They've took my mule, now they're burning my things to make me sign a contract and be a slave. But by—"

"There, Rob, let Millie come with me—we'll see Miss Smith. We must get land to rent and arrange somehow."

The mother sobbed, "The cradle—was baby's!"

With an oath the white man dashed the cradle into the fire, and the red flame spurted aloft.

The crimson fire flashed in Zora's eyes as she passed the overseer.

"Well, nigger, what are you going to do about it?" he growled insolently.

Zora's eyelids drooped, her upper lip quivered.

"Nothing," she answered softly. "But I hope your soul will burn in
hell forever and forever."

They proceeded down the plantation road, but Zora could not
speak. She pushed them slowly on, and turned aside to let the anger,
the impotent, futile anger, rage itself out. Alone in the great broad
spaces, she knew she could fight it down, and come back again, cool
and in calm and deadly earnest, to lead these children to the light.

The sorrow in her heart was new and strange; not sorrow for herself,
for of that she had tasted the uttermost; but the vast vicarious suffering for the evil of the world. The tumult and war within her fled, and a
sense of helplessness sent the hot tears streaming down her cheeks. She
longed for rest; but the last plantation was yet to be passed. Far off she
heard the yodle of the gangs of peons. She hesitated, looking for some
way of escape: if she passed them she would see something—she always saw something—that would send the red blood whirling madly.

"Here, you!—loafing again, damn you!" She saw the black whip
writhe and curl across the shoulders of the plough-boy. The boy
crouched and snarled, and again the whip hissed and cracked.

Zora stood rigid and gray.

"My God!" her silent soul was shrieking within, "why doesn't the
coward—"

And then the "coward" did. The whip was whirring in the air again;
but it never fell. A jagged stone in the boy's hand struck true, and the
overseer plunged with a grunt into the black furrow. In blank dismay,
Zora came back to her senses.

"Poor child!" she gasped, as she saw the boy flying in wild terror
over the fields, with hue and cry behind him.

"Poor child!—running to the penitentiary—to shame and hunger
and damnation!"

She remembered the rector in Mrs. Vanderpool's library, and his question that revealed unfathomable depths of ignorance: "Really, now, how do you account for the distressing increase in crime among your people?"

She swung into the great road trembling with the woe of the world in her eyes. Cruelty, poverty, and crime she had looked in the face that morning, and the hurt of it held her heart pinched and quivering. A moment the mists in her eyes shut out the shadows of the swamp, and the roaring in her ears made a silence of the world.

Before she found herself again she dimly saw a couple sauntering along the road, but she hardly noticed their white faces until the little voice of the girl, raised timidly, greeted her.

"Howdy, Zora."

Zora looked. The girl was Emma, and beside her, smiling, stood a half-grown white man. It was Emma, Bertie's child; and yet it was not, for in the child of other days Zora saw for the first time the dawning woman.

And she saw, too, the white man. Suddenly the horror of the swamp was upon her. She swept between the couple like a gust, gripping the child's arm till she paled and almost whimpered.

"I—I was just going on an errand for Miss Smith!" she cried.

Looking down into her soul, Zora discerned its innocence and the fright shining in the child's eyes. Her own eyes softened, her grip became a caress, but her heart was hard.

The young man laughed awkwardly and strolled away. Zora looked back at him and the paramount mission of her life formed itself in her mind. She would protect this girl; she would protect *all* black girls. She would make it possible for these poor beasts of burden to be decent in their toil. Out of protection of womanhood as the central thought, she must build ramparts against cruelty, poverty, and crime. All this in turn—but now and first, the innocent girlhood of this daughter of shame must be rescued from the devil. It was her duty, her heritage.

She must offer this unsullied soul up unto God in mighty atonement—but how? Here now was no protection. Already lustful eyes were in wait, and the child was too ignorant to protect herself. She must be sent to boarding-school, somewhere far away; but the money? God! it was money, money, always money. Then she stopped suddenly, thrilled with the recollection of Mrs. Vanderpool's check.

She dismissed the girl with a kiss, and stood still a moment considering. Money to send Emma off to school; money to buy a school farm; money to "buy" tenants to live on it; money to furnish them rations; money—

She went straight to Miss Smith.

"Miss Smith, how much money have you?" Miss Smith's hand trembled a bit. Ah, that splendid strength of young womanhood—if only she herself had it! But perhaps Zora was the chosen one. She reached up and took down a well-worn book.

"Zora," she said slowly, "I've been going to tell you ever since you came, but I hadn't the courage. Zora," Miss Smith hesitated and gripped the book with thin white fingers, "I'm afraid—I almost know that this school is doomed."

There lay a silence in the room while the two women stared into each other's souls with startled eyes. Swallowing hard, Miss Smith spoke.

"When I thought the endowment sure, I mortgaged the school in order to buy Tolliver's land. The endowment failed, as you know, because—perhaps I was too stubborn."

But Zora's eyes snapped "No!" and Miss Smith continued:

"I borrowed ten thousand dollars. Then I tried to get the land, but Tolliver kept putting me off, and finally I learned that Colonel Cresswell had bought it. It seems that Tolliver got caught tight in the cotton corner, and that Cresswell, through John Taylor, offered him twice what he had agreed to sell to me for, and he took it. I don't suppose Taylor knew what he was doing; I hope he didn't.

"Well, there I was with ten thousand dollars idle on my hands, paying ten per cent on it and getting less than three per cent. I tried to get the bank to take the money back, but they refused. Then I was tempted—and fell." She paused, and Zora took both her hands in her own.

"You see," continued Miss Smith, "just as soon as the announcement of the prospective endowment was sent broadcast by the press, the donations from the North fell off. Letter after letter came from old friends of the school full of congratulations, but no money. I ought to have cut down the teaching force to the barest minimum, and gone North begging—but I couldn't. I guess my courage was gone. I knew how I'd have to explain and plead, and I just could not. So I used the ten thousand dollars to pay its own interest and help run the school. Already it's half gone, and when the rest goes then will come the end."

Without, the great red sun paused a moment over the edge of the swamp, and the long, low cry of night birds broke sadly on the twilight silence. Zora sat stroking the lined hands.

"Not the end," she spoke confidently. "It cannot end like this. I've got a little money that Mrs. Vanderpool gave me, and somehow we must get more. Perhaps I might go North and—beg." She shivered. Then she sat up resolutely and turned to the book.

"Let's go over matters carefully," she proposed.

Together they counted and calculated.

"The balance is four thousand seven hundred and ninety-eight dollars," said Miss Smith.

"Yes, and then there's Mrs. Vanderpool's check."

"How much is that?"

Zora paused; she did not know. In her world there was little calculation of money. Credit and not cash is the currency of the Black Belt. She had been pleased to receive the check, but she had not examined it.

"I really don't know," she presently confessed. "I think it was one thousand dollars; but I was so hurried in leaving that I didn't look carefully," and the wild thought surged in her, suppose it was more!

She ran into the other room and plunged into her trunk; beneath the clothes, beneath the beauty of the Silver Fleece, till her fingers clutched and tore the envelope. A little choking cry burst from her throat, her knees trembled so that she was obliged to sit down.

In her fingers fluttered a check for—*ten thousand dollars!*

It was not until the next day that the two women were sufficiently composed to talk matters over sanely.

"What is your plan?" asked Zora.

"To put the money in a Northern savings bank at three per cent interest; to supply the rest of the interest, and the deficit in the running expenses, from our balance, and to send you North to beg."

Zora shook her head. "It won't do," she objected. "I'd make a poor beggar; I don't know human nature well enough, and I can't talk to rich white folks the way they expect us to talk."

"It wouldn't be hypocrisy, Zora; you would be serving in a great cause. If you don't go, I—"

"Wait! You sha'n't go. If any one goes it must be me. But let's think it out: we pay off the mortgage, we get enough to run the school as it has been run. Then what? There will still be slavery and oppression all around us. The children will be kept in the cotton fields; the men will be cheated, and the women—" Zora paused and her eyes grew hard.

She began again rapidly: "We must have land—our own farm with our own tenants—to be the beginning of a free community."

Miss Smith threw up her hands impatiently.

"But sakes alive! Where, Zora? Where can we get land, with Cresswell owning every inch and bound to destroy us?"

Zora sat hugging her knees and staring out the window toward the sombre ramparts of the swamp. In her eyes lay slumbering the madness of long ago; in her brain danced all the dreams and visions of childhood.

"I'm thinking," she murmured, "of buying the swamp."

Thirty-three

THE BUYING OF THE SWAMP

It's a shame," asserted John Taylor with something like real feeling. He was spending Sunday with his father-in-law, and both, over their after-dinner cigars, were gazing thoughtfully at the swamp.

"What's a shame?" asked Colonel Cresswell.

"To see all that timber and prime cotton-land going to waste. Don't you remember those fine bales of cotton that came out of there several seasons ago?"

The Colonel smoked placidly. "You can't get it cleared," he said.

"But couldn't you hire some good workers?"

"Niggers won't work. Now if we had Italians we might do it."

"Yes, and in a few years they'd own the country."

"That's right; so there we are. There's only one way to get that swamp cleared."

"How?"

"Sell it to some fool darkey."

"Sell it? It's too valuable to sell."

"That's just it. You don't understand. The only way to get decent work out of some niggers is to let them believe they're buying land. In nine cases out of ten he works hard a while and then throws up the job. We get back our land and he makes good wages for his work."

"But in the tenth case—suppose he should stick to it?"

"Oh,"—easily, "we could get rid of him when we want to. White people rule here."

John Taylor frowned and looked a little puzzled. He was no moralist, but he had his code and he did not understand Colonel Cresswell. As a matter of fact, Colonel Cresswell was an honest man. In most matters of commerce between men he was punctilious to a degree almost annoying to Taylor. But there was one part of the world which his code of honor did not cover, and he saw no incongruity in the omission. The uninitiated cannot easily picture to himself the mental attitude of a former slaveholder toward property in the hands of a Negro. Such property belonged of right to the master, if the master needed it; and since ridiculous laws safeguarded the property, it was perfectly permissible to circumvent such laws. No Negro starved on the Cresswell place, neither did any accumulate property. Colonel Cresswell saw to both matters.

As the Colonel and John Taylor were thus conferring, Zora appeared, coming up the walk.

"Who's that?" asked the Colonel shading his eyes.

"It's Zora—the girl who went North with Mrs. Vanderpool," Taylor enlightened him.

"Back, is she? Too trifling to stick to a job, and full of Northern nonsense," growled the Colonel. "Even got a Northern walk—I thought for a moment she was a lady."

Neither of the gentlemen ever dreamed how long, how hard, how heart-wringing was that walk from the gate up the winding way beneath their careless gaze. It was not the coming of the thoughtless, careless girl of five years ago who had marched a dozen times unthinking before the faces of white men. It was the approach of a woman who knew how the world treated women whom it respected; who knew that no such treatment would be thought of in her case: neither the bow, the lifted hat, nor even the conventional title of decency. Yet she must go on naturally and easily, boldly but circumspectly, and play a daring game with two powerful men.

"Can I speak with you a moment, Colonel?" she asked.

The Colonel did not stir or remove his cigar; he even injected a little gruffness into his tone.

"Well, what is it?"

Of course, she was not asked to sit, but she stood with her hands clasped loosely before her and her eyes half veiled.

"Colonel, I've got a thousand dollars." She did not mention the other nine.

The Colonel sat up.

"Where did you get it?" he asked.

"Mrs. Vanderpool gave it to me to use in helping the colored people."

"What are you going to do with it?"

"Well, that's just what I came to see you about. You see, I might give it to the school, but I've been thinking that I'd like to buy some land for some of the tenants."

"I've got no land to sell," said the Colonel.

"I was thinking you might sell a bit of the swamp."

Cresswell and Taylor glanced at each other and the Colonel re-lit his cigar.

"How much of it?" he asked finally.

"I don't know; I thought perhaps two hundred acres."

"Two hundred acres? Do you expect to buy that land for five dollars an acre?"

"Oh, no, sir. I thought it might cost as much as twenty-five dollars."

"But you've only got a thousand dollars."

"Yes, sir; I thought I might pay that down and then pay the rest from the crops."

"Who's going to work on the place?"

Zora named a number of the steadiest tenants to whom she had spoken.

"They owe me a lot of money," said the Colonel.

"We'd try to pay that, too."

Colonel Cresswell considered. There was absolutely no risk. The cost of the land, the back debts of the tenants—no possible crops could pay for them. Then there was the chance of getting the swamp cleared for almost nothing.

"How's the school getting on?" he asked suddenly.

"Very poorly," answered Zora sadly. "You know it's mortgaged, and Miss Smith has had to use the mortgage money for yearly expenses."

The Colonel smiled grimly.

"It will cost you fifty dollars an acre," he said finally. Zora looked disappointed and figured out the matter slowly.

"That would be one thousand down and nine thousand to pay—"

"With interest," said Cresswell.

Zora shook her head doubtfully.

"What would the interest be?" she asked.

"Ten per cent."

She stood silent a moment and Colonel Cresswell spoke up:

"It's the best land about here and about the only land you can buy— I wouldn't sell it to anybody else."

She still hesitated.

"The trouble is, you see, Colonel Cresswell, the price is high and the interest heavy. And after all I may not be able to get as many tenants as I'd need. I think though, I'd try it if—if I could be sure you'd treat me fairly, and that I'd get the land if I paid for it."

Colonel Cresswell reddened a little, and John Taylor looked away.

"Well, if you don't want to undertake it, all right."

Zora looked thoughtfully across the field—

"Mr. Maxwell has a bit of land," she began meditatively.

"Worked out, and not worth five dollars an acre!" snapped the Colonel. But he did not propose to hand Maxwell a thousand dollars. "Now, see here, I'll treat you as well as anybody, and you know it."

"I believe so, sir," acknowledged Zora in a tone that brought a sudden keen glance from Taylor; but her face was a mask. "I reckon I'll make the bargain."

"All right. Bring the money and we'll fix the thing up."

"The money is here," said Zora, taking an envelope out of her bosom.

"Well, leave it here, and I'll see to it."

"But you see, sir, Miss Smith is so methodical; she expects some papers or receipts."

"Well, it's too late tonight."

"Possibly you could sign a sort of receipt and later—"

Cresswell laughed. "Well, write one," he indulgently assented. And Zora wrote.

When Zora left Colonel Cresswell's about noon that Sunday she knew her work had just begun, and she walked swiftly along the country roads, calling here and there. Would Uncle Isaac help her build a log home? Would the boys help her some time to clear some swamp land? Would Rob become a tenant when she asked? For this was the idle time of the year. Crops were laid by and planting had not yet begun.

This too was the time of big church meetings. She knew that in her part of the country on that day the black population, man, woman, and child, were gathered in great groups; all day they had been gathering, streaming in snake-like lines along the country roads, in well-brushed, brilliant attire, half fantastic, half crude. Down where the Toomsville-

Montgomery highway dipped to the stream that fed the Cresswell swamp squatted a square barn that slept through day and weeks in dull indifference. But on the First Sunday it woke to sudden mighty life. The voices of men and children mingled with the snorting of animals and the cracking of whips. Then came the long drone and sing-song of the preacher with its sharp wilder climaxes and the answering "amens" and screams of the worshippers. This was the shrine of the Baptists—shrine and oracle, centre and source of inspiration—and hither Zora hurried.

The preacher was Jones, a big man, fat, black, and greasy, with little eyes, unctuous voice, and three manners: his white folks manner, soft, humble, wheedling; his black folks manner, voluble, important, condescending; and above all, his pulpit manner, loud, wild, and strong. He was about to don this latter cloak when Zora approached with a request briefly to address the congregation. Remembering some former snubs, his manner was lordly.

"I doesn't see," he returned reflectively, wiping his brows, "as how I can rightly spare you any time; the brethren is a-gettin' mighty onpatient to hear me." He pulled down his cuffs, regarding her doubtfully.

"I might speak after you're through," she suggested. But he objected that there was the regular collection and two or three other collections, a baptism, a meeting of the trustees; there was no time, in short; but—he eyed her again.

"Does you want—a collection?" he questioned suspiciously, for he could imagine few other reasons for talking. Then, too, he did not want to be too inflexible, for all of his people knew Zora and liked her.

"Oh, no, I want no collection at all. I only want a little voluntary work on their part." He looked relieved, frowned through the door at the audience, and looked at his bright gold watch. The whole crowd was not there yet—perhaps—

"You kin say just a word before the sermont," he finally yielded; "but not long—not long. They'se just a-dying to hear me."

So Zora spoke simply but clearly: of neglect and suffering, of the sins of others that bowed young shoulders, of the great hope of the children's future. Then she told something of what she had seen and read of the world's newer ways of helping men and women. She talked of cooperation and refuges and other efforts; she praised their way of adopting children into their own homes; and then finally she told them of the land she was buying for new tenants and the helping hands she needed. The preacher fidgeted and coughed but dared not actually interrupt, for the people were listening breathless to a kind of straightforward talk which they seldom heard and for which they were hungering.

And Zora forgot time and occasion. The moments flew; the crowd increased until the wonderful spell of those dark and upturned faces pulsed in her blood. She felt the wild yearning to help them beating in her ears and blinding her eyes.

"Oh, my people!" she almost sobbed. "My own people, I am not asking you to help others; I am pleading with you to help yourselves. Rescue your own flesh and blood—free yourselves—free yourselves!" And from the swaying sobbing hundreds burst a great "Amen!" The minister's dusky face grew more and more sombre, and the angry sweat started on his brow. He felt himself hoaxed and cheated, and he meant to have his revenge. Two hundred men and women rose and pledged themselves to help Zora; and when she turned with overflowing heart to thank the preacher he had left the platform, and she found him in the yard whispering darkly with two deacons. She realized her mistake, and promised to retrieve it during the week; but the week was full of planning and journeying and talking.

Saturday dawned cool and clear. She had dinner prepared for cooking in the yard: sweet potatoes, hoe-cake, and buttermilk, and a hog to be barbecued. Everything was ready by eight o'clock in the morning. Emma and two other girl helpers were on the tip-toe of expectancy. Nine o'clock came and no one with it. Ten o'clock came, and eleven.

High noon found Zora peering down the highway under her shading hand, but no soul in sight. She tried to think it out: what could have happened? Her people were slow, tardy, but they would not thus forget her and disappoint her without some great cause. She sent the girls home at dusk and then seated herself miserably under the great oak; then at last one half-grown boy hurried by.

"I wanted to come, Miss Zora, but I was afeared. Preacher Jones has been talking everywhere against you. He says that your mother was a voodoo woman and that you don't believe in God, and the deacons voted that the members mustn't help you."

"And do the people believe that?" she asked in consternation.

"They just don't know what to say. They don't 'zactly believe it, but they has to 'low that you didn't say much 'bout religion when you talked. You ain't been near Big Meetin'—and—and—you ain't saved." He hurried on.

Zora leaned her head back wearily, watching the laced black branches where the star-light flickered through—as coldly still and immovable as she had watched them from those gnarled roots all her life—and she murmured bitterly the world-old question of despair: "What's the use?" It seemed to her that every breeze and branch was instinct with sympathy, and murmuring, "What's the use?" She wondered vaguely why, and as she wondered, she knew.

For yonder where the black earth of the swamp heaved in a formless mound she felt the black arms of Elspeth rising from the sod—gigantic, mighty. They stole toward her with stealthy hands and claw-like talons. They clutched at her skirts. She froze and could not move. Down, down she slipped toward the black slime of the swamp, and the air about was horror—down, down, till the chilly waters stung her knees; and then with one grip she seized the oak, while the great hand of Elspeth twisted and tore her soul. Faint, afar, nearer and nearer and ever mightier, rose a song of mystic melody. She heard its human voice and sought to cry aloud. She strove again and again with that gripping, twisting pain—that awful hand—until the shriek came and she awoke.

She lay panting and sweating across the bent and broken roots of the oak. The hand of Elspeth was gone but the song was still there. She rose trembling and listened. It was the singing of the Big Meeting in the church far away. She had forgotten this religious revival in her days of hurried preparation, and the preacher had used her absence and apparent indifference against her and her work. The hand of Elspeth was reaching from the grave to pull her back; but she was no longer dreaming now. Drawing her shawl about her, she hurried down the highway.

The meeting had overflowed the church and spread to the edge of the swamp. The tops of young trees had been bent down and interlaced to form a covering and benches twined to their trunks. Thus a low and wide cathedral, all green and silver in the star-light, lay packed with a living mass of black folk. Flaming pine torches burned above the devotees; the rhythm of their stamping, the shout of their voices, and the wild music of their singing shook the night. Four hundred people fell upon their knees when the huge black preacher, uncoated, red-eyed, frenzied, stretched his long arms to heaven. Zora saw the throng from afar, and hesitated. After all, she knew little of this strange faith of theirs—had little belief in its mummery. She herself had been brought up almost without religion save some few mystic remnants of a half-forgotten heathen cult. The little she had seen of religious observance had not moved her greatly, save once yonder in Washington. There she found God after a searching that had seared her soul; but He had simply pointed the Way, and the way was human.

Humanity was near and real. She loved it. But if she talked again of mere men would these devotees listen? Already the minister had spied her tall form and feared her power. He set his powerful voice and the frenzy of his hearers to crush her.

"Who is dis what talks of doing the Lord's work for Him? What does de good Book say? Take no thought 'bout de morrow. Why is you trying to make dis ole world better? I spits on the world! Come out from it. Seek Jesus. Heaven is my home! Is it yo's?" "Yes," groaned the multitude. His arm shot out and he pointed straight at Zora.

"Beware the ebil one!" he shouted, and the multitude moaned. "Beware of dem dat calls ebil good. Beware of dem dat worships debbils; the debbils dat crawl; de debbils what forgits God."

"Help him, Lord!" cried the multitude.

Zora stepped into the circle of light. A hush fell on the throng; the preacher paused a moment, then started boldly forward with upraised hands. Then a curious thing happened. A sharp cry arose far off down toward the swamp and the sound of great footsteps coming, coming as from the end of the world; there swelled a rhythmical chanting, wilder and more primitive than song. On, on it came, until it swung into sight. An old man led the band—tall, massive, with tufted gray hair and wrinkled leathery skin, and his eyes were the eyes of death. He reached the circle of light, and Zora started: once before she had seen that old man. The singing stopped but he came straight on till he reached Zora's side and then he whirled and spoke.

The words leaped and flew from his lips as he lashed the throng with bitter fury. He said what Zora wanted to say with two great differences: first, he spoke their religious language and spoke it with absolute confidence and authority; and secondly, he seemed to know each one there personally and intimately so that he spoke to no inchoate throng—he spoke to them individually, and they listened awestruck and fearsome.

"God is done sent me," he declared in passionate tones, "to preach His acceptable time. Faith without works is dead; who is you that dares to set and wait for the Lord to do your work?" Then in sudden fury, "Ye generation of vipers—who kin save you?" He bent forward and pointed his long finger. "Yes," he cried, "pray, Sam Collins, you black devil; pray, for the corn you stole Thursday." The black figure moved. "Moan, Sister Maxwell, for the backbiting you did today. Yell,

Jack Tolliver, you sneaking scamp, t'wil the Lord tell Uncle Bill who ruined his daughter. Weep, May Haynes, for that baby—"

But the woman's shriek drowned his words, and he whirled full on the preacher, stamping his feet and waving his hands. His anger choked him; the fat preacher cowered gray and trembling. The gaunt fanatic towered over him.

"You—you—ornery hound of Hell! God never knowed you and the devil owns your soul!" There leapt from his lips a denunciation so livid, specific, and impassioned that the preacher squatted and bowed, then finally fell upon his face and moaned.

The gaunt speaker turned again to the people. He talked of little children; he pictured their sin and neglect. "God is done sent me to offer you all salvation," he cried, while the people wept and wailed; "not in praying, but in works. Follow me!" The hour was half way between midnight and dawn, but nevertheless the people leapt frenziedly to their feet.

"Follow me!" he shouted.

And, singing and chanting, the throng poured out upon the black highway, waving their torches. Zora knew his intention. With a half-dozen of younger onlookers she unhitched teams and rode across the land, calling at the cabins. Before sunrise, tools were in the swamp, axes and saws and hammers. The noise of prayer and singing filled the Sabbath dawn. The news of the great revival spread, and men and women came pouring in. Then of a sudden the uproar stopped, and the ringing of axes and grating of saws and tugging of mules was heard. The forest trembled as by some mighty magic, swaying and falling with crash on crash. Huge bonfires blazed and crackled, until at last a wide black scar appeared in the thick south side of the swamp, which widened and widened to full twenty acres.

The sun rose higher and higher till it blazed at high noon. The workers dropped their tools. The aroma of coffee and roasting meat rose in the dim cool shade. With ravenous appetites the dark, half-famished throng fell upon the food, and then in utter weariness stretched themselves and slept: lying along the earth like huge bronze earth-spirits, sitting against trees, curled in dense bushes.

And Zora sat above them on a high rich-scented pile of logs. Her senses slept save her sleepless eyes. Amid a silence she saw in the little grove that still stood, the cabin of Elspeth tremble, sigh, and disappear, and with it flew some spirit of evil.

Then she looked down to the new edge of the swamp, by the old lagoon, and saw Bles Alwyn standing there. It seemed very natural; and closing her eyes, she fell asleep.

___

Thirty-four

THE RETURN OF ALWYN

B les Alwyn stared at Mrs. Harry Cresswell in surprise. He had not seen her since that moment at the ball, and he was startled at the change. Her abundant hair was gone; her face was pale and drawn, and there were little wrinkles below her sunken eyes. In those eyes lurked the tired look of the bewildered and the disappointed. It was in the lofty waiting-room of the Washington station where Alwyn had come to meet a friend. Mrs. Cresswell turned and recognized him with genuine pleasure. He seemed somehow a part of the few things in the world—little and unimportant perhaps—that counted and stood firm, and she shook his hand cordially, not minding the staring of the people about. He took her bag and carried it towards the gate, which made the observers breathe easier, seeing him in servile duty. Someway, she knew not just how, she found herself telling him of the crisis in her life before she realized; not everything, of course, but a great deal. It was much as though she were talking to some one from another world—an outsider; but one she had known long, one who understood. Both from what she recounted and what she could not tell he gathered the substance of the story, and it bewildered him. He had not thought that white people had such troubles; yet, he reflected, why not? They, too, were human.

"I suppose you hear from the school?" he ventured after a pause.

"Why, yes—not directly—but Zora used to speak of it."

Bles looked up quickly.

"Zora?"

"Yes. Didn't you see her while she was here? She has gone back now."

Then the gate opened, the crowd surged through, sweeping them apart, and next moment he was alone.

Alwyn turned slowly away. He forgot the friend he was to meet. He forgot everything but the field of the Silver Fleece. It rose shadowy there in the pale concourse, swaying in ghostly breezes. The purple of its flowers mingled with the silver radiance of tendrils that trembled across the hurrying throng, like threads of mists along low hills. In its midst rose a dark, slim, and quivering form. She had been here—here in Washington! Why had he not known? What was she doing? "She has gone back now"—back to the Sun and the Swamp, back to the Burden.

Why should not he go back, too? He walked on thinking. He had failed. His apparent success had been too sudden, too overwhelming, and when he had faced the crisis his hand had trembled. He had chosen the Right—but the Right was ineffective, impotent, almost ludicrous. It left him shorn, powerless, and in moral revolt. The world had suddenly left him, as the vision of Carrie Wynn had left him, alone, a mere clerk, an insignificant cog in the great grinding wheel of humdrum drudgery. His chance to do and thereby to be had not come.

He thought of Zora again. Why not go back to the South where she had gone? He shuddered as one who sees before him a cold black pool whither his path leads. To face the proscription, the insult, the lawless hate of the South again—never! And yet he went home and sat down and wrote a long letter to Miss Smith.

The reply that came after some delay was almost curt. It answered few of his questions, argued with none of his doubts, and made no mention of Zora. Yes, there was need of a manager for the new farm and settlement. She was not sure whether Alwyn could do the work or not. The salary was meagre and the work hard. If he wished it, he must decide immediately.

Two weeks later found Alwyn on the train facing Southward in the Jim Crow car. How he had decided to go back South he did not know. In fact, he had not decided. He had sat helpless and inactive in the grip of great and shadowed hands, and the thing was as yet incomprehensible. And so it was that the vision Zora saw in the swamp had been real enough, and Alwyn felt strangely disappointed that she had given no sign of greeting on recognition.

In other ways, too, Zora, when he met her, was to him a new creature. She came to him frankly and greeted him, her gladness shining in her eyes, yet looking nothing more than gladness and saying nothing more. Just what he had expected was hard to say; but he had left her on her knees in the dirt with outstretched hands, and somehow he had expected to return to some corresponding mental attitude. The physical change of these three years was marvellous. The girl was a woman, well-rounded and poised, tall, straight, and quick. And with this went mental change: a self-mastery; a veiling of the self even in intimate talk; a subtle air as of one looking from great and unreachable heights down on the dawn of the world. Perhaps no one who had not known the child and the girl as he had would have noted all this; but he saw and realized the transformation with a pang—something had gone; the innocence and wonder of the child, and in their place had grown up something to him incomprehensible and occult.

Miss Smith was not to be easily questioned on the subject. She took no hints and gave no information, and when once he hazarded some pointed questions she turned on him abruptly, observing acidly: "If I were you I'd think less of Zora and more of her work."

Gradually, in his spiritual perplexity, Alwyn turned to Mary Cresswell. She was staying with the Colonel at Cresswell Oaks. Her coming South was supposed to be solely for reasons of health, and her appearance made this excuse plausible. She was lonely and restless, and naturally drawn toward the school. Her intercourse with Miss Smith was only formal, but her interest in Zora's work grew. Down in the swamp, at the edge of the cleared space, had risen a log cabin; long, low, spacious, overhung with oak and pine. It was Zora's centre for her settlement-work. There she lived, and with her a half-dozen orphan girls and children too young for the boarding department of the school. Mrs. Cresswell easily fell into the habit of walking by here each day, coming down the avenue of oaks across the road and into the swamp. She saw little of Zora personally but she saw her girls and learned much of her plans.

The rooms of the cottage were clean and light, supplied with books and pictures, simple toys, and a phonograph. The yard was one wide green and golden play-ground, and all day the music of children's glad crooning and the singing of girls went echoing and trembling through the trees, as they played and sewed and washed and worked.

From the Cresswells and the Maxwells and others came loads of clothes for washing and mending. The Tolliver girls had simple dresses made, embroidery was ordered from town, and soon there would be the gardens and cotton fields. Mrs. Cresswell would saunter down of mornings. Sometimes she would talk to the big girls and play with the children; sometimes she would sit hidden in the forest, listening and glimpsing and thinking, thinking, till her head whirled and the world danced red before her eyes. today she rose wearily, for it was near noon, and started home. She saw Alwyn swing along the road to the school dining-room where he had charge of the students at the noonday meal.

Alwyn wanted Mrs. Cresswell's judgment and advice. He was growing doubtful of his own estimate of women. Evidently something about his standards was wrong; consequently he made opportunities to talk with Mrs. Cresswell when she was about, hoping she would bring up the subject of Zora of her own accord. But she did not. She was too full of her own cares and troubles, and she was only too glad of willing and sympathetic ears into which to pour her thoughts. Miss Smith soon began to look on these conversations with some uneasiness. Black men and white women cannot talk together casually in the South and she did not know how far the North had put notions in Alwyn's head.

Today both met each other almost eagerly.

Mrs. Cresswell had just had a bit of news which only he would fully appreciate.

"Have you heard of the Vanderpools?" she asked.

"No—except that he was appointed and confirmed at last."

"Well, they had only arrived in France when he died of apoplexy. I do not know," added Mrs. Cresswell, "I may be wrong and—I hope I'm not glad." Then there leapt to her mind a hypothetical question which had to do with her own curious situation. It was characteristic of her to brood and then restlessly to seek relief in consulting the one person near who knew her story. She started to open the subject again today.

But Alwyn, his own mind full, spoke first and rapidly. He, too, had turned to her as he saw her come from Zora's home. He must know more about the girl. He could no longer endure this silence. Zora beneath her apparent frankness was impenetrable, and he felt that she carefully avoided him, although she did it so deftly that he felt rather than observed it. Miss Smith still systematically snubbed him when he broached the subject of Zora. With others he did not speak; the matter seemed too delicate and sacred, and he always had an awful dread lest sometime, somewhere, a chance and fatal word would be dropped, a breath of evil gossip which would shatter all. He had hated to obtrude his troubles on Mrs. Cresswell, who seemed so torn in soul. But today he must speak, although time pressed.

"Mrs. Cresswell," he began hurriedly, "there's a matter—a personal matter of which I have wanted to speak—a long time—I—" The dinner-bell rang, and he stopped, vexed.

"Come up to the house this afternoon," she said; "Colonel Cresswell will be away—" Then she paused abruptly. A strange startling thought flashed through her brain. Alwyn noticed nothing. He thanked her cordially and hurried toward the dining-hall, meeting Colonel Cresswell on horseback just as he turned into the school gate.

Mary Cresswell walked slowly on, flushing and paling by turns. Could it be that this Negro had dared to misunderstand her—had presumed? She reviewed her conduct. Perhaps she had been indiscreet in thus making a confidant of him in her trouble. She had thought of him as a boy—an old student, a sort of confidential servant; but what had he thought? She remembered Miss Smith's warning of years before—and he had been North since and acquired Northern notions of freedom and equality. She bit her lip cruelly.

Yet, she mused, she was herself to blame. She had unwittingly made the intimacy and he was but a Negro, looking on every white woman as a goddess and ready to fawn at the slightest encouragement. There had been no one else here to confide in. She could not tell Miss Smith her troubles, although she knew Miss Smith must suspect. Harry Cresswell, apparently, had written nothing home of their quarrel. All the neighbors behaved as if her excuse of ill-health were sufficient to account for her return South to escape the rigors of a Northern winter. Alwyn, and Alwyn alone, really knew. Well, it was her blindness, and she must right it quietly and quickly with hard ruthless plainness. She blushed again at the shame of it; then she began to excuse.

After all, which was worse—a Cresswell or an Alwyn? It was no sin that Alwyn had done; it was simply ignorant presumption, and she must correct him firmly, but gently, like a child. What a crazy muddle the world was! She thought of Harry Cresswell and the tale he told her in the swamp. She thought of the flitting ghosts that awful night in Washington. She thought of Miss Wynn who had jilted Alwyn and given her herself a very bad quarter of an hour. What a world it was, and after all how far was this black boy wrong? Just then Colonel Cresswell rode up behind and greeted her.

She started almost guiltily, and again a sense of the awkwardness of her position reddened her face and neck. The Colonel dismounted, despite her protest, and walked beside her. They chatted along indifferently, of the crops, her brother's new baby, the proposed mill.

"Mary," his voice abruptly struck a new note. "I don't like the way you talk with that Alwyn nigger."

She was silent.

"Of course," he continued, "you're Northern born and you have been a teacher in this school and feel differently from us in some ways; but mark what I say, a nigger will presume on the slightest pretext, and you must keep them in their place. Then, too, you are a Cresswell now—"

She smiled bitterly; he noticed it, but went on:

"You are a Cresswell, even if you have caught Harry up to some of his deviltry,"—she started,—"and got miffed about it. It'll all come out right. You're a Cresswell, and you must hold yourself too high to 'Mister' a nigger or let him dream of any sort of equality."

He spoke pleasantly, but with a certain sharp insistence that struck a note of fear in Mary's heart. For a moment she thought of writing Alwyn not to call. But, no; a note would be unwise. She and Colonel Cresswell lunched rather silently.

"Well, I must get to town," he finally announced. "The mill directors meet today. If Maxwell calls by about that lumber tell him I'll see him in town." And away he went.

He had scarcely reached the highway and ridden a quarter of a mile or so when he spied Bles Alwyn hurrying across the field toward the Cresswell Oaks. He frowned and rode on. Then reining in his horse, he stopped in the shadow of the trees and watched Alwyn.

It was here that Zora saw him as she came up from her house. She, too, stopped, and soon saw whom he was watching. She had been planning to see Mr. Cresswell about the cut timber on her land. By legal right it was hers but she knew he would claim half, treating her like a mere tenant. Seeing him watching Alwyn she paused in the shadow and waited, fearing trouble. She, too, had felt that the continued conversations of Alwyn and Mrs. Cresswell were indiscreet, but she hoped that they had attracted no one else's attention. Now she feared the Colonel was suspicious and her heart sank. Alwyn went straight toward the house and disappeared in the oak avenue. Still Colonel Cresswell waited but Zora waited no longer. Alwyn must be warned. She must reach Cresswell's mansion before Cresswell did and without him seeing her. This meant a long detour of the swamp to approach the Oaks from the west. She silently gathered up her skirts and walked quickly and carefully away.

She was a strong woman, lithe and vigorous, living in the open air and used to walking. Once out of hearing she threw away her hat and bending forward ran through the swamp. For a while she ran easily and swiftly. Then for a moment she grew dizzy and it seemed as though she was standing still and the swamp in solemn grandeur marching past—in solemn mocking grandeur. She loosened her dress at the neck and flew on.

She sped at last through the oaks, up the terraces, and slowing down to an unsteady walk, staggered into the house. No one would wonder at her being there. She came up now and then and sorted the linen and piled the baskets for her girls. She entered a side door and listened. The Colonel's voice sounded impatiently in the front hall.

"Mary! Mary?"

A pause, then an answer:

"Yes, father!"

He started up the front stairway and Zora hurried up the narrow back stairs, almost overturning a servant.

"I'm after the clothes," she explained. She reached the back landing just in time to see Colonel Cresswell's head rising up the front staircase. With a quick bound she almost fell into the first room at the top of the stairs.

Bles Alwyn had hurried through his dinner duties and hastened to the Oaks. The questions, the doubts, the uncertainty within him were clamoring for utterance. How much had Mrs. Cresswell ever known of Zora? What kind of a woman was Zora now? Mrs. Cresswell had seen her and had talked to her and watched her. What did she think? Thus he formulated his questions as he went, half timid, and fearful in putting them and yet determined to know.

Mrs. Cresswell, waiting for him, was almost panic-stricken. Probably he would beat round the bush seeking further encouragement; but at the slightest indication she must crush him ruthlessly and at the same time point the path of duty. He ought to marry some good girl— not Zora, but some one. Somehow Zora seemed too unusual and strange for him—too inhuman, as Mary Cresswell judged humanity. She glanced out from her seat on the upper verandah over the front porch and saw Alwyn coming. Where should she receive him? On the porch and have Mr. Maxwell ride up? In the parlor and have the servants astounded and talking? If she took him up to her own sitting-room the servants would think he was doing some work or fetching something for the school. She greeted him briefly and asked him in.

"Good-afternoon, Bles"—using his first name to show him his place, and then inwardly recoiling at its note of familiarity. She preceded him up-stairs to the sitting-room, where, leaving the door ajar, she seated herself on the opposite side of the room and waited.

He fidgeted, then spoke rapidly.

"Mrs. Cresswell—this is a personal affair." She reddened angrily. "A love affair"—she paled with something like fear—"and I"—she started to speak, but could not—"I want to know what you think about Zora?"

"About Zora!" she gasped weakly. The sudden reaction, the revulsion of her agitated feelings, left her breathless.

"About Zora. You know I loved her dearly as a boy—how dearly I have only just begun to realize: I've been wondering if I understood— if I wasn't—"

Mrs. Cresswell got angrily to her feet.

"You have come here to speak to me of that—that—" she choked, and Bles thought his worst fears realized.

"Mary, Mary!" Colonel Cresswell's voice broke suddenly in upon them. With a start of fear Mrs. Cresswell rushed out into the hall and closed the door.

"Mary, has that Alwyn nigger been here this afternoon?" Mr. Cresswell was coming up-stairs, carrying his riding whip.

"Why, no!" she answered, lying instinctively before she quite realized what her lie meant. She hesitated. "That is, I haven't seen him. I must have nodded over my book,"—looking toward the little verandah at the front of the upper hall, where her easy chair stood with her book. Then with an awful flash of enlightenment she realized what her lie might mean, and her heart paused.

Cresswell strode up.

"I saw him come up—he must have entered. He's nowhere downstairs," he wavered and scowled. "Have you been in your sitting-room?" And then, not waiting for a reply, he strode to the door.

"But the damned scoundrel wouldn't dare!"

He deliberately placed his hand in his right-hand hip-pocket and threw open the door.

Mary Cresswell stood frozen. The full horror of the thing burst upon her. Her own silly misapprehension, the infatuation of Alwyn for Zora, her thoughtless—no, vindictive—betrayal of him to something worse than death. She listened for the crack of doom. She heard a bird singing far down in the swamp; she heard the soft raising of a window and the closing of a door. And then—great God in heaven! must she live forever in this agony?—and then, she heard the door bang and Mr. Cresswell's gruff voice—

"Well, where is he?—he isn't in there!"

Mary Cresswell felt that something was giving way within. She swayed and would have crashed to the bottom of the staircase if just then she had not seen at the opposite end of the hall, near the back stairs, Zora and Alwyn emerge calmly from a room, carrying a basket full of clothes. Colonel Cresswell stared at them, and Zora instinctively put up her hand and fastened her dress at the throat. The Colonel scowled, for it was all clear to him now.

"Look here," he angrily opened upon them, "if you niggers want to meet around keep out of this house; hereafter I'll send the clothes down. By God, if you want to make love go to the swamp!" He stamped down the stairs while an ashy paleness stole beneath the dark-red bronze of Zora's face.

They walked silently down the road together—the old familiar road. Alwyn was staring moodily ahead.

"We must get married—before Christmas, Zora," he presently avowed, not looking at her. He felt the basket pause and he glanced up. Her dark eyes were full upon him and he saw something in their depths that brought him to himself and made him realize his blunder.

"Zora!" he stammered, "forgive me! *Will* you marry me?"

She looked at him calmly with infinite compassion. But her reply was uttered unhesitantly; distinct, direct.

"No, Bles."

Thirty-five

THE COTTON MILL

The people of Toomsville started in their beds and listened. A new song was rising on the air: a harsh, low, murmuring croon that shook the village ranged around its old square of dilapadated stores. It was not a song of joy; it was not a song of sorrow; it was not a song at all, perhaps, but a confused whizzing and murmuring, as of a thousand ill-tuned, busy voices. Some of the listeners wondered; but most of the town cried joyfully, "It's the new cotton-mill!"

John Taylor's head teemed with new schemes. The mill trust of the North was at last a fact. The small mills had not been able to buy cotton when it was low because Cresswell was cornering it in the name of the Farmers' League; now that it was high they could not afford to, and many surrendered to the trust.

"Next thing," wrote Taylor to Easterly, "is to reduce cost of production. Too much goes in wages. Gradually transfer mills South."

Easterly argued that the labor was too unskilled in the South and that to send Northern spinners down would spread labor troubles. Taylor replied briefly: "Never fear; we'll scare them with a vision of niggers in the mills!"

Colonel Cresswell was not so easily won over to the new scheme. In the first place he was angry because the school, which he had come to regard as on its last legs, somehow still continued to flourish. The ten-thousand-dollar mortgage had but three more years, and that would end all; but he had hoped for a crash even earlier. Instead of this, Miss Smith was cheerfully expanding the work, hiring new teachers, and especially she had brought to help her two young Negroes whom he suspected. Colonel Cresswell had prevented the Tolliver land sale, only to be inveigled himself into Zora's scheme which now began to worry him. He must evict Zora's tenants as soon as the crops were planted and harvested. There was nothing unjust about such a course, he argued, for Negroes anyway were too lazy and shiftless to buy the land. They would not, they could not, work without driving. All this he imparted to John Taylor, to which that gentleman listened carefully.

"H'm, I see," he owned. "And I know the way out."

"How?"

"A cotton mill in Toomsville."

"What's that got to do with it?"

"Bring in whites."

"But I don't want poor white trash; I'd sooner have niggers."

"Now, see here," argued Taylor, "you can't have everything you want—day's gone by for aristocracy of old kind. You must have neighbors: choose, then, white or black. I say white."

"But they'll rule us—out-vote us—marry our daughters," warmly objected the Colonel.

"Some of them may—most of them won't. A few of them with brains will help us rule the rest with money. We'll plant cotton mills beside the cotton fields, use whites to keep niggers in their place, and the fear of niggers to keep the poorer whites in theirs."

The Colonel looked thoughtful.

"There's something in that," he confessed after a while; "but it's a mighty big experiment, and it may go awry."

"Not with brains and money to guide it. And at any rate, we've got to try it; it's the next logical step, and we must take it."

"But in the meantime, I'm not going to give up good old methods; I'm going to set the sheriff behind these lazy niggers," said the Colonel; "and I'm going to stop that school putting notions into their heads."

In three short months the mill at Toomsville was open and its wheels whizzing to the boundless pride of the citizens.

"Our enterprise, sir!" they said to the strangers on the strength of the five thousand dollars locally invested.

Once it had vigor to sing, the song of the mill knew no resting; morning and evening, day and night it crooned its rhythmic tune; only during the daylight Sundays did its murmur die to a sibilant hiss. All the week its doors were filled with the coming and going of men and women and children: many men, more women, and greater and greater throngs of children. It seemed to devour children, sitting with its myriad eyes gleaming and its black maw open, drawing in the pale white mites, sucking their blood and spewing them out paler and ever paler. The face of the town began to change, showing a ragged tuberculous looking side with dingy homes in short and homely rows.

There came gradually a new consciousness to the town. Hitherto town and country had been ruled by a few great landlords but at the very first election, Colton, an unknown outsider, had beaten the regular candidate for sheriff by such a majority that the big property owners dared not count him out. They had, however, an earnest consultation with John Taylor.

"It's just as I said," growled Colonel Cresswell, "if you don't watch out our whole plantation system will be ruined and we'll be governed by this white trash from the hills."

"There's only one way," sighed Caldwell, the merchant; "we've got to vote the niggers."

John Taylor laughed. "Nonsense!" he spurned the suggestion. "You're old-fashioned. Let the mill-hands have the offices. What good will it do?"

"What good! Why, they'll do as they please with us."

"Bosh! Don't we own the mill? Can't we keep wages where we like by threatening to bring in nigger labor?"

"No, you can't, permanently," Maxwell disputed, "for they some-time will call your bluff."

"Let 'em call," said Taylor, "and we'll put niggers in the mills."

"What!" ejaculated the landlords in chorus. Only Maxwell was silent. "And kill the plantation system?"

"Oh, maybe some time, of course. But not for years; not until you've made your pile. You don't really expect to keep the darkies down forever, do you?"

"No, I don't," Maxwell slowly admitted. "This system can't last al-ways—sometimes I think it can't last long. It's wrong, through and through. It's built on ignorance, theft, and force, and I wish to God we had courage enough to overthrow it and take the consequences. I wish it was possible to be a Southerner and a Christian and an honest man, to treat niggers and dagoes and white trash like men, and be big enough to say, 'To Hell with consequences!' "

Colonel Cresswell stared at his neighbor, speechless with bewilder-ment and outraged traditions. Such unbelievable heresy from a North-erner or a Negro would have been natural; but from a Southerner whose father had owned five hundred slaves—it was incredible! The other landlords scarcely listened; they were dogged and impatient and they could suggest no remedy. They could only blame the mill for their troubles.

John Taylor left the conference blithely. "No," he said to the committee from the new mill-workers' union. "Can't raise wages, gentlemen, and can't lessen hours. Mill is just started and not yet paying expenses. You're getting better wages than you ever got. If you don't want to work, quit. There are plenty of others, white and black, who want your jobs."

The mention of black people as competitors for wages was like a red rag to a bull. The laborers got together and at the next election they made a clean sweep, judge, sheriff, two members of the legislature, and the registrars of votes. Undoubtedly the following year they would capture Harry Cresswell's seat in Congress.

The result was curious. From two sides, from landlord and white laborer, came renewed oppression of black men. The laborers found that their political power gave them little economic advantage as long as the threatening cloud of Negro competition loomed ahead. There was some talk of a strike, but Colton, the new sheriff, discouraged it.

"I tell you, boys, where the trouble lies: it's the niggers. They live on nothing and take any kind of treatment, and they keep wages down. If you strike, they'll get your jobs, sure. We'll just have to grin and bear it a while, but get back at the darkies whenever you can. I'll stick 'em into the chain-gang every chance I get."

On the other hand, inspired by fright, the grip of the landlords on the black serfs closed with steadily increasing firmness. They saw one class rising from beneath them to power, and they tightened the chains on the other. Matters simmered on in this way, and the only party wholly satisfied with conditions was John Taylor and the few young Southerners who saw through his eyes. He was making money. The landlords, on the contrary, were losing power and prestige, and their farm labor, despite strenuous efforts, was drifting to town attracted by new and incidental work and higher wages. The mill-hands were more and more overworked and underpaid, and hated the Negroes for it in accordance with their leaders' directions.

At the same time the oppressed blacks and scowling mill-hands could not help recurring again and again to the same inarticulate thought which no one was brave enough to voice. Once, however, it came out flatly. It was when Zora, crowding into the village court-house to see if she could not help Aunt Rachel's accused boy, found herself beside a gaunt, overworked white woman. The woman was struggling with a crippled child and Zora, turning, lifted him carefully for the weak mother, who thanked her half timidly. "That mill's about killed him," she said.

At this juncture the manacled boy was led into court, and the woman suddenly turned again to Zora.

"Durned if I don't think these white slaves and black slaves had ought ter git together," she declared.

"I think so, too," Zora agreed.

Colonel Cresswell himself caught the conversation and it struck him with a certain dismay. Suppose such a conjunction should come to pass? He edged over to John Taylor and spoke to him; but Taylor, who had just successfully stopped a suit for damages to the injured boy, merely shrugged his shoulders.

"What's this nigger charged with?" demanded the Judge when the first black boy was brought up before him.

"Breaking his labor contract."

"Any witnesses?"

"I have the contract here," announced the sheriff. "He refuses to work."

"A year, or one hundred dollars."

Colonel Cresswell paid his fine, and took him in charge.

"What's the charge here?" said the Judge, pointing to Aunt Rachel's boy.

"Attempt to kill a white man."

"Any witnesses?"

"None except the victim."

"And I," said Zora, coming forward.

Both the sheriff and Colonel Cresswell stared at her. Of course, she was simply a black girl but she was an educated woman, who knew things about the Cresswell plantations that it was unnecessary to air in court. The newly elected Judge had not yet taken his seat, and Cresswell's word was still law in the court. He whispered to the Judge.

"Case postponed," said the Court.

The sheriff scowled.

"Wait till Jim gets on the bench," he growled.

The white bystanders, however, did not seem enthusiastic and one man—he was a Northern spinner—spoke out plainly.

"It's none o' my business, of course. I've been fired and I'm damned glad of it. But see here: if you mutts think you're going to beat these big blokes at their own game of cheating niggers you're daffy. You take this from me: get together with the niggers and hold up this whole capitalist gang. If you don't get the niggers first, they'll use 'em as a club to throw you down. You hear *me*," and he departed for the train.

Colton was suspicious. The sentiment of joining with the Negroes did not seem to arouse the bitter resentment he expected. There even came whispers to his ears that he had sold out to the landlords, and there was enough truth in the report to scare him. Thus to both parties came the uncomfortable spectre of the black men, and both sides went to work to lay the ghost.

Particularly was Colonel Cresswell stirred to action. He realized that in Bles and Zora he was dealing with a younger class of educated black folk, who were learning to fight with new weapons. They were, he was sure, as dissolute and weak as their parents, but they were shrewder and more aspiring. They must be crushed, and crushed quickly. To this end he had recourse to two sources of help—Johnson and the whites in town.

Johnson was what Colonel Cresswell repeatedly called "a faithful nigger." He was one of those constitutionally timid creatures into whom the servility of his fathers had sunk so deep that it had become second-nature. To him a white man was an archangel, while the Cresswells, his father's masters, stood for God. He served them with dog-like faith, asking no reward, and for what he gave in reverence to them, he took back in contempt for his fellows—"niggers!" He applied the epithet with more contempt than the Colonel himself could express. To the Negroes he was a "white folk's nigger," to be despised and feared.

To him Colonel Cresswell gave a few pregnant directions. Then he rode to town, and told Taylor again of his fears of a labor movement which would include whites and blacks. Taylor could not see any great danger.

"Of course," he conceded, "they'll eventually get together; their interests are identical. I'll admit it's our game to delay this as long possible."

"It must be delayed forever, sir."

"Can't be," was the terse response. "But even if they do ally themselves, our way is easy: separate the leaders, the talented, the pushers, of both races from their masses, and through them rule the rest by money."

But Colonel Cresswell shook his head. "It's precisely these leaders of the Negroes that we mush crush," he insisted. Taylor looked puzzled.

"I thought it was the lazy, shiftless, and criminal Negroes, you feared?"

"Hang it, no! We can deal with them; we've got whips, chain-gangs, and—mobs, if need be—no, it's the Negro who wants to climb up that we've got to beat to his knees."

Taylor could not follow this reasoning. He believed in an aristocracy of talent alone, and secretly despised Colonel Cresswell's pretensions of birth. If a man had ability and push Taylor was willing and anxious to open the way for him, even though he were black. The caste way of thinking in the South, both as applied to poor whites and to Negroes, he simply could not understand. The weak and the ignorant of all races he despised and had no patience with them. "But others—a man's a man, isn't he?" he persisted. But Colonel Cresswell replied:

"No, never, if he's black, and not always when he's white," and he stalked away.

Zora sensed fully the situation. She did not anticipate any immediate understanding with the laboring whites, but she knew that eventually it would be inevitable. Meantime the Negro must strengthen himself and bring to the alliance as much independent economic strength as possible. For the development of her plans she needed Bles Alwyn's constant coöperation. He was business manager of the school and was doing well, but she wanted to point out to him the larger field. So long as she was uncertain of his attitude toward her, it was difficult to act; but now, since the flash of the imminent tragedy at Cresswell Oaks had cleared the air, with all its hurt a frank understanding had been made possible. The very next day Zora chose to show Bles over her new home and grounds, and to speak frankly to him. They looked at the land, examined the proposed farm sites, and viewed the living-room and dormitory in the house.

"You haven't seen my den," said Zora.

"No."

"Miss Smith is in there now; she often hides there. Come."

He went into the large central house and into the living-room, then out on the porch, beyond which lay the kitchen. But to the left, and at the end of the porch, was a small building. It was ceiled in dark yellow pine, with figured denim on the walls. A straight desk of rough hewn wood stood in the corner by the white-curtained window, and a couch and two large easy-chairs faced a tall narrow fireplace of uneven stone. A thick green rag-carpet covered the floor; a few pictures were on the walls—a Madonna, a scene of mad careering horses, and some sad baby faces. The room was a unity; things fitted together as if they belonged together. It was restful and beautiful, from the cheerful pine blaze before which Miss Smith was sitting, to the square-paned window that let in the crimson rays of gathering night. All round the room, stopping only at the fireplace, ran low shelves of the same yellow pine, filled with books and magazines. He scanned curiously Plato's Republic, Gorky's "Comrades," a Cyclopædia of Agriculture, Balzac's novels, Spencer's "First Principles," Tennyson's Poems.

"This is my university," Zora explained, smiling at his interested survey. They went out again and wandered down near the old lagoon.

"Now, Bles," she began, "since we understand each other, can we not work together as good friends?" She spoke simply and frankly, without apparent effort, and talked on at length of her work and vision.

Somehow he could not understand. His mental attitude toward Zora had always been one of guidance, guardianship, and instruction. He had been judging and weighing her from on high, looking down upon her with thoughts of uplift and development. Always he had been holding her dark little hands to lead her out of the swamp of life, and always, when in senseless anger he had half forgotten and deserted her, this vision of elder brotherhood had still remained. Now this attitude was being revolutionized. She was proposing to him a plan of wide scope—a bold regeneration of the land. It was a plan carefully studied out, long thought of and read about. He was asked to be co-worker—nay, in a sense to be a follower, for he was ignorant of much.

He hesitated. Then all at once a sense of his utter unworthiness overwhelmed him. Who was he to stand and judge this unselfish woman? Who was he to falter when she called? A sense of his smallness and narrowness, of his priggish blindness, rose like a mockery in his soul. One thing alone held him back: he was not unwilling to be simply human, a learner and a follower; but would he as such ever command the love and respect of this new and inexplicable woman? Would not comradeship on the basis of the new friendship which she insisted on, be the death of love and thoughts of love?

Thus he hesitated, knowing that his duty lay clear. In her direst need he had deserted her. He had left her to go to destruction and expected that she would. By a superhuman miracle she had risen and seated herself above him. She was working; here was work to be done. He was asked to help; he would help. If it killed his old and new-born dream of love, well and good; it was his punishment.

Yet the sacrifice, the readjustment was hard; he grew to it gradually, inwardly revolting, feeling always a great longing to take this woman and make her nestle in his arms as she used to; catching himself again and again on the point of speaking to her and urging, yet ever again holding himself back and bowing in silent respect to the dignity of her life. Only now and then, when their eyes met suddenly or unthinkingly, a great kindling flash of flame seemed struggling behind showers of tears, until in a moment she smiled or spoke, and then the dropping veil left only the frank open glance, unwavering, soft, kind, but nothing more. Then Alwyn would go wearily away, vexed or disappointed, or merely sad, and both would turn to their work again.

Thirty-six

THE LAND

Colonel Cresswell started all the more grimly to overthrow the new work at the school because somewhere down beneath his heart a pity and a wonder were stirring; pity at the perfectly useless struggle to raise the unraisable, a wonder at certain signs of rising. But it was impossible—and unthinkable, even if possible. So he squared his jaw and cheated Zora deliberately in the matter of the cut timber. He placed every obstacle in the way of getting tenants for the school land. Here Johnson, the "faithful nigger," was of incalculable assistance. He was among the first to hear the call for prospective tenants.

The meeting was in the big room of Zora's house, and Aunt Rachel came early with her cheery voice and smile which faded so quickly to lines of sorrow and despair, and then twinkled back again. After her hobbled old Sykes. Fully a half-hour later Rob hurried in.

"Johnson," he informed the others, "has sneaked over to Cresswell's to tell of this meeting. We ought to beat that nigger up." But Zora asked him about the new baby, and he was soon deep in child-lore. Higgins and Sanders came together—dirty, apologetic, and furtive. Then came Johnson.

"How do, Miss Zora—Mr. Alwyn, I sure is glad to see you, sir. Well, if there ain't Aunt Rachel! looking as young as ever. And Higgins, you scamp—Ah, Mr. Sanders—well, gentlemen and ladies, this sure is gwine to be a good cotton season. I remember—" And he ran on endlessly, now to this one, now to that, now to all, his little eyes all the while dancing insinuatingly here and there. About nine o'clock a buggy drove up and Carter and Simpson came in—Carter, a silent, strong-faced, brown laborer, who listened and looked, and Simpson, a worried nervous man, who sat still with difficulty and commenced many sentences but did not finish them. Alwyn looked at his watch and at Zora, but she gave no sign until they heard a rollicking song outside and Tylor burst into the room. He was nearly seven feet high and broad-shouldered, yellow, with curling hair and laughing brown eyes. He was chewing an enormous quid of tobacco, the juice of which he distributed generously, and had had just liquor enough to make him jolly. His entrance was a breeze and a roar.

Alwyn then undertook to explain the land scheme.

"It is the best land in the county—"

"When it's cl'ared," interrupted Johnson, and Simpson looked alarmed.

"It is partially cleared," continued Alwyn, "and our plan is to sell off small twenty-acre farms—"

"You can't do nothing on twenty acres—" began Johnson, but Tylor laid his huge hand right over his mouth and said briefly:

"Shut up!"

Alwyn started again: "We shall sell a few twenty-acre farms but keep one central plantation of one hundred acres for the school. Here Miss Zora will carry on her work and the school will run a model farm with your help. We want to centre here agencies to make life better. We want all sorts of industries; we want a little hospital with a resident physician and two or three nurses; we want a coöperative store for buying supplies; we want a cotton-gin and saw-mill, and in the future other things. This land here, as I have said, is the richest around. We want to keep this hundred acres for the public good, and not sell it. We are going to deed it to a board of trustees, and those trustees are to be chosen from the ones who buy the small farms."

"Who's going to get what's made on this land?" asked Sanders.

"All of us. It is going first to pay for the land, then to support the Home and the School, and then to furnish capital for industries."

Johnson snickered. "You mean youse gwine to git yo' livin' off it?"

"Yes," answered Alwyn; "but I'm going to work for it."

"Who's gwine—" began Simpson, but stopped helplessly.

"Who's going to tend this land?" asked the practical Carter.

"All of us. Each man is going to promise us so many days' work a year, and we're going to ask others to help—the women and girls and school children—they will all help."

"Can you put trust in that sort of help?"

"We can when once the community learns that it pays."

"Does you own the land?" asked Johnson suddenly.

"No; we're buying it, and it's part paid for already."

The discussion became general. Zora moved about among the men whispering and explaining; while Johnson moved, too, objecting and hinting. At last he arose.

"Brethren," he began, "the plan's good enough for talkin' but you can't work it; who ever heer'd tell of such a thing? First place, the land ain't yours; second place, you can't get it worked; third place, white folks won't 'low it. Who ever heer'd of such working land on shares?"

"You do it for white folks each day, why not for yourselves," Alwyn pointed out.

"'Cause we ain't white, and we can't do nothin' like that."

Tylor was asleep and snoring and the others looked doubtfully at each other. It was a proposal a little too daring for them, a bit too far beyond their experience. One consideration alone kept them from shrinking away and that was Zora's influence. Not a man was there whom she had not helped and encouraged nor who had not perfect faith in her; in her impetuous hope, her deep enthusiasm, and her strong will. Even her defects—the hard-held temper, the deeply rooted dislikes—caught their imagination.

Finally, after several other meetings five men took courage—three of the best and two of the weakest. During the Spring long negotiations were entered into by Miss Smith to "buy" the five men. Colonel Cresswell and Mr. Tolliver had them all charged with large sums of indebtedness and these sums had to be assumed by the school. As Colonel Cresswell counted over two thousand dollars of school notes and deposited them beside the mortgage he smiled grimly for he saw the end. Yet, even then his hand trembled and that curious doubt came creeping back. He put it aside angrily and glanced up.

"Nigger wants to talk with you," announced his clerk.

The Colonel sauntered out and found Bles Alwyn waiting.

"Colonel Cresswell," he said, "I have charge of the buying for the school and our tenants this year and I naturally want to do the best possible. I thought I'd come over and see about getting my supplies at your store."

"That's all right; you can get anything you want," said Colonel Cresswell cheerily, for this to his mind was evidence of sense on the part of the Negroes. Bles showed his list of needed supplies—seeds, meat, corn-meal, coffee, sugar, etc. The Colonel glanced over it carelessly, then moved away.

"All right. Come and get what you want—any time," he called back.

"But about the prices," said Alwyn, following him.

"Oh, they'll be all right."

"Of course. But what I want is an estimate of your lowest cash prices."

"Cash?"

"Yes, sir."

Cresswell thought a while; such a business-like proposition from Negroes surprised him.

"Well, I'll let you know," he said.

It was nearly a week later before Alwyn approached him again.

"Now, see here," said Colonel Cresswell, "there's practically no difference between cash and time prices. We buy our stock on time and you can just as well take advantage of this as not. I have figured out about what these things will cost. The best thing for you to do is to make a deposit here and get things when you want them. If you make a good deposit I'll throw off ten per cent, which is all of my profit."

"Thank you," said Alwyn, but he looked over the account and found the whole bill at least twice as large as he expected. Without further parley, he made some excuse and started to town while Mr. Cresswell went to the telephone.

In town Alwyn went to all the chief merchants one after another and received to his great surprise practically the same estimate. He could not understand it. He had estimated the current market prices according to the Montgomery paper, yet the prices in Toombsville were fifty to a hundred and fifty per cent higher. The merchant to whom he went last, laughed.

"Don't you know we're not going to interfere with Colonel Cresswell's tenants?" He stated the dealers' attitude, and Alwyn saw light. He went home and told Zora, and she listened without surprise.

"Now to business," she said briskly. "Miss Smith," turning to the teacher, "as I told you, they're combined against us in town and we must buy in Montgomery. I was sure it was coming, but I wanted to give Colonel Cresswell every chance. Bles starts for Montgomery—"

Alwyn looked up. "Does he?" he asked, smiling.

"Yes," said Zora, smiling in turn. "We must lose no further time."

"But there's no train from Toombsville tonight."

"But there's one from Barton in the morning and Barton is only twenty miles away."

"It is a long walk." Alwyn thought a while, silently. Then he rose. "I'm going," he said. "Good-bye."

In less than a week the storehouse was full, and tenants were at work. The twenty acres of cleared swamp land, attended to by the voluntary labor of all the tenants, was soon bearing a magnificent crop. Colonel Cresswell inspected all the crops daily with a proprietary air that would have been natural had these folk been simply tenants, and as such he persisted in regarding them.

The cotton now growing was perhaps not so uniformly fine as the first acre of Silver Fleece, but it was of unusual height and thickness.

"At least a bale to the acre," Alwyn estimated, and the Colonel mentally determined to take two-thirds of the crop. After that he decided that he would evict Zora immediately; since sufficient land was cleared already for his purposes and moreover, he had seen with consternation a herd of cattle grazing in one field on some early green stuff, and heard a drove of hogs in the swamp. Such an example before the tenants of the Black Belt would be fatal. He must wait a few weeks for them to pick the cotton—then, the end. He was fighting the battle of his color and caste.

The children sang merrily in the brown-white field. The wide baskets, poised aloft, foamed on the erect and swaying bodies of the dark carriers. The crop throughout the land was short that year, for prices had ruled low last season in accordance with the policy of the Combine. This year they started high again. Would they fall? Many thought so and hastened to sell.

Zora and Alwyn gathered their tenants' crops, ginned them at the Cresswells' gin, and carried their cotton to town, where it was deposited in the warehouse of the Farmers' League.

"Now," said Alwyn, "we would best sell while prices are high."

Zora laughed at him frankly.

"We can't," she said. "Don't you know that Colonel Cresswell will attach our cotton for rent as soon as it touches the warehouse?"

"But it's ours."

"Nothing is ours. No black man ordinarily can sell his crop without a white creditor's consent."

Alwyn fumed.

"The best way," he declared, "is to go to Montgomery and get a first-class lawyer and just fight the thing through. The land is legally ours, and he has no right to our cotton."

"Yes, but you must remember that no man like Colonel Cresswell regards a business bargain with a colored man as binding. No white man under ordinary circumstances will help enforce such a bargain against prevailing public opinion."

"But if we cannot trust to the justice of the case, and if you knew we couldn't, why did you try?"

"Because I had to try; and moreover the circumstances are not altogether ordinary: the men in power in Toomsville now are not the landlords of this county; they are poor whites. The Judge and sheriff were both elected by mill-hands who hate Cresswell and Taylor. Then there's a new young lawyer who wants Harry Cresswell's seat in Congress; he don't know much law, I'm afraid; but what he don't know of this case I think I do. I'll get his advice and then—I mean to conduct the case myself," Zora calmly concluded.

"Without a lawyer!" Bles Alwyn stared his amazement.

"Without a lawyer in court."

"Zora! That would be foolish!"

"Is it? Let's think. For over a year now I've been studying the law of the case," and she pointed to her law books; "I know the law and most of the decisions. Moreover, as a black woman fighting a hopeless battle with landlords, I'll gain the one thing lacking."

"What's that?"

"The sympathy of the court and the bystanders."

"Pshaw! From these Southerners?"

"Yes, from them. They are very human, these men, especially the laborers. Their prejudices are cruel enough, but there are joints in their armor. They are used to seeing us either scared or blindly angry, and they understand how to handle us then, but at other times it is hard for them to do anything but meet us in a human way."

"But, Zora, think of the contact of the court, the humiliation, the coarse talk—"

Zora put up her hand and lightly touched his arm. Looking at him, she said:

"Mud doesn't hurt much. This is my duty. Let me do it."

His eyes fell before the shadow of a deeper rebuke. He arose heavily.

"Very well," he acquiesced as he passed slowly out.

The young lawyer started to refuse to touch the case until he saw— or did Zora adroitly make him see?—a chance for eventual political capital. They went over the matter carefully, and the lawyer acquired a respect for the young woman's knowledge.

"First," he said, "get an injunction on the cotton—then go to court." And to insure the matter he slipped over and saw the Judge.

Colonel Cresswell next day stalked angrily into his lawyers' office.

"See here," he thundered, handing the lawyer the notice of the injunction.

"See the Judge," began the lawyer, and then remembered, as he was often forced to do these days, who was Judge.

He inquired carefully into the case and examined the papers. Then he said:

"Colonel Cresswell, who drew this contract of sale?"

"The black girl did."

"Impossible!"

"She certainly did—wrote it in my presence."

"Well, it's mighty well done."

"You mean it will stand in law?"

"It certainly will. There's but one way to break it, and that's to allege misunderstanding on your part."

Cresswell winced. It was not pleasant to go into open court and acknowledge himself over-reached by a Negro; but several thousand dollars in cotton and land were at stake.

"Go ahead," he concurred.

"You can depend on Taylor, of course?" added the lawyer.

"Of course," answered Cresswell. "But why prolong the thing?"

"You see, she's got your cotton tied by injunction."

"I don't see how she did it."

"Easy enough: this Judge is the poor white you opposed in the last primary."

Within a week the case was called, and they filed into the courtroom. Cresswell's lawyer saw only this black woman—no other lawyer or sign of one appeared to represent her. The place soon filled with a lazy, tobacco-chewing throng of white men. A few blacks whispered in one corner. The dirty stove was glowing with pine-wood and the Judge sat at a desk.

"Where's your lawyer?" he asked sharply of Zora.

"I have none," returned Zora, rising.

There came a silence in the court. Her voice was low, and the men leaned forward to listen. The Judge felt impelled to be over-gruff.

"Get a lawyer," he ordered.

"Your honor, my case is simple, and with your honor's permission I wish to conduct it myself. I cannot afford a lawyer, and I do not think I need one."

Cresswell's lawyer smiled and leaned back. It was going to be easier than he supposed. Evidently the woman believed she had no case, and was weakening.

The trial proceeded, and Zora stated her contention. She told how long her mother and grandmother had served the Cresswells and showed her receipt for rent paid.

"A friend sent me some money. I went to Mr. Cresswell and asked him to sell me two hundred acres of land. He consented to do so and signed this contract in the presence of his son-in-law."

Just then John Taylor came into the court, and Cresswell beckoned to him.

"I want you to help me out, John."

"All right," whispered Taylor. "What can I do?"

"Swear that Cresswell didn't mean to sign this," said the lawyer quickly, as he arose to address the court.

Taylor looked at the paper blankly and then at Cresswell and some inkling of the irreconcilable difference in the two natures leapt in both their hearts. Cresswell might gamble and drink and lie "like a gentleman," but he would never willingly cheat or take advantage of a white man's financial necessities. Taylor, on the other hand, had a horror of a lie, never drank nor played games of chance, but his whole life was speculation and in the business game he was utterly ruthless and respected no one. Such men could never thoroughly understand each other. To Cresswell a man who had cheated the whole South out of millions by a series of misrepresentations ought to regard this little falsehood as nothing.

Meantime Colonel Cresswell's lawyer was on his feet, and he adopted his most irritating and contemptuous manner.

"This nigger wench wrote out some illegible stuff and Colonel Cresswell signed it to get rid of her. We are not going to question the legality of the form—that's neither here nor there. The point is, Mr. Cresswell never intended—never dreamed of selling this wench land right in front of his door. He meant to rent her the land and sign a receipt for rent paid in advance. I will not worry your honor by a long argument to prove this, but just call one of the witnesses well known to you—Mr. John Taylor of the Toomsville mills."

Taylor looked toward the door and then slowly took the stand.

"Mr. Taylor," said the lawyer carelessly, "were you present at this transaction?"

"Yes."

"Did you see Colonel Cresswell sign this paper?"

"Yes."

"Well, did he intend so far as you know to sign such a paper?"

"I do not know his intentions."

"Did he say he meant to sign such a contract?"

Taylor hesitated.

"Yes," he finally answered. Colonel Cresswell looked up in amazement and the lawyer dropped his glasses.

"I—I don't think you perhaps understood me, Mr. Taylor," he gasped. "I—er—meant to ask if Colonel Cresswell, in signing this paper, meant to sign a contract to sell this wench two hundred acres of land?"

"He said he did," reiterated Taylor. "Although I ought to add that he did not think the girl would ever be able to pay. If he had thought she would pay, I don't think he would have signed the paper."

Colonel Cresswell went red, than pale, and leaning forward before the whole court, he hurled:

"You damned scoundrel!"

The Judge rapped for order and fidgeted in his seat. There was some confusion and snickering in the courtroom. Finally the Judge plucked up courage:

"The defendant is ordered to deliver this cotton to Zora Cresswell," he directed.

The raging of Colonel Cresswell's anger now turned against John Taylor as well as the Negroes. Wind of the estrangement flew over town quickly. The poor whites saw a chance to win Taylor's influence and the sheriff approached him cautiously. Taylor paid him slight courtesy. He was irritated with this devilish Negro problem; he was making money; his wife and babies were enjoying life, and here was this fool trial to upset matters. But the sheriff talked.

"The thing I'm afraid of," he said, "is that Cresswell and his gang will swing in the niggers on us."

"How do you mean?"

"Let 'em vote."

"But they'd have to read and write."

"Sure!"

"Well, then," said Taylor, "it might be a good thing."

Colton eyed him suspiciously.

"You'd let a nigger vote?"

"Why, yes, if he had sense enough."

"There ain't no nigger got sense."

"Oh, pshaw!" Taylor ejaculated, walking away.

The sheriff was angry and mistrustful. He believed he had discovered a deep-laid scheme of the aristocrats to cultivate friendliness between whites and blacks, and then use black voters to crush the whites. Such a course was, in Colton's mind, dangerous, monstrous, and unnatural; it must be stopped at all hazards. He began to whisper among his friends. One or two meetings were held, and the flame of racial prejudice was studiously fanned.

The atmosphere of the town and country quickly began to change. Whatever little beginnings of friendship and understanding had arisen now quickly disappeared. The town of a Saturday no longer belonged to a happy, careless crowd of black peasants, but the black folk found themselves elbowed to the gutter, while ugly quarrels flashed here and there with a quick arrest of the Negroes.

Colonel Cresswell made a sudden resolve. He sent for the sheriff and received him at the Oaks, in his most respectable style, filling him with good food, and warming him with good liquor.

"Colton," he asked, "are you sending any of your white children to the nigger school yet?"

"What!" yelled Colton.

The Colonel laughed, frankly telling Colton John Taylor's philosophy on the race problem,—his willingness to let Negroes vote; his threat to let blacks and whites work together; his contempt for the officials elected by the people.

"Candidly, Colton," he concluded, "I believe in aristocracy. I can't think it right or wise to replace the old aristocracy by new and untried blood." And in a sudden outburst—"But, by God, sir! I'm a white man, and I place the lowest white man ever created above the highest darkey ever thought of. This Yankee, Taylor, is a nigger-lover. He's secretly encouraging and helping them. You saw what he did to me, and I'm warning you in time."

Colton's glass dropped.

"I thought it was you that was corralling the niggers against us," he exclaimed.

The Colonel reddened. "I don't count all white men my equals, I admit," he returned with dignity, "but I know the difference between a white man and a nigger."

Colton stretched out his massive hand. "Put it there, sir," said he; "I misjudged you, Colonel Cresswell. I'm a Southerner, and I honor the old aristocracy you represent. I'm going to join with you to crush this Yankee and put the niggers in their places. They are getting impudent around here; they need a lesson and, by gad! they'll get one they'll remember."

"Now, see here, Colton,—nothing rash," the Colonel charged him, warningly. "Don't stir up needless trouble; but—well, things must change."

Colton rose and shook his head.

"The niggers need a lesson," he muttered as he unsteadily bade his host good-bye. Cresswell watched him uncomfortably as he rode away, and again a feeling of doubt stirred within him. What new force was he loosening against his black folk—his own black folk, who had lived about him and his fathers nigh three hundred years? He saw the huge form of the sheriff loom like an evil spirit a moment on the rise of the road and sink into the night. He turned slowly to his cheerless house shuddering as he entered the uninviting portals.

Thirty-seven

THE MOB

When Emma, Bertie's child, came home after a two years' course of study, she had passed from girlhood to young womanhood. She was white, and sandy-haired. She was not beautiful, and she appeared to be fragile; but she also looked sweet and good, with that peculiar innocence which peers out upon the world with calm, round eyes and sees no evil, but does methodically its simple, everyday work. Zora mothered her, Miss Smith found her plenty to do, and Bles thought her a good girl. But Mrs. Cresswell found her perfect, and began to scheme to marry her off. For Mary Cresswell, with the restlessness and unhappiness of an unemployed woman, was trying to atone for her former blunders.

Her humiliation after the episode at Cresswell Oaks had been complete. It seemed to her that the original cause of her whole life punishment lay in her persistent misunderstanding of the black people and their problem. Zora appeared to her in a new and glorified light—a vigorous, self-sacrificing woman. She knew that Zora had refused to marry Bles, and this again seemed fitting. Zora was not meant for marrying; she was a born leader, wedded to a great cause; she had long outgrown the boy and girl affection. She was the sort of woman she herself might have been if she had not married.

Alwyn, on the other hand, needed a wife; he was a great, virile boy, requiring a simple, affectionate mate. No sooner did she see Emma than she was sure that this was the ideal wife. She compared herself with Helen Cresswell. Helen was a contented wife and mother because she was fitted for the position, and happy in it; while she who had aimed so high had fallen piteously. From such a fate she would save Zora and Bles.

Emma's course in nurse-training had been simple and short and there was no resident physician; but Emma, in her unemotional way, was a born nurse and did much good among the sick in the neighborhood. Zora had a small log hospital erected with four white beds, a private room, and an office which was also Emma's bedroom. The new white physician in town, just fresh from school in Atlanta, became interested and helped with advice and suggestions.

Meantime John Taylor's troubles began to increase. Under the old political regime it had been an easy matter to avoid serious damage-suits for the accidents in the mill. Much child labor and the lack of protective devices made accidents painfully frequent. Taylor insisted that the chief cause was carelessness, while the mill hands alleged criminal neglect on his part. When the new labor officials took charge of the court and the break occurred between Colonel Cresswell and his son-in-law, Taylor found that several damage-suits were likely to cost him a considerable sum.

He determined not to let the bad feelings go too far, and when a particularly distressing accident to a little girl took place, he showed more than his usual interest and offered to care for her. The new young physician recommended Zora's infirmary as the only near place that offered a chance for the child's recovery.

"Take her out," Taylor promptly directed.

Zora was troubled when the child came. She knew the suspicious temper of the town whites. The very next day Taylor sent out a second case, a child who had been hurt some time before and was not recovering as she should. Under the care of the little hospital and the gentle nurse the children improved rapidly, and in two weeks were outdoors, playing with the little black children and even creeping into classrooms and listening. The grateful mothers came out twice a week at least; at first with suspicious aloofness, but gradually melting under Zora's tact until they sat and talked with her and told their troubles and struggles. Zora realized how human they were, and how like their problems were to hers. They and their children grew to love this busy, thoughtful woman, and Zora's fears were quieted.

The catastrophe came suddenly. The sheriff rode by, scowling and hunting for some poor black runaway, when he saw white children in the Negro school and white women, whom he knew were mill-hands, looking on. He was black with anger; turning he galloped back to town. A few hours later the young physician arrived hastily in a cab to take the women and children to town. He said something in a low tone to Zora and drove away, frowning.

Zora came quickly to the school and asked for Alwyn. He was in the barn and she hurried there.

"Bles," she said quietly, "it is reported that a Toomsville mob will burn the school tonight."

Bles stood motionless.

"I've been fearing it. The sheriff has been stirring up the worst elements in the town lately and the mills pay off tonight."

"Well," she said quietly, "we must prepare."

He looked at her, his face aglow with admiration.

"You wonder-woman!" he exclaimed softly.

A moment they regarded each other. She saw the love in his eyes, and he saw rising in hers something that made his heart bound. But she turned quickly away.

"You must hurry, Bles; lives are at stake." And in another moment he thundered out of the barn on the black mare.

Along the pike he flew and up the plantation roads. Across broad fields and back again, over to the Barton pike and along the swamp. At every cabin he whispered a word, and left behind him grey faces and whispering children.

His horse was reeking with sweat as he staggered again into the school-yard; but already the people were gathering, with frightened, anxious, desperate faces. Women with bundles and children, men with guns, tottering old folks, wide-eyed boys and girls. Up from the swamp land came the children crying and moaning. The sun was setting. The women and children hurried into the school building, closing the doors and windows. A moment Alwyn stood without and looked back. The world was peaceful. He could hear the whistle of birds and the sobbing of the breeze in the shadowing oaks. The sky was flashing to dull and purplish blue, and over all lay the twilight hush as though God did not care.

He threw back his head and clenched his hands. His soul groaned within him. "Heavenly Father, was man ever before set to such a task?" Fight? God! if he could but fight! If he could but let go the elemental passions that were leaping and gathering and burning in the eyes of yonder caged and desperate black men. But his hands were tied—manacled. One desperate struggle, a whirl of blood, and the whole world would rise to crush him and his people. The white operatore in yonder town had but to flash the news, "Negroes killing whites," to bring all the country, all the State, all the nation, to red vengeance. It mattered not what the provocation, what the desperate cause.

The door suddenly opened behind him and he wheeled around.

"Zora!" he whispered.

"Bles," she answered softly, and they went silently in to their people.

All at once, from floor to roof, the whole school-house was lighted up, save a dark window here and there. Then some one slipped out into the darkness and soon watch-fire after watch-fire flickered and flamed in the night, and then burned vividly, sending up sparks and black smoke. Thus ringed with flaming silence, the school lay at the edge of the great, black swamp and waited. Owls hooted in the forest. Afar the shriek of the Montgomery train was heard across the night, mingling with the wail of a wakeful babe; and then redoubled silence. The men became restless, and Johnson began to edge away toward the lower hall. Alwyn was watching him when a faint noise came to him on the eastern breeze—a low, rumbling murmur. It died away, and rose again; then a distant gun-shot woke the echoes.

"They're coming!" he cried. Standing back in the shadow of a front window, he waited. Slowly, intermittently, the murmuring swelled, till it grew distinguishable as yelling, cursing, and singing, intermingled with the crash of pistol-shots. Far away a flame, as of a burning cabin, arose, and a wilder, louder yell greeted it. Now the tramp of footsteps could be heard, and clearer and thicker the grating and booming of voices, until suddenly, far up the pike, a black moving mass, with glitter and shout, swept into view. They came headlong, guided by pine-torches, which threw their white and haggard faces into wild distortion. Then as bonfire after bonfire met their gaze, they moved slowly and more slowly, and at last sent a volley of bullets at the fires. One bullet flew high and sang through a lighted window. Without a word, Uncle Isaac sank upon the floor and lay still. Silence and renewed murmuring ensued, and the sound of high voices in dispute. Then the mass divided into two wings and slowly encircled the fence of fire; starting noisily and confidently, and then going more slowly, quietly, warily, as the silence of the flame began to tell on their heated nerves.

Strained whispers arose.

"Careful there!"

"Go on, damn ye!"

"There's some one by yon fire."

"No, there ain't."

"See the bushes move."

Bang! bang! bang!

"Who's that?"

"It's me."

"Let's rush through and fire the house."

"And leave a pa'cel of niggers behind to shoot your lights out? Not me."

"What the hell are you going to do?"

"I don't know yet."

"I wish I could see a nigger."

"Hark!"

Stealthy steps were approaching, a glint of steel flashed behind the fire lights. Each band mistook the other for the armed Negroes, and the leaders yelled in vain; human power can not stay the dashing torrent of fear-inspired human panic. Whirling, the mob fled till it struck the road in two confused, surging masses. Then in quick frenzy, shots flew; three men threw up their hands and tumbled limply in the dust, while the main body rushed pellmell toward town.

At early dawn, when the men relaxed from the strain of the night's vigil, Alwyn briefly counselled them: "Hide your guns."

"Why?" blustered Rob. "Haven't I a right to have a gun?"

"Yes, you have, Rob; but don't be foolish—hide it. We've not heard the last of this."

But Rob tossed his head belligerently.

In town, rumor spread like wildfire. A body of peaceful whites passing through the black settlement had been fired on from ambush, and six killed—no, three killed—no, one killed and two severely wounded.

"The thing mustn't stop here," shouted Sheriff Colton; "these niggers must have a lesson." And before nine next morning fully half the grown members of the same mob, now sworn in as deputies, rode with him to search the settlement. They tramped insolently through the school grounds, but there was no shred of evidence until they came to Rob's cabin and found his gun. They tied his hands behind him and marched him toward town.

But before the mob arrived the night before, Johnson feeling that his safety lay in informing the white folks, had crawled with his gun into the swamp. In the morning he peered out as the cavalcade approached, and not knowing what had happened, he recognized Colton, the sheriff, and signalled to him cautiously. In a moment a dozen men were on him, and he appealed and explained in vain—the gun was damning evidence. The voices of Rob's wife and children could be heard behind the two men as they were hurried along at a dog trot.

The town poured out to greet them—"The murderers! the murderers! Kill the niggers!" and they came on with a rush. The sheriff turned and disappeared in the rear. There was a great cloud of dust, a cry and a wild scramble, as the white and angry faces of men and boys gleamed a moment and faded.

A hundred or more shots rang out; then slowly and silently, the mass of women and men were sucked into the streets of the town, leaving but black eddies on the corners to throw backward glances toward the bare, towering pine where swung two red and awful things. The pale boy-face of one, with soft brown eyes glared up sightless to the sun; the dead, leathered bronze of the other was carved in piteous terror.

Thirty - eight

ATONEMENT

T hree months had flown. It was Spring again, and Zora sat in the transformed swamp—now a swamp in name only—beneath the great oak, dreaming. And what she dreamed there in the golden day she dared not formulate even to her own soul. She rose with a start, for there was work to do. Aunt Rachel was ill, and Emma went daily to attend her; today, as she came back, she brought news that Colonel Cresswell, who had been unwell for several days, was worse. She must send Emma up to help, and as she started toward the school she glanced toward the Cresswell Oaks and saw the arm-chair of its master on the pillared porch.

Colonel Cresswell sat in his chair on the porch, alone. As far as he could see, there was no human soul. His eyes were blood-shot, his cheeks sunken, and his breath came in painful gasps. A sort of terror shook him until he heard the distant songs of black folk in the fields. He sighed, and lying back, closed his eyes and the breath came easier. When he opened them again a white figure was coming up the avenue of the Oaks. He watched it greedily. It was Mary Cresswell, and she started when she saw him.

"You are worse, father?" she asked.

"Worse and better," he replied, smiling cynically. Then suddenly he announced: "I've made my will."

"Why—why—" she stammered.

"Why?" sharply. "Because I'm going to die."

She said nothing. He smiled and continued:

"I've got it all fixed. Harry was in a tight place—gambling as usual—and I gave him a lump sum in lieu of all claims. Then I gave John Taylor—you needn't look. I sent for him. He's a damned scoundrel; but he won't lie, and I needed him. I willed his children all the rest except two or three legacies. One was one hundred thousand dollars for you—"

"Oh, father!" she cried. "I don't deserve it."

"I reckon two years with Harry was worth about that much," he returned grimly. "Then there's another gift of two hundred thousand dollars and this house and plantation. Whom do you think that's for?"

"Helen?"

"Helen!" he raised his hand in threatening anger. "I might rot here for all she cares. No—no—but then—I'll not tell you—I—ah—" A spasm of pain shot across his face, and he lay back white and still. Abruptly he sat up again and peered down the oaks. "Hush!" he gasped. "Who's that?"

"I don't know—it's a girl—I—"

He gripped her till she winced.

"My God—it walks—like my wife—I tell you—she held her head so—who is it?" He half rose.

"Oh, father, it's nobody but Emma—little Emma—Bertie's child—

the mulatto girl. She's a nurse now, and I asked to have her come and attend you."

"Oh," he said, "oh—" He looked at the girl curiously. "Come here." He peered into her white young face. "Do you know me?"

The girl shrank away from him.

"Yes, sir,"

"What do you do?"

"I teach and nurse at the school."

"Good! Well, I'm going to give you some money—do you know why?"

A flash of self-consciousness passed over the girl's face; she looked at him with her wide blue eyes.

"Yes, Grandfather," she faltered.

Mrs. Cresswell rose to her feet; but the old man slowly dropped the girl's hand and lay back in his chair, with lips half smiling. "Grandfather," he repeated softly, He closed his eyes a space and then opened them. A tremor shivered in his limbs as he stared darkly at the swamp.

"Hark!" he cried harshly. "Do you hear the bodies creaking on the limbs? It's Rob and Johnson. I did it—I—"

Suddenly he rose and stood erect and his wild eyes stricken with death stared full upon Emma. Slowly and thickly he spoke, working his trembling hands.

"Nell—Nell! Is it you, little wife, come back to accuse me? Ah, Nell, don't shrink! I know—I have sinned against the light and the blood of your poor black people is red on these old hands. No, don't put your clean white hands upon me, Nell, till I wash mine. I'll do it, Nell; I'll atone. I'm a Cresswell yet, Nell, a Cresswell and a gen—" He swayed. Vainly he struggled for the word. The shudder of death shook his soul, and he passed.

A week after the funeral of Colonel Cresswell, John Taylor drove out to the school and was closeted with Miss Smith. His sister, installed once again for a few days in her old room at the school, understood that he was conferring about Emma's legacy, and she was glad. She was more and more convinced that the marriage of Emma and Bles was the best possible solution of many difficulties. She had asked Emma once if she liked Bles, and Emma had replied in her innocent way,

"Oh, so much."

As for Bles, he was often saying what a dear child Emma was. Neither perhaps realized yet that this was love, but it needed, Mrs. Cresswell was sure, only the lightning-flash, and they would know. And who could furnish that illumination better than Zora, the calm, methodical Zora, who knew them so well?

As for herself, once she had accomplished the marriage and paid the mortgage on the school out of her legacy, she would go abroad and in travel seek forgetfulness and healing. There had been no formal divorce, and so far as she was concerned there never would be; but the separation from her husband and America would be forever.

Her brother came out of the office, nodded casually, for they had little intercourse these days, and rode away. She rushed in to Miss Smith and found her sitting there—straight, upright, composed in all save that the tears were streaming down her face and she was making no effort to stop them.

"Why—Miss Smith!" she faltered.

Miss Smith pointed to a paper. Mrs. Cresswell picked it up curiously. It was an official notification to the trustees of the Smith School of a legacy of two hundred thousand dollars together with the Cresswell house and plantation. Mrs. Cresswell sat down in open-mouthed astonishment. Twice she tried to speak, but there were so many things to say that she could not choose.

"Tell Zora," Miss Smith at last managed to say.

Zora was dreaming again. Somehow, the old dream-life, with its glorious phantasies, had come silently back, richer and sweeter than ever. There was no tangible reason why, and yet today she had shut herself in her den. Searching down in the depths of her trunk, she drew forth that filmy cloud of white—silk-bordered and half finished to a gown. Why were her eyes wet today and her mind on the Silver Fleece? It was an anniversary, and perhaps she still remembered that moment, that supreme moment before the mob. She half slipped on, half wound about her, the white cloud of cloth, standing with parted lips, looking into the long mirror and gleaming in the fading day like midnight gowned in mists and stars. Abruptly there came a peremptory knocking at the door.

"Zora! Zora!" sounded Mrs. Cresswell's voice. Forgetting her informal attire, she opened the door, fearing some mishap. Mrs. Cresswell poured out the news. Zora received it in such motionless silence that Mary wondered at her want of feeling. At last, however, she said happily to Zora:

"Well, the battle's over, isn't it?"

"No, it's just begun."

"Just begun?" echoed Mary in amazement.

"Think of the servile black folk, the half awakened restless whites, the fat land waiting for the harvest, the masses panting to know—why, the battle is scarcely even begun."

"Yes, I guess that's so," Mary began to comprehend. "We'll thank God it has begun, though."

"Thank God!" Zora reverently repeated.

"Come, let's go back to poor, dear Miss Smith," suggested Mary.

"I can't come just now—but pretty soon."

"Why? Oh, I see; you're trying on something—how pretty and becoming! Well, hurry."

As they stood together, the white woman deemed the moment opportune; she slipped her arm about the black woman's waist and began:

"Zora, I've had something on my mind for a long time, and I shouldn't wonder if you had thought of the same thing."

"What is it?"

"Bles and Emma."

"What of them?"

"Their liking for each other."

Zora bent a moment and caught up the folds of the Fleece.

"I hadn't noticed it," she said in a low voice.

"Well, you're busy, you see. They've been very much together—his taking her to her charges, bringing her back, and all that. I know they love each other; yet something holds them apart, afraid to show their love. Do you know—I've wondered if—quite unconciously, it is you? You know Bles used to imagine himself in love with you, just as he did afterward with Miss Wynn."

"Miss—Wynn?"

"Yes, the Washington girl. But he got over that and you straightened him out finally. Still, Emma probably thinks yours is the prior claim, knowing, of course, nothing of facts. And Bles knows she thinks of him and you, and I'm convinced if you say the word, they'd love and marry."

Zora walked silently with her to the door, where, looking out, she saw Bles and Emma coming from Aunt Rachel's. He was helping her from the carriage with smiling eyes, and her innocent blue eyes were fastened on him.

Zora looked long and searchingly.

"Please run and tell them of the legacy," she begged. "I—I will come—in a moment." And Mrs. Cresswell hurried out.

Zora turned back steadily to her room, and locked herself in. After all, why shouldn't it be? Why had it not occurred to her before in her blindness? If she had wanted him—and ah, God! was not all her life simply the want of him?—why had she not bound him to her when he had offered himself? Why had she not bound him to her? She knew as she asked—because she had wanted all, not a part—everything, love, respect and perfect faith—not one thing could she spare then—not one thing. And now, oh, God! she had dreamed that it was all hers, since that night of death and circling flame when they looked at each other soul to soul. But he had not meant anything. It was pity she had seen there, not love; and she rose and walked the room slowly, fast and faster.

With trembling hands she drew the Silver Fleece round her. Her head swam again and the blood flashed in her eyes. She heard a calling in the swamp, and the shadow of Elspeth seemed to hover over her, claiming her for her own, dragging her down, down . . . She rushed through the swamp. The lagoon lay there before her presently, gleaming in the darkness—cold and still, and in it swam an awful shape.

She held her burning head—was not everything plain? Was not everything clear? This was Sacrifice! This was the Atonement for the unforgiven sin. Emma's was the pure soul which she must offer up to God; for it was God, a cold and mighty God, who had given it to Bles—her Bles. It was well; God willed it. But could *she* live? Must she live? Did God ask that, too?

All at once she stood straight; her whole body grew tense, alert. She heard no sound behind her, but knew he was there, and braced herself. She must be true. She must be just. She must pay the uttermost farthing.

"Bles," she called faintly, but did not turn her head.

"Zora!"

"Bles," she choked, but her voice came stronger, "I know—all. Emma is a good girl. I helped bring her up myself and did all I could for her and she—she is pure; marry her."

His voice came slow and firm:

"Emma? But I don't love Emma. I love—some one else."

Her heart bounded and again was still. It was that Washington girl then. She answered dully, groping for words, for she was tired:

"Who is it?"

"The best woman in all the world, Zora."

"And is"—she struggled at the word madly—"is she pure?"

"She is more than pure."

"Then you must marry her, Bles."

"I am not worthy of her," he answered, sinking before her.

Then at last illumination dawned upon her blindness. She stood very still and lifted up her eyes. The swamp was living, vibrant, tremulous. There where the first long note of night lay shot with burning crimson, burst in sudden radiance the wide beauty of the moon. There pulsed a glory in the air. Her little hands groped and wandered over his close-curled hair, and she sobbed, deep voiced:

"Will you—marry me, Bles?"

L'Envoi

Lend me thine ears, O God the Reader, whose Fathers aforetime sent mine down into the land of Egypt, into this House of Bondage. Lay not these words aside for a moment's phantasy, but lift up thine eyes upon the Horror in this land;—the maiming and mocking and murdering of my people, and the prisonment of their souls. Let my people go, O Infinite One, lest the world shudder at

The End

Reader's Companion

1. By the end of the novel, *The Quest of the Silver Fleece* reveals itself as a tale largely concerned with exploring the complex issues of morality in American life. Considering W.E.B. Du Bois's seeming affinity for the power of the "Word" throughout the story, how would you assess his characterization of Zora's mother, the witch Elspeth? Described as "old . . . black and wrinkled with yellow fangs, red hanging lips and wicked eyes," Elspeth potentially represents many things for Du Bois racially. What are the racial implications of her crude characterization? What is to be made of the nature and fact of her death? How important is her ghostly "return" toward the end of the book?

2. As a place of both oppression and redemption for Zora, the swamp is a contradictory location throughout the novel. What is the significance of Zora's early departure from its confines? Is her flight to Miss Smith's school and ultimately to the North a necessary one? What is Du Bois's interest in staging her triumphant return to the school, the South, and the swamp? Why

must the cabin of Elspeth be made to "tremble, sigh and disappear" from its boundaries by novel's end?

3. At the outset, Bles and Zora quickly forge what seems to be an important bond. What is the significance of their differences? What larger issues of black life loom at the heart of their coupling?

4. The romantic pairing of Zora and Bles is soon ruptured when it is revealed that Zora has lost her "innocence" and is not "pure" due to her early sexual compromise by her master. Why is the issue of purity so important to Bles? How does gender figure in his quick and summary refusal of Zora as a suitable partner? How are traditional conceptions of female virture complicated by Du Bois's representation of Zora's and other black girls' brutal violation? What is Du Bois suggesting about the nature and character of the institution of slavery?

5. Zora's beauty and intelligence are the subject of much speculation and interest throughout. Compare her characterization in the novel's early stages to her depiction toward its end. What differences emerge? How are her training at Miss Smith's school and her relationship to Mrs. Vanderpool significant? What is Du Bois suggesting about the role of education in ending black suffering? Why is it important that Du Bois has placed a black woman at the center of this novel of black pain and resistance?

6. Through different means, Bles and Zora acquire knowledge and education and emerge as vanguards in their community. What issues of class are at work here? How significant is language? How does Du Bois's famous notion of "The Talented Tenth" figure in the novel?

7. A central figure throughout, Miss Sarah Smith is presented as a white woman whose "noble efforts" over three decades to maintain a "Negro school" confirm her commitment to the upward mobility of black people. Looking at her expressions in defense of black humanity and those declaring her contempt for white exploitation and superiority, how would you describe her notions of race in America? Has she succeeded in transcending its pitfalls? Or does she continue to support some notions of white subjectivity and superiority?

8. As a title, *The Quest of the Silver Fleece* is well chosen. Not only is the novel concerned with that special crop of cotton Zora and Bles succeed in producing in the swamp, but it is more generally interested in examining the historically central role of cotton in determining the economic future of the nation's inhabitants. What is the connection between race and capitalism in the novel? What issues of morality does Du Bois bring up in this context? What is to be made of Bles's negotiation of this complex terrain? How significant is Zora's socially conscious economic venture toward the end of the book?

9. At the moment of his death, Colonel Cresswell grants Emma, his mulatto and previously unacknowledged granddaughter, a measure of financial legacy. Two hundred thousand dollars and the Cresswell home and plantation are later revealed as bequeathed to Miss Smith's school. What is the significance of Colonel Cresswell's deathbed generosity? How do you view the issue of white philanthropy throughout the novel?

10. Upon his return to the South after his "failure" in Washington, Bles asks Zora to marry him and she refuses. Why does Zora decline this offer? What accounts for her change of heart by novel's end? Why is it significant that ultimately *she* asks for Bles's hand in marriage?

About the Author

W.E.B. Du Bois (1868–1963) is regarded as one of the most influential black leaders of the twentieth century. Born in Great Barrington, Massachusetts, Du Bois attended Fisk University and then Harvard University, going on to conduct sociological work at the University of Pennsylvania. His first collection of essays, *The Souls of Black Folk*, has been called by many the most important book ever written by an African American. Published in 1903, it identified the color line as the defining problem of the twentieth century.

Du Bois helped found America's premier civil rights organization, the NAACP, and moved to New York in 1910 to found *The Crisis*, the association's magazine. He also wrote two novels, *The Quest of the Silver Fleece* (1911) and *Dark Princess: A Romance* (1928). From the 1920s and into the 1940s, Du Bois's writings became more militant and controversial as he spoke out vehemently against imperialism, and he continued his essay writing in books like *Black Folk: Then and Now* (1934) and *Dusk of Dawn: An Essay Towards an Autobiography of a Race Concept* (1940). After moving to Ghana at the behest of President Kwame Nkrumah, Du Bois died at ninety-four as a Ghanaian citizen.